# FINAL ROUND

## Alan Parr

MINERVA PRESS
LONDON
MIAMI   RIO DE JANEIRO   DELHI

FINAL ROUND
Copyright © Alan Parr 2001

All Rights Reserved

ISBN  0  75411  730  8

First Published 2001 by
MINERVA PRESS
315–317 Regent Street
London W1B 2HS

Printed in Great Britain for Minerva Press

# FINAL ROUND

## Author's Note

WHAT you are about to read is a work of fiction. Occasionally, actual names of people, cities, towns, events and boxing venues have been used to help provide a sense of era and atmosphere.

I apologise to all boxers, both amateur and professional, who were champions and challengers at the time (1967 to 1994) of my story. I hope they are not offended that their hard-earned place in history has been taken by a load of fictional characters.

During forty years spent in and around boxing, many people have provided me with entertainment, education, argument, inspiration and, in some cases, friendship. I take this opportunity to record my thanks, in no particular order, to:

Tony Sibson, Keith and Kath Sibson, Mick Greaves, Chris Pyatt, Dan McAlinden, Marvin Hagler, Tony McKenzie, Shaun Cummins, Adey Allen, Mickey Duff, Frank Warren, Barry Hearn, Mike Barrett, Johnny Griffin, Ron Gray, the late George Biddles, Carl Gunns, David Jones, Peter Moss, Colin Hart, Fred Burcombe, Ron Olver, Ian Darke, Reg Gutteridge, Harry Carpenter, Des Lynam, Gary Newbon, the late Sam Burns, Jarvis Astaire, Jimmy Tibbs, Terry Lawless, Frank Black, Mick Inskip, the late Jim Knight, Ken Squires, Norman Jones and all members of the Leicester Ex-Boxer's Association.

Finally, heartfelt thanks also to my wife Jill for her continued support and belief.

*PART ONE*

H IS WHOLE BODY ached. His head was throbbing, his hearing muffled. He sat, arms resting heavy on his lap, trying to ignore the increasing pain in his hands.

Years of hard, brutal experience had told him this was going to be tough but, even so, he was surprised at how bad he felt. Glistening with sweat, he took another deep breath, trying to fill his lungs with enough oxygen to give him the energy to battle on.

Gradually, the noise of the excited crowd in the vast arena entered his senses again and he began to take notice of the familiar face in front of him. A concerned but calm face. The lips were moving.

'It's time to step up a gear. You've got to push him back. There's not much in it but you've gotta fucking work. You've come too far to toss this away. This is what you've wanted, it's what you've worked for. Don't let it slip away.'

The phrases struck home. 'What you've wanted... what you've worked for...'

Oh yes, he wanted it all right and he'd certainly worked for it. Right back when he was a kid, he'd dreamed of a moment such as this. It was what his life was all about. No one could say he hadn't worked to achieve his ambition. Not just the years of physical grind, the punishment meted out to his body, but the setbacks which had taxed his ability to pick up the pieces and carry on.

How many times had he felt like giving up? How often had he questioned the wisdom of carrying on, of trying to rebuild? Surely there was more to life than this torture? But, in his quieter, more reflective moments, he knew that the hard knocks were there to test him, to mould his character – and they made the moments of triumph even sweeter. So, he had dug deep into his mind and heart and summoned up the energy, the will and the strength to reach out again for his Holy Grail: champion of the world.

Now, here he was, eighteen years on from when he first laced his gloves and only minutes from his sworn destiny. Yes, this was what he wanted, what he'd worked for. He knew these should be the defining moments. The time when he called on every last drop of energy, skill and desire and made all those eighteen roller coaster years worthwhile.

But sitting on the ring stool, as his handlers feverishly worked to rouse him for more gigantic efforts, his shoulders sagged and his ears again became clogged, shutting out the words and the noise of the crowd as his thoughts wandered.

They didn't know, did they? He was the only one who knew. Just him. No one could help him, the problem was his – and it was the biggest of his life. He knew he had to find the answer. There was no shirking this one. And time was running out. He'd been threatened before. Sure, he knew some nasty people but he'd shown he could take care of himself. He wasn't afraid of anything or anybody. Threats! What were they? Just words.

But this was different. This time he knew it was the business. These people were for real. And, for the first time, he was worried. In fact, he was scared. Not for himself, understand, but for—

'Seconds out… for round seven…'

# Chapter One

The bottle, which Johnny Willis saw only at the last moment, whistled over his shoulder and shattered the long bar mirror, sending hundreds of glass splinters cascading among the optics. Another Saturday night spectacular.

Willis, scanning the small, smoke-filled room, took in the chaos and moved swiftly towards the nub of the trouble. Six feet tall, with broad shoulders and a deep chest stretching his white sports shirt, Willis was a formidable sight.

He targeted the biggest of the five hooligans who seemed intent on wrecking the pub. Shaven-headed and taller than Willis, bulging arms and neck decorated with tattoos. The message in pigment was clear: hard man. But not hard enough. A blistering punch sent him crashing into a table, bottles and glasses spilling onto the worn carpet. Willis then spun to his right and delivered another crunching blow to deck a second youth.

The tumult in the crowded pub diminished to a babble at the sight of this one-man clean-up operation. The squealing women and startled men who had decided – wisely or as cowards – to stay clear of the trouble looked on in admiration. Panic over.

'Okay, that's enough… we're off,' shouted one of the youths still standing. 'We're not messing with you. Just cool it. Come on lads, let's get the fuck out of here.'

Willis, brown eyes blazing beneath his black hair, took a deep breath, jutting out his massive chest.

'That's right, piss off – and take your scum pals with you.' A quiet, menacing tone. 'And don't bother coming back. Ever.'

Doug Jones stood transfixed among the debris behind the bar. Overweight with fair, thinning hair, the landlord wore heavy black-framed spectacles with lenses that resembled the bottom of a beer bottle. He was sweating profusely as Willis returned to his company, and his glass of Coke, at the bar.

'Thanks, I'm lucky you were here,' said Jones. 'Will you have a drink?'

'It's okay, I'm happy with this Coke. But these lads might enjoy a pint.' Willis nodded at his three companions.

'Sure thing – three pints coming up.'

As Jones pulled the drinks he looked at the swarthy young man. Some gypsy stock in there? A light of recognition flickered in his eyes. 'Say, don't I know you? I'm sure I've seen you somewhere.'

'You should do, mister,' said the shortest of Willis's associates. 'Johnny here's going to be a world champion, ain't you pal?'

Willis smiled, showing perfect white teeth.

The landlord set down the pints. 'Of course, you're Johnny Willis. I saw you boxing as a kid. You were quite tasty then. But you've certainly grown. What are you, a middleweight?'

'Not yet. I'm around eleven stone, still light-middle. But I'm growing and filling out. Reckon to be a middleweight soon.'

'How old are you?' Jones reached for a broom to start sweeping up the broken glass beneath his feet.

'Twenty. I'm turning pro next week – so I'll have to avoid nights like these,' he laughed. 'I can't afford trouble, you know. Do you have a lot of bother with these tearaways?'

Jones leaned on his broom. 'Funnily enough, that's the third time in a couple of weeks,' he said. 'Not the same guys, but the trouble just starts out of the blue. Point is, they come in quiet enough and you'd never guess they'd start anything. It's almost as though they've planned it.'

'The town's getting a bit rough, 'specially on Saturday nights. Ever thought about security?'

'What, bouncers on the door, you mean?'

'That sort of thing. They'd keep the riff-raff out. If you don't watch it, you'll be losing your regulars.' Willis glanced around the room. There was an uneasy peace but some drinkers were preparing for an early departure.

'I know what you mean. But this is only a small pub. I don't make a fortune, you know.'

'You'll make even less if this carries on,' said Kenny Willis. He was Johnny's eldest brother by three years, with similar dark features, but was a couple of inches shorter. He sported a half-moon scar under his left eye, collected in a fight with a glass-wielding thug. Kenny had taken his reprisal that night. With the aid of a bar stool, he battered his assailant to within a gasp of his life, and got six months' detention for it. That was five years back. Although he still walked on the wild side with his other younger brother Colin, he'd been clever enough to avoid another trip to the cells.

'These lads might be able to help you out, if you're interested,' suggested Johnny.

Jones looked at the trio – the brothers and their friend Pete Payne. The shortest, Payne had a solid physique. The landlord turned back to Willis. 'What do you mean?'

'These two are my brothers, Kenny and Colin, and this is our friend Pete.' They nodded at Jones. Little smiles. Eyes cold.

'Believe me, they can look after themselves. They've started a security firm. Quite a few mates are interested in that line of work. As I said, this town's getting a bit rough. We reckon people will stop going out at nights, 'specially at weekends, if things don't get better. That won't be good for you, will it?'

Jones rested his broom against the wall and surveyed the glass splinters on his shelves. A couple of spirit bottles had also perished in this latest incidence of crazy violence. 'So, what are you saying?' he asked.

'Quite simple,' said Kenny. 'We put a couple of guys on the door and guarantee no bother. In the unlikely event that some fucking nutter does act up, we'll deal with him quickly, like Johnny here did tonight. But it won't come to that. In fact, if there's any bother after the first two weeks, we'll give you back our fee every night it happens. There, that's confidence for you.'

'Sounds good. But, as I say, I don't earn a fortune out of this place. How much do you charge?'

'It's gonna get mighty expensive if this trouble keeps happening. How much for that mirror, for instance? And you'll lose punters. What about the police and the brewery? They're not gonna be happy with a lot of bother, fights all the time. Do you wanna lose your licence? And, don't forget, one day you might get hurt.' Kenny paused, letting Jones contemplate the worst scenario. 'Look,' he continued, 'we'll be reasonable. P'raps you don't need cover every day, say just at weekends – Friday to Sunday. That's three days and nights. For a couple of blokes, we'll say fifty quid a time.'

'You mean a hundred and fifty a weekend? That's a lot of dough. I'd need to sell plenty of beer for that.'

Jones wiped his damp brow with a bar towel as Kenny picked up his pint and took a long swallow. He set the empty glass back on the bar. 'It's cheaper than thirty of those a night. You'll be well covered. I know that and so do you.'

'And it's cheaper than replacing that sodding mirror every week,' threw in Colin. 'You know it makes sense. Jeez, it's an offer you can't refuse.' The four young men smiled.

Payne dug into the inside pocket of his black leather jacket and drew out a business card. 'Here, take this.'

The fat landlord took it. 'Doors Limited, Security Specialists,' he read. No address, no names, just two phone numbers.

'Ring either of those numbers,' said Payne, 'someone'll answer. If you think there's gonna be bother at any time, we'll get somebody here pronto. No charge. That's a bonus. But, believe me, once these toerags get to know we're about, this pub won't have any trouble. Punters will flock here and you'll make a mint. You keep a good pint and we'll keep the peace.'

Jones stared at the card in his right hand and flicked it with his thumb, meditating. Their sales pitch was good. 'How about a trial run?'

'Trial?' said Kenny. 'Let's just agree we'll do the job. If you're not satisfied, then you can pay us off. But don't expect us to come running back if you get into fucking bother again. Okay?'

Jones studied the card again and shrugged. 'Suppose you're right.' Looking at Johnny, he asked, 'Is this your business?'

The handsome young boxer smiled. 'No, I've got my reputation to think about. It's not good for a boxer to be on the door, you know? Things like tonight I can well do without. I only sorted it because I didn't fancy being clouted by a stray bottle. That one only just missed. Anyway, I'm well tucked up in bed before you pull your last pint. I run early every morning and I go to the gym every day. I haven't got the time for all this. It's down to my brothers, it's their business. But you'll be in safe hands.

They're good.'

Willis glanced at his watch. 'Bedtime,' he said and turned to Kenny. 'I'll see you later. You'd better stay here just in case those idiots get brave and decide to come back. I'll walk home. Here's the car keys.' He turned to Jones and offered his hand across the bar. 'You won't regret doing business with these guys,' he said. Jones's palm was damp.

'Sure, and thanks for your help. Good luck with the boxing. Perhaps I'll see you around.'

'You can always buy a ticket to one of my fights. In fact, you could sell a few in here. Colin looks after that sort of thing. He'll let you have what you want.'

Willis headed for the door. Many pairs of eyes followed him across the room. 'Goodnight all,' he said to the room and was gone into the warm August night air. But he didn't head for the road. Instead, he walked round to the ill-lit car park at the rear of the pub. The gang of five were leaning against his car, two of them drawing heavily on cigarettes. The burly tattooed thug stood up as Willis approached.

'Watch the paintwork.'

'Sorry, Johnny,' he said. The others all moved away from Willis's six-year-old racing green Rover. One day it would be a Jag or Merc, or even a Roller. 'Everything go all right?'

'Sure, job's done. You lads did just fine. Kenny's gonna pay you when he comes out. He won't be much longer. Didn't hurt you, did I?'

'Not much. But I'm glad you hit me on the fucking chest and not the jaw. I was bleeding worried for a second. Mind you, I could have done without falling into that fucking table. That fucking hurt,' he laughed, rubbing the back of his head.

'Don't worry. Few more rucks like tonight and we'll have the town sewn up. The word will soon get round and every pub'll want us on the door. We've got six already. Not bad for a coupla weeks, eh?

'When we've finished with this little scam, you'll have regular jobs on the door. No worries. Okay, lads, see you around – be good.'

The Willis family lived in a drab, brown-brick three-bedroom house at the end of a scruffy cul-de-sac on a sprawling Midlands council estate. Johnny had the luxury of his own bedroom. A closet, really, cramped with a divan bed, small chest of drawers and a single wardrobe. Kenny and Colin shared the biggest room. The third, middle-sized room was occupied by Mary, their beautiful, auburn-haired seventeen-year-old sister. She was the one person Willis loved and protected above all others. While aggressive in his ambition to earn his fortune from his fists, he was particularly driven by a desire to take Mary out of this depressing existence. Nothing would be too good for her.

That was more than could be said for his mother. Connie, an ash blonde, would not see forty-five again but still dressed and behaved as if she was a thirtysomething. There was no helping her. Never had been.

She had once been a curvaceous woman whose cleavage and face, usually in that order, commanded the attention of many a young man. She could have done well for herself. Instead, she opted for the good time. Dancing, drinking and indulging in the pleasures of the flesh that any able-bodied man could provide. And there had been many takers, including the father of her four children.

Danny Willis, too, was a free spirit – a hybrid of Irish and gypsy stock. Connie adored him. They shared wild, passionate times, always ready for a party. No one quite knew what Danny did for a living. But there was always money to spend, food on the table and a seemingly endless supply of alcohol. You name it, Danny had it. Beer, spirits, even champagne. It all flowed in the Willis household.

Danny was a likeable rogue; a ruggedly good-looking charmer with a silver tongue. He lived on his wits and wasn't averse to a bit of thieving. Needs must – and he and Connie had expensive needs. Each day was there to be lived to the full. Tomorrow would look after itself. Hope springs eternal, he'd say, not realising or caring that he was quoting Alexander Pope.

For seven fruitful years, Danny and Connie partied. They never married, never even discussed the possibility. The four children were conceived in nights, even days, of lust. Their lovemaking was fierce, passionate. The three boys and a girl all had swarthy complexions, deep brown eyes and hearts as big as houses. But it wasn't long before Connie started to lose her bloom. Her figure drooped and broadened. Her face sagged under the weight of a burgeoning double chin.

At thirty, Connie looked forty, and Danny flew the nest. Or rather, he left home one drizzly September morning, just a month after the birth of Mary. With a lilting 'Cheerio' he was gone. For ever.

Connie waited a couple of days – sometimes 'business' prevented Danny from getting home on the same day he left – before trying to find him. She didn't, of course, ring the police but she spoke to friends and phoned hospitals. No one had seen or heard from him. And neither would they. He had disappeared, leaving Connie with her four kids aged from one month to six years.

Connie was heartbroken. But the good times did not come to a shuddering halt. Friends rallied round, offering drinks, invitations to parties and hand-me-down clothes for the children. But her offspring were never Connie's priority. She was, and always would be, the good-time party girl.

Over the years, she bestowed her favours on almost any man, to satisfy her lust for a penetrating penis and, more importantly, the cash a fleeting lover would donate. She wasn't a prostitute, didn't walk the streets or advertise in phone booths. But the defining, dividing line was thin. Connie turned the front room of 36 Johnson Close into her boudoir. As her brood grew up, it was a practical solution to the ever-increasing demands for space. It was there she entertained male friends, or held parties. With growing frequency, she fell into a lonely, drunken slumber. Day or night. At least she didn't have to climb the stairs.

Kenny had a few vague memories of his father. Mostly he remembered the noise of the parties. He would lie in his bed, listening to the throb of loud music from the record player, smelling cigarette smoke and hearing the laughter and general hubbub of folk enjoying the good life. Pure escapism.

When the front door closed on the last guest, he'd hear his parents laughing and giggling as they stumbled up the creaky stairs. Then, a few minutes later, his mother would be squealing and shouting, his father grunting and gasping, the bed springs rhythmically squeaking. Silence would finally envelop the darkened house. All that he could remember. But he'd no recollection of his father teaching him anything. Not reading, writing or how to ride a bike. He never seemed to have the time.

Colin, born a year after Kenny, had even vaguer memories. And, if there hadn't been photographs on the sideboard, Johnny wouldn't remember what his father looked like. Mary, of course, knew nothing of him.

What Mary did learn, from a very young age, was how to keep house. She cleaned, cooked, washed, ironed and yet, remarkably, remained cheerful and attentive to her own appearance. Later on, Connie, in rare sober moments, would offer her teenage daughter advice on dress and make-up. Mary matured rapidly into a woman, a beautiful woman in both spirit and appearance.

Kenny, the titular head of this disparate family, left school at sixteen and worked as a builder's labourer. He liked the physical work and the banter among the men and was respected not just for his output but for his attitude. Kenny was strong and ever willing to demonstrate it with a punch on the nose.

Kenny later persuaded his bosses to give Colin a job – and no one messed with those boys. A handy pair of scrappers, they didn't need asking twice to prove their prowess. Say the wrong thing and the Willis boys waded into action. Young as they were in a hard man's world, Kenny and Colin were not to be taken lightly.

But the toughest of the Willis bunch was young Johnny. A gutsy kid, always getting into scrapes and scraps, in the streets and at school, he threatened a teacher when he was only eight years old.

A promising footballer, dominant in midfield with his fierce tackling and almost maniacal determination to win, he possessed a thunderous shot. Not surprisingly, his sports master was impressed.

'You could be a professional if you carry on like this, Johnny,' said Mr Bates one afternoon after a games lesson. The headstrong Willis, then just nine years old, had won every tackle, passed with precision and whacked in two goals from the edge of the penalty area. What power from one so young!

Mr Bates debated picking Johnny for the school under-elevens soccer team. He was big for his age and could certainly look after himself. But trouble was always on Johnny's shoulder. He took his knocks, didn't complain about the odd kick on his shins or foul committed in the heat of competition. But he wouldn't accept any backchat or insults. Especially against his family. Call Connie 'a slag' and, true as that might be, you paid for it.

When it happened during one inter-class match, Mr Bates had to drag Willis off his fallen, battered foe.

'What's going on, Willis?' shouted the teacher as he held Johnny firmly by the shoulders. The boy gazed evenly at Mr Bates, a man he liked and respected. But he said nothing.

'Willis, listen to me, I've had both your brothers here. They were good footballers, but not a patch on you. But, if you carry on flaring up like this, I fear for you. What gets into you?'

Johnny never averted his eyes. He knew he was a good player and he liked soccer. But nobody called him or his family names. Family honour was more important than any game. When their dad walked out, the young Willises formed an impervious bond, looking after themselves and each other. That was the number-one priority.

Now, Johnny remained silent as Mr Bates turned his attention to the stricken lad on the floor. The boy, wiping his bloodied nose on a shirtsleeve, stifled a sob and slowly got to his feet. Frightened, he didn't look at Willis. He thought the kid was crazy.

'Go and wash your face, son. Bryant, you go with him and make sure he's all right.' The concerned teacher turned back to Johnny. 'Will you tell me what that was all about? If you carry on like this, I can't pick you for the team.'

'Sorry, sir, can't say. It was between me and him, that's all.'

Bates scrutinised the youngster's earnest face and then posed the question which would change Johnny's life. 'If you really want to fight, why don't you do it properly?'

'What do you mean, sir? I hit pretty good.'

'No, Willis, I mean why don't you join a boxing club? Learn to box properly in a ring with other boys who can fight a bit.' At the very least, thought Mr Bates, it would channel some of his aggression into a more fitting place. It might be the making of the boy. 'Think about it, Willis. There's a decent club in town and I know the trainer. If your mother agrees, I could take you along there. We'd need her permission. But, for now, you'd better get changed. You're sent off for fighting.'

Willis, head still high, made for the touchline but stopped in his tracks and turned. 'Sir?' he said.

'Yes, Willis, what is it?'

'I'll try the boxing. Don't worry about my Ma, she won't mind a bit.' And off he went to the dressing room with a fresh challenge, a new life, stretching before him.

Willis was an instant hit at the Friar Amateur Boxing Club. Harry Riley, a wiry, flat-nosed old pug of a man, had been trainer at the club for almost thirty years. He'd packed in the pro game after a lengthy but largely unsuccessful career around the small halls of Britain. Riley wasn't easily impressed but his eyes shone as soon as Willis pounded the heavy punchbag.

The kid not only had serious power for a youngster – 'Wot, only nine? That's a bit young but, okay, I'll have a look,' Riley had told Bates over the telephone – but his balance was superb. He was also nimble.

After three rounds on the bag, Willis was sweating, his arms weary. But his heart was pounding with a contentment he'd never known, not even when winning crunching tackles or slamming in long-range goals.

'Okay, son, that'll be all fer tonight,' said Harry, putting a gnarled hand on his shoulder.

Only it didn't quite sound like that to young Johnny. He looked at the veteran trainer. Flat nose, hanging eyebrows and cauliflower left ear. The slurred words seemed to escape from the old man's nose. After more than 150 fights and thousands of rounds sparring, Harry's speech was less than intelligible to the untrained ear.

Harry noticed the lad's shoulders slump and disappointment crease his fresh face. 'Whatsupson?'

Again, it took Willis a few seconds to understand the question. Then, brushing a lock of black hair back off his damp brow, he asked, 'Don't I get to fight, then?'

'Box, sonny, yer mean box. Anyone can 'ave a fight. I teach boxing. And, no, not tonight. Need to look atya some more. You've got plentya time, sonny. Seeya tomorra, eh?' He ruffled Willis's hair.

The next night – and every night the gym was open – Willis was there. Pounding the bag, learning to skip, shadow-boxing in front of a large, grimy mirror and watching everyone else working out. But he didn't get to box. Never stepped inside the ring.

Clearly the youngest at the club, it didn't stop him complaining to anyone who would listen. 'I want to fight, I mean, box. Why won't he let me?' They all smiled but still he didn't get to put on the big sparring gloves. He enjoyed training sure enough but, after all, he was there to swap a few punches. To show everyone how good he really was.

'Time enuff yetawhile,' was all Harry said. Until one night, when Willis was about to pull on the bag gloves for his nightly pounding, Harry stood in front of him. 'Shadder-box to warmup. Then yer can box. Lad over there'll do fer yer.'

And so young Willis finally got his wish. But, as Harry tied on the big gloves, the boy felt his stomach tighten – should he go to the toilet? – and there was a slight trembling in his arms. His legs felt weak. Butterflies. The nervous tension which every athlete needs before a performance.

Across the ring, a slightly taller, older lad beat his gloved fists together, waiting for the first bell. He'd show the new kid what it was all about.

'Just go steady, Pete,' ordered Harry. 'It's not a contest, justa spar.' But he didn't tell Willis.

At the sound of the bell, Willis forgot all about trembling limbs and knotted stomach. He moved swiftly into the centre of the ring where he was puzzled to see his opponent with both arms extended towards him. Pete Payne, six victorious schoolboy bouts to his credit, was even more surprised when Willis pushed a left jab into his face and followed with a jolting right hand that landed heavily on his chest.

'Whoa,' shouted Harry from outside the ropes. 'Yer gotta touch gloves.'

'Oh,' said Willis.

'It's okay,' mumbled Payne through his white gumshield. He'd make the kid pay for those cheap shots.

They touched gloves. Payne got up on his toes and circled to his left, pumping out a left lead straight at Willis's nose. Followed by another. And a third.

All three punches landed. Unexpected tears formed in Willis's eyes. There was a buzzing inside his head, a warm, stinging sensation around his nose. He didn't feel pain, just shock. He'd been hit before but, somehow, this was different. He felt anger welling up inside him.

He charged forward, swinging his right hand and ran smack into another left jab, his own wild punch flailing the air. In that instance, Willis recognised what old Harry meant when he said, 'Anyone can fight – I teach boxing.'

Payne was giving him his first boxing lesson.

Harry called time after two minutes. Willis had landed barely three glancing blows, but the lesson was well learned. He went home to his bed, aching and feeling his bumps, but determined to improve. Under Harry's watchful eye, he did improve. Swiftly.

After a month, there was little to choose between the two boys. They jabbed, slipped punches and swapped snappy right crosses. They also became friends. Willis respected Payne for his skills, for showing him that there was more to boxing than just bravado. Payne recognised that his young new sparmate was a quick learner and he respected Willis's power and grit.

'You're coming along great,' he told Willis as they dressed after one session.

'Thanks. I'm gonna be world champion, you know.' Payne laughed but Willis just stared at him. 'It's no joke. No point doing anything unless you're gonna be the best. I'll be the best.'

You could be right, thought Payne, impressed by his young pal's confidence.

Old Harry was certainly delighted with this spunky kid. Not only did he have natural balance and power in both hands but he was strong and willing to learn. Most of all, he had character. He took his knocks and came back even more determined. He's a nugget, a little diamond, thought Harry. If he doesn't lose his way, there's no telling where he might finish up.

## Chapter Two

Boxing changed Willis's life. Suddenly, in his hands, was the promise of a career with which he could achieve his goal. He could see a way out of the mean estate streets. Willis dreamed of a lifestyle of comfort and riches for him and beloved, put-upon sister Mary.

He was dedicated in training. He listened, watched and worked hard. He rarely missed a gym session and this took him off the streets, a territory in which his brothers were gathering a reputation.

They had little respect for the law. If they wanted something, they took it. Corner shops were easy prey. Create a commotion and – hey presto! – food, magazines, sweets, drinks, anything that could be smuggled out under jackets and sweaters or in pockets was snaffled.

From those petty beginnings, Kenny and Colin progressed to burglary – but not on their own patch. What the folk of Burnmoor Estate had, they deserved. Anyway, the pickings were richer in big detached houses or on the private developments. The rich folk could afford to lose a VCR, music centre or microwave. They'd be insured and, if not, that was their greedy misfortune.

Electrical goods were easy to sell. Second-hand shops and carboot merchants would buy them at a reasonable price. Kenny and Colin used their growing gang of pals to sell the stuff on.

The brothers also adopted a Robin Hood attitude. If someone in the neighbourhood wanted a TV or some such appliance, they'd supply it. Stealing to order, they didn't need to harbour goods for long. So their reputation grew and, good lads, they looked after their friends. In return, no one would dream of betraying the Willis boys.

Johnny avoided these activities except when his brothers wanted a special lookout or a smaller, fitter body to gain access on a job. Then he would oblige – but only after training. Mary worried about her lawless brothers but kept her counsel. Connie, too, said nothing.

For a time all three Willis boys boxed. The elder pair had decided one night to accompany their kid brother to the gym to ensure everything was okay. But, in their late teens, Kenny and Colin defected to other pursuits; pubs, clubs, girls and getting money. The dedication needed for boxing wasn't for them.

Kenny's incarceration for his vicious use of a bar stool also signalled the end of his boxing. When he emerged from the institution, he was a tough eighteen-year-old and even more determined to make money by whatever means he could. Colin, having maintained their 'business' interests during Kenny's absence, was happy to leave behind the demands of regular training. Boxing had served its purpose, consolidating their status as a duo handy with their fists.

Johnny prospered under old Harry and, later, a new assistant trainer, Ron Brown. Brown had been a good amateur. He once reached the national ABA welterweight quarter-finals but was never interested in punching for pay. He was skilful but too light-hitting. After sixty-seven contests his face bore few marks of battle.

Now thirty years old, Brown was barely above his ten stone seven pounds fighting weight. A self-employed painter and decorator, he maintained his fitness, worked on the pads with his young charges and occasionally sparred, passing on invaluable ring craft.

Willis and Brown struck up a rapport. Brown invited him to his home, a neat semi-detached house he shared with his petite wife Helen and their four-year-old twin daughters. Over sandwiches and tea, the trainer impressed Willis with stories of fighters and fights. He loaned the boy boxing books and maga-zines and they watched video tapes of some of the greats. Sugar Ray Robinson and Joe Louis, Rocky Marciano and Muhammad Ali, Marvin Hagler and Roberto Duran. It was all part of Willis's boxing education, fuelling his aspirations and increasing his knowledge of the sport's history and demands.

'It's a hard life, Johnny. Very few get to the top. For every champion, there's thousands who never make it. You've got to have ability but you need luck and, above all, determination.'

Willis would listen and nod. 'I'll do it,' he'd say. 'I'm gonna be champion of the world. It's the only reason to fight. I'll do whatever it takes.'

By the time he was fifteen, Willis hadn't lost in twenty-four contests. He had also won his first national title, a schoolboy championship, which led to his selection for England Schools against Wales in Cardiff.

Willis had never journeyed so far from home but he stopped his Welsh rival in the second round. His name began to appear in the amateur section of the *Boxing News* and his regional evening newspaper, the *Westhampton News*, recorded his progress. At first he appeared only in the results at the end of reports on Friar ABC shows. Then, as an unbeaten prospect, he was mentioned in the closing paragraphs. When he won his national title, he became headline news.

It wasn't a big headline – 'Willis storms to schools crown' across two columns – but there was a picture. The *News* sent a photographer to his school and he was taken out of lessons to pose, smiling, with his trophy. It was rare for someone from the Burnmoor Estate to be in the papers, unless it was for a court appearance.

Willis took the publicity and fuss in his stride. It didn't alter his outlook, although it gave Mary yet another job. She started a scrapbook. It pleased Willis that his sister was so obviously proud of his achievements. Connie barely managed to say 'well done' although she became more enthusiastic when her men friends praised Johnny and even started to turn up at his fights. Kenny and Colin encouraged their building mates to follow his career. 'Our kid's going places,' they'd tell anyone who'd listen.

Payne was probably most thrilled. Willis's best pal didn't sustain his own boxing rise, as three consecutive defeats dented his confidence and ambition. But they still enjoyed regular sparring sessions. 'You're a champ now, Johnny. You're on the way to that world title,' he said.

Brown understood the euphoria and, though the talk was grossly premature, he built on Willis's single-minded purpose.

'You're getting what you work for, Johnny. Keep at it, but remember this. There's an old saying: "No gain without pain." You're a winner now but, along the line somewhere, one day, it will go wrong. You can go out in the rain with an umbrella but you won't dodge all the spots. Randy Turpin said that, I think. Point is, it depends how you handle the knocks. Even Ali was beaten.'

Willis listened. He knew life wasn't easy and his chosen path was a rugged one. But he would come through. He had all the incentives. Failure wasn't even a fleeting consideration.

'I'll be fine, don't you worry about that,' he assured his trainer.

In the next two years, Willis chalked up another sixteen victories, adding a Junior ABA crown to his championship record. Mary's scrapbook grew and Willis got to know and respect Bob Mercer, the boxing writer on the *News*.

Brown made the introductions after one gym session. Mercer, a balding, bespectacled divorcee in his mid-forties, had been around boxing for thirty years, as a fan and then as a reporter. Well known among the Midlands boxing fraternity, he was on more than nodding terms with the big-time operators.

He'd covered world championship boxing in America – he'd even shaken hands with Don King and Bob Arum – and reported from many European capitals as well as the big London shows. But he retained a love for the grassroots of the sport. Mercer was just as happy covering Friar ABC shows as he was watching Ali–Cooper or Minter–Hagler.

But, most of all, Mercer was a boxer's man. Brown told Willis several stories of how the reporter had advised and helped boxers, himself included, and his first interview with Mercer left an impression on the teenager. It was really no more than a casual chat, not a question-and-answer session, but he made Willis feel important. And that from a man who had spoken to Ali!

What really surprised Willis was that their conversation – how long had it been, twenty minutes at most? – turned into a long article; a mini-feature accompanied by archive photographs taken in the previous two years. It appeared in the *News* just two nights after their meeting and an excited Mary brought it to his attention. Under the bold headline 'Johnny's world' with a subsidiary heading which declared 'Young Willis putting town on boxing map' Mercer wrote:

Johnny Willis, the first Westhampton boxer to win a Junior ABA title since featherweight Michael Turner 32 years ago, has one target in life – to be world champion.

This 17-year-old has emerged from the Burnmoor Estate to be not only the leading light of the Friar ABC but probably the most exciting talent to come out of the Griffin Road gymnasium.

A former schoolboy champion and England schools international, in eight years he has compiled an impressive record of 40 contests without a defeat. And, proof of his power punching, the light-welterweight has won 28 inside the distance.

World championships, of course, are a long way off but veteran Friar trainer Harry Riley and his assistant Ron Brown, remembered for his rousing ABA quarter-final which he lost to Liverpudlian Jackie Jones in 1974, believe they have unearthed a gem.

'From the first day he came here, just a scrawny nine year old, I could see he was special,' recalls Riley. 'He not only had talent but he was keen. All he wanted to do was fight.'

Brown adds: 'He's been a delight to train. He listens, he learns and he's always in the gym. I doubt if there is a better young 10-stoner in the country.'

Willis faces his first year in the seniors next season but Brown is convinced his young champion is ready for open competition. 'He's a strong lad and still growing. His punching power gets more impressive each year. I should know – I get the jolts right through my arms when we work on the pads.'

But Willis is more than just a knock-out specialist. He has a snappy, jolting left lead and is not one to take unnecessary punches. 'I'm lucky to have Harry and Ron. They're good trainers,' says quietly spoken Willis, whose two elder brothers Ken and Colin also boxed at Friar until a couple of years ago.

Willis also gives credit to his regular sparring partner, welterweight Pete Payne. 'He was the first lad I ever sparred with. He gave me a right pasting,' laughs Willis. 'He's my best mate now and I owe a lot to him. He showed me there was more to this game than just having a scrap.'

So, just how far does Willis think he can go? 'I've always said I want to be a world champion. If I do well in the next two or three years, I'll probably turn pro. There's no rush, I'm still learning, but this is a hard game just to win plastic trophies and cups. I know the pro game is even harder but I wouldn't want to be just a six-round fighter. The real money is in titles and you've got to aim for the top.'

Although he has big ambitions and is certainly a firm believer in his ability, Willis, who works as a supermarket shelf-stacker, is modest and certainly grateful to those who have helped him along the way. So far, he has more than repaid them for their assistance.

It's still early days, but keep an eye out for young Johnny Willis. The teenager is putting Westhampton back on the boxing map.

Nothing seemed to daunt Willis. Not even when, in his first senior bout at Doncaster, he met Clive Richards. Black as Yorkshire coal and twice as hard, Richards was a seasoned campaigner in his mid-twenties. With gloves held high, he forced his way in close to unleash rib-bruising hooks. He was also adept at an illegal forearm smash and used his head as a battering ram.

'You've got to use your jab, Johnny,' said Brown at the end of the first round. 'Stick it in his face when he comes in. Knock him off his stride. And use your legs. Don't stand and trade. He's a tough bastard.'

Willis had other plans. As instructed, he rammed home two left leads at the start of the second round, which momentarily stopped Richards in his tracks. But the Tyke bustled inside, rushed Willis to the ropes and attempted an audacious butt. The referee ignored the offence but Willis locked his left arm around Richards's neck and gave it a mighty wrench.

The packed partisan crowd roared their disapproval. This time, the referee stepped in. 'Don't do that again or you'll be out of this ring like a shot,' he warned Willis, wagging his finger. Willis simply looked nonchalantly over the official's shoulder at Richards. He was rolling his neck, attempting to ease the pain.

'Box on.'

Richards stormed forward, ready to show the young upstart what rough fighting was all about. From a crouched position, he launched a swinging right at Willis's groin. It never landed. Willis sent a scything right on to Richards's temple and the black man hit the canvas in a sitting position.

He was up at the count of six and took the rest of the mandatory 'eight' on his feet. He gained a few more seconds of recovery as the referee wiped his gloves, looked into his eyes and asked whether he was able to continue. Richards nodded – and quickly wished he hadn't.

Willis, swiftly across the ring, feinted to throw another big right and, as the Doncaster man swayed to avoid the blow, he was caught flush on the jaw with a sizzling left hook. It was all over before Richards even fell to the canvas. After starting the count, the referee abandoned the idea. Richards lay motionless on his left side, gumshield half out of his mouth.

Brown rubbed Willis's face with a towel. 'Smart work, Johnny. What a punch! A real peach!'

'He shouldn't have tried the fucking rough stuff. Wouldn't last five minutes on our estate.'

'He didn't last five minutes here. You'd better go over to him,' said Brown, nodding in the direction of the opposite corner.

Richards had been plopped onto his stool and the doctor was looking into his eyes, asking simple questions. 'Where are you? How many fingers am I showing?'

Willis went over and tapped his opponent sportingly on the head. 'Hard luck. You okay?' he said in a flat voice.

'Sure,' said Richards, not yet sufficiently recovered to rise off his stool. 'I'll live. Good punch.'

'Thanks. Be lucky.' Willis turned away and put on his dressing gown. He received polite applause from the stunned but grudgingly admiring crowd when he was announced 'the winner by count-out in thirty-five seconds of the second round'.

Willis collected his prize; a canteen of cutlery in a box which had clearly seen better days.

'Looks like we'll be able to flog this junk back,' he said to Brown in the dressing room. 'Seems it's done the rounds for some time.'

'I'll ask when I collect the expenses,' Brown said.

'How much are we on?'

'I asked for thirty-five quid.'

The Doncaster club's treasurer was happy to buy back the cutlery. It saved buying new prizes at inflated prices. But he haggled over the value.

'Must be worth at least forty quid,' claimed Brown.

'Nay, lad, twenty. Not a 'pennorth more.'

'You're kidding? We've not come all this way for a poxy twenty-quid prize. Give us thirty-five and the same in exes. That's fair.'

'I remember thee boxing, our Ronnie. Tricky Charlie then, I recall. I'll give thee thirty – if lad promises to come back again. Reet poplar he were.'

'Didn't sound too popular to me.'

'Mebbe they didn't show it. But crowd loved 'im. I can tell. Thirty pounds, is it?'

'Make it thirty-five and I'll definitely bring him back. For better exes, of course.'

'You bugger! Okay, thirty-five it be. But you'll sign for forty-five. Got to keep books in order, you know.'

'Not a bad night. A win and seventy quid,' said Willis, taking the money from Brown. 'Here, twenty for the petrol.'

'Give me ten. That'll be fine. You've earned it.'

'Okay, Ron. Thanks. There'll be bigger pay days down the road. Just you see. This is only the start. We'll come back here any time, if they can find someone to fight me.'

'They'll find someone, don't you worry. They'll be looking for revenge. I know these folk. Be warned, you did well tonight, a good win against a hard opponent. But there's a lot harder out there.'

Willis smiled and put his hand on his trainer's shoulder. 'You worry too much. Anyway, shouldn't you phone old Harry and tell him how we got on? I'm gonna let Mary know.'

Mary never watched her brother box. 'I couldn't bear it, seeing you hit,' she would shudder. 'No, never. You carry on. It's what you like and you're good at it. I'm pleased for you. But don't ask me to come with you. Just let me know you're all right. That's all I ask.'

She's more like a mother than a younger sister, thought Willis. No, that's not right. Ma doesn't give a fuck what's happening to me. All she worries about is herself, her men and her parties.

How Mary puts up with it, I don't know. One day, I'll get her out of this mess. That's a promise. And bollocks to Ma. She'll have to fend for herself then.

'Hi, Mary, it's me, Johnny,' he virtually shouted down the phone. 'Can you hear me?'

'Yeah – just a minute.'

He heard the receiver being placed on the table and then voices rise in the background. The loud music eventually subsided. Mary was back. 'Sorry, Johnny. I've asked Ma to turn the music down for a bit.'

'Having another party, is she? Who's there?'

'Just a few friends.'

'All men, I bet.'

'No, silly. It's the normal bunch. You know, Maggie, Beth, Arnie, that crowd. Oh, and that new guy of hers, whatsisname?'

'Dick?'

'That's him. Works at your place, doesn't he?'

'He's in the offices. Anyway, don't let them keep you up late. School in the morning.'

'Don't worry. But what about you? You sound okay. Are you?'

'Fine. No problems. Won in the second.'

'Second! That's great. Well done, Johnny. Some more cuttings for the scrapbook?'

'Don't think so. Not from up here. Ron'll ring Bob Mercer with the news in the morning. That's about all.'

'Still, it's a good start with the big boys, isn't it?'

'Big boys?' Willis laughed. 'Seniors, Mary, not big boys.'

'Same thing. You're with the big boys now.'

'Sorry, Mary, has she turned the music up again? I can hardly hear you.'

'Yeah, never mind Johnny. Don't put any more money in the box. I'll see you in the morning. Well done. Love you.'

'Okay sis. Love you… Damn,' he said as the line went dead. Bet she couldn't hear me because of that fat cow and her loud music, he thought. The neighbours would complain if it wasn't for fear of getting a back-hander from our Kenny. More's the pity. We could do with more peace and quiet, especially now that Mary's studying so hard.

'You know, Ron,' he said as they climbed into the trainer's van, 'my ma's a selfish bitch. Doesn't care about anyone but herself. She really puts on Mary. Treats her like a slave, not a daughter. I don't know how sis puts up with it.'

Brown was used to occasional outbursts from Willis. Very much a private person, the boy usually he kept his thoughts to himself. But his mother upset him. Brown tried to placate Willis.

'I don't suppose it's been easy for her. Not when your dad left her with four young kids. Think about it, Johnny.'

'That's the point. I can't remember her doing anything. It's always been her friends and the neighbours who were there for us. Mrs Thompson across the road fed us more jam sandwiches than Ma ever did. She's never bothered where we were, what we were doing. Nothing. No, that's not quite right. She always knew where Mary was because she did the work. The work Ma should have been doing. Not some schoolkid. I know this much, if there's justice in this world then, one day, Ma will get her comeuppance. She'd better not come to me for help. Bollocks to that.'

Brown glanced across the darkened interior of the van, noting Willis's stern profile as he glared straight ahead. He means it, he thought. 'I know how you feel. But blood's thicker than water, you know. In time you may think differently.'

'Uh,' replied Johnny.

And then silence.

It was three months before Willis went back to Doncaster. He'd won four more bouts, one on his home show in the first round. Another perfect left hook.

Harry joined them this time. It was rare for the old trainer to close the gym for a night but he wanted to be there. Like Brown, he knew the Tykes wanted revenge and he wasn't going to allow any funny business.

'Strength in numbers,' he mumbled when Brown asked him why he wanted to be there.

'I can handle it, Harry.'

'That's as maybe. No harm in making sure. They're a cunning bunch, just like the Cockneys.'

The old pug was right.

Shaun Tomkins, a stocky ginger-haired bruiser, was the proposed opponent. Harry went wild at the weigh-in. 'Yer can't call him a light-welter,' he shouted at the Doncaster matchmaker. 'Chrissakes! He's bigger than welterweight. We're not 'aving this.'

'Okay, Shaun's a bit heavy. But he's only ten-eight and he's not the class of your kid. We've seen his punch,' countered the matchmaker.

'Look 'ere. Johnny's only ten-two and that's too much to give away. He's only seventeen years old, fer Chrissakes.'

'All I'm saying is, your kid's got class. Shaun 'ere... well, he's a decent fighter but, honest, he'll do well to last with yon Willis.'

'Bullshit,' interjected Brown. 'Weight's important and you know it.'

The matchmaker sighed. 'That's it, then. You've come for nowt. We've no one else to fight him.'

'We'll need exes,' said Brown. 'It's cost us to get here. It's not our fault you've got nobody.'

'Just a minute.' It was Willis. Turning to the matchmaker, he said, 'There's three of us. Give us fifty quid expenses and the same again for a prize. I bet you've still got some knives and forks knocking about.'

'That's 'undred pounds,' said the matchmaker.

'That's it. I'll take your man, big as he is. But I want paying for it.'

The matchmaker rubbed his bristly chin and looked across at the club's treasurer. 'What d'ya think, Gerry?'

'It's a lotta brass. How's rest o' bill?'

'Not bad. But this'd be top fight.'

'Worth paying for, then,' cut in Willis.

The two canny Yorkshire men looked at him. Cocky bugger, they thought. Shaun'll bring him down a peg or two. The treasurer nodded and the matchmaker said, 'It's a deal. Fight's on at your terms. Four rounds, though.'

'Whoa,' said Harry loudly. 'Johnny's never boxed four in his life. An' he's not gonna do it givin' six pound away.'

'Look, for 'undred quid—'

'It's okay,' said Willis. 'Deal's done. But I'm not going on last.

We've a long way to get home.'

'Fine. Second after interval do?'

'Thanks, but no later.'

Back in the dressing room, crowded with a dozen boxers and their seconds, Riley was livid. 'What d'yer think yer up to, Johnny?'

'What's up, Harry?'

'I come up 'ere to look after yer interests. And what d'yer do? Yer takes over.'

'Sorry, Harry, but I want the fight. And I want the money. It's a good deal.'

'Good deal? Listen, sonny, there's never a good deal with these Tykes. They'll be 'specting blood and it won't be theirs. Believe me.'

Willis laughed. 'Harry, you worry too much. There's not a problem.'

Brown shook his head. 'I know you're confident, Johnny. But Harry's right. It's a lot of weight to give away. And four rounds?'

'Four rounds! I won't need four rounds.'

'Look,' said Riley, 'I'm not knocking yer boxing. Yer good, I know that. But yer've a lot to learn. Don't go poking yer nose in. Making matches is not yer job. Leave that to us.'

'Sorry, Harry. I wasn't being flash.'

'Flash? I 'ope not. Anyway, what's done's done. C'mon, Ron, we've helluva job. Let's get 'im ready.'

But Willis was ready. Not stripped for action but, mentally, he was prepared. He liked the odds stacked against him. It had always been that way. In life, in school, in sport. He smiled to himself.

Harry was clearly worried. Perhaps he's had his day, thought Willis. Too old now. Ron, who busied himself organising the kit, getting the gloves and wrapping Johnny's hands, seemed to thaw. He's come to terms with it, thought Willis.

'How do they feel?' asked Brown when he'd finished applying the gauze and tape.

Willis smacked each fist alternately into his palms. 'Fine. How do you feel?'

Brown gazed into Willis's brown eyes, clipped him lightly on the jaw and grinned. 'You're a cool one, Johnny Willis. You'll do for me. But be careful out there. Have a look at him. Don't do anything rash.'

The smoky hall was packed as the Westhampton trio made their way through the expectant crowd to the small ring. Many of the spectators had seen Willis dispatch Richards but they knew Tomkins was something else. He was the best fighter in the club, perhaps the whole of South Yorkshire. The Midland gypsy would get sorted tonight.

Willis anticipated a furious start from Tomkins, but it didn't happen. And there was another thing. He was a southpaw.

'Chrissakes,' mumbled Harry when the two boxers squared up. 'He's a fucking lefty as well.'

Willis hadn't boxed many right-hand lead boxers but he'd not had any trouble handling them. He hadn't had much trouble in any contest.

Tomkins was compact. Elbows tucked in, he moved his head from side to side and pawed out his extended right arm to measure the range. Willis kept on his toes and made the first move, a light double jab. Both punches landed on Tomkins's forehead and the Yorkshire man replied with a flashing right that caught Johnny on his left ear. It didn't hurt but it stung. The guy could obviously punch his weight.

'Hands up,' he heard Ron shout above the roar of four hundred Yorkshire throats.

It was a cagey first round.

'Get some snap in yer jab,' Riley implored as Brown gave Willis a swallow of water from the bottle. 'Yer only poking it out.'

That's the idea, thought Willis, and he continued to prod and poke through the second three minutes.

Tomkins, who stole the round with his own jab and a couple of straight lefts to the midriff, grew in confidence. 'Nowt much to 'im,' he told his corner. 'Jab's nowt.'

'Step up pressure, then, Shaun. See what he's made of,' his trainer said. Shaun nodded and bit hard on his water-rinsed mouthpiece.

The storm Willis had anticipated finally arrived. Tomkins thrust out a right lead and rushed in, clubbing to the body with both hands. Willis grabbed him and pulled him to the ropes. The referee ordered 'break'.

Tomkins was all aggression, pumped up. But he maintained his discipline, weaving his head, keeping his elbows tucked by his sides. Willis got on his toes, moving left and right, prodding with his left glove. Tomkins contemptuously brushed it aside and prepared to launch a mighty attack. As he stormed forward, Willis dropped on to the heels of his boots and rammed a jab into Tomkins's face.

It was the first solid lead Willis had thrown and Tomkins unwittingly added to its impact with his rush forward. The blow landed square on his nose, drawing blood. Tomkins was stunned, surprised by the strength of the jab. Where did he get that from? And, before he could cover up or respond, Willis cracked him with a vicious left hook.

Tomkins, almost in slow motion, started to fall. His legs had turned to jelly and he reached out with his left arm to cushion his impact on the canvas. Then another punch, a right hook which he saw only as a red blur, altered the course of his tumble. He crashed on to his back, but he didn't know it. He was concussed.

Harry's mouth gaped. Brown leaped out of his crouch by the ring post, wet sponge still in his right hand. He thrust it into the air and clenched his fist, sending water running down his arm.

'Yes!' he shouted, clambering into the ring as the referee bent over the stricken Tomkins, pulling out his bloodied mouthpiece. 'Come here, you beauty,' Brown said, spraying Willis with what water remained in the sponge.

Harry, still hardly believing what he had witnessed, pulled himself through the ropes. He tapped Willis on his firm stomach. 'Yer did great, son, just great.'

Willis smiled. 'You worry too much, Harry.'

'I tell you, Bob, he's something special.' Brown was on the telephone to Mercer early the next morning. 'That Shaun Tomkins is a good fighter, experienced, and he had a big weight advantage. I don't mind telling you, I was worried. They said he was ten-eight but he looked bigger.'

'What did Johnny weigh?'

'They said ten-two but I know he was more. They'd fixed the

scales. Johnny's growing and I can't see him making light-welter, but I don't know where he'd lose weight. There's not an ounce of fat on him. Anyway, that's another story. Point is, he not only knocked the guy out but he set him up.'

'What d'you mean? How did he set him up?'

'He conned him. It was beautiful. I'm telling you, Bob, he's got a fantastic boxing brain. He's not just a kid with a punch.'

'I've seen him, Ron. I know he's got a good jab and he moves well. He opens them up for the big finish.'

'But this was different. Listen, Harry and me were worried because Johnny didn't have any power in his jab. Just shoving it out, like, and I began to think, "Maybe he's taken on too much." You know, like it was a bigger step than he thought and he was just trying to get through the four rounds. Oh yeah, I forgot to tell you, it was a four-rounder.'

'That was a big step.'

'Sure. But Johnny wanted it. That's the point, see? He'd been so confident beforehand and then, in the ring, he's not the usual Johnny.'

'Hesitant?'

'Not really. Just not firing all-out, not taking charge as he does. But it was all part of his plan. He got this Shaun character believing that he really didn't have a dig. And, come the third round, he starts to go after Johnny. Then – wham! Johnny caught him coming in with a tremendous jab, straight on the hooter. It shook him up. But the best was to come. Johnny whipped in a left hook to the jaw and then smacked him with a right as he fell. That was it, good night and thank you. I'm telling you, he was terrific.'

'Sounds like it, Ron. I'll get a few paragraphs in tonight's editions. Thanks for the call. Keep in touch.'

'Sure thing, Bob. I know you can't write all that in the paper. People wouldn't understand. They just want to know that he knocked the guy out. But I thought you'd like to know. You understand the game, Bob.'

'Quit the flattery, Ron. But you're right, fans just love to see the big knock-out punch. They don't bother about the build-up. I'll see you at the gym one night.'

Mercer put the phone down. He thought for a moment, looked up at the clock and saw it was only fifteen minutes to nine. Plenty of time to write the latest on young Willis. He picked up the phone again and dialled a London number.

'Good morning. Is Mr Sellers there? It's Bob Mercer from the *Westhampton News* here. Thanks.'

Lew Sellers was a veteran boxing manager. Known in some quarters as Lew the Jew, he was in his sixtieth year. He'd managed champions since the late 1950s and was one of the most influential men in the fight game. He didn't manage mugs. He didn't need to. His record ensured that he had the pick of the leading amateurs and, in some ways, that made his job easier. But Sellers, a short man with wavy hair and a contented paunch, would bristle at the suggestion. 'It wasn't always like this, you know,' he would say. 'I worked bloody hard to be a success. I've travelled up and down the country at godforsaken hours with six-round fighters. It's not always been champions and top purses. No way.'

'Hello, Bob, long time since I heard from you. What's doing?'

'It's been a while. Then again, it's some time since you had a fighter from around here.'

'More's the pity. We could do with some fresh blood from the Midlands. I've always liked the area. Had some good fighters from your way.'

'That's why I'm calling. It's early days yet, but I thought I'd mark your card about a young amateur called Johnny Willis.'

'Junior champ. That him?'

'Yes. He's not eighteen yet but I think he'll be a good 'un. It's my guess it won't be long before he thinks about turning pro. I've just had his trainer on the phone. He won again last night, a knock-out up in Doncaster. That makes forty-six wins out of forty-six.'

'Will he be in the ABAs this year?'

'Probably next year. He's growing all the time. Supposed to be light-welter but I don't think he can make ten stone. He'll probably be welterweight next season. He's worth keeping an eye on.'

'Are you close to him, Bob?'

'Not really. Just getting to know him. Lives on one of the

council estates. Got two elder brothers who boxed for a while. Couple of hard cases.'

'What about the boy? Is he a clean-living lad or what?'

'Haven't heard anything bad. He trains hard, seems dedicated enough. But he's young and, as you know, Lew, a lot can happen.'

'Sure. Well, thanks for the call, Bob. Appreciate it. Keep me in touch. I might even treat you to dinner next time you're down this way.'

Mercer laughed. Sellers had a reputation for being careful, if not mean, with his money. 'I'm still waiting for that drink you promised me a year ago,' said the reporter.

# Chapter Three

Willis, much to his annoyance, didn't compete in the Amateur Boxing Association championships that year. His trainers agreed that he should wait until he developed into a full welterweight.

'There's plenty of time, Johnny,' reasoned Brown. 'I know you want to have a go at the nationals but you can't make light-welter and I'm not sure you're ready to step up to ten-seven just yet. There's seasoned men in the championship. Past champions and internationals, as well. Be patient. Time's on your side.'

He had four more club contests, all victories, only one going the distance. That was an off night at the end of the season when Willis confessed to feeling a bit jaded. 'Couldn't get going,' he moaned.

'It's okay,' said Ron. 'Everybody has one of those nights. You still won and that's what matters. It's been a long season. You can ease off in the summer and get yourself refreshed. Just tick over in the gym coupla times a week, nothing strenuous. Keep the pipes open.'

But there was more to it than an off night. Willis had quit his job. Shelf-stacking was boring. Apart, that is, from fumbling about with the girls. Most were a good laugh. Some were not bad-looking, either and Willis discovered that his growing fame, his minor celebrity, was an added attraction for the opposite sex.

Shirley Collins, a nineteen-year-old checkout operator, was especially enamoured – and endowed. Blessed with luxuriant, long, black hair and high cheekbones, Shirley used her deep-set, smouldering violet eyes to send out signals. She'd pucker up pink lips, smooth her hands slowly over rounded hips, push a consid-erable chest towards Willis and, in a husky voice, promise, 'One day, if you're very good, Johnny, this could be yours.'

That day, in fact, turned out to be a Saturday night. At Shirley's suggestion, they went to the cinema. With the lights dimmed and Clint Eastwood taking on the world's bad guys, they enjoyed two hours of exploration.

'Don't be in such a rush, Johnny,' she said as her eager suitor grasped at her right breast. 'Take your time. Give me a proper kiss.' Their lips locked, moistening as Shirley flicked her tongue into Willis's mouth. 'That's better.'

Her violet eyes sparkled as she rested a hand on his thigh. They kissed again; a long, lingering union. Willis murmured with unexpected pleasure as Shirley guided his hand back to her bra-less breast. Through her dress, he felt the firm mound of flesh and rubbed his fingers against the hard nipple. Shirley squirmed in her seat. She ran fingers through the back of his hair and slipped her tongue again into his mouth, gently nibbling his when Willis responded.

All too soon, Clint had rid the planet of bad guys. 'Time to go, Johnny,' said Shirley, caressing his cheek and then straightening her clothes. 'Walk me home?'

'Sure, if I dare stand up,' he smiled, looking at his aching, bulging crotch.

'Seems a pity to waste that,' she said and, for the first time, lightly brushed his straining manhood. Taking him by the hand, she said, 'C'mon, home time.'

They walked for nearly two miles, stopping occasionally for another kiss, until Shirley said, 'Here we are.'

'Here' was a pre-war semi-detached house, bordered by shoulder-high privet hedges. The house was in darkness.

'No one at home?' he asked.

'Yes, there is,' said Shirley, noticing a flash of disappointment cross Willis's eyes. 'But Mum and Dad will be in bed. They always go about eleven. Come in for a coffee.'

They entered through the front door and Shirley switched on the hall light.

'That you, Shirl?' came a gruff voice from above.

'Yes, Dad. Just brought a friend in for a coffee. That okay?'

'Okay, luv. Keep the noise down.'

'Course, Dad. We'll be in the kitchen.' She took Willis by the hand and led him down the passage.

The kitchen was spacious, with fitted imitation-pine cup-boards and work surfaces, a shiny white oven, washer and refrigerator. In the centre of the room was a large wooden table.

'Very nice,' whispered Willis. 'Real home comforts.'

Shirley looked at him and, with a quick smile, pecked his lips. 'Shut the door. Coffee first. It'll give them time to get off to sleep.'

'Time?'

'Yes, time, silly. I told you that was too good to waste.' She looked in the direction of Willis's now subsided groin. 'Oh, where's it gone?'

'Don't worry. It's only resting. In between rounds, like.'

Shirley made mugs of coffee which they drank, leaning against the sink. They spoke in whispers until, with mugs drained, Willis looked into this remarkable girl's eyes. Would she know he was a virgin? He certainly wasn't going to tell her.

'What you thinking, Johnny?'

'Uh, just what lovely eyes you have.'

'Is that all?'

'No... course not,' he faltered. 'You've got a lovely face altogether and...'

'And what?' She swayed her hips and posed, hands on her slender waist, bosom jutting and raven tresses tumbling over her shoulders.

Willis studied her for a few seconds. 'And what a picture!'

A short, throaty chuckle and then that husky voice again. 'Well, Johnny, I think you've been a good boy. This could be your day. What do you say?'

He said nothing, but he took her in his arms and bent to kiss her warm mouth, tasting the coffee and last remnants of pink lipstick. She sighed and let Willis guide her backwards until her buttocks rested against the edge of the table.

'Steady, tiger,' she said, unbuttoning his shirt and running her fingers against his firm hairless chest. 'Mmm... smooth as a baby's bum but as hard as iron. Just what I like.' She slipped the shirt down over his shoulders and then leaned into him. 'Undo my zip.'

Her dress slithered slowly down, uncovering proud breasts, and wriggled over her hips and thighs to reveal white panties and black hold-up nylons. Shirley stepped out of the dress, her full breasts quivering as she kicked the garment to one side. Willis felt a twinge in his groin.

The near-naked girl put her hands on Willis's waist and pulled him close, her face upturned, eyes pleading. They kissed and Willis felt hands unbuckling and then unzipping his trousers. Hands slid inside the waistband of his boxer shorts, fingers lightly walking down his buttocks. God, what a touch! Then – oh God! Oh God! – a hand circled his erect shaft, gently stroking, caressing it upwards towards his stomach. Oh God!

Trousers around his ankles, Willis stood transfixed, holding on tight as Shirley, still fondling his throbbing penis, tugged at his boxers with her free left hand. He stepped clumsily out of his trousers and shorts, causing Shirley to release him.

'Take my knickers off.'

He bent before her. She placed her hands on the top of his head and he eased her panties down. He saw a thick, dark bush and a damp patch on her knickers as she stepped out of them. Pressing his face into her smooth, soft stomach, he automatically kissed her navel. She shuddered as he slowly stood, tongue trailing up her pale torso to stiff, brown nipples. He kissed and suckled them as she again grasped his erection and, standing on tip-toes, settled her buttocks on the table edge.

Willis, reluctantly, left her breasts. They kissed as she coiled her legs around his hips and guided him towards her moist mound. She fed the seeping, bulbous end into the warm cavity and whispered into his ear. 'Fuck me slowly. Be gentle.'

Gradually, he eased into her. His primeval urge was to pump furiously, to feel power surge through his loins, but he held back, controlled his lust and rhythmically, like a piston, sated himself. All too soon he felt his passion swelling and throbbing, ready to explode.

'It's coming,' he gasped.

Shirley clung to his neck. That husky whisper. 'Let it come, lover.'

And, with strangled gasps, he enjoyed a moment never to be repeated. His first release of seed into a woman, spurting, shooting into a dark, wet void. Shirley bit into his neck and trembled, beads of perspiration running between her breasts. She clamped her legs firmly around him, savouring the moment, her flared nostrils relishing the scent of their union.

'God, Johnny, that was good,' she said at length, kissing his brow, nose and, finally, his mouth.

He smiled down at her. Fuck me, he thought, I'm good at this, too.

It was a long, hot summer and the obsessed young lovers bloomed. Willis, invited to Sunday tea, was courteous to Shirley's parents, a genuine politeness which stemmed from his pleasure at being welcomed into a quiet, normal household. What a difference to the bedlam of 36 Johnson Close!

The idyll became heaven during the first two weeks of July when Mr and Mrs Collins flew to Crete for their annual holiday. Willis virtually moved in. He met Shirley at the end of each working day and they gloried in their freedom and the sharing of new experiences. For the first time they slept in a bed and spent complete nights together.

Willis even missed gym sessions, but he didn't give it a second thought. The delights and mysteries of Shirley's sexual prowess consumed him. She was nothing if not imaginative in their couplings, using different positions and places around the house. One balmy evening, they daringly mated on the lawn while neighbours feasted at a barbecue next door, only a six-foot fence shielding them. Furtiveness added to the pleasure.

Shirley was an ardent, seductive teacher and Willis was a compliant, faithful pupil. But he was far from passive and quickly learned when to take control and the precise moment to use his developing sensual skills to lift his eager lover to wild ecstasy. Thanks to Shirley's confident coaching, he was a considerate partner. 'Don't be in a hurry. Enjoy the moment. Control the urges. Pleasure me and you'll get even more pleasure,' she said.

Willis's excitable drive didn't always allow him to meet her wishes. But such was his stamina – a combination of youth and physical training – he did not disappoint. He would spill his seed but still maintain a powerful erection. Then he'd bring voluptuous Shirley to a writhing, convulsive orgasm, and not just once, or even twice, in their prolonged sessions.

'That was wonderful, Johnny,' she'd say, sprawled across his chest, fingers teasing his firm abdomen.

'Carry on doing that and I'll start again.'

'Uh… promises, promises.' Teasing in her husky voice, casually rubbing her palm over his stirring member. And on they would go into the night.

Yet, even as their relationship grew, Willis's guard remained. His independence and shell of self-preservation were always there, protecting him from suffering a major disappointment. One day, this will all be over, he told himself. We'll both move on. It's just a brief moment, soon to be a memory. There are more important things. Like boxing. Being a champion. Earning money.

Money was a problem as Willis had no real income. He signed on for benefit but had no intention of taking up the menial employment opportunities he was offered. Kenny and Colin helped out and he reciprocated by assisting in their various activities.

Colin latched on to new and easy pickings; credit card and chequebook thefts.

'It's amazing how people leave them lying around. They're in wallets, in drawers, even just left on a table. They're asking us to nick 'em. So why not?' he would say.

They did and it fell to Johnny to use them. He stocked the larder, buying disposable goods at various supermarkets. Better still, some suckers even left a pin number in their wallets. Cashpoints surrendered hundreds of pounds before the victim reported the loss. Then a hole-in-the-wall would simply gobble up the card.

In August, with the new boxing season looming, Willis resumed serious training. It was unusually hard work and old Harry chided him. 'Whatya being doin' with yerself? Yer look knackered.'

That, Willis thought, wasn't far from the truth, After training, he'd rush off to indulge himself with Shirley. He didn't need anyone to tell him what was happening. The romps had to have a downside. Time to cool it, take a step back. What did he want? To be a stud or a champion?

Shirley had been good to him. He liked the girl, but he had to tell her. Would she understand? It's not as if we can't see each other, he thought. Just calm it down. Oh, what the hell! It's my life. What does it matter what she thinks? Shirl's had a good time, too. She's had plenty from me – plenty of cock certainly. If she doesn't understand, well, that's tough. There's more important things in *my* life.

He told Shirley while her parents were away for the weekend, visiting relatives in Scotland. They lay naked on top of the bed, recovering, Shirley resting on his chest. He idly twisted her raven locks around his fingers.

'Look, Shirl, you know what I do?'

'You and your brothers, you mean?'

'No, me. My boxing.'

'Course I do.'

'The new season's starting and I must get back to serious training.'

'Thought you'd started.'

'I have. But it's an important year. I've got to keep my mind on boxing. No distractions, like. I'm going for the ABAs. They're the biggest thing outside the Olympics.'

'What, even bigger than this?' she teased, wrapping her fingers around his flaccid penis.

'That's just what I mean.' The harsh rising edge of his voice startled her. 'I can't be messing about all the time. Even old Harry said the other day that I looked knackered.'

Shirley sat up, folding her legs into the lotus position. Her damp, dark bush glistened but Willis didn't look. No distractions.

'What're you saying, Johnny?'

'I'm not very good with words.' He paused. 'We've had a great time and you know I really like you. But, boxing's my game. It's what I'm good at and – no, don't say anything.' He stopped again as Shirley swallowed unspoken words. She tossed her hair across her back and stared, anxiously waiting.

'I can't carry on seeing you like this,' he said. 'It's too much.'

Silence filled the bedroom. Eventually, in a familiar husky tone, Shirley spoke. 'You want to finish?'

'That's up to you, Shirl. I'd like to keep seeing you. But I can't be coming round as often. That might not be enough for you. I don't really know what you want.'

'Don't you? I want you, Johnny. Always have, since the first day I saw you stocking baked beans.' Then, almost afraid to ask, fearful of the possible gut-wrenching answer, she said, 'Is there someone else?'

'What? Don't be daft. Unless boxing's someone else.'

Shirley chewed a ringlet of hair, her eyes boring into the handsome, swarthy face lying on the white, creased pillow. He continued to gaze at the ceiling but it was a picture she consigned to her memory. She pulled the damp hair out of her mouth, smoothing it into place behind her ear.

'Okay, Johnny, let's see what happens. I want to be number one in your life but I guess that can't be. I want to see you when I can but I'm only nineteen. I won't just sit round waiting like some old maid.'

Willis turned his head and gazed up into deep, violet eyes. The nipples on her round breasts pointed at him. He would miss her, all of her. He smiled and sat up, planting a firm but quick kiss on her lips.

'I wouldn't expect you to hide away. As you say, that would be a waste,' he said, reaching for his jeans and sweatshirt draped over a bedside chair.

'What're you doing?'

'Time to go.'

'Why? Mum and Dad won't be back until late. You can stay a while longer. Another fuck at least.'

'No. Best I go now. Thanks for the offer, but I've gotta get up early in the morning. Time I started roadwork again. Got to rebuild my stamina.'

Shirley watched him dress. They exchanged another disappointing perfunctory kiss and she heard him walk down the stairs and out of the front door. She went to the window and tapped on the glass. He turned, raised his arm and gave her a warm smile, flashing brilliant white teeth. Then he was through the gate and gone. Shirley turned to the rumpled bed, flopped down and sobbed.

Willis started to hum an old Morecambe and Wise Show

closer – 'When you're smiling, the whole world smiles with you' – and briskly walked towards the Burnmoor Estate. That went okay, he thought. Well done, Johnny.

Training went even better. Once he'd made his decision and confronted Shirley, the burden was lifted from his shoulders. He was focused again.

'Good session, Johnny. You're looking like your old self,' praised Brown.

'Cheers, Ron. I feel better. P'raps I shouldn't have taken so much time out of the gym. I felt kinda rusty, but it's all started to flow again. I can feel it in my blood.'

'That's good. You'll need a couple of contests before the ABAs. It's a long, hard road. Something like ten bouts to get all the way.'

'Can't wait.'

Within a month, Willis was fighting fit. He scaled around ten-eight and Brown noticed, as he towelled him down after each training session, how he was filling out. His chest was deeper, broader and the long muscles in his arms and down his back – where the power came from – were getting firmer.

'Watch your diet, Johnny. There's not much surplus here. You'll need to dry out. Stop taking too many liquids or you'll bugger it up. You've got to make ten-seven.'

'You worry too much, Ron.' The normal response.

He weighed ten-eight for his season pipe-opener, hardly raising a sweat and knocking over a hapless, overwhelmed opponent in two rounds. He was a few ounces lighter three weeks later. That time he won in the first, a superb left hook under the ribs sending his victim sinking to his knees, gasping for air.

The championships started in similar fashion. Three quick victories as he marched almost untouched through area rounds into the Midlands final. There, to his disappointment, his opponent from Coventry failed to make the weight, by a whopping two pounds.

'Looks like he didn't wanna know,' said old Harry. 'Yer scared 'im off.'

That was fanciful; an old-fashioned attempt to further boost an already confident boxer. Willis didn't take any joy from being named Midlands welterweight champion without having earned it in a contest. He used his frustration to batter the next man in three rounds, scoring knock-downs in each round. The referee finally stepped in after the East Anglian fighter crashed to the canvas for the fifth time.

Mercer followed Willis's progress with growing anticipation and professional excitement. The eighteen-year-old was improving constantly and had been called up to train with the Young England squad at Crystal Palace.

Brown worked him hard on the pads but there was now a distinct lack of quality sparring in the Griffin Road gym. Payne was ever-willing but Willis never got out of second gear with his pal.

'It's getting to be a problem,' Brown confided in Mercer.

'Take him to the pros, then. It could do him good. I know it's against the rules but all the top lads do it.'

'I'll think about it. At least he gets the occasional useful spar at the Palace.'

'How does he get on down there?'

'Okay, I think. You know Johnny, doesn't say much. I had a chat on the phone with the coach and he seemed pleased enough. No complaints.'

'Well, think about the pros. If you need any help, just give me a call. There is one thing in his favour, of course. The ABA fights come round about every two weeks now. That's busy enough.'

'True – but it'll get harder. We're down south next and those London guys are no slouches.'

So it proved. Willis needed a couple of decisions to maintain his progress against southern opposition and then he was through to the All-England finals at Gloucester. Just three more victories to claim the title.

At the end of March, he got the call. He was watching a video tape of Marvin Hagler when the telephone rang. He ignored it until its persistence persuaded him to stop the tape.

'Johnny, is that you, Johnny?'

'Yes, who's this?' The huskiness seemed familiar but he was

preoccupied. He loved that Hagler–Hearns fight.

'It's me, Shirl. I must see you.'

'Shirl?' Then blinding recognition. How could he forget? 'Shirl. How are you? How y'doing?'

'Okay, I suppose. You haven't called for months, not since Christmas. I must see you.'

'Haven't you been reading the *News*? I'm busy at the moment, you know. It's the All-England finals next week. I'm two fights from the ABA final.'

'I know. You're doing really well and I'm pleased. I wouldn't call, but it's important.'

'Why? What is it?'

'I can't tell you over the phone. I need to see you. It's important.'

Willis let the words dangle in the air. What on earth was going on? Didn't she understand that he had to concentrate on next week's fight? What could possibly be more important than that?

'Johnny, are you still there? Johnny?' The voice was urgent now.

'Yeah, yeah. Can't it wait until after next week? I'm really tied up at the moment.'

'No, it can't wait. Surely you can spare me some time?'

'Shirl, I told you a long time back that boxing is my priority—'

'I know that,' she interrupted. 'But you found time at Christmas. Or was that just because you fancied a bit?'

This was turning ugly. 'Don't get sharp with me, Shirl. I reckon we'd better stop right there.'

'No, Johnny,' she almost shouted down the receiver. She sensed she'd got his attention and continued, quietly. 'Okay, I didn't want to tell you like this but... I'm pregnant, Johnny. I'm having our baby. Your baby.'

## Chapter Four

'How did it happen? I thought you were on the pill?'

Willis, twiddling distractedly with a beer mat, sat at a corner table in The Rose and Crown, a backstreet pub near to the supermarket. He'd agreed to meet Shirley at the end of her shift.

'I was... I am.' She paused. 'I don't know. How do these things happen? There's no hundred-per-cent guarantee, you know.'

'Suppose not. What you gonna do?'

'Do? What can I do?'

Willis looked into her eyes. They were still that amazing deep-violet colour but the sparkle was missing, replaced by worry. She certainly looked older than twenty.

'How long has it been?'

'Since Christmas. I've missed two periods. I'm due again soon.'

'And you're sure?'

'Sure? I know if I have a period or not. If you mean am I sure I'm pregnant, then I'm only assuming. I haven't had morning sickness or anything.'

'I don't really mean that,' said Willis.

Shirley looked at him in disbelief. 'Is it yours, you mean? Of course it bloody is! What do you think I am, a sodding tramp? Johnny Willis, you'd better get it into your head that you're gonna be a dad and that's that.'

'Sorry, Shirl, but it's been a long time since last summer. I don't know who you've been seeing. As you said, you wasn't gonna sit at home like an old maid.'

'No, I wasn't. But that didn't mean I was going out to fuck any Tom, Dick or Harry that came along. In fact, I've hardly been out at all. Believe it or not, when you came round... when we did it at Christmas... well, that was the first time since you walked out.'

'I didn't walk out.'

'Call it what you like, Johnny, but you didn't come back, did you? You didn't even call me or just pop into the supermarket to see me. I reckon that's walking out.'

'It wasn't like that. You knew I had to get back to my boxing. That's my life, my future.'

'And what about mine? I've got your kid in here. What sort of future am I gonna have? And what about the kid?'

Silence shrouded their corner of the musty room. Jeez, thought Willis, I can't be doing with this. Lumbered with a kid at my age. It wouldn't be fair on anyone.

'You don't have to have it.'

Shirley didn't explode. She knew, even understood, he might react this way. But it was a life. You don't just terminate a life. That's murder. 'No, I don't have to have it. But I can't kill it. Could you live with that?' she said.

Willis looked down at the table and brushed a spot of liquid off the surface with the beer mat. Yes, I could live with that, he mused. It would be better than having an unwanted child and I know all about that. God, what shall I do?

At length, he said, 'I haven't had the best family life, you know. No father about. I wouldn't want that for another poor sod. Because, whatever happens, Shirl, I'm not rushing into marriage. No way. Get me?'

'I don't expect that. But you had to know. And I'm not gonna do this all on my own. The least you can do is stand by me, offer some support.'

'Support! Fine chance of that. I've got no job and I'm sponging off my brothers. I've nothing to give.'

'It's not just money, Johnny. There's you. You can give time. Be there, for me and your child.'

'That's easily said, Shirl. Look, I could promise you all sorts of things but I'm being honest.' He paused. Here comes the crunch, she thought. 'I can't do it. Sorry. I've got my life to think about. When I get some money behind me it might be different but now... well, there's no chance. That's how it is.'

Now Shirley exploded. 'You are one mean, selfish bastard, Johnny Willis! You can't just walk away, I won't let you. You have responsibilities and if you're anything like the man you claim to be, you'll meet them. You can't turn your back and pretend nothing's happened.'

Tears welled in her eyes and she rummaged in her bag for tissues. Willis watched as she wiped her eyes, sniffled, blew her nose and finally rolled the tissue into a ball, clenching it in the palm of her hand, before looking up at him.

His face was set. Not a flicker of emotion. One cold bastard. It must have been his upbringing. Upbringing? That's a laugh, she thought. He didn't have one. He's a wild child, that's what he is. Perhaps she, and her baby, would be better off without him.

But, as she continued to examine his face and search his brown eyes, she thought that, however deep inside it was buried, there was some goodness there. She knew he cared about her and the child. He simply didn't want anyone to contend with life the way he did, to approach each day as if it was war. Him against the world, with no one to help. Or, at least, no one he would ask. Yet, wasn't he prepared to let her fend for herself?

'Haven't you anything to say?' she asked.

'Nothing else. I'm sorry. I know it's a mess but...' His words trailed away with a shrug.

'So, what do you expect me to do?'

He shrugged again. 'I don't know what you'll do. But,' and he stood, ready to leave, 'if it was me, I'd get rid of it.'

She looked up at him. 'I guess you're going, then.'

'I've got to get to the gym. I told you, it's the All-England finals next week.'

'Yes, the bloody All-England finals. That's all that matters to you, isn't it?'

Her raised voice prompted the plump woman behind the bar to look across at the pair. Bit of a lover's tiff, she thought.

'At the moment, yes. I don't suppose you understand what it means to me.'

Shirley scoffed, wiped her nose again and then picked up her bag. 'I won't ask you to walk me home. But you can't turn your back on us. You'll hear from me again, you know.'

Willis nodded. "Spect so.' And, without another word, he sauntered out of the pub.

Shirley reached into her bag for more tissues as the tears

streamed down her face and her breath came in great sobs. The woman moved out from behind the bar.

'You all right, love? Can I get you anything? Blokes, they're bastards, aren't they?'

Shirley blew her nose, trying to compose herself. 'Some are,' she said and rose from her seat to leave. 'Thanks for caring.'

The Gloucester Leisure Centre was packed for the clashes of England's top amateur boxers. The champions of four regions – London, west, Midlands and north – met in two semi-finals. The winners progressed to the following week's British semi-finals and there they would meet either the Scottish or Welsh champion. The two victors would clash at Wembley in the finals in May.

Willis was drawn against the northern counties title-holder, Jason Beard. A rugged Liverpudlian, he'd been outpointed at this stage twelve months earlier.

'Could've been harder,' said Mercer. 'The London lad, Brian Adams, is favourite.'

Brown studiously wrapped Willis's hands. 'There's nothing easy now. We know that. Suppose Johnny's the outsider?'

'He's the unknown element, although they must respect an unbeaten record and his Young England stuff.'

'They'll respect him even more after tonight.'

Old Harry coughed. 'I'm going outside for a bit. Don't want anything, do yer?'

Nobody did. What was there to want? Unless you were Harry and needed a few puffs on a cigarette to calm the nerves. 'He gets more nervous than the boxers. Get him to brush his teeth, Ron,' Willis joked. 'I hate that smell of smoke when he leans over me in the corner.'

The show ran in weight order – light-flyweight up to super-heavyweight. In the middle of the programme, Willis was in the second welterweight bout.

He strolled into the hall, hands taped but still wearing his tracksuit, to meet his brothers and a few friends who had travelled in a hired mini-coach. A coach had also made the trip from Westhampton.

'You've got some support tonight, Johnny,' said Colin. They sat at the rear of the hall as two featherweights locked in furious head-to-head battle. 'Your fame's spreading.'

'Bob's write-ups in the *News* have helped. He reckons I should do this scouser.'

'Sure you will. Just be yerself and don't worry about him. He lost here last time, he'll do it again tonight. He's used to it now.'

Willis grinned. 'If it was all that fucking simple, eh?'

A roar from the crowd turned their attention to the ring. One of the featherweights was scrambling about on the canvas.

'That's one gone,' said Kenny as the lad from Birmingham struggled to regain his footing. 'Quite fancied him, as well. Where's the other kid from?'

'Liverpool,' said Payne, flicking through the programme. 'Same club as Beard.' Nothing more was said, but the point had been made.

'Time to go. See you later,' said Willis and made his way around the back of the hall to the dressing room.

When he next emerged, Adams had flattened his man in the first. It had been a bad night for the Midlands with only two progressing, one of them rather fortunately on a cut-eye stoppage.

There was a good reception for Willis, not only from the Westhampton travellers and other Midlands fans but from a spattering of followers who had been impressed by him on previous nights. But it was nothing like the roar that greeted Beard's introduction.

'Jeez,' said old Harry. 'Them scousers always make a din. But they know their boxing.'

Willis stood, head bowed, concentrating. Shuffling his feet in the corner he fixed his gaze on a dried blood spot on the canvas. He didn't look across at Beard, a thickset twenty-five-year-old who had tattoos running the length of both arms. On his chest, a fiery dragon poked above his white vest.

Willis decided to open with a solid jab. Get some early respect. But he was surprised when Beard moved his head just enough for the punch to pass harmlessly over his left shoulder. At the same time, he shot a light right into Johnny's ribs. Another jab, but Beard ducked under it before sending a harder right to the stomach.

Clever, a counter-puncher. I'll feint him, Willis thought. He motioned to start a third jab but held back, waiting for that split-second reaction from the Liverpudlian. He got it, but not how he'd anticipated. A snappy left hook came out of the arc lights and crashed against Willis's temple, sending him reeling into the ropes. What a strange sensation!

Beard chased after him and Willis was aware of a huge roar rising somewhere in the distance. His head pounded. Everything was moving in slow motion. Beard hammered another left and right to his face. What the fuck? he thought. I've gotta get moving. What's happened to my legs? Why won't they move?

Another thudding left landed to the side of his face, turning him sideways into the ropes. As he looked down, he saw Mercer. The reporter was looking up into his face, showing no emotion, no concern, no encouragement, no nothing.

He saw a red glove heading again for his face, but this time he managed to sway back on the ropes and the punch whistled through the smoke-laden atmosphere. Then, somehow, his arms worked again and he grabbed the Liverpudlian.

They wrestled and struggled on the ropes before the referee sternly shouted 'break' and Beard forced himself out of Willis's grip. Thank God, his legs were working again! Willis moved into the centre of the ring. As the buzzing in his head stopped, he watched for Beard's next move. It came as a surprisingly clumsy attempt to land a haymaking right hand. Amateur!

Willis leaned back and, as the punch missed, he moved in with a short, straight right that thudded against Beard's jaw. The effect was devastating. Beard's forward momentum stopped, his hands dropped to his side and he slumped to his knees. The Leisure Centre crowd was, momentarily, stunned into silence. Then a roar bounced off the brick walls and rang around the steel rafters.

Willis was pointed to a neutral corner. He looked across and Brown signalled for him to go in. Both hands, finish it. Old Harry looked amazed, mouth agape. Across the ring, Mercer was watching Beard being counted, occasionally glancing across at Willis. Taking it all in, eh, Bob? he thought.

Beard was on his feet at 'six', probably more surprised than hurt. A game 'un, thought Willis. The spring wasn't back in his legs but Willis hustled across the canvas and landed a rapid left, bouncing off a defensive glove on to Beard's nose. Beard started to move away to his left and instinctively, Willis launched a rocket right hand. This time it was all over.

Willis knew it, the crowd knew it, the referee knew it. But Beard was unaware as he crashed on to his back, his head thumping the canvas. His big chest heaved and there was a slight twitch in his left foot. The referee pulled out the gumshield and ensured the supine boxer was not choking on his tongue.

The pandemonium around the arena ceased, leaving just a simmer of excited voices. Brown slipped a towel around Willis's neck as Beard suddenly came to his senses and attempted to sit up. The doctor, one knee on the canvas, ordered him not to move. He carried on talking to him and, eventually, allowed Beard's cornermen to help him on to a stool.

Willis watched, but he didn't really see. His mind was occupied with one thought: will it be a Scot or Taff next?

It was John Dickson, a Scottish international from Larkhall. Only twenty, his pedigree was impressive. Former Scottish Youth champion, runner-up and then Scottish champion. Three international victories, against Sweden, Holland and Denmark.

As Brown drove up the M6 to the Preston Guildhall, Willis slumbered in the back of the van. Riley mumbled on about the times he had been robbed in the Lancashire town.

'Bloody 'omers, them refs, all of 'em,' he insisted.

But Brown was concerned about tonight, not six-round slug-fests from forty years ago. Willis had been hurt by Beard. It was the first time that the youngster had been staggered and the trainer was not sure how he would emerge from the experience. True, he'd produced an incredible knock-out but that was in the heat of the battle. A week after the experience, he wasn't certain how Willis would react. No doubt about it, things were getting tougher.

Willis, in fact, had taken note of one pertinent paragraph in Mercer's report:

Willis was hurt, no denying that. His legs wobbled, he sagged into the ropes just above me and took three or four blows without responding. Willis has never looked so close to defeat as he was in Gloucester last night. He looked destined for the canvas, or even intervention by the referee, when suddenly he grabbed his Liverpudlian tormentor. His powers of recovery were immense and he proceeded to produce the knock-out of the night, if not the championships.

Willis didn't need to read any more. He knew that Mercer had stared up at him, professionally detached, assessing the situation, watching for signs of weakness and strength. And that was the point, he thought. I was rattled but I came through. Just like Ron told me; you can take an umbrella out in the rain but you won't dodge all the spots. Randy Turpin, was it? Anyway, I know I'm strong and I can take the punches if I have to. I'm gonna be ABA champion. And that's just for starters.

The Preston bout was an anticlimax. Dickson was a cagey performer and, not surprisingly, wary of Willis's power. Willis found it difficult to land clean blows and there was too much holding and mauling. It was only in the last round that Dickson chanced his arm. But a couple of solid left leads and one stinging right cross from Willis had the rangy Scot withdrawing into his shell again.

Willis got a unanimous decision but there was little in it. Just like the contest had been, he was subdued in the dressing room despite reaching the ABA finals at his first attempt.

'I looked bad out there, didn't I, Ron? Was it really bad?'

'You did just fine, son. Don't forget, he's very experienced and can make anyone look bad.'

'That's just it, Ron. I didn't get to him. He spoiled and I didn't have the fucking answer.'

'It's all experience. Don't be hard on yerself. It's a good win and it's been a long, hard grind. The finals are in three weeks. We'll have a few days off and then start to work on Brian Adams.'

'It's Adams, is it?' Willis hadn't even thought about the second semi-final.

Mercer stepped in. 'The ref stopped it in the last. But the Welsh kid wasn't up too much. Probably the weakest to make it this far.'

'I've got it all to do, then,' said Willis, wearily tugging off his boots. 'I'll be glad when I can have a rest.'

But rest didn't come easy. Night after night, he lay in his small bed, usually listening to the party noise from downstairs, wondering what his life was all about. What's the purpose? Why couldn't Shirl understand? Why didn't she realise that they were both too young to have a kid? Their whole lives lay ahead of them, why muck it up now? Women! Look at his mother – she didn't have any ambitions beyond the next party or a wham-bang between the sheets with some half-drunk lay. That's not for me, nor Mary, he thought. She's a good girl, the sort any man would be happy to share the rest of his life with. Clean, honest, caring and a good worker. I'll look after her. And God help any bloke who doesn't treat her right. They'll answer to me, that's for certain.

Wembley Arena! The thought of it sent chills down Willis's spine. Think of all the big fights, the big names, and you think of Wembley. And tomorrow, he'd be there, fighting for the ABA welterweight championship.

Mercer and a *News* photographer visited the gym to prepare a full preview. Mary pasted it across two pages of her scrapbook.

'Think I'll get a new book, a bigger one, for next season,' she said. 'There'll be a lot of stories like this one, I know there will.'

Willis put an arm around his sister's cool, white shoulders and kissed her brow. 'You're doing a grand job. Reckon you'll make a perfect secretary when you leave school. Think about it. You're good at organising things.'

'You've got to type and do that shorthand stuff, Johnny. I can't do that.'

'You could learn.'

'I don't have the time. Anyway, I'll be happy in a factory, or a shop. Don't think I'd fancy office work. It's not me, really.'

Willis eased off his training in the four days before the final but he was conscious of his weight. He often hadn't eaten or taken a drink in the twenty-four hours before his ABA contests. He didn't want to risk being overweight and ruled out. That would be a disaster.

He scaled ounces inside the ten-seven limit. Adams, an angular black fighter who was surrounded by pals in bright woolly hats, was a pound lighter. They exchanged nods but no words and waited in line to see the doctor.

'Arrogant pig,' said Kenny.

'I don't like him much either,' said Colin.

'Tell you what, I wish I was our Johnny. I'd like to bash his smug fucking mug in.'

'Yeah. But Johnny'll do the job just fine. P'raps we should look after his mates.'

They laughed. Payne, with a wry smile, shook his head. 'You two! What a bleeding pair.'

'What? What do yer mean, Pete? Nothing wrong with us, pal,' said Kenny, slapping him on the back. 'C'mon, let's get a drink.'

Willis was dry, too. 'I could spit feathers,' he told Brown, taking massive gulps of water from a cold bottle.

'Not too much, Johnny. You'll get stomach cramps. C'mon, we'll get a bit of chicken and a pot of weak tea. That'll do nicely.'

When they returned to the vast arena with its ten thousand seats, Willis watched some of the work that went on behind the scenes for a big sporting occasion.

Television people were sorting cables. Others were walking around talking and listening to responses in their headsets. The ring was being finished, ropes tightened, canvas stretched and tested, corner swing stools secured. Programme sellers stood around in bunches, chatting before going to their stations. Stewards checked seat rows and numbers. This was big, the biggest night of the year in amateur boxing. And Willis was a part of it.

'Really somethin', innit?' said Harry.

'Sure is, Harry, sure is,' said Willis, soaking up the atmosphere of the old arena. Voices echoed around the near-empty hall. Just wait until the crowd gets in, he thought.

'How's yer feeling?'

'Great. No problem. Reckon I'll have a lie down, though. Where's the dressing room?'

An ABA official took them along a door-lined corridor. 'Let's see, Willis... you're in here I think. Yep, this is the one,' he said.

His name – and those of two other boxers – was printed on a sheet of notepaper and pinned to the dark red door. The room was sparse. A few chairs, a washbasin and a massage table in the middle, with a door leading to the showers and toilet. No one else in the room.

'Reckon I'll have a rest on that,' Willis nodded in the direction of the table.

'Fine,' said Riley. 'I'll find Ron. Reckon he's collecting the expenses. You be okay?'

There was a knock on the door and the same ABA official popped his bald head around the door. 'Ah, thought I'd better give you this,' he said. It was a pale blue envelope.

'Thanks,' said Willis, surprised to see it addressed to him, c/o Wembley Arena. 'You gonna find Ron, then?' he said to Riley. The old trainer was curious to see the contents of the envelope.

'Yeah, sure, I'm off then.'

'Don't have too many smokes.'

Willis fingered the envelope. It felt like a card. The postmark was Westhampton. Someone wishing him well? Perhaps it was Mary. It's the sort of thing she'd do.

He unsealed the flap and took out a gold greetings card emblazoned with the words 'Good Luck'. His eyelids twitched as he read the neatly written words inside. He placed the card on the table and then picked it up again.

NO BABY. GOOD LUCK TONIGHT. LOVE SHIRLEY.

What did it mean? Had she had an abortion? No, bet it had all been just a scare. A false alarm. Women do miss periods, don't they? What a silly bitch. Putting me through all this! Still, everything's rosy now.

He strolled into the adjoining room, ripped up the card and envelope, dropped them into the toilet bowl, took a leak and flushed.

The story was splashed across the front page of the *Westhampton*

*News*. It was mentioned on radio and at the end of the recorded highlights on BBC television. It was no more than Harry Riley deserved. He'd treasured the young Willis from the start – was it really nine years ago? – and helped develop him into a special talent.

The welterweight final was the best fight of the championships. Willis, dragging up every last ounce of energy and determination, produced a rousing last round against Adams. He'd never had such a hard fight. Give-and-take all the way, the boxers collapsed into each other's arms in mutual respect at the final bell. They could hardly speak but Adams sportingly gasped, 'You've nicked it.'

'Don't know. It's bleedin' close.'

'Enjoyed it. Do it again some time... for money.'

They shook hands with the opposition trainers but, as they crossed paths on the return journey, Adams said, 'Your old guy looks a bit dodgy.'

Dodgy? What did he mean? Willis looked to his corner where Riley was clutching the top rope. Brown was talking earnestly to him.

'I'm okay, nothin' wrong at all,' insisted the perspiring old-timer, watching Willis approach. 'C'mon kid, let's get that sash off yer. They'll want it for another bout.'

Riley struggled with the bow on the red ribbon around Willis's waist. Brown, noticing the old man's trembling hands, took over. 'Come 'ere, let me do it. You get Johnny' s mouthpiece.'

Willis had removed the gumshield from his mouth and he passed it to Harry. 'You all right? You look a bit – pasty.' He nearly said 'dodgy'.

'Don't you start. I've had enuff from 'im. It's nothing, just a bit tired. Anyway, well done, kid. Reckon yer did enuff in the last to make sure. Yer've dun yerself proud, Johnny. Whatever the result—'

The trainer was cut short as the referee called both boxers back into the centre of the ring. Again they shook hands and then stood, one either side of the official, nervously jigging and staring out into the crowd.

'Lords, ladies and gentlemen... the result of the 1986 ABA

welterweight championship. By a majority decision of 59–58, 58–59, 59–58, the winner and ABA champion is – J Willis, of Midlands—'

The rest of the MC's words were lost to Willis. He leaped into the air and shoved his right arm skywards, wallowing in the cheers of the vast crowd. Finally, he turned again to Adams.

'Bad luck,' he said.

'Yeah, it happens.'

It was then, in Willis's moment of glory, that Harry, standing on the ring apron, let out a sudden groan and slumped into the ropes. Before Ron could reach him, he collapsed in a heap and rolled down the steps. The Wembley house second managed to grab him and gently laid him on the floor.

Willis rushed across the ring and looked down at Harry's frail figure as a doctor started to examine him, feeling for a pulse. 'Bring a stretcher,' he said.

But by the time they'd carried Harry to the medical room, the old pug was dead. His fists were tightly clenched.

*PART TWO*

H E SLUMPED ON the stool and let his head droop. Blood dripped on to his heaving chest. More problems.

It was bad. He could tell that from the anxious look in the eyes gazing down at him. It didn't matter how calm these guys appeared to be in the corner, their eyes gave them away. Just like looking into an opponent's eyes. The windows to their fears. He'd learned that much over these eighteen long years.

He felt the pressure of the swab on his left eyebrow. The doctor hovered on the ring apron, peering at the wound and talking to his handlers. 'It's okay, all under control,' he heard. He smiled inwardly, knowingly. No way would they let any quack stop this. If only his other problem was as easy to settle.

His mind wandered. Ironic, isn't it? Here I am, exposed to thousands of people, naked all but for shorts and boots. And yet none of them can see. They haven't a clue what I'm thinking, what I'm going through. They don't know what I know. It's all so simple to them – black and white. Beat the other guy and you're a champion. If only that was all!

What a night. It's tough, the toughest yet. But nothing's ever been easy. No, never has been and probably never will. Don't expect it to be. But this makes everything else trivial. C'mon, get a grip, stop messing about. Make a decision. It's gone long enough—

The voice broke into his thoughts, returning him to the din of his hostile surroundings. 'You may never get another chance like this. Don't let it slip. You can beat this guy. You'll never forgive yourself if you don't give everything,' it said.

Forgive myself? If only he knew! This isn't just about me, is it? Okay, it's my problem and no one can help. It's my choice. But what would he do? What would anyone do in my position? he thought.

'Listen, listen to me. What the hell's up with you? Is it your hands? Well, you've gotta grit your teeth and get on with it. Don't let yourself down. You'll regret it for the rest of your life.'

Too true, too bloody true.

'Seconds out... for round eight...'

## Chapter Five

For the first time in his life, Willis felt a sense of loss. He'd been too young to understand or feel anything when Danny left, but this was different. Harry Riley had been a vital part of his life for nine years.

He sat at the back of the small crematorium, flanked by Brown and Mercer.

'Good turnout,' whispered Mercer.

'Lot of people I don't know,' said Willis. 'Didn't realise Harry was so well known.'

'You've got to remember Harry was in boxing nearly all his life. There's people here he used to box with. And he trained their sons, even their grandkids. Generations have gone through Harry's hands.'

'I didn't realise. It's something special, isn't it?'

'He was special. Devoted his life to boxing and hardly earned a penny from it. The club will miss him. He'll take some replacing.'

The clergyman spoke of Harry's sixty-six years, recalled his army service, boxing career and how he devoted time and energy to Friar ABC and the youth of Westhampton. How many people had he helped, taking them off the streets and demonstrating the benefits of discipline? He spoke of Harry's widow and their forty-three years of marriage, two daughters and three grandchildren. And he said that Harry probably left this world just how he would have wished; in the corner of a boxing ring having just seen one of his young men become a champion.

That brought a lump to Willis's throat. His mouth was dry. Altogether, a most unfamiliar sensation. Brown noticed and put a reassuring hand on his knee. Willis glanced at him and forced a half-smile. 'He was a good man,' he said. 'I'm glad I knew him.'

'He was glad to know you. You gave him a lot of happiness.'

That was when the first tears formed in Willis's eyes. He'd never felt such emotion. Yes, he'd cried before, but that was in frustration or anger. This was different. These tears were for someone else.

Mourners gathered outside to look at the wreaths. Talking in hushed tones, shaking hands in greeting, some even hugging and back-slapping. There were kisses for the women, particularly for Mrs Riley, a small, white-haired lady who walked with the aid of a stick. Willis realised that he didn't know her. He'd rarely spoken to Harry about his family.

He walked along the rows of wreaths, slowly reading the cards of sympathy, until he heard a light, faltering voice behind him. 'You're Johnny, aren't you?'

He turned and saw it was the widow. 'Yeah, I am… Mrs Riley.'

'Very pleased to meet you, son.' She offered her gloved hand. It was so small and frail in his own but he didn't let go. 'Harry was very fond of you. He said you'd be a champion. I'm glad he lived to see the day. He hadn't been well for years. I told him to stop smoking, or at least cut down, but no, he couldn't do it. He tried, though. Didn't always succeed but he tried. And you can't beat a trier. He always said that.'

She looked up at Willis's face and back down at his hand, which was still lightly holding hers. 'You've got good hands, Johnny. Kind hands. Anyone ever tell you that?'

Willis was in awe of the old lady, admiring the way she bore herself at a time of such grief. She spoke so nicely, not like Harry. He wished he'd met her before.

'No, they haven't, Mrs Riley.'

'I can tell a person by their hands, you know. Harry told me about you. I know you've not had it easy. Despite all that, I think you're a good lad.'

Willis felt her hand being drawn away. 'Must be moving along,' she said. 'We're having a cup of tea and a few sandwiches at home. Would you like to come?'

Willis hadn't even thought about such a thing. Funerals were new to him. 'That's very kind of you, Mrs Riley, but I can't. I'm going back home with my brothers. They used to box, you know.'

The old lady searched his face with small, red-rimmed, pale-blue eyes. 'I know. To tell you the truth, Harry didn't think their heart was in it. It was something they did because you were there. Is that right?'

'Don't rightly know, Mrs Riley. They're good lads. Know how to fight, if you know what I mean.'

'Yes. Mary.'

'What?'

'Mary – call me Mary. That's my name.'

'I've a sister called Mary. A lovely kid. Coming up to sixteen now.'

'Poor girl! Three brothers. Bet you lads give her a hard time.'

Willis laughed. 'No, she looks after us. We daren't get in her bad books.'

'She helps your mother, then? She must be pleased.'

The iron curtain came down. Suddenly, but as politely as possible, he excused himself. 'Been nice meeting you, Mrs Riley. I really liked your husband. Harry was very good to me. But I must be getting along.'

'Nice to meet you, too. Don't forget, the name's Mary.' She smiled sweetly, without parting her lips. 'Perhaps you'll pop round to see me one day? I've got lots of Harry's old boxing programmes, posters and things. Boxes of them. If you're interested in that kind of thing?'

'I'd like to see them. Yeah, I will pop round. Thanks very much, er, Mary.'

Again, she offered her hand. Willis took it gently, gave it a little squeeze and, surprising himself, leaned down to kiss her cheek. 'Bye for now. You take care.'

He reluctantly turned away to seek out his brothers for the drive back to Johnson Close. Ma will never turn out to be a beautiful old lady like that, he thought. And then it dawned on him. Mary Riley was old enough to be his grandmother. And he hadn't even got grandparents.

Brown found his assistant for Friar ABC, another ex-fighter who had been a regular spectator at club shows. Vic Grant, a wiry fifty-year-old with crinkly blond hair, had boxed for the RAF but didn't continue in civvy street. On leaving the forces, he gained employment as a car mechanic and now had his own small repair business, supplementing his income by trading in cheap vehicles.

He wasn't anything special as a trainer but, as Brown put it, 'He's willing, knows the game and can look after the young kids and novices. He's happy with that and so am I.'

Willis took a summer break from the gym. He ran occasionally and, most days, put himself through an exercise regime to keep his body toned.

He also visited Mary Riley. Sitting in the cosy front room of the tiny terraced house, he looked through Harry's memorabilia, sipping tea out of an old china cup.

'I can read the leaves,' the old lady declared one day. 'Would you like that? By the looks of you, you've got some Romany in your blood.'

'To be honest, I'm not sure I believe that sort of thing, Mary,' he said.

But she did it anyway. 'You're going to be a success,' she said, before adding, 'It won't be a bowl of cherries, though. I see ups and downs.'

'Nothing new there then,' said Willis lightly. Mrs Riley frowned but remained silent. 'What is it? Something bad?'

'Oh, I don't know. Perhaps I'm losing my touch. It's a long time since I did this sort of thing.'

'What is it? Tell me.'

'Well,' she said and paused again. 'Have you ever been in trouble with the law?'

'No.'

'Done anything bad? Got away with it?'

Willis thought for a moment. 'Not really bad, no.'

'Oh, well. As I say, it's a long time since I did this. Perhaps I'm reading it all wrong.'

'Tell me what you see.'

'I may be getting this wrong, Johnny. Oh dear, I'm a silly old fool. I shouldn't have started this.'

'Don't worry. I told you, I'm not sure I even believe this stuff. But you've got me curious. What is it? Tell me, please.'

'There's a break... a gap. Some sort of pause in your life. I don't know what causes it, except it's not good. That's why I ask if you've done something bad, something you might have to answer for.'

'No, can't think of anything. When's all this supposed to happen?'

'That's the trouble, I can't really see. But I don't think you'll be much older. Oh, dear me! I shouldn't be saying such things.'

The old lady was distraught but Willis laughed, rose from his chair and kissed her powdered cheek. 'Don't get upset. Give me the cups. I'll put them in the sink.'

When he returned from the cramped kitchen, Mrs Riley was still agitated, rubbing the back of her left hand with the palm of her right.

'C'mon, Mary, settle down. It's nothing to worry about.'

'I'm sorry, Johnny. I really am a silly old fool. Take no notice of me. Harry always said I was potty, not quite all there. Perhaps he was right, you know.' She smiled winsomely.

She seemed her usual self by the time Willis left her watching her favourite TV soap. As he walked down the narrow street – just like Coronation Street, he thought – storm clouds loomed in the June sky. Better get a move on. He edged between two parked cars and started to hurry across the narrow street as a dark blue Escort screeched to a halt beside him.

'Look where you're fucking going, you dozy bastard!'

Willis was startled by the near miss. He hadn't been looking. But he walked around the front of the car and towards the driver's door. 'What did you say?'

The driver, in his mid-twenties, was alone. He shouted through the open window, 'I could've run you over, you daft git. Look where you're going.'

Willis pulled the door open. 'Get out,' he ordered.

'You what?'

'Get out. Or I'll fucking pull you out.'

'That's it.'

The driver unbuckled his safety belt and started to swivel out of his seat. As he put his right foot onto the road, Willis slammed the door, smashing it against the unsuspecting man's shin. He yelled in pain but Willis pulled the door back – and banged it again on to the battered leg with a bone-shattering whack. The driver screamed.

Willis slung the door open again, bent into the car and grabbed his victim's throat. 'Just watch your fucking tongue, mate. It'll get you in serious trouble.' With a mighty push, he shoved the driver away and swung the door again, catching the victim's leg for a third time.

Passers-by looked on in astonishment. It had all happened in seconds; the screech of tyres, vehement accusations and the savage, calculated assault.

Mary Riley, roused by the commotion, heaved herself up on her stick and hobbled to the tiny front window. She saw Willis striding around a corner and out of sight. She didn't notice the blue Escort or the people gathering around just one hundred yards along the street. Wonder if Johnny saw anything, she thought. I'll ask him next time he visits. If I remember, that is. And, with that, she turned back to the television.

Great drops of rain fell from the black skies and Willis sought shelter in a pub. He called home from a pay phone in the bar and Kenny agreed to pick him up in the van, a vehicle which had multiple purposes. It got him around town, was ideal for loading up stolen goods – and it was a mobile love nest. The Fuckmobile, he named it.

Willis ordered an orange juice, bringing glances from the roughnecks standing at the bar. No one spoke.

'All right lads?' he said. A few mumbles and scraping of feet.

'Sorry about old Harry.' This came from a small character, sandy hair jutting from beneath a paint-splattered cap. 'Your trainer. You are Johnny Willis, aren't you?'

Willis looked him over. It didn't take long. 'Yeah. Thanks. Harry was a good man.'

'I live a couple of doors away from them. Mary'll miss 'im. She doted on 'im and 'im on 'er, like. Nice couple. Are you gonna turn pro now?'

'Not yet.'

'Gonna defend your ABA title, then?' said a second stranger with brawny arms, pint pot dwarfed in his hand.

'I'll be in the championships but I don't think it'll be welter-weight. Moving up to light-middle.'

'Aye, you're a big lad. Haven't seen you around here before.'

'I've just been to see Mary – Mrs Riley.'

'That's nice,' said Sandy Hair. 'Good, that is. You're a good lad to do that.'

That's two people who think I'm a good lad, mused Willis. Bet that fucking car driver doesn't. And he grinned inwardly.

Willis bowled over a Swede in one round for Young England at Norwich and earned himself a senior call-up for a match in Finland – his first trip abroad. Kenny drove him to Peterborough and they waited nearly all day to get Willis's first passport. 'Fucking bureaucrats,' summed up Kenny.

Willis stood amazed in the midst of the hustle and bustle of Heathrow Airport. Lost and confused until he found the meeting point by a British Airways desk, he enjoyed the experience of his first flight. Not bad for a kid from the Burnmoor, he thought. All expenses paid trip abroad just to punch some guy's nose in. Not bad at all, Johnny.

Willis also appreciated the camaraderie of the team, the leg-pulling and the underlying feeling that they were all in this together. He shared a room with middleweight Dean Gregory, a seasoned international from London's St Pancras, and quickly learned to appreciate his streetwise humour.

'Brought your carrots, Johnny?'

'What?'

'Carrots – what you Midlanders eat up there. You're fuckin' carrot crunchers.'

'Better than them slimy jellied eels, or stodgy pie and mash.'

Gregory laughed.

Willis overwhelmed his Finnish opponent, forcing the referee to halt proceedings in the final round after the home boxer took a third standing count.

'Well done,' said Mercer over the telephone when Willis returned to the Burnmoor Estate. 'It's good to win any international but especially good away from home on your début.'

'Thanks. But the Finns weren't up to much. We won easy.'

'That's as maybe. It'll do you no harm when it comes to turning pro. Thought much about that?'

'Not a lot. I'm just bothered about this season and the ABAs. Then we'll see.'

'When the time comes, if you want any help, you know where I am. There's a couple of managers I know who are following you with interest.'

'Yeah? Who?'

'Lew Sellers, for one. You've heard of him, I take it?'

'Sure. Top man. But I didn't think he'd be interested in a carrot cruncher like me.'

Mercer laughed. 'I can tell you've been with the Cockneys. Carrot cruncher, indeed. Insulting bastards. Bet you didn't let them get away with that.'

'It's all a bit of fun. We had a laugh. Taking the piss seems a way of life with them.'

'That's true. Keep your sense of humour and you'll be okay. Anyway, well done. If I can help any time, don't hesitate to ask.'

Birmingham's George Barnett, the top manager and promoter in the Midlands, cornered Willis after the area championships.

An average welterweight, Barnett found his niche as a manager, matchmaker and then as a promoter. Now, at forty-five and a portly thirteen stone, thanks to some sumptuous living, he was truly a big man in the British fight game.

'When you think about turning pro, give me a call,' he said. Cigar smoke curled around the centre parting of his brown hair. 'We can do business. You could be a big star, the biggest draw in the Midlands. Sign with me and there'll be money up front, regular fights and good matches.'

'What do you think?' Willis asked Mercer later, over the phone.

'He's the best around here, all right. Runs a lot of shows and he'll make the right matches for you. But you could do better. Don't rush into anything and don't make any promises. Above all, don't sign anything.'

'He's offering money to sign.'

'How much?'

'He didn't say. How much am I worth?'

'That depends. Cash up front is one thing but what about

purse money? You'll be a big ticket-seller and that means you'll want good pay days from the start.'

Willis's following was increasing, and not only in Westhampton. He always got a warm reception on the ABA trail and *Boxing News* had picked up on his popularity, making him the featured fighter in most reports.

But a headline he didn't anticipate came after his second ABA final appearance. He stormed to Wembley and was a hot favourite to beat Scotland's Ally McIntyre, who had reached the finals for the first time on his fifth attempt.

It seemed easy when a glancing left hook caught McIntyre off-balance in the opening exchanges and the Scot toppled over. He was quickly up, shaking his head. 'Just a slip, ref,' he protested, but he was given a standing count.

Willis knew he hadn't connected properly but was still confident enough to press forward, seeking to land a better, solid punch. McIntyre retreated behind a left jab which, while light, was swift, pecking into Willis's face and chest.

This pattern continued in the second round. Willis chased but failed to land any effective punches as McIntyre dodged, weaved and picked up points with his flicking left hand.

'Cut him off in the corners,' said Brown. 'He's pinching it. Keep your head moving; don't give him a target. A big last round should do it. He'll tire. He can't keep running.'

McIntyre duly ran out of steam in the last half of the round and Willis rocked the Scot several times with hard punches to the head. His huge following in the packed arena roared their encouragement but he didn't put McIntyre down until a left hook sent him tumbling to the canvas as the bell sounded.

'Two knock-downs, that should clinch it,' said Brown.

He was wrong. A year on from his biggest triumph, Willis, for the first time, was the loser. The majority decision brought howls of disapproval from the packed Wembley bleachers but McIntyre didn't care. He jumped and waved wildly to his Scottish supporters, celebrating his biggest win and the upset of the finals night.

Willis managed to say 'Well done' to the beaming McIntyre but he felt drained. It was his first defeat in nearly seventy contests. He couldn't wait to leave the ring.

Later, *Boxing News* would proclaim 'Willis outsmarted' in a banner headline while Mercer's report in the *Westhampton News* ran under the headline 'Title disaster' with a subheading, 'Willis loses unbeaten record to smart Scot.'

Opinion in the dressing room centred on Willis being robbed.

'He never took a step forward...'

'Knocked down twice and he gets the title...'

'Never laid a glove on yer...'

'The judges must be bent...'

'What do you have to do to win?'

Payne clapped his arm around him and whispered in his ear. 'Don't worry about it. You couldn't go on winning for ever. No fucker can.'

But Willis was inconsolable. He sat, head bowed, looking at his boots as perspiration dripped on to the floor. Finally, he looked up at no one in particular, and said, 'Bollocks to it. I'm finished with the amateurs. I wasn't at my best and he was tricky. But I thought I'd done enough to win. Fuck 'em.'

That's when he decided to telephone Barnett. Next morning. No waiting. It was time to get some money – serious money.

## Chapter Six

Barnett was quick to call a press conference. It was an indication of the promoter's stature and Willis's prospects that journalists from most of the area's daily regional newspapers, local radio and TV stations gathered at the Westhampton Post House.

'Johnny Willis can go all the way to the top,' Barnett told the gathering, waving his ever-present cigar. 'I'm very pleased to have signed him and it's good that he's staying in the Midlands.'

Barnett constantly and famously waged verbal war with the big London promoters, complaining that they profited off the back of lucrative TV contracts which were denied to provincial promoters. His capture of Willis, he knew, would be a major disappointment to them.

'We've some good, honest fighters in the Midlands but this boy will set boxing alight. I'll give everyone a chance to come and see him. We'll start with a show here, right in his home town, probably in early September.

'I won't go into any details. That's a private matter between Johnny and myself. But I'll tell you that a three-year contract has been lodged with the British Boxing Board of Control and Johnny's passed his medicals. We're ready to start rolling. This is a great day for Midlands boxing.'

Sitting next to his manager, wearing his England tracksuit, Willis smiled when a reporter from the *Birmingham Mail* asked, 'Did you ever think of going to London?'

'Thought about it. But I'd rather stay at home. I'm not keen on living in London. I don't see why I can't be a success from Westhampton. After all, I didn't do too badly as an amateur. Until the last fight, that is.'

'You would have had big TV exposure…'

'And there's no reason why he can't get it,' interrupted Barnett. He pointed his cigar at the journalist. 'I do work with the London boys, you know. They'll want to use Johnny. He's too good a fighter for them to ignore. But I'll make sure we get a proper deal. Now, if there are no more questions, there are drinks and sandwiches at the bar, gentlemen. You've got the press releases detailing Johnny's background and record and you know you can always reach me on the phone. If you don't ring me, you know I'll always ring you.'

That brought laughter from the media men. They were used to calls from Barnett at all times of day and night. He had a reputation for not sleeping.

'Happy with everything?' Mercer asked Willis as the last of the visiting journalists reluctantly left the bar to return to their offices. Mercer's story was already printed. He'd got an exclusive from Barnett so that the *News* would, indeed, be first with the news.

'Sure, Bob. Why not? It's a good deal.'

'Is it?'

'I think so. Between you and me, George has paid me ten thousand and he says I'll have a dozen fights in the first year.'

'How much a fight?'

'No less than two grand, to start with. That's all for me, no percentages. He'll make his money on the promotions.'

'I'm sure he will. He's a good promoter. He's handled British champions, as you know. It could turn out okay.'

'You don't sound convinced.'

Mercer pushed his spectacles on to the bridge of his nose with his forefinger. 'I'm not saying anything's wrong. But you're hot property, Johnny, and boxers get only one bite in this game. Managers and promoters can go on for ever. Remember that. You've got to make the most of what you've got, this one chance.'

'You think I should've gone to London?'

'I'm not saying that. This could be a good deal. It could work out. But, to be honest, London's the heart of the game. Maybe you're big enough for it to work here. Time will tell and, at the moment, it's on your side. Anyway, I wish you luck. Who's going to train you?'

'Ron's applying for a licence, George says he'll look after his money – I won't have to pay him. My money's mine.'

'Ron's happy with that?'

'Yes. He had a chat with George last week. We're gonna carry on at the Friar and I'll sometimes go over to George's gym in Brum for sparring. Should work out okay.'

Willis spent some of his money buying an old but clean Rover from Vic Grant. He gave a few hundred each to Kenny and Colin – 'Thanks for helping me out' – and proudly presented Mary with enough cash to fit her out with a new wardrobe. He also bought some new trainers, sweatshirts and jeans. And, at Mary's suggestion, he bought his first suit along with a few shirts and ties. Connie got nothing.

Willis enjoyed driving. It gave him independence. He got to the gym with ease and buzzed around town with his brothers as they set up the pub and club security business. He hadn't taken a driving test but there was time enough for that later. The Rover was taxed and insured in Kenny's name. Simple. Job done.

Brown usually drove them up the M6 to Birmingham to the gym above the White Horse pub, where Barnett had a dozen boxers working out. Two of them became Willis's regular sparring partners, a Walsall light-heavyweight named Stu Jones and a local black middleweight, Herman Browne.

Willis could unload his big punches against the thirteen-stone Jones, a ponderous but strong character, while Browne was speedy without being too heavy-handed. They had regular eight-round sessions and, by the time Barnett announced that Willis would make his debut at a dinner show in Solihull, he was fit and strong at just over eleven stone.

'I'm sorry for his fans that Johnny's not boxing in Westhampton but it hasn't been possible to arrange a suitable venue,' Barnett told Mercer. 'I hope we'll be able to do something next time. I promise his Westhampton fans they'll get enough chances to support him.'

Barnett's idea, in fact, was to give Willis a low-key début. It would be testing enough without having to appear in front of hundreds of expectant home supporters. He also knew Mercer would provide excellent coverage in the *News* that would sustain, maybe increase, interest in his young protégé.

The promoter elected to use one of his major dinner clubs which was always a sell-out. Four hundred and fifty members and guests at £65 per person. It was good business. Even allowing for the cost of catering and hire of the impressive hall, four annual shows left him with a tidy profit. More than enough to keep him in cigars!

Most of the dinner-jacketed audience used the night to mix business with pleasure. They invited guests to lay the ground for deals, consolidate links or offer thanks for past business, but many were also keen boxing supporters. They gave Willis a warm reception when the spotlight picked him out in a new crimson gown, shorts and boots.

'Seems odd, going out there without a vest on,' he said to Colin in the dressing room. His brothers and Payne had special passes to watch the match from a small balcony.

Willis glowed with health. When Brown stripped him of his robe, the boxer's oiled, rippling muscles gleamed under the lights.

Colin Eaves, a Manchester journeyman with sixty-four scraps under his belt, leaped at the larger-than-normal pay. Barnett reasoned that he would survive three or four rounds.

Eaves, pug nosed and somewhat flabby, was flat-footed but defended himself adequately. Elbows tucked in, hands held high, he wasn't a big target but Willis probed with his solid jab, mixed in some rib-crunching hooks and produced a sizzling right cross for a dramatic third-round conclusion.

The members applauded loudly and agreed that the youngster had potential. Barnett grinned through his blue cigar smoke. Willis happily contemplated adding another two thousand pounds to his new bank account and his trio of supporters declared, 'We're off to get pissed. Well done, Johnny.' Everyone, including the well-paid Eaves, went home happy.

When he entered 36 Johnson Close, Willis was surprised to see a shaft of light under the door of the back room. He knew Connie was out – either at a party or comatose in the front room, he didn't care which – and he had, as usual, telephoned Mary with the news of his success. He expected her to be in bed.

He pushed open the door and saw Mary, with her back to him, at the ironing board. She glanced over her shoulder as he entered and Willis saw immediately that she'd been crying.

'What's up? Why've you been crying? Why aren't you in bed?'

Mary sniffled. 'I've got to get this lot done.'

'It's gone one o'clock. You have been crying, haven't you? What's going on?'

'It's silly, nothing to get worked up about.'

'It's her, isn't it? What's the cow been up to now?'

'Johnny, don't talk about Ma like that. She is your mother, give her some respect.'

'Respect? Look, sis, I know what you do for her and it's great, it really is. I don't know how you do it. You know how I feel. I don't care about her – not like you do. Sorry, but there it is. Now, tell me, what's been going on?'

Mary put down the iron, wiped her reddened eyes with the back of a hand, and turned to face her brother. 'Ma had one of her tantrums, that's all. You know how it is. It just came out of the blue. Said she hadn't got anything to wear because I hadn't ironed her best blouse. I said she'd plenty to wear. Then she just went wild, ranting and raving, as she does.'

'When was this?'

'After you phoned. I told her you'd won and she said "Good" and then started on about her blouse.'

'Hang on, sis, you don't cry when she shouts at you. What else happened?' As he asked the question, Willis noticed a red mark on Mary's left cheek. 'Come here, let me look at your face.'

'It's nothing.'

'Nothing! She's hit you, the cow.'

'Johnny! Don't! Don't call her that.'

'She is a cow. Why'd she hit you? Christ, you do everything for her. I'll sort her out.'

'No, Johnny, leave it. Don't make it worse. She'll have forgotten all about it by the time she gets home.'

'She might, I won't. Come here, sis.'

Willis kissed his sister's brow, smelling the fragrance of her shampoo and feeling the soft warmth of her trembling body as they held each other. Eventually, Mary released him. 'I've just got this T-shirt of yours to finish and then I'm done,' she said.

'Forget that. You get off to bed.'

'Promise you won't say anything to Ma? Let it drop.'

'If you say so, sis. But I'm not happy.' Willis, fists clenched at his side, vowed that such a thing would never happen again. Over my dead body, he thought.

Mary made her way upstairs. Willis went into the kitchen, made a mug of instant coffee and took it into the front room, settling down in his mother's lumpy armchair. In the dark, he sipped his drink and brooded, waiting for Connie.

The slamming of car doors woke him from a slumber. He peered across at the luminous dial of his mother's bedside clock. Three o'clock in the morning. It wasn't Connie. Kenny and Colin were laughing, speaking in loud drunken whispers as they stumbled into the hall.

'Fucking great night,' slurred Colin. 'That bird was really up for it. What a blow job.'

'That's all you were fit for. Surprised you got it hard for that.'

'What d'yer mean? I could've given her one. No problem. But it was wrong time of the month.'

Kenny slapped his brother on the back. 'Only kiddin', Col. Anyway, we've gotta be up in the morning. Don't forget we're going to Nottingham.'

'Shit. Can't we give it a miss?'

'No. It's good dough. C'mon, Col, yer can do it in yer sleep.'

'Sleep… that's what I need.'

They stomped noisily up the stairs, bouncing off the wall. Minutes later they were snoring, spread out fully clothed on their beds. Nutters, thought Willis. Don't give a damn about anything. But they wouldn't be pleased if they knew Connie had smacked Mary.

Another half-hour passed before Willis heard the click-click of heels on the pavement, followed by fumbling attempts to put a key in the door. A few curses later, Connie was in. Willis was glad that she was alone. She switched on the light and gasped, startled, when she saw her youngest son lounging in the chair.

'God, Johnny, you gave me a start. What're you doing?'

'Waiting for you,' he said evenly.

'Why? What's up?'

'What's up? You should know.'

'What? Don't talk in riddles. It's late.'

'I know what the time is. And I know what you've been doing.'

Connie removed her coat, slung it over the bed and sat down heavily next to it. She looked at Johnny and, for a fleeting moment, she thought how much he resembled Danny. Same swarthy skin, same black hair and those deep-set dark eyes. Yes, the eyes. But they were staring coldly at her.

'Been to a party. Nothing wrong in that. Anyway, it's no business of yours what I do.'

'It is when it involves Mary,' said Willis, rising from the chair and moving across the room to tower over his mother.

'Mary? What's Mary got to do with anything?'

Willis glared down at the slatternly blonde who reeked of stale cigarette smoke. He felt hatred bubbling up inside him. He clenched his fists, striving to maintain control, feeling the bile rise in his throat. Quietly, he said, 'You lay one more finger on her and it'll be the last thing you do.'

'What? Who d'you think you are to speak to me like that? I'm your mother and don't you forget it.'

'I wish I could. You're no mother. You can rot in hell for all I care. Just don't ever, ever do that to Mary again. Understand?'

'Get out of my room. Go to bed.'

Willis struggled to contain his urge to strike out, to smash his fists into that full mouth smeared with ruby lipstick.

'I'm going. It makes me sick being in the same room as you. But I mean it. Leave Mary alone or you'll regret it. That's a promise.' He slammed the door behind him and climbed the stairs in a rage.

Connie, suddenly sober, tried to recollect what she'd done to Mary. What on earth was he talking about?

He's going mad. Probably all that boxing. Too many slaps to the head. And then she remembered. Slaps.

'Well, well,' she said softly to herself, standing up to undress. 'Johnny certainly loves his sister. God help any bloke who crosses her. They'll be a dead man.'

She slid wearily between the sheets and her coat slipped into a heap on the carpet. But he wouldn't really hurt me, she thought as she drifted off into sleep. Would he?

Willis's next fight, three weeks later, was another club show, a smaller affair in Stoke-on-Trent. It took only ninety-five seconds to batter a rangy, black Welshman, Solomon 'The Kid' Driscoll, to defeat. Down three times, Driscoll wisely took the full count on one knee, rubbing gingerly at his broken nose as it poured blood on to the canvas.

'Great stuff, Johnny,' said Barnett. 'How do you fancy boxing at home?'

'Sure, George, any time. I don't mind where I fight. Just keep bringing 'em along.'

'Reckon it's time to see what sort of following you've got. I've lined up the Coldstream Lane baths. You'll top the bill. Eight rounds.'

'Eight rounds. More money, then.'

Barnett blew a plume of cigar smoke into the air. 'Sure, more money. You'll be on two and a half grand – plus ticket sales. Five per cent, after VAT, of all the tickets you sell.'

Mercer revealed details of the fight a week later in the *News*. Payne, with the Willis brothers, set about selling tickets. Capacity was set at eight hundred, with ringside seats costing fifty pounds down to ten for back-of-the-hall tickets. Barnett pitched the majority of seats at twenty-five pounds and reasoned he could gross twenty-five thousand on a sell-out. Not that he expected a full house at this early stage in Willis's career. But he hadn't reckoned on the persuasive sales pitch of Payne and the Willis boys.

From their base at The Casino, they had security men working at twenty pubs and clubs. And regular customers were 'persuaded' to buy a ticket for the fight. In fact, no fight ticket, no admission for the weekend's drinking. Anyway, didn't they want to see Johnny belt the shit out of some poor bugger?

'He's gonna be a world champion,' Payne repeated time after time, night after night. 'It'll cost you a lot more to see him then. It'll be a great night. Of course there'll be a bar. How many tickets do yer want?'

All the doormen were versed in the homily. It was another nice little earner from the Willis boys. Johnny insisted they would receive the full five per cent – after VAT, of course. He wasn't interested in the ticket commission, his profit would come later through bigger purses. A fighter with a big following commands bigger pay. Let the workers keep their bits and pieces – I'll rake in the thousands, he thought. That's the name of the game. Just keep pushing the tickets, lads.

Barnett did his bit to make the event special. Two weeks before the big night, he announced that the opponent would be from the continent; a truly international show. In truth, because Willis's reputation was already high, it was cheaper to bring in a moderate European rather than pay an inflated price for a home-based opponent.

Chomping on the inevitable fat cigar, he phoned Mercer. 'I'm bringing over a fighter from Belgium. My agent's been working on this for a fortnight and he's come up with a decent guy called... let me see... yes, Claude Renard. He's twenty-four, been a pro for two years and lost only two of thirteen fights. Don't know a lot more but you can ring Bertie Fosse if you like. He's the agent. Have you got his number?'

'I know Bertie. You wouldn't know how this Renard lost the two fights, would you?'

'Points. Bertie says he hasn't been stopped. It'll be a good fight, Bob.'

'Bet he can't punch.'

'Aw, c'mon, Bob.' The reporter envisaged blue smoke being blown towards the ceiling. 'We're not in the business of knocking over our honeypot, are we? You've got a good story. International boxing in Westhampton, local kid's the star. What more could you want? Give it a good show, Bob.'

'Sure. When's Renard coming over?'

'Probably the day before the fight. Flights and hotels aren't cheap. But you'll get the chance to see him. Probably book them into The Post House. They should do me a deal after that press conference. Cost me an arm and a leg for you lads to get sozzled.'

'Worth every penny to you, George. How's ticket sales?'

'Thought you might know more about that. Those Willis lads say they're doing okay. What do you reckon to them? They seem lively.'

'They are. Not quite sure what they do. I know they're in the building trade but they're well known around the town. Used to box a bit. I know Kenny's been in a spot of bother. Beat up some guy and did a few months in detention.'

'Willis doesn't strike me like that. Nice kid to handle.'

'Yes, he's a decent sort. He's popular. Built quite a following in the amateurs. It'll be interesting to see what sort of crowd turns up.'

'Well, we're giving it a go. These small shows don't sell many tickets in advance. Usually depends on the walk-up on the night. If there's nothing on the telly, they'll turn out. Give it plenty of coverage in the *News*, Bob. I'd like to run a few shows over there.'

'Keep feeding me the lines, George. If I get the stuff before anyone else, we'll run it a lot bigger.'

'I know that. By the way, I'll be inviting some of the footballers to the fight. But you can run that story later. Another line, eh?'

But the Westhampton City team wasn't invited. They were involved in an away Cup replay. 'Just my luck,' wailed Barnett. 'Bound to knock our gate.'

The promoter, however, was stunned at the weigh-in when Colin turned up with only fifteen unsold tickets and a bag full of money.

'You've done well,' Barnett beamed.

'It's all worked out. The account's in the bag with the money. Do yer wanna check it now?'

Barnett's wife, Hilary, was in a dressing room, checking ticket stubs, fingers sliding efficiently over a calculator. Ten minutes later, she declared, 'Fine. It all adds up, Mr Willis. Thank you very much. That's nearly four hundred tickets you've sold.'

'Johnny's popular.'

That Willis had trained exceptionally hard for his first eight-rounder was illustrated when he tipped the scales at ten stone and thirteen pounds. The match was made at eleven-two and Brown was confident that Willis would comfortably last the eight rounds – if necessary. Willis had natural strength and stamina and had trained so conscientiously that there was no need to dry out. He had just a cup of weak tea and two rounds of toast before the weigh-in.

Renard, a pale, lean man without visible scars on his angular face, was exactly eleven-two. He smiled warmly as he shook hands with Willis, posing for photographers.

Renard spoke little English – as Mercer had discovered the previous night, conducting an interview instead with his manager Jean Rives – but he tapped Willis on his rippling midriff and said, 'Is good.'

Willis smiled back, brought his left arm up in front of his chest and clenched his fist. 'This better,' he said.

The Belgian shrugged and turned to his manager, who translated rapidly. Then Renard laughed. 'We see, we see.'

Mercer gleaned a couple of facts from Rives in their interview. Renard had not had thirteen fights but sixteen and he had lost five, all on points against quality opposition. He'd won only three contests inside the distance but Rives insisted, 'He's a clever boxer. Never been knocked down. Your man had better be prepared for a long, hard fight.'

It was a point Mercer emphasised in his preview.

Willis has never gone beyond three rounds and tonight he could be going into the unknown. Renard's manager, Jean Rives, claims that his 24-year-old boxer has never been knocked down and his five points defeats were all close. 'Renard probably deserved a draw in a couple of them,' says Rives, 'but he was boxing away from home.'

All that may be managerial hype but Renard, a spidery six-footer, has clean looks and professes to rely on boxing skills rather than brawn or a big punch. He may not be able to hurt Willis, who has a strong chin, but the man from Ostend appears confident of taking the former ABA champion all the way.

Willis, for his part, will be keen to impress on his home professional début. Promoter George Barnett says tickets have sold well and believes he could be close to an 800 sell-out. And that means a lot of people will be at the Coldstream Lane baths with huge expectations. Does that add pressure on the 20-year-old's shoulders?

'I expect a lot from myself,' says Willis. 'Obviously, I want to put on a good show in front of my own people. I appreciate that they are turning out to support me and I won't let them down. That's a promise.

'I don't know much about Renard but George tells me he's a strong man. I'll find out on the night. It won't matter if it goes the distance, as long as I win and win well. I'm not bothered about eight rounds. I've sparred more than that in a night. I've trained hard.'

Willis, after opening his paid career with two quick victories, understandably has confidence but I have a sneaking feeling that Renard may be crafty enough to teach him a few things tonight.

And that, after all, is the purpose of the exercise. Willis needs to develop in the pro ring. His punching power is not in dispute and, on occasions in the amateur ring, he has displayed a smart boxing brain.

I think he will need all those assets tonight but, barring injuries or cuts, I take him to win, probably around the sixth round.

Willis didn't read Mercer's assessment until he was in the dressing room.

'Seems you've respect for this guy,' he said when Bob popped in to wish him well.

'I don't think he's a mug. But I don't think George has brought him over to beat you. That wouldn't make sense.'

'Anything can happen.'

'It can. But I don't doubt you'll win. It's just simply a fact that you're on a learning curve. You should learn from each fight, just like you did when you started in the amateurs.'

Willis nodded thoughtfully. 'I've come a long way since then. But I know what you mean.'

'Okay, Johnny. Just go out there and do the business. Don't worry about him, or the crowd. Do it your way. It's been good enough so far.'

'Cheers, Bob. See you later.'

Barnett had packed one side of the six-fight bill with his own boxers. Willis's middleweight sparmate, Herman Browne, shared his dressing room. He was in the chief supporting bout.

'I'd like to see how Herman's doing.'

'Sorry, Johnny,' said Brown. 'We need to warm up. We'll be on as soon as Herman's done. Let's get you oiled up.'

The trainer rubbed oils into Willis's torso and arms and then, holding his fingers, shook the fighter's arms. 'That's it, relax those muscles. Don't be tense,' he said.

'I'm fine, Ron. You worry too much.' They both smiled. A

roar from the crowd told them something dramatic was happening in the arena. 'Hope Herman wins,' said Willis. 'He's a good lad, smart boxer.'

Another roar. Seconds later the door burst open. Harry Marshall, the whip – the man responsible for ensuring that the fighters were ready to enter the ring – bustled into the room.

'You nearly ready?' he asked.

'Almost,' said Brown. He was checking his medical bag, making sure he had Willis's mouthpiece. 'What's happened?'

'Fight's been stopped. The fourth, I think.'

'Who won? Herman?'

'No. He ran into a coupla right-handers.'

'Shit,' said Willis under his breath.

'Better get the gloves on,' said Marshall. 'Fifteen-minute interval and then you're on. Okay? I'll be back in ten.'

Willis put on his crimson robe and sat down while Ron gloved him up.

Browne, accompanied by his trainer and Barnett, came in. He slumped on a chair, shaking his bowed head. 'Can't believe it,' he muttered.

'You got caught by a lucky punch,' said Barnett. 'It happens. I'll get you a return and you can put the record straight. You okay?'

'I just didn't see it. What was it, a right hand?'

'A big swinger.'

'Sucker punch. Fuckin' sucker punch. Fuckin' hell.' Silence.

Ron asked Willis, 'How do they feel?'

He banged his gloved fists together. 'Fine. Give me a swill of water.'

Willis gargled and spat the liquid into a washbasin. Then he walked over to Herman and placed a gloved hand on his shoulder. 'Sorry, mate. You okay?'

Herman looked up, his eyes sad and hurt. 'Sure, man. Shit happens. You go out there and stuff that Belgy.'

Renard was first into the ring, to a muted but polite reception. He bowed to all four sides of the compact hall and went to his corner, jiggling up and down on his toes as the house lights dimmed. A spotlight played around before settling on the corner of the baths from which Willis would emerge.

The buzz of the crowd erupted into a deafening explosion as the local prospect appeared and headed for the red corner. Willis was surprised by the boisterous reception but he kept his head down, concentrating. He picked out a few familiar voices on the short walk and, at the ring steps, he saw his brothers and Pete sitting near his corner.

'Be lucky,' mouthed Pete. Willis smiled before climbing the steps, straddling the ropes and provoking another enthusiastic cheer as he danced into the centre of the ring with his hands held aloft.

'A showman already,' said Mercer to a fellow reporter.

Willis was pumping inside, bubbling with energy. Lifted by an adrenaline rush, he barely listened to the introductions or formal instructions from the referee. Let's get going, he thought.

Renard, wearing black and white striped shorts and white boots adorned with black tassels, was grim-faced. At the bell, he did the sign of the cross on his chest, muttered to himself, and went straight to the centre of the ring. He adopted a low crouch, left shoulder pointing towards Willis. He snaked a left towards Willis's chest and Johnny countered with a left hook which whistled through the air.

Renard, from his crab-like stance, weaved and swayed, jabbing spasmodically at Willis's stomach. Occasionally he backed off, stood upright and clapped his gloves together. But, each time Willis advanced, he resumed his crouch. Willis had difficulty finding range. Punching down at the low, elusive target didn't suit him.

Towards the end of the round, in desperation, Willis slammed a wide right almost on Renard's spine, which brought a swift rebuke from the referee. Renard, walking around the edge of the ring, shook his head in silent admonishment.

'You've got to get him to stand up,' said Brown, rather obviously, between rounds. 'Bend your knees, bring the punches up at him.'

Willis tried. But, as he moved closer, the Belgian stood up and walked away. The crowd howled. Willis tried again. The Belgian grabbed him and they wrestled in mid-ring before the referee parted them.

The crowd became restless as this dreary pattern repeated itself in rounds three and four. It was a stinker. A plaintive voice pierced the gloom from the back of the hall. 'C'mon, Willis, 'it 'im, fer Godsake.'

Willis, searching his boxing brain for a solution, didn't hear the exhortation but continued to throw punches that all too frequently missed the target. By round five he was arm-weary. He settled for prodding out his jab, trying to line up a more damaging right cross. But Renard was good at what he did and effective in a negative manner, picking up points with jabs to the body.

Barnett puffed anxiously on his cigar. Willis didn't look good. In fact he looked bad, a novice. This isn't good box office, he thought. Why the hell's Bertie Fosse dug up this guy for me? Fucking agents! I'll have words with him.

Renard, to everyone's surprise, showed more aggression in the sixth. He stood up, exchanged jabs to the face and even threw his first right of the fight. It fell short and he resumed his crab style.

In the seventh, Willis gave up. He prodded a few downward jabs and then, only feet away from Renard in the centre of the ring, stood with hands held low and wide. The gesture simply asked the disappointed crowd: 'What do you expect me to do?'

Renard grinned and stood upright. He knew he'd mentally worn down his young, inexperienced rival.

But in a flash, Willis brought up a sizzling left hook which caught the relaxed Renard flush on the jaw. The Belgian reeled across the ring into the ropes. He'd paid dearly for losing concentration. Renard had been outfoxed.

Then Willis was in front of him, slamming away with both hands. As the crowd, roused from their torpor, rose to their feet, Renard was knocked off his.

With his right arm clinging to the rope above his head, he sat on the canvas, blood seeping down his face from a cut over his right eye. He could hear the referee. 'Six... seven...'

Time to get up, pull himself together and get back to basics. Frustrate the young Brit. Only a round and a bit to go.

'Eight...'

Up you get, he thought. But his legs failed him. He tried

pulling himself up on the ropes but his legs buckled underneath him. He slipped untidily back on to the seat of his striped shorts.

'Nine...' The referee waved his arms to signal the end of the fight. The crowd was frenzied as Willis's left arm was held aloft. All the tedium of the affair was forgotten. Willis had produced a dramatic knock-out. That was all that mattered.

Brown wiped the perspiration from Willis's face and chest before slipping the towel around his neck and draping the dressing gown across his shoulders. 'Well done, Johnny. That was smart work.'

Willis grinned at his breathless trainer. 'No problem. I told you, Ron, you worry too much.'

## Chapter Seven

'I tell you, it'll work like a dream. Hundred per cent perfect. Can't fail.'

Willis still wasn't convinced of brother Colin's latest scheme to make thousands. 'Why do I need to be involved? I said I'll give you the money. Isn't that good enough?'

'No, it's not. Look, Johnny, you know Vic Grant best. He'll listen to you. You explain to him and he'll go along with it. I know he will.'

'Tell me again.'

'It's simple. You get Vic to buy a car, cheap like, probably from an auction. Probably got heavy mileage or been banged up in a smash, something like that. Anyway, say we get it for two grand, maybe three. We value it on insurance for double that. Okay?'

'Yeah, I'm okay with that.'

'The thing is, we use five different insurance companies. It means laying out a few quid but not for too long. After a few weeks, we report the car stolen. The police give us a crime number and we tell the insurances.

'Then – and this is the best bit – we torch the car. Burn it real good so that no one knows what sort of state it was in. They won't know whether it was worth two or six grand, see. Then we get Vic to take it to his garage and wait for the insurance guys to look it over. He tells 'em when they can see the car. That makes sure they don't arrive at the same time.

'They won't give us the full value, the cheating bastards never do. But it could be worth anywhere between a ten- and fifteen-grand profit. Vic'll get a bung and so will the two insurance lads I told you about.'

'What about them? Who're they?'

'Me and Kenny met them down The Casino a few times. They've watched you fight. Anyway, they're settlers or somethin' and we got talking one night. They told us about the strokes people pull. Injuries, flood-damaged goods, arson, that sort of thing. It's amazing what people get up to, really is.'

'They're willing to go along with this?'

'Sure. In fact, we'll use them for a coupla insurances. They're safe as houses. They don't get overpaid and I reckon they're not too lucky on the tables. They won't say "No" to a few easy quid. Now, what do you say? Are you in or what?'

'If they're that safe, why don't you just use them? Why spread it around? Why add to the risk?'

'Risk? It's a piece of piss, Johnny. Honest. These guys reckon that so many cars get stolen they don't have the time to check 'em out properly. They won't even follow up the crime number. They just accept it. When cars are found, battered to bits or burnt out, the assessors are so busy, all they're bothered about is knocking off a few hundred quid. Besides, five times three grand is better than two times, ain't it? All for one job, one car. C'mon, Johnny, it's a beauty.'

'I'll have a word with Vic. See what he says. He might not go for it.'

'Course he will. Tell him he's on a nice earner.'

'How much? If he's interested, he's bound to ask.'

'Ah!' said Colin and paused. 'Tell him, he could be in for a grand. That's if we get a decent payout. It all depends on the mark-up from the car. Bigger the margin, bigger the profit.'

Grant had reservations. 'I wouldn't say no to a thousand pounds, Johnny. Course I wouldn't. I can get you a car, no problem with that. But I'm not sure about getting involved with assessors. That could be dodgy for me. I'm taking a big risk there. I'm in deep that way already.'

'I know what you're saying, Vic. But these insurance guys, they reckon it's easy.'

'Maybe. But I'm still taking the risk. Let's put it this way,' he wiped his hands on an oily rag, 'if I do it, it's surely worth more than a grand?'

'You'll do it for a bigger cut?'

'I'm not saying I want to get involved. I need to think about it. But I wouldn't take the risk just for a grand. I could lose my business, get sent down.'

'I understand what you mean. I don't think it's that risky but I'll have another word with Col. See if he can come up with more. Anyway, will you start looking for a car?'

'That's not a problem, Johnny. That's the easy bit. I'll leave it with you, then.'

Willis explained the garage man's reluctance to Colin. 'Don't worry, Johnny. I'll see to him.'

'Nice premises you've got here. Be a pity to lose them, wouldn't it?' said Colin.

'Lose them?' said Vic.

'Yeah, you know. If they got burnt down or blew up.'

Kenny wandered around the rear of the garage. He kicked a tall metal canister. 'These tanks can be dangerous. Highly volatile,' he said.

Vic looked from one brother to the other. 'Jeez,' he said. Two minutes later, he accepted a deal. Two per cent of the profit.

Mary lay back in the steamy bath water. She rubbed soap on her flat stomach and over her well-rounded breasts, conscious of their firm nipples. She raised her right leg out of the water, toes pointing at the far wall. She admired the slim calf and slender ankle and ran a hand over the taut thigh. Her wet, hairless skin felt so smooth. She did the same with her other leg. She closed her eyes, right hand sliding between her thighs and thought of Pete, as she soaped the mass of dark pubic hair. No one else had ever touched her there. Not in nineteen years. She let her fingers play among the sodden, flattened hairs. Perhaps she should trim them, like those girls did in the magazine she'd found when cleaning under Kenny's bed. Neat, shaped, not a wild sprouting like hers. Some were bald. Didn't like them. A slim rectangle was better. Yes, that would be nice. Bet Pete would like that.

Mary sat up and watched the soapy water swill over her thighs and lap against her pubis. She reached for her razor. First the armpits and then she'd do it. A birthday present to herself. And, maybe, just maybe, for Pete as well.

Payne patted the aftershave around his jaw and throat, sensitive to the cleansing sting, sniffing the fresh hint of cedar. He combed a parting in his recently cropped fair hair and looked approvingly at the reflection in the mirror.

He wandered, naked, back into his bedroom, pulled open a wardrobe door and struck a fighter's pose in front of the full-length mirror. His shoulders were wide and his torso tapered to a slim, fat-free waist.

'Still in shape, son,' he told his reflection as he reached for his one suit. Dark blue with deep red threads weaving through it, he had bought it off the peg from Marks and Spencer. He lay it carefully on the bed next to the new white shirt, still in its wrapping.

Wear a suit and tie, Johnny had said. It's Mary's birthday and we're gonna give her a proper posh night out. Dinner at a fancy restaurant. Tablecloths, wine glasses and waiters who call you 'Sir' and 'Madam'. We'll make it a night she'll always remember.

You bet, thought Pete. Just give me the chance.

Mary considered her choices. Thanks to Johnny, she'd now got some nice clothes. The white halter-neck top and black skirt, with the gold St Christopher pendant, the beautiful gift she'd had from Johnny on her eighteenth birthday. That should be classy enough. Get dressed up, Johnny told her. We're going to Mario's, top Italian restaurant. Prepare to be spoilt. And Johnny certainly spoils me, she thought, pulling white bikini panties over her talcum-powdered pubic creation.

Can't believe the last two years. Johnny's done really well. Unbeaten in twenty fights, contender for the British title, loads of money. Famous, too. On TV, in the papers, presenting trophies, even opening fêtes. Our Johnny – a celebrity!

And his new flat. Okay, it's only rented but he had to get away from here. That was a close call, Colin and his stupid insurance job. That could've ruined Johnny. Thank God Colin took the rap. It was his mad idea after all.

At the dressing table, Mary applied subtle eyeliner, lipstick and brushed her shoulder-length hair. She glanced at the framed picture of her brother with his ABA belt. You've come a long way, she thought. Nice flat, nice car, money. People might think you've changed, but you're still Johnny. That will never change. Look at tonight. My nineteenth birthday, a special occasion, and you'll insist on paying the bill for us all. Me and the four musketeers: my three brothers and their pal Pete. Ah, yes, Pete. Wonder what Johnny'd think about me and Pete...

Pete saw Willis's BMW pull up at the kerbside as he slipped on his jacket and checked the pockets. House key, tissues, a wad of money and some loose change. And a packet of condoms.

Time to go. Time to give Mary the best night of her life. Johnny said so, didn't he?

The three brothers raised their wine glasses.

'To you, sis,' said Johnny. 'The best sister anyone could wish for.'

'To Mary,' they said in unison.

Mary, radiant at the attention, fingered the gold chain at her neck and a broad, captivating smile lit her face. She picked up her glass and looked across the table at Johnny. 'Thanks for a wonderful night. Thanks, all of you. And that includes you, Pete.' Her spectacular brown eyes focused on the man next to her.

'Course it does,' said Colin, his face still pallid from long months without the benefit of sunshine. 'Best pal anyone could have – man or woman.'

'Well, I don't know about—'

'C'mon, cut the crap,' interrupted Kenny. 'Do yer wanna get the violinist over?'

The brothers laughed. Mary lightly put a hand on Payne's shoulder and leaned to kiss his cheek. 'Don't mind Kenny,' she said, 'it's only 'cause nobody says anything nice about him.'

'What d'yer mean, sis? My probation officer said a lot of nice things about me. And she weren't half bad, either.'

'But she must've been half blind,' ribbed Payne. They all laughed again and a grinning Kenny wagged a warning finger at his friend.

'What d'you wanna do next, sis?' asked Johnny. 'Go clubbing, a disco, bit of dancing? Maybe The Casino? Or I'll get a table at the Comedy House if you like. What'll it be?'

Mary looked at her new watch, a birthday gift from her brothers. 'Not for me, thanks all the same, Johnny. I've had a great night but I'd better be getting home now.'

'Why? It's only just after ten. Night's young.' Then, with sudden anger, he spat, 'Nothing to do with Ma, is it?'

'No, course not. She told me to enjoy myself.'

'I bet.'

Mary ignored the sarcasm in his voice. 'Honestly, I've really enjoyed myself but I'm on early shift tomorrow. Up at six.' She glanced at Pete. 'Will one of you call me a taxi?'

'If you're really going, I'll run you home,' said Johnny. 'You're not going home alone.'

'I'll be fine in a taxi. You lads carry on and enjoy yourselves. Have some beers or something. I'm sure Kenny's dying for a pint. Wine's not your idea of a drink, is it?'

'Don't worry about me, sis. I'll drink owt. 'Specially if it's free,' Kenny said, heartily patting Johnny on the back.

'I'll take you home,' insisted Johnny. 'I picked you up and I'll make sure you get back safely.'

'No need,' said Payne suddenly. 'I'm not long for my bed. Got a big day ahead. I'll take Mary in a cab and you lot go to The Casino. Make a night of it, Johnny. God knows you'll be back in training for long enough.'

Mary smiled. 'Are you sure, Pete? I'll be all right in a taxi on my own.'

'Won't hear of it. I've gotta get one, anyway. We may as well share. Johnny'll feel better about it, won't you?'

The boxer frowned as he looked at his best friend, then switched his gaze to Mary, his beloved sister. She smiled sweetly, comfortingly, back at him.

'Fine. If you're sure, Pete. Don't you fancy an hour at The Casino?'

'Not tonight. I'll see Mary home and be off to bed. See you lads later.'

Mary so wanted it to be good the first time. After all, this was a precious gift. She'd never be a virgin again. She'd always liked

Pete. Even as a kid, when he first came home with Johnny after training, she'd liked him. Only then, she was an embarrassed seven-year-old. Now it was different. Had been for some years, even before she left school.

And she knew Pete liked her. She could tell. The sly, appraising looks as he sat waiting for Johnny, when she was ironing or cleaning or sewing. He didn't think she noticed, but she did. Women did, didn't they? Sixth sense.

Now, as Pete wrapped his strong arms around her, it was confirmed. His embrace was firm but tender. Not crushing, just secure.

The restrained glow from the bedside lamp cast shadows across the room, giving out just enough light for her to look into his eyes. To see the desire, the expectancy, that she had to see. Not love; she didn't expect that. Not yet, anyway.

On the bed, they kissed, gently at first and then hungrily. Clothes were scattered hastily on to the floor until they were naked. Mary's bosom heaved and her back arched as Payne slid fingers through her newly styled pubic region. She held him tight, seeking his mouth as she opened her legs.

'Damn. The rubbers are in my jacket.' Payne pulled reluctantly away, fumbled in his jacket and tore impatiently at the condom packaging.

Mary held out her hand, took the contraceptive and gently rolled it over his fat erection. Then she lay back, spreading her legs. 'It's my first time,' she murmured.

'God,' said Payne as he gingerly entered. Mary felt soft kisses on her neck but the real pleasure came from much lower. No pain, only pleasure. Slowly, tenderly, Pete gave her a first time to treasure. A birthday to remember.

As the taxi pulled away, Payne looked up at the darkened bedroom. Mary's shadow image waved. Payne leaned back in the seat, wound down a window and tossed the empty contraceptive packet into the August midnight air. All three used. What a girl.

He closed his eyes and relived the moments. He'd never had such pleasure. It wasn't just fucking. It felt so different to those other times. He'd known nice girls, but this was different. Mary was different. But what to do about Johnny?

Mary was Johnny's inspiration, his driving force. Willis wanted success for himself but he craved it equally for Mary. Boxing could propel them both towards a better life. Nothing would stop Johnny in that quest. That's why, in Johnny's analysis, a world title was all-important.

But what about tonight's happening in his sister's bedroom? What would he think of his oldest, best pal? Payne knew he wouldn't – couldn't – tell him. Nor would Mary. But he couldn't turn away from her, not now.

Johnny will understand, he thought. He's not that possessive. He must know that men lust after Mary. Surely it's better to have her in the hands of his trusted best mate? Trusted? See her home safely, Pete. Sure, Johnny.

Two minutes after Payne's taxi drove out of Johnson Close, the blue BMW purred to a halt outside number 36. Willis looked up. Lights out. Curtains closed at Mary's bedroom window.

Well done, Pete, you're a mate, he thought, before contentedly setting off back to The Casino. I can concentrate on the cards now, he mused. I need to stop this fucking losing run.

## Chapter Eight

Barnett tossed the letter on to his desk. Bastards! he thought. They've done it again. Turned me over. There's no way the fight's worth that much. Never!

He sucked on his cigar, leaned back in the leather chair and blew smoke at the ceiling. Fifteen grand for a challenger on a sixty-forty split. No way they're paying Brian Adams £22,500. He won't even get what Johnny's getting. Still, it's a good pay day for Johnny and my twenty per cent's pretty tidy, he mused.

Barnett jotted figures on a pad. He'd made a purse bid of twenty thousand pounds to the British Boxing Board of Control. Twelve for Adams, eight for Willis. Good offer. Big attraction in the Midlands – Willis challenging Adams for his British light-middleweight title. But, as the Board letter informed him, it had gone to Harry Jacobs.

Probably be a supporting bout on a big London show, Barnett thought. Adams won't get twelve thousand. Probably done a deal for ten, or even less. Bugger him. I'm only gonna pick up three grand. Could've made twenty on my own show. Shit. Why wouldn't they cut a deal with me? Could've been a good joint promotion up here. Plenty in the pot for all of us. Greedy bastards.

Barnett ground his cigar butt into the ashtray. They've got home advantage. Paid for it, through the nose. Then he smiled. Willis beat him in the ABA final at Wembley. He can do it again. Course he will. And then I'll be in the driving seat. Kiss my ass, you greedy Cockney bastards. He lit another cigar and picked up the phone.

Mercer walked across the editorial floor and stopped at the sports editor's desk. 'Got a good one, Mac,' he said.

Bill McKenzie, a sandy-haired Scot in his late fifties, took his pipe from between tobacco-stained teeth and looked up from the page proof he was reading. 'What's that, Bob?'

'Johnny Willis has got his British title fight. George Barnett's just been on the phone.'

'Will it be here?'

'Unfortunately not. Looks like London. Harry Jacobs put in the top offer.'

'That's a pity. Could've done with a big fight here. Would've made a lot of stories.'

'Still will.'

'Not the same, laddie. More interest if it was here, not London.'

'C'mon, Mac, you know Willis is good copy. There's a lot of people interested in him. They'll go down there to support him. Hundreds will go.'

The sports editor nodded and scribbled an alteration on the page proof. 'Better get it written. We'll make a hole for it on the back.'

'It's worth more than a hole,' said Mercer fiercely. 'It's a big story. Westhampton kid fighting for a British title? It could be his first step to even greater things.'

'Okay. But don't forget City are playing tomorrow night. We haven't got all the space in the world, laddie. Get it written, but keep it tight.'

'Tight? I've already got loads of quotes from Barnett and I'm gonna give Willis a call. You want his reaction, don't you?'

'Sure. But keep it tight,' McKenzie said again. 'I'll find some room overnight for you. You can do a full job for tomorrow's paper. Okay?'

'We've got this to ourselves, Mac. It's not been officially announced by the Boxing Board yet.'

'Good. We'll put an exclusive tag on it. But don't overdo it. No room.'

McKenzie left his seat and carried the corrected page proof to the composing room.

'Doesn't know a fucking good story from shit,' Mercer said, storming back to his desk. 'Bet there's all sorts of crap in the paper. Fucking City! That's all he's bothered about. Football!'

'Get it written, Bob,' shouted the chief sports sub-editor. 'I heard what you said. I'll give it a decent show on the back page. Don't worry, old son.'

'Cheers, Mike. I know you'll do your best. Wish you could convince that Scottish hack.' And he picked up the phone.

Willis looked in disbelief at his bank statement. He took a swig of orange juice and leaned against the kitchen sink. Where's all the money gone? he thought. Chrissakes, I thought I'd got more than that. Just a coupla grand? Jeez. And then there's the marker at The Casino. What's that, about £800 now? Stuff 'em. They'll have to wait. Could do with a fight. Wonder if George's working on anything. I'll give him a call later. Time we heard about the title fight.

The telephone ring cut into his thoughts. He wandered into the lounge, still clutching the bank statement.

'Just been thinking about you, George,' he said, slumping into an armchair.

'Why's that?'

'Wondering if you'd got anything lined up for me. It's been a long summer. Could do with some dough.'

'Summer's over, Johnny,' said Barnett. 'You're about to enter the autumn of your content.'

'What's that mean?'

'The British title. Harry Jacobs won the bid.'

'Yeah? Beat you, did he?'

'In a way, Johnny, in a way. But it's a winner for you. Loads of dough.'

Willis looked at the statement in his lap. 'Loads? How much is loads?'

'Twelve grand.'

The boxer made a quick mental calculation. He was getting used to percentages. 'That's over nine for me, ain't it, George?'

'No, Johnny. It means twelve. I've still to see the contracts, of course, but our end of the purse is fifteen. Good news, eh?'

'You don't know how good, George. When and where?'

'Before the end of October, but I reckon they might want it for last week in September at Wembley. Jacobs always starts his season with a show there. Will you be ready?'

Another quick calculation. Five weeks away. 'You bet. I'll take Adams next week if I have to.'

'How's the weight?'

'Good. Around eleven-six,' he lied. 'Six pound's nothing to lose.'

Willis was nearer twelve stone. Restaurant food and a growing intake of lager at The Casino meant he'd fleshed out since his last contest in May. But it wasn't a problem. Two weeks of hard physical work and he'd be back on track.

'Okay. I'll be in touch as soon as I hear from Jacobs. By the way, I've let Bob Mercer know. He'll probably be giving you a call today. Okay? Be lucky, son.'

'Cheers, George. Just one thing, is there any chance of—' The phone went dead before Willis could ask for an advance on his purse. 'Shit!' he muttered.

Still, I can get through five weeks, he thought. It's back to the graft. Fuck The Casino. Anyway, I'll rob 'em blind after the title fight. Twelve grand. My luck's changed. Look out, here comes the high roller.

Willis knew it was bad the moment his right hand bounced awkwardly off Herman Browne's headguard. The pain shot from his knuckles, through the back of his hand and along his forearm. He backed off and shook his arm.

'You okay?' Browne mumbled through his blood-smeared gumshield.

'Think so. Caught your fucking hard nut a bit wrong, that's all.'

The sparmates touched gloves and continued their workout. Brown, leaning on the ropes, noticed that Willis used his right only once more and he winced when it landed on Herman's shoulder.

'That'll do for tonight,' said the trainer as the three-minute clock buzzed to end the round. 'Let's get those gloves off.'

Willis gritted his teeth as Brown pulled off the right glove. When he unwrapped the crêpe bandage, his fears were confirmed. The back of the hand and wrist were swollen and a vivid bruise was forming.

'It's not good, Johnny. Let's get it into the ice bucket.'

With a towel draped over his head, Willis sat on a bench. Sweat dripped off the end of his nose, forming a puddle between his feet. For three weeks he had worked hard, losing weight, building up stamina and honing his boxing with up to ten rounds of sparring each night. He felt good. Knew he was on track to be at peak fitness to take Adams and have a coveted Lonsdale Belt strapped around his waist. Until now.

The mood in the Friar gym was subdued. Herman sat down next to Willis and removed his own hand bandages. 'How is it?' he asked.

Willis didn't look up. 'Probably just bruised. It'll go in a coupla days.'

Brown didn't agree. 'It's worse than that,' he declared after feeling the swollen hand. 'Could be a bone broken. You'll need an X-ray.'

'Fuck,' said Willis, feeling twelve thousand pounds slipping through his aching fingers.

Jacobs was furious. 'When did this happen? I'll need a doc's note. Fucking hell! Why didn't you tell me before?'

Barnett eased the receiver from his ear to lessen the boom of the London promoter's rasping voice. He waited for the tirade to cease, then lied. 'I told you, Harry, it only happened a coupla days ago. We thought it might just be bruising. But it's worse, he's damaged a bone, a carpus or something. I'll send you the doc's report but the fight's off.'

'Bollocks,' said Jacobs. 'What a fucking pisser.'

'We're not best pleased, either. Johnny's really pissed off. He's trained hard for this.'

'Bollocks,' repeated Jacobs. 'I've only got forty-eight hours to find a replacement.'

'You can't let Adams defend the title. We've got a contract.'

'Shit to that. Your lad's out. It's not my fault; I've got a show to think about. The Board'll accept a substitute. They'll have to.'

'I'll object. All we're asking for is a postponement. He's injured and the Board must back us. Johnny's the official challenger.'

'Protest all you like. Fact is, I've got Adams lined up for the European title. This was just a warm-up.'

So that's it, thought Barnett. That's why he put in a ridiculous bid. 'Where's that leave us?' he said.

'In the cold. Your kid's missed the boat. I'll get a sub in and then it's the European. We'll give up the British title after winning that. You're looking at least six months down the road before the Board come up with someone to fight your kid for the vacant title.'

Barnett knew the Londoner was right. It was a bad break for Willis.

Willis was desperate. Three weeks after Adams retained his title by knocking out an overmatched late substitute, he badly needed money. Barnett advanced him a grand in lieu of his next purse but he still owed The Casino eight hundred, and it would be another six weeks before he could start punching again. God only knew when his next fight would be.

His share of the door-security business was useful but it was pin money. It wouldn't even pay the rent on the flat. That's why Kenny's proposal was tempting. He had to consider it.

'We'll go in and do the job, you just drive the car,' said Kenny. 'Village post offices always have a few grand in cash for pensioners and whatnot. Col's worked it all out.'

Willis parked in the narrow side street and he watched in the rear-view mirror as Colin and Kenny sauntered back towards the corner post office.

The plan was simple. Colin had surveyed the place, knew the layout. They'd pull on balaclavas, barge in, bang the counter with baseball bats to frighten everybody and bolt the door. Load the holdalls with cash, shut everyone in the back room and exit by the rear door. Through the yard, out the gate and round the corner back into the car. Five minutes maximum. Job done.

Willis looked at the dashboard clock. It was two minutes since his brothers had clambered out, but it seemed like an hour. He concentrated on the corner up ahead on the opposite side of the street. They should be coming soon. He fingered the ignition key, ready to start the motor, concentrating on the corner. Then came the tap at the passenger door window.

Shit! Willis saw the blue serge, silver buttons and ruddy complexion of a stooping constable. He pressed the button and the window slowly descended.

'You can't park here, sir.'

'Sorry. I'm just waiting for someone. Shouldn't be long.'

'There's a car park up there.' The constable obligingly pointed along the street. 'It's free,' he added with a smile.

'Right. Didn't know. Thanks.'

'That's all right.' He straightened up and Willis pressed the window button but let it go as the constable's face appeared again. 'Say, aren't you Johnny Willis?'

Willis's mouth dried. He flicked his tongue over his gums. 'Sorry?'

'Johnny Willis. Aren't you him, the boxer?'

Willis glanced along the street. His brothers had just turned the corner at a brisk walking pace, with bats, balaclavas and a disappointing haul of cash stuffed into their holdalls. They faltered but, without conferring, sauntered on towards the car.

'That's me,' Willis told the policeman.

'Thought it was.' The constable was pleased with his powers of observation. 'How's the hand?'

'Lot better,' said Willis, making a fist. His forearm rested on the steering wheel. 'Ah, here they are.'

Colin walked to the offside rear door and opened it. Kenny approached the policeman on the pavement, 'Afternoon. Everything all right, officer?' he said, putting his hand on the door handle.

The constable took a pace back, allowing Kenny to open the door. Willis started the engine. But the low roar of the BMW did not stifle the shouts from the bottom of the street.

'There they are! Stop them, officer – they've robbed me!'

The constable looked from Kenny to the anguished postmaster, who had emerged from the front of the post office. He turned back to Kenny, glanced at the holdall. 'What's going on?'

The postmaster began a staggering run towards them.

'Shit,' said Kenny, dropping his holdall.

'Say that again,' said Colin, putting his holdall on the car roof.
Willis switched off the engine.

'He doesn't know anything about this,' said Kenny, loud enough for Johnny to hear. 'He thought he was picking us up after shopping. That's all.'

*PART THREE*

T HAT'S BETTER. GOT in a few good shots and the cut didn't bother me much. I know I can beat him.

He looked around the ringside. Still looked normal. Nothing out of the ordinary for a big fight night. A lot of familiar faces and even more strangers. It's the strangers you have to worry about. Can't trust a stranger. What if it's him? Or that oily bastard over there?

'That's more like it. Good round.'

The voice was encouraging. Eyes bright with excitement. 'Keep the pressure on. He's eating jabs.'

The wet, cold sponge was squeezed onto the back of his neck and a swab pressed on the gashed eyebrow. They're earning their money tonight. So am I.

Whoever said this is the loneliest place in the world knew something. It's hard enough just trying to beat the other guy. You don't need any other problems, any other decisions to make. You've gotta concentrate three minutes at a time. Let your mind wander and – bingo! – it can be all over. One punch. Put to sleep. Not in dreamland, though. No, it's all dreams over.

Get back to reality. Concentrate. Focus. Easily said. I can't just shrug this off. I must decide. What's most important?

I'm still not convinced. Why should I be? Threats! They mean nothing, absolutely sweet FA. It's action that counts.

'Four rounds to go. Keep your foot on the gas. Go get 'im.'

'Seconds out... for round nine...'

## Chapter Nine

Mary Riley handed Willis a cup of tea. She'd read the reports, in the *Westhampton News*, about Johnny's arrest, his release and the subsequent court case. But this was the first time Willis had visited since his brothers had been sentenced.

'Want to tell me about it?'

'Not a lot to tell.' Willis stirred a spoonful of sugar into the weak brew. 'Truth is, I needed money. I drove my brothers to a job. It was hairy for a time but Kenny and Colin said I knew nothing about the robbery. In fact, Kenny said I should drive my car because that would make it obvious I knew nothing about it. What sane bloke would drive his own motor as a getaway car? That's what he said. I know the police didn't believe us but they couldn't prove it. They couldn't make it stick. I wasn't charged.'

'You were lucky.'

'Yeah,' agreed Willis thoughtfully. 'I was even luckier that Mary told me to take my driving test. She wouldn't come in the car with me until I passed. So they couldn't even nab me for driving without a licence. Funny, eh?' He shook his head ruefully. Then he added, 'But I feel bad, being free when Kenny and Colin are doing three years.'

'They've looked after you,' she said softly. 'Make the most of it. You've still got a career in front of you.'

'Sure. That's what Colin said.'

The old lady scrutinised Willis's solemn features. 'You don't seem convinced.'

'I feel I should've held my hands up as well. Doesn't seem right, them taking all the blame.'

'At least this way you can get on with your boxing, make something of yourself. That's what you want, isn't it? You don't really want to be stealing and robbing, do you? It's not a way to live.'

Willis looked into her small, watery eyes and shook his head. 'I was desperate. Needed money, that's all.'

'But that's not the way to do it, Johnny. You're a good boy, really. My Harry always said so and he was a good judge. And I agree with him. Let this be a lesson to you. Keep your nose clean, don't ruin your life. Stay out of trouble, concentrate on boxing. You've got a chance to make something of yourself. Don't waste it.'

'You're right, of course you are. I won't get involved again.'

'Good,' said Mrs Riley, smiling. 'Remember when I read the leaves? The gap in your life I couldn't understand? Perhaps this was it. How long's it been since you had a fight?'

'More than six months. I couldn't think about it until after the trial. Didn't want to know.'

'Well, it's over. You've got to move on. What about the British title?'

'Some way off.' He paused. 'If I hadn't bust my hand, all this wouldn't have happened. I'd be champion now with money in the bank.' Another pause. 'Adams fights for the European next week. If he wins, he'll give up the British. If he loses, I guess it'll be some time before he's ready to defend. Anyway, I need a coupla warm-ups.'

'At least you'll get some money.'

'True. Trouble is, I need it now. In fact, I need it like yesterday. I'm well behind with the rent on the flat.'

Mrs Riley heaved herself upright with the aid of her stick. 'I haven't got a lot, Johnny, but Harry left a bit of insurance. You can have a few hundred until you're back on your feet. How much do you need?'

Willis stood and took the old lady in his arms. He looked down at her. 'No way, Mary. It's very kind but I couldn't.'

'I manage on my pension. It's better you have it than lose your flat. I know you'll pay me back.'

'No, Mary, really, I couldn't. Thanks all the same.' Then, almost as an afterthought, he said, 'They say a hungry fighter's a dangerous fighter. Well, they'd better watch out – I'm starving.' And, for the first time in months, he smiled.

Barnett got Willis back into action at Stoke with a two-round win over a timid Frenchman and then agreed a deal with Jacobs. An eight-rounder on a TV show, followed by the title fight with Adams, who'd been on the wrong end of a disputed decision in Paris.

The TV fight, at the Royal Albert Hall against a stocky Mexican, was over in five rounds. The clash with Adams was set for Wembley, first week in June.

Willis cleared his rent arrears and even settled The Casino debt. It didn't leave much in the bank but he was focused. It was ten months late but he was finally getting his chance at the British title. Nothing would stop him winning that.

He ran in the mornings, worked out in the gym each afternoon and sparred in the evenings, going back to Johnson Close every night for supper cooked by Mary. Sometimes, he slept in his old room. It seemed the right thing to do with Kenny and Colin both being away.

Mary was still adamant that she wouldn't move in with him. 'I've got Ma to look after. You can take care of yourself but honestly, Johnny, she wouldn't eat properly if I wasn't here.'

'Boozed out of her head, that's why. And those fags she's smoking have a funny smell. She's killing herself with booze and drugs. I should worry.'

'She's a sad woman,' said his sister. 'It must've really hurt when Dad left.'

'It happens to other people. They don't go to pieces for the rest of their lives. Anyway, she has a good time. With you around she doesn't have to do a damn thing. She doesn't care what she's doing to your life.'

'I'm okay.'

'Okay? You hardly go out. A beautiful young girl like you shouldn't be chained to the kitchen sink. When d'you enjoy yourself?'

'You know Pete takes me out when he can get away from The Casino. We go to the pictures. Have a meal or a drink.'

Willis looked thoughtfully at his sister. 'Yeah,' he said eventually. 'Pete's a good pal. He's keeping things ticking over for Kenny and Colin, The door business is quite an earner for them and they'll need something when they get out.'

Mary smiled. 'Pete likes me, you know.'

'Sure he does, sis. So he should. Good girl like you.' Then with sudden realisation, he asked, 'What about him? What d'you think of Pete?'

'I like him, course I do.'

'Like? Is that all?'

'Bit more than like, I suppose. But don't you say anything to him. I'll be mad if you tell him.'

'C'mon, sis. I wouldn't say anything to upset you. Pete's a good bloke and I trust him with you. I know you're special to him.'

'Why, what's he said?' she asked.

'Nothing. He hasn't said anything. But I can tell by the way he looks at you. How he treats you. He cares a lot for you, you must know that.'

'We're good friends. Let's face it, we've known each other a long time.'

'Childhood sweethearts, eh?'

Mary felt colour rising in her cheeks. 'Give over, Johnny. We were hardly sweethearts. I was just a little kid.'

'There's something going on now, though. I can sense it.'

'That's enough. We're pals, that's all.'

'For now. But who knows what's gonna happen?'

'That's right. Who knows?'

'Ah,' said Willis triumphantly. 'So there is something to it. At least, you'd like there to be.'

'Okay, I've said I like him a lot. But I don't want you saying anything. Pete's got to make his own mind up. Don't you force anything.'

Willis smiled. 'Course not, sis.'

'Johnny...'

Mercer read the brief news story from the Press Association news agency and shook his head. Willis isn't having any luck, he thought. He reached for the phone and dialled the boxer's number. Willis answered it on the fourth ring.

'Hi, Johnny, it's Bob. Suppose you've heard the news?'

'What news, Bob?'

'About Adams.'

'Adams? What's he done?'

'You haven't heard?' Mercer was surprised but said quickly, 'Just had a story from the PA. Adams failed his brain scan.'

'What? You've gotta be kidding?'

'No, Johnny, sorry. It says he failed the scan and can't box again. Course, they can have another scan but it looks like the fight's off.' He didn't add 'again'.

'Shit! I don't fucking believe it.' He paused. 'Sorry, Bob, didn't mean to swear like that. Thanks for letting me know.'

'Sorry it's bad news. I thought George would've told you. He must have heard from the Board.'

'Yeah. I'll give him a call, find out what's happening. Bollocks!'

'Okay, Johnny. Let me know if there's any developments. The PA story doesn't say what the Board are doing about the title. They'll probably wait until Adams has had a second scan.'

'Suppose so. Okay, Bob, thanks again. I'll call you. Bye.'

Mercer replaced the receiver and the phone rang almost immediately. It was Lew Sellers, manager of Adams.

'What's going on with Willis?' he asked.

'What d'you mean, Lew?'

'You know Adams is out, don't you?'

'Just got the story. Rough on your lad.'

'It's serious, Bob. The scan picked up a shadow on his brain. We'll have another scan but it doesn't look good. They say he's healthy enough, it's not life-threatening or anything. But it looks like his boxing days are over.'

'Boxers have been cleared by second scans.'

Sellers ignored the comment. 'I can't understand what your lad's up to. It's a perfectly good offer,' he said.

'Offer?' said Mercer. 'What offer, Lew?'

'Thought you'd know. Look, I'd better not say any more. Best you get hold of George Barnett.'

Mercer knew the old fight manager was playing games. 'Mark my card, Lew. All off the record. I won't say anything to Barnett.'

'I trust you, Bob, but we've never had this conversation. Harry Jacobs has offered Willis the same money to fight Ray Peterson for the vacant title. All he wants is the right to stage his first defence if he wins. Same money again.'

Peterson, rated at nine, was also managed by Sellers. But the Southern Area champion was on the slide. Two years of regular sparring with Adams had taken their toll on the twenty-eight-year-old scrapper.

'Sounds good for Willis,' said Mercer. 'But – and forgive me for being cynical, Lew – what's the catch?'

Sellers bristled. 'There's no fucking catch. It's just good business. Good for everyone. Obviously, if Adams gets the all-clear next time, he'll want his title back. And we're making sure we get the right to stage that fight. Nothing wrong in that.'

'And if he doesn't get the all-clear?' persisted the reporter.

'Willis gets a good purse for his first defence.'

'Okay, Lew. Thanks for that. I'll get on to it.'

'Keep in touch.'

Mercer considered his next call. How to approach Barnett and draw out the facts? Not easy. Should I phone Willis first? he wondered.

Sellers put his phone down and looked across the office at Jacobs. 'The shit's about to hit the fan, Harry,' he told his partner. 'Willis is as good as ours.'

Barnett scribbled financial permutations on his pad. Adams's misfortune had opened up a golden gate; he could now stage Willis's title challenge and didn't have to settle for a mere percentage of Willis's purse. He would promote the show and pocket much more. Okay, the kid's had some bad publicity but he's still a popular fighter. A British title fight in Westhampton is a big deal.

That's what he told Willis when he phoned. I'll get the Board to nominate someone to fight you for the vacant title and we'll stage it in Westhampton, he'd said. The money won't be as big, but it'll be good. And we'll have the title. When you're champion, the money follows. Believe me, Johnny, I know what's best. We don't need London.

Willis, having surprisingly extracted the promise of a two-thousand-pound advance from Barnett, was satisfied when he put the phone down.

The promoter, too, was contented. He puffed merrily on his cigar. It's an ill-wind, he thought. But it became uncomfortably chilly for him when Mercer came on the line.

Barnett enthusiastically told him about his plans. 'It's a great story for you, Bob. Exclusive,' he concluded.

The reporter agreed but asked, 'What about the contract with Jacobs?'

'Kaput,' said Barnett. 'That was for Adams–Willis, nothing else.'

'Course,' said Bob. 'But Johnny's sold a lot of tickets already. I understand Jacobs is still keen to use him on the June show.'

'Where'd you hear that?'

'Is it true?'

Barnett leaned forward, elbows on his desk and blustered down the phone. 'What Jacobs and Co. want isn't always what happens!'

'So, it is true. What's the deal, George? You can tell me.'

'Deal? There isn't a fucking deal. I've told you, I'm gonna put it on in Westhampton. Isn't that the best news for you?'

'If it's true, George.'

'Whadya mean?'

'Have you told Willis about Jacobs's offer?'

'Why should I?' Then suddenly, Barnett asked, 'What offer?'

'You tell me, George. Look, I get to hear whispers from the lads in London. You know we exchange titbits.'

'Whispers? Newspaper talk!' But Barnett knew Mercer was on to something. He changed tack. 'Tell me what you've heard.'

'Why the fuck didn't you tell me in the first place? What's going on, George?' Willis fumed.

'Calm down, son. There's lots that a manager doesn't tell his fighter. We're paid to negotiate, to make the deals. Your job is to fight and to concentrate on training. Okay?'

'It's not okay. If there's a good offer on the table, I should know about it. And this sounds fucking good to me, George. I get twenty-four grand for two fucking fights. Are you gonna come up with that kinda dough? No, you're not.'

'There's more to it than that. You've got your independence.

You don't wanna be tied down to Jacobs.'

'It's only two fights. That's not "tied down". Anyway, if it's such a bad deal, why're you telling me about it now? C'mon, George, tell me.'

'Because rumours get about—'

'Rumours! It's not rumours, George. It's fucking fact. They're offering me twenty-four-fucking-grand for two fights. You'll get six. That's not bad, is it?'

'I know the money's good but you've got to look at the broader picture, Johnny. They only want the second fight in case Adams gets the all-clear. If we don't accept, we can do what we like as champion.'

'If he does get cleared, the Board will insist I defend against him anyway. What will you do then, George, outbid Jacobs? You didn't manage it last time.'

'I can push the purse up, make a big offer based on what we'd have to pay Adams.'

'And I take a pay cut?'

'No. Whatever I pay Adams, you'll still get twelve grand.'

'But not for the first fight – you told me that. You said I wouldn't be on the same money as Jacobs offered. Good, but not as big, you said. That means I get less from you in two fights. It's not good business.'

Barnett sighed. 'Johnny, I've always done well by you, haven't I?'

'Until now.'

'I've paid you more than I need at times. I've been happy to break even on some shows and I've paid over the odds for opponents to keep your record going. Why? Because I believe in you. Because I know we can hit the jackpot together.'

Willis remembered something Mercer once told him. 'Fighters come and go, George,' he said. 'They have one career. Managers and promoters go on for ever. This is my one career and I'll fight anybody, anywhere, for the right money. Tell me, George, what is the right money for me? No, don't bother, I'll fucking tell you. The right money is the best money. The most I can get for each fight. That fucking right, George?'

'Look, Johnny, we're not gonna fall out over a coupla grand.

I'll make sure you get your twelve grand each time.'

'Damn right you will, George. You'll ring Jacobs and tell him we accept.'

Barnett ground his half-smoked cigar into the ashtray, gripped the phone tightly and snapped, 'Don't tell me what to fucking do. I'm the manager, you're just the fighter.'

'That so, George? Just the fighter? Don't forget, you work for me. You take a percentage for working for me. And if I'm not happy, I'll get somebody else to do the deals.'

'Like fuck you will. We've got a three-year contract.'

'Yeah, which is over in September.'

'I've got an option for another three years if you win the British title.'

'Bollocks to your option. You can forget that.'

'No way.'

'That case, forget the title fight. And fucking forget me. I'll never fight for you again.'

The phone went dead.


In the kitchen at 36 Johnson Close, Mary prepared fish and salad for Johnny and his visitor. In the bathroom, Connie pampered herself, relaxing in a warm bubble bath. She was off to bingo and then the pub. In the backroom, Willis sat at the table and complained to Mercer.

'Barnett thinks he's being clever. I know his game. He wants me to win the title and then he'll have me by the balls. Three more fucking years.'

'Would that be too bad?'

'I don't trust him any more. It's not just because he didn't tell me about the offer. He was thinking about himself, not me. He wanted more money from his own show. Probably get more than me. So, I told him to forget it. Said I'll never fight for him again. So now he's accepted Jacobs's deal and backed me into a corner.'

'What you gonna do?'

'Fuck knows. What can I do? I can't turn down a British title fight. I'll have to sign the contract.'

Mercer lit a menthol cigarette. 'You don't have to turn it down but there is a way out.'

'Is there?'

'Injury. It happens. Get your doctor to give you a certificate. Get a postponement and then sit out your contract.'

Doctor Thomas finished examining Willis's swollen right hand.

'The good news is, there's nothing broken this time. How did it happen?' he asked.

'On the heavy bag.'

'Well, I recommend rest for at least a week, preferably two.'

'But I've got a fight in three weeks.'

'You can keep fit, but there's no way you should be using that hand. Rest is the only solution.'

'But I need to spar.'

'Out of the question. If I were you, I wouldn't think about boxing for six weeks. The longer you rest the hand, the better for you. Anyway, I'm sure it's too painful to use right now.'

Willis agreed. The doctor signed a certificate. He would be unable to box for six weeks.

## Chapter Ten

Mercer made the first approach in August. Sellers suggested Willis should telephone him.

'He's still under contract for another month. I can't be accused of poaching. Let him approach me,' he said.

They met in Sellers's main turf accountant's office in central London. As they exchanged handshakes, Sellers couldn't resist asking, 'How's the injury?'

'Fine now,' said Willis, grinning to acknowledge the conspiracy.

'Shame about the title fight. Hopefully, there's no long-term damage.' This time, Sellers smiled. 'You know Don, don't you?'

'We've met briefly,' said Willis.

Don Murray, a broad-shouldered six-footer, came out from behind a desk and proffered his giant right hand. Murray had been an average light-heavyweight but he was now one of the world's top matchmakers.

'Pleased you could come.' The hint of a Scottish accent lingered despite forty years spent in the south of England. The son of a docker, Murray was the fifty-one-year-old wheeling, dealing power behind Jacobs's promotions.

They all sat and Sellers got down to business.

'I understand you're not renewing your contract with George Barnett. I don't need to know the reasons but let's make it clear that you've approached me. Okay?'

Willis agreed. 'There are several managers sniffing around, but I'm not doing anything until I've listened to you. I know you've had a lot of champions.'

Sellers ran a hand through his grey-flecked brown hair. 'You have talent. Now's the time to find out how much. To see how far you can go.'

'All the way to the world title.'

'A lot of fighters have said things like that in this office. Some have been exceptional, given it a good shot. But not many make it. It takes something special to be world champion.'

'I'll do it.'

Sellers glanced at Murray. 'You're still young,' said the matchmaker. 'What are you, twenty-two?'

'I was twenty-three in May.'

'The next two years will be big. You can make your mark. If you keep yourself right, stay dedicated, you can be fighting for the world title when you're twenty-five. That means you could have some good years as champion.'

'Sounds great to me.'

'First things first,' said Sellers. 'There's the British title and we need to get you international experience. You've gotta be able to handle all sorts of styles. Then there's the European. Plenty of money to be made with that title. European champions are automatically ranked in the world top ten. It's valuable.'

'How long would that take?'

'Depends on you. You've got a decent record and reputation already. A warm-up, then the British title. Perhaps another couple of fights before we press for European recognition.'

'What all boxers need,' interjected Murray, 'is the right matches, the right results and the right money. You'll get all those with us if you do your bit.'

'What sort of money are we talking?' asked Willis.

'I don't pay signing-on fees,' said Sellers firmly. 'Does that bother you?'

'Depends.'

'On what?'

'On what sort of money I'll get.'

Sellers again looked towards Murray, who raised an eyebrow.

'Let's put it this way,' said the manager. 'We'll get you the British title fight in no time. For ten-rounders, minimum of fifteen grand. And it'll get better.'

'What's your cut?'

'Nothing, until you hit thirty grand a fight. Then it's twenty-five per cent.'

Willis grinned. 'I'd be as well stopping at twenty-nine grand, then.'

'We're talking no less than a hundred thousand this season,' said Murray. 'That's for starters. All you've got to do is keep winning, knocking 'em over like you've done so far. Brian Adams says you're one tough cookie – and he should know.'

'How is he?'

'Back in the gym. Having another scan soon. I'll take you to the gym later. You can have a look round, meet the guys. Brian'll probably be there.'

'Do you want me to move down here?'

'Your choice, son,' said Sellers. 'It's better if you train here sometimes. The sparring's good. But if you're happier at home, then stay there. The choice is yours.'

'I'll think about it. Fact is, I'll have to think about a lot of things. It all sounds good, but I need a bit of time. Okay?'

'Of course,' said Sellers. 'Your contract isn't up yet. We'll get together again when you're free.'

'I'll drive you to the gym,' said Murray. 'You may as well have a look while you're here.'

The gym was in Soho, above another of Sellers's betting shops, surrounded by sex emporiums. Murray knew everyone. Doormen at the strip clubs nodded, temporarily idle waiters waved through restaurant windows and street vendors issued cheery greetings.

A sweat-soaked Adams was skipping rope, winding down his session, when Willis walked in. Surprised to see his old, possibly next, rival, he nodded a greeting.

The gym was well equipped and the ring sizeable. Willis was impressed.

'We work in shifts,' said Murray, 'starting at eleven and running through to about seven. There's no hanging about; you do your work and get out. There's plenty of quality sparring. No mugs here.'

Adams shuffled over as Murray went to answer a phone call. He offered his hand. 'How's things, Johnny?'

'Fine. What about you?'

'Dunno. Failing the scan was a bastard. But it might be a glitch. It happens.'

'Here's hoping.'

'Yeah. Anyway, what brings you here?'

'My contract's up soon. Fancy a change.'

'Signing for Lew?'

'Probably. Haven't decided yet. I'd like to know a bit more.'

Adams wiped his brow with a towel and draped it over his head. 'If you wanna wait while I change, we can have a cuppa and chat in the caff over the road. My sister's coming for a lift home,' he said.

'Sure. I can get any train. No rush.'

'Which station?'

'St Pancras.'

'I'll give you a ride, if you like. Won't be long.'

Adams walked off to have a brief conversation with Murray. The matchmaker ended it with a slap on the boxer's sodden back and headed for Willis. He was reading the faded, old fight posters on the walls.

'See you're down the bill on one of these,' he said as Murray approached.

'Always down the bill, me. Some good fighters in those days. I wasn't cut out to be a champion. But the game's always been in my blood.'

'Matchmaking keeps you involved, then?'

'You could say that.' Murray changed tack. 'Brian says he's taking you for a cuppa. He'll fill you in about our set-up. Good to see you, Johnny, but I've gotta fly.'

No hard sell there, thought Willis. But they're used to handling the best. I've still got to prove myself.


Mary didn't recognise the cultured southern voice of the girl on the phone who asked to speak to Johnny.

'Sorry, he's not here at the moment. Can I take a message?'

'I'm Vanessa, personal assistant to Mr Michael Greene. Who am I speaking to?'

The names didn't mean anything to Mary. 'I'm Mary, Johnny's sister,' she replied.

'Ah. Well, hello, Mary.'

'Hello.'

'Would you ask Johnny to ring Mr Greene when he comes in?

I'll give you the number.'

'Sure, but I don't know how late he'll be. He's in London.'

'In that case, I'll give you the office number and Mr Greene's personal mobile number. If it's after six, call the mobile.'

Vanessa dictated the numbers, politely ended the call and immediately told her boss that Willis might phone on his return home from London.

He's down here, thought Greene. Hope he hasn't done anything yet.

Over mugs of tea, Adams answered Willis's questions.

'It's a good organisation. I don't know too much about how they work it, but they're tied in. Jacobs, Sellers and Murray; they're a team, a big team at that. Got all the contacts.'

'What about money?'

'They pay well. Do a few deals but they've been fair with me. In fact, Lew's offered me the chance to train as a settler if the boxing goes belly-up.'

'Settler?'

'Yeah, in the betting shop. I've already done a bit of work behind the counter, taking the bets. It's a mug's game.'

'Why do it then?'

'What? No, I mean gambling's a mug's game.'

'Oh, gotcha.'

'Here's Natalie.' Adams looked over Willis's shoulder.

Before Willis could turn, Adams's sister arrived at their corner table. As she bent to kiss her brother, all Willis saw was a mass of glossy blue-black ringlets and an enormous brown bosom.

She looked down at Willis. In a lilting voice, eyes mockingly wide open, she said, 'Who've we got here? Where've you been hiding this handsome hunk, Bri?'

'Calm down, Nat. This is Johnny Willis. You know, the guy who beat me in the ABA final.'

Willis took in Natalie's radiant features. But, most of all, he noticed her body. A gaping white cotton shirt was knotted beneath the impressive cleavage, a gold stud gleamed from her navel and a short, pleated red skirt billowed around lean thighs.

Natalie offered her hand, nails painted a brilliant white.

'Pleased to meet you, honey,' she said. Full mouth, white teeth glistening.

Willis accepted the hand and looked into the stunning, beacon-bright eyes, like chocolate drops in fresh snow.

'Likewise,' he said, holding on to her hand. Natalie made no move to withdraw it.

'Okay if I join you for a while?' She dropped a red duffle bag to the floor.

Willis released her hand and drew a chair back from the table. She leaned back in the chair and swung her right leg over her left knee, dangling a white leather ankle boot near to Willis's calf. Occasionally, her jiggling foot tapped Willis leg. She didn't apologise, but grinned, searching Willis's face for a reaction. He smiled back.

Her stunning entrance removed all thoughts of boxing from Willis's brain. Adams recognised the effect.

'Natalie's a model,' he said.

'I can believe it.'

'You should try it, honey,' said Natalie. 'You've got the looks. And all the equipment, I shouldn't wonder.'

'Never thought about it.'

'I've got contacts if you're interested.'

'Reckon he's got enough on his plate at the moment,' said Adams. 'Boxing's a full-time job, Nat.'

'Pity.' Natalie's eyes roved Willis's face and broad shoulders. 'What you down here for?'

Willis explained, manfully ignoring Natalie's foot as it rubbed nonchalantly, playfully along his calf.

'Hope you're not in a rush to leave,' she said.

'Brian says he'll drive me to the station.'

'No need for that.' She looked at her brother. 'Reckon I'll show your friend a few of the sights. I'm in no hurry to get home.' She turned to Willis. 'What do you say, honey? Fancy a bite to eat and some fun?'

They dined in a small Italian restaurant and over a carafe of house red, Natalie regaled Willis with risqué tales from some of her assignments. Bit-parts in soft-porn videos had helped pay for her enlarged chest.

'Bigger tits, bigger parts, if you see what I mean,' she said and waved to a trio of girls as they entered the restaurant. 'They've been on the afternoon shift. Dancers.'

Willis looked across. They were all scantily dressed and carried duffle bags.

'Those bags seem popular.'

'Tools of the trade. Perfect for carrying a change of clothes, make-up and other bits and pieces.'

'Can't get many clothes in there.'

'You'd be surprised, honey.' She flashed a broad grin. 'Anyway, we don't wear much, do we?'

'Just about enough. What sort of dancers are they? Strippers?'

'No, proper dancers, been in real shows. Felicity, the one with red hair, she's done summer seasons in Blackpool and Bournemouth. But they do strip as well. It keeps the money coming in.'

'What about you?'

'Am I stripper, you mean?' She laughed, wide-mouthed, eyes gleaming. 'Not really. Not on stage. But I like to dance and I have been known to take my clothes off. Especially for the right man. Fancy a dance, Johnny?'

'Where?'

'There's a club round the corner. Disco music. Real cool.'

Cool wasn't how Willis would have described it. The small room was sweltering as gyrating, sweating bodies crammed the tiny dance area.

Natalie was an energetic dancer and the strobe lighting did much for her. The swaying and bouncing of her body also did much for Willis. He could see why she was such a popular girl, constantly waving a fluttering hand at people. The volume of the beat made conversation impossible. Eventually, Natalie grabbed his hand and led him to an empty booth at the back of the room.

'Enough dancing for now.'

Willis wiped his brow with a paper napkin. 'Better than a workout,' he said as a waitress put down a bottle of wine and two glasses.

'On the house, honey,' said Natalie. 'Ginny's a pal of mine.'

'Who's Ginny?'

'The guy in the roll-neck sweater at the bar. He owns the place.'

Willis spotted a tall, slim ginger-haired man, adorned with gold jewellery. Chains, rings and an identity bracelet. Only the music prevented Willis from hearing the jangle as Ginny waved to Natalie.

'Worth a few bob,' he said.

'Maybe. He was a good dancer in his day. Knee trouble finished him. Then he started this place.'

'Ginny's a funny name.'

'Look at his hair. He was known as Ginger, but over the years, it's become Ginny. Suits him better, the daft old queen. Look out, he's coming over. Probably fancies you.'

She laughed as she got up to air kiss Ginny on both cheeks. She introduced Willis and he was surprised by the firm grip of Ginny's warm, damp palm.

'Nice to see a new face,' he said. 'Nat looking after you, darling?'

'Sure,' said Willis, trying to think if anyone had ever called him 'darling' before.

'Don't try moving in, Ginny.' Natalie slipped an arm around Willis's waist. 'He's mine tonight.'

'Rules me out, then. Afraid he'd be straight. The good-looking ones always are, more's the pity.'

'He's a boxer. Good as well. He even beat Bri.'

Ginny whistled and appraised Willis. A slow up-and-down gaze.

'Well, I never. Beat Brian, did you? You must be good.'

Willis grinned, warming to the affected character.

'It was some time ago and there wasn't a lot in it. Brian's a good fighter.'

He glanced at Natalie, who smiled up at him as she put her other arm around him and hugged. Willis felt her breasts squash against his chest. He slipped an arm over her shoulders.

'I'll leave you two lovers to enjoy yourselves,' said Ginny. 'Nice to see you, Nat. Hope to see you again Johnny, real soon. Bye-ee.' He waved and made his way back to the bar.

'Won't be a tick,' said Natalie suddenly.

She weaved between tables in pursuit of Ginny. Willis watched the pair converse and saw Ginny throw his head back, laughing. Then he looked in Willis's direction, still grinning. He withdrew something from a trouser pocket and handed it to Natalie. She kissed his cheek.

Natalie returned, sliding onto the leather booth seat. Her left thigh pressed against Willis.

'What made him laugh?'

'Ginny's always laughing.'

'But he looked at me. Does he think I'm funny? He's the queer 'un.'

'Don't get upset, honey.' Natalie ran a hand through his hair and leaned into his shoulder. 'I just asked him for a favour.'

'What sort of favour makes him laugh?'

'I told him you were dying to see his bedroom.'

'You what?' Willis turned to face Natalie. 'Why the hell did you say that?'

Natalie flashed white teeth at him. Her eyes were again wide, mocking him.

'Not afraid, are you? It's a nice room. You'll like it. Like it a lot.'

'Like it? I'm not going anywhere near it, wherever it is. You won't catch me in a poof's bedroom.'

'Not even with me? That's a crying shame.'

'What? With you?'

'With me. That's why I asked Ginny if I could borrow his key.'

'Why didn't you say that?' Willis relaxed back into his seat.

'Let's finish the wine. Then we can go upstairs to the flat.'

'Upstairs? Is that where it is?'

'Sure, honey. The door next to the bar. Straight up the stairs and we're in heaven.'

Willis stood, picked up the wine and the two glasses. 'C'mon, *honey*,' he said. 'Let's finish the bottle in heaven.'

Mary left the note on the table in the back room and Willis read it when he got home around noon. It had been a long night. Natalie proved as energetic in bed as she had on the dance floor. They'd finally fallen asleep somewhere around two. When they left at eight, there was no sign of Ginny.

'Probably gone off with a friend,' said Natalie, fishing a sweater out of her duffle bag. She handed Willis a toothbrush.

When he came out of the bathroom, Natalie had dressed. Figure-hugging white sweater, black leather trousers, white pumps and a red beret perched at a jaunty angle.

'Sure do get a lot in that bag,' he said.

'You should get one for the next time.' Her smile lit up the room. 'Then you won't look such a mess in the morning.' She pointed at Willis's crumpled sweatshirt and jeans, lying in a heap by the bed.

They hailed two taxis. One took Natalie home to Bethnal Green and the other dropped Willis at St Pancras in time for a mid-morning Intercity back to Westhampton. They didn't arrange to meet again but Willis knew they would. He was going to sign with Sellers.

But now there was this message. Michael Greene was a thrusting young Londoner who'd burst on to the boxing scene and, in the last three years, he'd threatened Jacobs's promotional dominance.

Greene had a stable of champions. His promotions, staged in the capital and around the country, were broadcast on satellite television. No harm in talking to him.

Willis picked up the phone and dialled the office number. What a pity I hadn't known last night when I was in London, he thought. My fault; should have rung Mary. Still, I *was* busy.

## Chapter Eleven

Greene's chauffeur, a burly thirtysomething in a bulging dark suit, wouldn't have looked out of place on a nightclub door.

Willis rode in the back of the Bentley from St Pancras to the Greene mansion, near Muswell Hill. Old, ornately framed oil paintings – landscapes and portraits – dominated the wood-panelled sitting room. Greene greeted him there. Slim with short, fair hair, the promoter dressed casually in grey slacks and a white shirt. But he oozed wealth.

Willis sat back in a leather sofa and wondered how one man could have so much, so soon. Greene was, after all, only thirty-nine. Born in 1951, according to the boxing annuals. And he hadn't acquired all this overnight.

Generations of the Greene family had, in fact, been in the building industry. Michael's father, William, had been the most successful, expanding the business and making a second fortune in the property market. As an only child, Michael enjoyed a private education, then joined the firm as a financial director. On his own, he bought properties. He was also a fearless, but not reckless, dealer on the stock markets.

William Greene was a fight fan. A regular ringsider at Jacobs's big Wembley shows, he'd readily stumped up cash to launch Michael's career as a promoter. It quickly paid dividends. Greene secured backing from sponsors, negotiated TV contracts and, importantly, signed top amateurs who rapidly marched through the professional ranks. For five years he'd worked hard to earn respect and, in the following three years, climbed to a prominent position within the sport. Talented professionals switched allegiance to his camp.

Sitting in the grandeur of Greene's house, Willis sensed why the man was a success. Perhaps some will rub off on me, he thought.

Greene, pacing the polished floor, got quickly to the point.

'Barnett gave your career a start,' he said, 'but he can't take you any further. Sellers and Murray could do a job but they're the old boys. They're losing touch. In a few years, they'll be finished as a power. Dinosaurs. They've had their day.

'Things are changing. Boxing is showbusiness now. Fanfares and national anthems – old hat! All in the past. You've got to give it plenty of *oomph*. Lights, music, lasers, the big entrances. It keeps the fans interested, on the edge of their seats. Makes them feel they're at an event, the place to be. And they come back for more.

'Believe me, Johnny, things are different now. The old way of doing business is dying. Why should a boxer do deals with his management. Take less than he's entitled to? Put up the money and give the fighter what he's worth, that's what I do.

'I've got a good set of fighters and I'll get more. My shows make profit. That means I make money and my fighters make money. I give punters what they deserve; proper fights, not mismatches. On a Michael Greene promotion the punters get at least ten fights. What does that mean, Johnny? I'll tell you. It means more work for my boxers. More work equals more money. And that's the name of the game, isn't it?'

Willis nodded. 'I don't know too much about promoting,' he said. 'I'm a fighter. But I know you're doing well, I've seen your shows on TV. And then there's this place.' He waved his arm around the room.

Greene sat down next to him. 'There's no reason why you can't have a place like this, Johnny. There's big money to be had nowadays and it's getting bigger. I know – I deal with the right people. My boxers get what they're worth. I'm up front and fair with them. No deals, no paybacks. What the fight's worth, the fighter gets.'

'What's that mean to me? What's the bottom line?'

'The bottom line, Johnny, is what we make it.' Greene stood and walked around the back of the sofa, pausing to put a manicured hand on Willis's shoulder. 'I won't go into detail until I know you're really interested. But, I'll tell you this, I think you can be world champion. And, with me, you'll be a millionaire. Did Sellers tell you that?'

'No. We didn't go that far.'

'Didn't think so.' He sat down alongside Willis again. 'Obviously, I don't know what they offered. But I'll guarantee you'll be better off with me.'

'We talked a bit of money, nothing definite.'

'Bit of money! Such as?'

'Over a hundred grand in the first year.'

'How many fights? What titles?'

'They said the British and European, probably five or six fights.'

'Five or six fights! In a year? That's rubbish!' Greene stood up again, took three paces and suddenly turned. 'Wouldn't you rather have ten fights and bank three or four hundred thousand?'

'Sure.'

'That would be our target then,' said Greene, sitting again. 'If you're interested, we can talk real business. And I don't just mean boxing.'

'What else is there?'

'If we're going to be partners, I don't want you stuck miles away in the Midlands. I want you near me.'

'Partners?'

'The way I see it, I won't be your manager. Technically, you'll be self-managed. I'll be your promoter and adviser. A partnership.'

'If I'm self-managed, you don't get a percentage.'

'That's right, Johnny. I won't work on commission. As I said, my shows make profit and, therefore, I make money. There's one stipulation. You box solely on my promotions. Not for anybody else. Think about it.'

Willis thought. 'What about titles? What if you don't make the deal? Or if you lose a purse bid. What then?'

'I'm your adviser, Johnny. If someone outbids me, it'll mean megabucks. Then I'll work for you, do all the arranging. The rôle of a manager, if you like.'

'And what do you get out of it?'

'As adviser, I'd receive twenty per cent. After all expenses, not off the top. We're talking net, not gross. For example, I won't take twenty grand out of a hundred. First, we deduct expenses; training and sparring, travel, trainer's fees and all that. Then I take my commission. Understand?'

Willis understood. Then he said, 'Living down here's not cheap. I'm not sure about that.'

'Not a problem, Johnny. I have property in Islington, very handy for the gym. You can have a flat at reasonable rent. Have a look first but I know you'll like them. A few of my fighters are in there and they're happy with the arrangement.'

Willis smiled. A good business sideline.

'I know it's a lot to think about,' said Greene, 'but there's even more I can do for you.'

'Yeah? Tell me.'

'You're a good-looking guy. With the fame that's coming your way, you can cash in.'

'Not modelling,' laughed Willis.

Greene grinned. 'What's so funny? Why not?'

'Somebody suggested something along those lines a coupla nights ago.'

'They're not wrong. My wife runs an agency. In fact, we employ some of the girls to carry the inter-round boards. Some act as hostesses – glorified waitresses, really – for sponsors at post-fight get-togethers. Gillian, that's my wife, gets all sorts of contracts. Catalogues, advertising, that sort of thing. Not page three or men's magazines, nothing cheap or sordid. Anyway, that's one for the future. When you're a star, eh?'

He slapped Willis's thigh and grinned.

'Sure. One for the future. What about the present?'

'That's for you to decide. If you haven't decided already.'

'Almost there.'

'What's the problem? Living down here?'

'No,' said Willis. A vision of Natalie's mighty breasts suddenly came to mind. 'That's not it. Although I'd like to look around – where was it?'

'Islington.'

'Yeah, Islington. No, that's not a problem.' He paused and looked straight into Greene's hazel eyes. 'What am I worth, up front?'

Greene's neck twitched. An involuntary habit, thought Willis. Or a nervous reaction, like his jumping up and down and pacing around. So much energy!

'If you agree to our partnership, then I will, of course, make you an offer. That goes without saying. I'd say twenty-five thousand with a minimum of ten fights. Ten thousand now, the rest after five fights. Would that be a deal?'

Willis didn't hesitate. 'Deal,' he said, spat in his palm and offered his right hand.

'A gypsy's bond, eh? Well, I'll shake on it, Johnny, but I'll want you to sign a contract. That okay?'

'Whatever you want, partner.'

They shook hands.

Not everybody was pleased when the news broke. Mercer complained to Willis that he hadn't been told before it appeared in the national press.

'Sorry, Bob, I didn't think.'

'I don't like missing a story on my own doorstep, especially when I've tried to help. Anyway, I thought you'd be signing with Lew Sellers.'

'This is a better deal.'

'Hope you're right. Greene is making waves and certainly changing things, but I'm not convinced about him. He puts on good shows but his fighters really earn their money. No easy matches with him.'

'I don't expect it easy, Bob. I'm looking for titles and they don't come easy. Anyway, I like him. He talks straight.'

'I wish you luck. But don't forget you're a Westhampton kid. Your supporters come from here, not London. Keep in touch, let me know what's happening. That way we keep your fans informed. I can't rely on press releases from his office.'

'I'll have a word with Michael, make sure he keeps you up to date. And I'll let you have my phone number once I've moved.'

'Good. I'll look you over when you're settled in. It'll make a good story; you in your new set-up.'

'Okay. And thanks for what you did, Bob. The Sellers business, I mean.'

'Have you spoken to him?'

'Yeah, I rang him. He wasn't too pleased. Said that Greene

would burn me out and use me to make his mark.'

'Lew could be right. Keep your eyes open and be on your guard. They can be sharp operators.'

'So was Barnett.'

Mercer chuckled. 'Just keep your guard up.'

'I will. Just because I like Michael doesn't mean I trust him. I'm not completely potty, Bob.'

Moving to Islington meant he wouldn't be able to see Mrs Riley too often.

'Don't you worry about me, Johnny,' she said. 'You're on your way and that's great. This could be the making of you. I hope you don't mind me saying this, but I think it's best you're leaving town.'

'You're probably right. A fresh start, eh?'

'That's it, Johnny. A fresh start. From what you tell me, this Michael Greene knows what he's doing. He could be perfect for you. And there's not much to keep you here, is there?'

'Not a lot. I just wish I could get Mary to come with me. But she won't leave Ma.'

'That's not surprising. She loves your mother, cares for her. And would it be right to take her away? She's happy here, not like you.'

'Suppose you're right. She's got Pete. I think they're getting quite serious, you know.'

'There you are, then. It's best she stays.'

Willis nodded. 'Then there's Ron. We've been through a lot together. He's been good to me, right from when I was a kid, just like Harry was. I like having him around.'

'I'm sure you can work something out. He can't train you any more but that doesn't mean he can't be in your corner, does it?'

'Mary, you're a gem. What would I do without you?' He kissed the old lady's cheek. 'I'm gonna see Ron now, make him an offer.'

'He won't refuse,' she said and winked.

Ron readily accepted. 'Just let me know when and where. I'll always be glad to be in your corner.'

'It'll be good money.'

'Pay me what you think's right. I don't think we'll fall out over money, not after all this time.'

Willis had two more items on his agenda. He got visiting orders to see Colin in Winson Green and Kenny in Leicester. He told his brothers of his plans, of the ideas he had for when they were released and they were pleased. But he didn't like seeing them locked up.

Finally, he took Mary and Pete out for dinner. Pete would continue handling ticket sales. Mary again rejected Johnny's pleas to join him.

'Look after her, Pete,' he said.

Now the way was clear for him to leave Westhampton.

Mary sat in the back room eating toast and flipping through a Sunday supplement. Willis had been gone a week. Pete had left her bed only an hour ago.

Connie, wrapped in a worn, white towelling robe, hair still damp from her bath, tramped in. She poured a cup of tea but declined Mary's offer of breakfast. She sat down opposite her daughter at the table.

'You can tell me to mind my own business,' Connie said suddenly, 'but please be careful.'

'About what?' Mary asked.

'Pete.' Before Mary could say anything, she continued, 'I know you're sleeping together.'

'We're careful.'

'You must be. I know Johnny and Pete are best mates but I know how your brother thinks about you. Going out together is one thing but, well, sharing a bed is different. God knows what Johnny'd do if something happened.'

'It's not a fling, Ma. Pete and me are serious. He wanted to tell Johnny but I thought it best for him to settle down in London first. He's got a lot to be getting on with. We'll tell him at Christmas.'

'Why Christmas?'

'We're thinking of getting engaged then.'

'Engaged! Oh, Mary!'

Connie put her mug down heavily on the table and raised both hands to her mouth. To Mary's surprise, tears trickled down her mother's pale cheeks. Mary, who had never seen Connie cry, couldn't understand the emotional outburst.

'What's wrong?' she asked.

Connie shook her head, reaching in a pocket for a tissue. Sobs racked her body.

'It's all right, Ma. If we get engaged it doesn't mean I'll be leaving you. We're not planning to get married for a long while. I'll still be here with you.'

'It's not that.' Connie tried to compose herself. 'I've been alone nearly all my life. Don't take that wrong. You've been a good daughter, more than I deserve.'

'Don't say that. It's been hard for you since—'

'No,' said Connie sharply. 'It's nothing to do with Danny leaving. Nothing at all.' She blew her nose and wiped her eyes with a sleeve of the robe. Mary waited, perplexed. 'You probably think I'm being selfish again,' she went on. 'But I'm not. Honestly, I'm happy for you. Getting engaged! So proper! Pete seems a nice lad and I can tell you think a lot of him. Perhaps something good is gonna come out of all this bleeding mess.'

Connie started to cry again. Mary reached across the table to hold her hand. 'It's okay, Ma. I know how hard it's been for you.'

'No, no, no – you don't understand.' Connie shook her head. 'You don't know anything about it.'

Eventually, she stopped sobbing and with trembling fingers, she lit a cigarette.

'I'll tell you something now, Mary, but you must promise not to breathe a word to anyone. Promise?'

'Promise.'

'Not a soul. Especially not Johnny. Understand?'

'I promise.'

Connie drew hard on her cigarette. 'You've never asked about your grandparents, probably 'cause I never encouraged family talk. But you must have wondered?'

Mary nodded.

'Plain fact is I don't know who they are,' Connie continued. 'I was born in 1940, just after the war started. I never knew my mother or father. P'raps she didn't even know who he was. There was a lot of us kids like it then. War babies. Abandoned.' Another long draw on her cigarette. She was calm now. Her voice was devoid of emotion, matter-of-fact.

'I remember being brought up in a home, orphanage I suppose. Then I was palmed out to foster parents. Never seemed to stay for long. Some were good, some were horrible. You never knew what to expect.

'Anyway, by the time I was fourteen, I'd what you might call "grown" quite a lot. You know, developed. A big bust, blonde hair and quite a pretty face. God, look what's happened to that.'

She laughed, a hollow, mirthless laugh. Stubbing out the cigarette, she again rubbed a sleeve across her face before continuing.

'I was abused,' she said flatly.

Mary gasped. 'No! Oh, Ma—'

Connie held up her right hand. 'Don't be sorry. Truth is, he was quite gentle, loving. I hadn't had much loving. I enjoyed it, the attention. I was wanted, needed even. And I looked forward to having him touch me, make love to me. Can you understand that?'

'Think so.'

'Trouble was, it was too much of a good thing. I think his wife became suspicious and I was on my way again. But I'd had a taste, Mary. Felt the other side, what it was to be loved. Okay, I know now that it was wrong. Knew then, I suppose. But I was a kid in a woman's body and I wanted to be loved. I didn't want to be shuttled all over the place.

'Them head doctors would probably put me on a couch and say I craved affection or something. Well, it was true and, God help me, I haven't been able to stop. I love to be loved. Well, it's not even love. Wanted's enough, even if it's only for a few minutes. Wham, bang! Know what I mean?'

Mary nodded. 'But what about Danny?' she asked.

Connie took a deep breath and pulled the robe tightly round her.

'Ah, what about Danny? A great man, Danny. He loved me and I loved him.' She lit another cigarette. 'I wronged him. Just the once, mind. It was Christmas. I was drunk. No excuse, I know. But the guy was a handsome bastard. Fancied him like fuck, I did. Anyway, Danny found out. Don't ask me how, I don't know to this day. Some evil nosy bastard must've told him.'

She took another drag, eyes closed. Her head drooped and she spoke to the table top.

'We didn't even row. No great argument or anything. Just after you were born he said he knew what'd happened. Didn't make a scene, even said it didn't matter. But next day he went off and that was that. I tried to find him. But I never heard of him again.'

Mary broke the silence. 'I'm sorry, Ma, I don't know what to say. It's so sad.'

Connie looked up and shook her head. 'Not sad, just life. My life and your life. I know, I know, any other mother might've leaned on her kids. For comfort and love, like. Tried to protect 'em. But I couldn't. It's a hard world out there and I thought you'd all got to stand on your own feet.

'The lads can look after themselves. Blokes do. Okay, they get in trouble and I'm not happy about that. But they'll survive. Ken and Col, they'll be okay. As for you... well, you've got a big heart. Plenty of love in you.' She smiled and lit another cigarette off the glowing end of the last one.

'You haven't mentioned Johnny,' Mary said.

Connie blew out smoke. Her sad, weepy eyes turned on Mary.

'He's different, very different. Hates me. Know he does.'

'But, Ma—'

'Don't say anything.' She paused. 'The other two, they don't think too much. Just get on with things. And you – you're a lovely gal, a good 'un. Don't complain, turned out well.' She inhaled deeply and coughed. 'But I worry about Johnny. He thinks too much. Easily hurt, you know. Oh, he's a fighter all right and I don't just mean his boxing. Won't be walked on, knows where he's going, what he wants. Wants it bad. Too much, p'raps. That's the danger. I worry for him.'

'Johnny'll be all right. He'll make something of his life. He'll really be somebody one day,' Mary replied.

Connie stubbed out the cigarette and stood up. 'Hope you're

right. You know him best.' She shuffled to the doorway and turned. 'Remember your promise. Not a word to anyone. Certainly not Johnny.'

*PART FOUR*

T HIS IS TORTURE. Pure madness. I must be going potty.

And my hands. They've never hurt so much. Something's gone wrong. Probably it's his hard skull. Made of sodding concrete. Christ, he takes a fair wallop.

'Listen to me.' Right in the left ear. Pushing the swab over my eye and bellowing in my ear. 'This is serious. You've gotta protect the cut. Box him. Busy with the jab. Keep moving. D'you hear?'

I hear. Yeah, yeah, yeah. But it's not what I want to hear. What the hell's going on?

They're all just looking at me. Blank faces. Bloody blank faces. C'mon! Someone give me a sign. Give me something for Chrissakes. Shit! It's bloody hopeless.

'C'mon!' Eyes looking straight into him. Searching his mind, his heart. 'Three more rounds. Just like an amateur fight. You can do it. Dig deep, my son.'

I know, I know. I can do it. Deep breaths. Mouthpiece in. Bite hard. Get on your feet again.

'Seconds out... for round ten...'

## Chapter Twelve

Freddie Thomson sniffed, drawing a sharp intake of air up his squashed nostrils as he draped damp bandages over the training-ring ropes. All the boxers gone. Tidy up and get home to Betty. Steak pie tonight.

Greene, on a rare visit to the Islington gym, sat on a bench, right elbow on thigh, chin resting on his fist.

'We've got a winner,' said Thomson. 'All he needs is experience.'

Greene nodded at the trainer's brief appraisal of Willis. He valued Thomson's opinion. He had been a good fighter, a middleweight contender. At thirty-nine, pushing forty, he was still a hard-bodied thirteen stone. Better than that, he was a talented trainer. A disciplinarian, too. No nonsense.

'He seems to train well,' said Greene.

Thomson sniffed again and rubbed his thick fingers through his cropped fair hair as he considered his reply.

'Can't fault him. Always on time, gets on with his work. Strong kid. Good learner.'

Thomson sat next to Greene and adopted a similar pose. Two thinkers. He turned his head, blue eyes resting on Greene's thoughtful face.

'Got a problem?'

Greene straightened his back, lifted his arms and linked fingers behind his neck. He didn't respond but debated within himself. Inside three weeks Willis had dumped an American in one round and then an Argentinian in five. Nothing special about the opposition. Hand-picked. Both fights were live on TV and he'd looked good, just as planned. But the next step concerned Greene. He inhaled deeply and his neck twitched and he stood. He started pacing.

'I could get him a British title shot,' he suddenly announced.

'Great.'

'Not too soon?'

'Nah. He's ready. Fact is, sooner the better. Don't know how long he'll stay at eleven stone.'

Greene stopped pacing. 'Seriously?'

'Nothing urgent. But he's still filling out. What is he, twenty-three?'

Greene nodded.

'Another year at most, I reckon,' said Thomson. 'He's got the frame for a middleweight. Good upper body, plenty of power.'

'But you say he needs experience?'

'Yeah, for bigger stuff. Not domestic. He can take anybody in Britain. Anyway, he was lined up to fight that poor sod Adams, wasn't he? Before he failed his scan.'

Greene nodded again. 'He wasn't certain to beat Adams. That might've been too quick for him.'

Thomson got off the bench and removed his leather jacket from a peg.

'Nah. From what I've seen of him this past month, Willis would've done him. I'd bet on it.'

Greene smiled. 'You and your betting!'

Thomson grinned back. 'I know a favourite when I see it. In my book, Willis is odds-on for the British title, whoever he meets.'

'Gary Dillon.'

'Ah,' said Thomson.

Dillon had relinquished the British welterweight title. Only one defeat in thirty-two fights, and a losing battle with the scales. Two wins since at light-middle. He was a clever box-fighter from Nottingham.

Thomson zipped up his jacket. 'When?' he asked.

'There's the rub. The Board want a new champion pretty quick after all that messing about with Adams.'

Thomson raised a quizzical eyebrow. 'So?'

'I'm working on December. There's a TV date, two weeks before Christmas. I've sewn up Dillon's people. All I need is a site.'

'Obvious Midlands fight, innit?'

'Yes. There's a place in Westhampton. Small ice stadium. Bit tight. Might get three thousand in.'

Thomson pulled a bunch of keys from a jacket pocket and tossed them in the air, letting them land in his broad palm.

'That's your side of the business. Mine's getting the fighters ready. What is it, six or seven weeks? That's plenty for Willis. He's in good nick already.'

Greene looked at the keys dangling from Thomson's fingers. 'Ready to go?'

'Raring,' Thomson said and grinned. 'Bet Willis will be, too.'

Natalie arched her back, pelvis thrusting into Willis's plunging groin. Knees drawn up, thighs wide and taut, she synchronised with Willis's increasing rhythm. Thrust meeting push. Perfect timing, like a metronome. Then the crescendo. Surging, racing to the finale.

'Yes, yes, oh yes! God!'

The climax, in harmony. Mutual satisfaction. Heavenly. The advantage of fit lovers. Willis relaxed, his tense arms slackening, body slowly dipping until his chest rested on Natalie's phenomenal silicone hillocks.

She nuzzled his damp throat with little kisses and nips, her arms wrapped around his broad muscular back. Then a ringing. Startling, piercing.

'Shit,' said Willis, pushing up and reaching for the bedside telephone. 'Hello,' he said tersely, still embedded between Natalie's thighs.

'Johnny. It's Freddie. *Awright?*'

'Yeah, sure. What's up?'

Natalie trailed her fingernails down his chest and stomach and tickled among his damp pubic hair with an impudent grin. He smiled back.

'Got a proposition for you,' said Freddie Thomson.

'Speak English, Freddie.'

'Thick sod. I'll get you a *dickshunary*. You can read, I take it.'

'Very funny.'

Freddie chuckled. 'Proposition, my son, bit of business for you to think about.'

'Right,' said Willis, flinching as Natalie playfully squeezed his testicles. 'What'd that be?'

'Night at the dogs. London Stadium. They want you to hand over a prize for the big race. What d'you say?'

'London dogs? Why me?'

'You're a star, my son. A sodding big-time Charlie. Get used to it.'

'I don't know, Freddie. I've done a few things back home. Opened garden fêtes and shops. That sort of thing. But the London dogs, that's different.'

'Nah, nothing to it. Hand over a tin pot and a cheque, pose for coupla photos. S'easy money.'

'Money?'

'Yessir. Money. Coupla hundred – cash. All down to expenses, my son. Bit of free betting money, eh?'

Willis pondered. Natalie, having lost his attention, wriggled clear. Willis settled back on to his haunches and watched Natalie's buttocks jiggle towards the bathroom.

'You still there, Johnny?'

'Yeah, sorry. Just thinking.'

'Congratulations.'

'Arsehole.'

'Articulated.'

'What?'

'Never mind. What about the dogs?'

'How do I get there?'

'With me, my son. I'll take you.'

'Okay. When?'

'Thursday night.'

'What's today?'

'Blimey! I'll get you a calendar as well, shall I? It's Tuesday, just after nine. At night, that is. Not doing anything, are you?'

'What? No, actually I've just... oh, on Thursday you mean?'

'What else? Pay *attenshun*.' A sniff. Then realisation dawned. 'Blimey, my son. You got somebody there?'

'Yeah. But it don't matter now.'

'Sorry. Look, I'll fuck off, leave you to it.'

'No problem, Freddie. I'll see you at the gym tomorrow. That's Wednesday. We'll sort the dog thing then. Okay?'

'Fine. See you at three.'

'Okay. By the way – it's ar-tic-u-late, not articulated. That's a big lorry.'

Willis replaced the receiver and headed for the bathroom. Natalie was splashing about. Never done it in the bath before…

Willis casually leaned against the wall, studying the form card. But he had a sneaky eye on Thomson.

'Won't be a tick,' he'd said and shouldered his way to join three characters near the bar. They were thickset, their sloping shoulders draped in well-cut suits. Dripping in gold at wrists and throats, with bottles of Pils at their elbows.

'Johnny! Over here, my son,' Freddie signalled to him.

He shoved off the wall and edged through the crowd.

'Three pals,' said Thomson and sniffed. 'Fight fans and they know their dogs. Arty, Benny, Terry, this is Johnny.' Popular, this letter 'y'.

Their handshakes were firm but nothing macho. Pleased to meet you. How's tricks? Backed any winners?

'Freddie's giving me bum tips. Costing me a fortune.'

'One of them nights, John,' said Benny. Or was it Arty? And why John? What's happened to my 'y'? he thought.

'Got one for the big race,' said Terry.

'Yeah?'

'The one dog. Decent odds. Should get threes at least.'

'Right. Thanks,' said Willis.

'Johnny's presenting the prize for that,' said Thomson. 'We've gotta be trackside. Won't have time to work the line for the odds.'

'Pity,' said Terry.

'We'll look after it,' said Benny. Or Arty. 'What do you want?'

'I'll go fifty,' said Thomson.

'What about you, John?'

Willis looked at Thomson. He'd got two hundred coming to him. 'Fifty will be fine,' he said.

'Sure? It's a good thing, ain't it, Art?'

So that was Benny. The one who didn't use the 'y'.

'Can't fail,' said Arty. 'It's the only reason we're here.'

'Make it a century?'

'Is that what you're having?'

Benny smiled. Shrugged his shoulders. 'More than that, John. But it's down to you. Your choice.'

Willis looked at Thomson again. The trainer sniffed, deadpan.

'Ton it is,' he said, fingering the notes in his trouser pocket. They were all twenties. He separated five and drew them out, offering them to Benny but he didn't move a muscle. Terry reached across and took them.

'Right. We'd better be getting trackside,' said Thomson. 'Gotta find Albert and his gang for the presentation. See you later.'

The trainer led Willis out of the bar and down a flight of stairs towards the offices. 'Albert'll be around here somewhere,' he said.

'Albert? Who's Albert?'

'Albert Davies. I told you. Wish you'd pay *attenshun*. He's the guv'nor, stadium boss. He'll be with you for the presentation. Make the announcement, introduce you. And he'll have your bunce.'

'Bunce?'

'Money, where you come from.'

'Right. Bunce.'

They found Albert Davies in his office, a half-empty whisky bottle on his desk and a tray of empty glasses next to the amber liquid. Albert was squat and grey-haired, about fifty. And, once he opened his mouth, clearly from Sarf London.

'Ava sherbert?' he asked.

'S'okay, Albert. Johnny's in training. Not drinking tonight.'

Willis smiled. 'Glass of water will do fine.'

'*Warter*! Right, warter it is. Mandy, sort a glass of warter for our friend 'ere.'

Mandy, roll-neck cream wool sweater bulging in the right area, swivelled on a chair behind her desk. She went to a small refrigerator, opened it and squatted. Round hips stretched her black ski pants. No visible knicker line. She emerged with a bottle of spring water, poured a glassful and slowly walked towards Willis.

'There y'are,' she said softly, not taking her eyes off the glass as she put it into Willis's hand. She had a round face and bleached hair in a pageboy cut.

Glass delivered, Mandy retreated to the desk where race cards were stacked high. Willis caught her glancing back at him. He smiled, raising the water to his lips. She turned her head away.

'Thanks for coming,' said Albert. 'S'nice to get a new celeb along.'

The office walls were dotted with photographs of past presentations in thin black frames.

'My pleasure,' said Willis. 'But I don't know about the celebrity bit.'

'You're a celeb all right, cocker. Dog people are fight people. They know you. Fact is, crowd's bigger than normal for a Thursday. Mind you, it'll be better on Saturday. Bonfire night. Fireworks before racing.'

'Fireworks. Won't that spook the dogs, Albert?' asked Thomson.

'Not really. Anyways, some of the mutts could do with a rocket up their arse.'

Grins all round, even Mandy. Davies flicked his wrist and peered at a leather-strapped watch.

'We'd better get out there. Don't wanna miss the race. Might give the prize to wrong geezer.' He laughed. Willis and Thomson smiled politely and Mandy grimaced.

The one dog breezed home.

Willis stood under a wavering spotlight, a large silver trophy gleaming on a cloth-covered trestle table next to him. Albert's voice crackled over the public address system and wind whistled down the microphone. The small gathering in front of the main stand applauded Willis's introduction and he handed over the trophy and cheque to the owner's wife. Middle-aged, wearing a silly hat, she offered a powdered cheek. Willis obliged with a peck, aware of a camera click and flash.

Albert led the way back to his office.

'Sure you won't ava sherbert?' He filled his own glass.

'No thanks, Albert,' said Thomson. 'We must shoot. Johnny's got an early morning run.'

'Course,' said Albert. He swigged the whisky. 'Mandy. Give Johnny 'ere the envelope.'

Mandy opened a drawer in her desk. She withdrew a manila envelope, got up, smoothed her pants over her hips and headed for Willis, eyes fixed on the floor.

'Thanks, Mandy,' he said.

'Pleasure,' she said and looked up. A hesitant smile played on her full lips, head tilted to one side. 'Any chance of an autograph?'

'Sure.'

She almost sprinted the short return journey to her desk and plunged again into a drawer. Willis, tucking the envelope into his inside jacket pocket, walked over to the desk. Mandy gave him a pen and an old Albert Hall boxing programme, folded back at a page bearing his picture.

'Where'd you get this?'

'I was there,' she said. 'With me boyfriend.'

'Right. Who do I sign it to, you or him?'

'Me, please. He's history. Blew him out that night.'

'Oh, why's that?'

'He's a jealous prat.'

'Not good that. Jealousy.'

'Naah. He didn't like it 'cause I fancied you. And now here y'are. Fancy that.'

Willis looked up from the programme. Mandy was smiling, eyes sparkling straight at him. He smiled and then wrote, *To Mandy with love, Johnny Willis xxx*

He handed the pen and programme back to her. She read the message.

'Thanks a lot,' she beamed, then stretched up and kissed his lips. Not so shy, after all.

'Ready, Johnny?' said Thomson, walking towards the door.

Polite thank yous and farewells dispensed with, they made their way back to the bar. More money to collect. The trio hadn't moved – same positions at the bar, full Pils bottles at their elbows.

'Wha' did I tell you?' beamed Arty. 'Romped home.'

'You were right,' said Thomson. 'Can't fault you.'

'Nice little earner,' said Benny.

'Nice little wedge,' said Terry. He pushed his right hand towards Willis's groin. A roll of notes. 'Got fours. Better than we thought.'

'Cheers,' said Willis, peeling off a couple of notes. 'Have a drink with me.'

'No need,' said Benny. 'Been our pleasure, ain't it, Art?'

Arty nodded. 'Any time.'

Thomson put a ten-pound note on the bar, setting one of the Pils bottles on top. 'Nah, we insist. Have a drink,' he sniffed.

'You're a gent, Fred. But there's no need,' said Benny.

'Enjoy,' said Thomson. 'But we've gotta push off. Beat the crowd, get Johnny back to Islington.'

'Islington,' said Benny. 'One of Greene's pads, eh?'

'That's right,' said Thomson.

'Nice drum, John?'

'Yeah, suits me. Handy for the gym.'

'Nice area,' said Terry. 'Pop over sometimes. Not often. Norf of the river.'

'Bit off our manor,' said Arty. 'Ain' it, Benny?'

Benny nodded, his dark eyes focused on Willis.

'Well,' said Benny, offering his hand, 'see you again some time.'

'Nice friends,' said Willis as he settled into Thomson's Escort.

'Better friends than enemies.'

'Bet that's the truth. Thought we were in a gangster movie.' He started to count his money.

'It'll all be there,' said Thomson.

'What happened with you? Thought you were having fifty on?'

'I did.' Sniff.

'I didn't see any money.'

'Fast hands, Johnny, still got fast hands, my son.' He glanced at Willis and grinned. 'You didn't see the other fella, did you?'

'What other fella?'

'Little chap. Hat on. He's their runner. Places the bets. Slipped him my fifty.'

'I'll know another time.'

'Another time?'

'Yeah. Have to do it again. Been a good night. Interesting.'

'Not to mention profitable.'

'There is that, of course. It helps.'

'Don't always win, though.'

When Willis got out of the warm car, he held the door open and leaned back in. 'Thanks, Freddie.'

'Glad you enjoyed it, my son.'

'Yeah, like I said, must do it again. I like going to the dogs.'

Thomson sniffed. 'My old dutch says I've been going to the dogs for years.'

Inside his flat, Willis emptied his pockets on to the bedside table and stripped naked. He counted his bundle of money. Yes, five hundred quid. Then he opened the manila envelope and pulled out the notes, wrapped in a sheet of white paper. He counted them, tens and twenties. Another two hundred. Not a bad night. Six hundred quid profit.

Shit! I didn't give Freddie anything, he thought. Sort it to-morrow.

He stacked the notes and folded them once, fat in his hand. Nice little wedge, indeed. He picked up the sheet of paper. It wasn't blank. The printed heading ran: London Greyhound Stadium. Damn, he thought. Freddie said it'd be expenses. Tax free, nothing in writing.

But it wasn't an invoice. Just a telephone number and a name – *Mandy*.

Not shy at all.

Willis loved Saturday mornings. They were the best. He didn't have to get up for a run. Road work! It was necessary for stamina, but five thirty was an ungodly hour to get up.

He almost opened his eyes. Squinting, he saw the clock. Nearly eight thirty. Lids down again. Another half-hour.

Ring… ring… Shit! Damn phone.

'Yeah?' he yawned.

'Johnny? Thought you'd be back now.'

'Back?'

'From your road work.'

Another yawn. 'Don't run on Saturday, Michael.'

'Don't you? Ah, well.' A pause. 'Got some news for you. Good news.' Silence. 'Johnny. You still there?'

'Uh uh.' His eyes were still closed. 'I'm listening. News, you said.'

'British title fight,' said the promoter.

Willis's eyes popped open. 'British title!'

'That's right. Against Gary Dillon.'

'When?'

'December. You've got six weeks, Freddie says that's enough.'

'No problem.' Willis sat up. His mind raced. Been here before, twice. Gotta be third time lucky. Nothing can go wrong this time, he thought. 'That's great, Michael. Just fucking great.'

'Thought you'd be pleased.'

'You're not kidding. British champion! Just think of it.'

'We'll go over the details next week.'

'Yeah, sure.'

'Just one more thing. Don't you want to know where?'

'Yeah, but it doesn't really matter. Anywhere'll do for a title.'

'Glad to hear it. But I've got a bit of an advantage. Westhampton – at the ice rink.'

Willis let it sink in. 'Back home,' he muttered.

'What? What was that, Johnny?'

'Great. I said great.'

'Well, have a good weekend. Get down to the graft next week. Okay?'

'Yeah. Six weeks, eh?'

'Bye, Johnny.'

'Right. Bye, Michael... oh, before you go. Will you let Bob know?'

'Who?'

'Bob, you know, Bob Mercer.'

'Don't worry about that. It's all in hand,' Greene lied.

'It's just that I let him down before. I promised he'd be first in future.'

'Bob'll get the beat on it. Before the press conference. We'll need plenty of local publicity.'

'Bob'll do it. Play fair with him; he's a good man.'

'Okay, Johnny. By the way, press conference will probably be Wednesday afternoon. It's gonna be a quick, hard sell.'

'I train at three.'

'No problem. I'll have it wrapped up in good time.'

'Cheers, Michael.'

Willis balanced the dead phone in his hand, tapping it on his knee. Mary! Must let her know, he thought. He leaned to dial, then stopped and sat back. No, I'll get up there. Tell her, take her out for a meal. Celebrate. This time it's gonna be okay. British champion! I can feel it in my water. Or should that be *warter*? And he glanced at the huddled body next to him. Bottle-blonde fringe. Bright blue eyes dreamily fixed on his face.

'Morning. Sorry about that. Did I wake you?'

'Mmm.' She stretched beneath the sheets. 'Important, was it?'

'You could say that. Look, I know we're supposed to have the day together, but I've gotta go.'

'Go?'

'Yeah, back home.'

'Something wrong?'

'No, far from it. Just something I've gotta do.'

'What about tonight? Fireworks at the dogs?'

'Sorry, Mandy. I'll be stopping over at home. There'll be other times.' He bent to plant a kiss on her squat nose. A warm arm circled his neck and pulled him towards moist lips.

'Spare five minutes, can't you?'

'How about an hour?'

'Even better.'

## Chapter Thirteen

Mary heard footsteps approach the front door and a key turned in the latch.

'Anyone home? Hello, anyone in?'

Mary scrambled out of bed. She pulled on a bathrobe and put a forefinger to her lips.

'Be quiet,' she whispered. 'Stay there.'

Payne nodded.

Mary closed the bedroom door behind her and made for the stairs. 'Coming, Johnny,' she shouted.

Willis stood at the bottom of the stairs.

'There you are,' he said. 'Didn't know whether you'd still be at work.'

'Early shift. Got home at three. I was just having a lie down. What're you doing here?'

'Surprise. Aren't you glad to see me?'

'Course I am, silly.' She hugged and kissed her brother and they walked into the kitchen.

'Want a drink? Coffee? Tea?'

'Murder a tea.'

Mary filled the kettle. 'So, what brings you home? Why didn't you phone?'

'Wanted to surprise you. I've got some news.'

She switched on the kettle and dropped two tea bags in the pot. 'What's that then?' she asked.

Willis watched his sister open a drawer and remove two spoons.

'I'll tell you if you'll stand still a minute.'

She turned to him. Her tousled hair was trapped beneath her collar. Willis reached behind her neck and flipped it clear.

'That's better,' he said.

'Thanks,' she said, folding her arms. 'What's your news then?'

'British title fight. In six weeks at the ice rink.'

'Oh Johnny, that's great! Does that mean your friend passed his whatsit... scan, or whatever it's called?'

He hadn't thought of Brian Adams as a friend. Suppose he was, in a way. Not so much as Natalie, but a friend, nonetheless.

'No, he didn't. He's finished with boxing.'

'Oh dear.' Mary poured the boiled water into the pot. 'What's he doing now?'

'Helping out in a gym and working in a betting shop. He's a funny bloke. Says the customer's always right, except in a betting shop. Funny, eh?'

'Yeah. But he's right.'

Willis picked up his mug of tea. 'Anyway, I'm here to take you out to celebrate. I'll give Pete a ring and we'll go for a meal. Slap-up job.'

Mary thought of Payne, upstairs in her bed. She used both hands to lift the mug to her mouth and sipped, then shook her head.

'Don't ring Pete. I'm phoning him at six. Before he goes to The Casino.'

'Course. He'll be working tonight. What an idiot, I forgot that.'

'He's doing seven until one.'

'Right, tell you what. We'll go out, just the two of us, and then go on to The Casino. See Pete there. What d'you think?'

'That'll be lovely. I'll tell Pete when I phone.'

'No. Don't tell him. Let's surprise him.'

'Okay.' Mary smiled. 'You're really chuffed, aren't you? I've never known you so excited.'

'Yeah, well, I feel everything's coming right at last. I just feel it. Know what I mean?'

Mary nodded. 'I can guess. I'm pleased for you.'

'For us,' he said. 'For us, sis. This is the start. I'll be British champion in six weeks. Then there's the European title. I can really make it big in the next coupla years. Then you can get out of this shit'ole.'

'Oh Johnny,' she laughed. 'One step at a time. You're like a kid at Christmas.'

'Christmas! Yeah, we'll have a great Christmas this year. Why don't you come down to London? Spend it with me. We'll have a great time.'

Mary put her mug down. 'No. You come up here, Johnny. I can't leave Ma on her own. It wouldn't be right.'

Willis's face darkened. 'Come on, sis. She'll probably be at some party or other. Why bother about her? Have some fun.'

'We've always had Christmas dinner here. All of us.'

'Suppose you're right. Won't be much fun for Kenny and Col this year, poor bastards. Banged up for Christmas. That's gotta be fucking awful.' Willis drained the last of his tea.

'Want another?' asked Mary.

'No, that was fine. Have you heard from them?'

'Yeah. Colin wrote this week. Letter's behind the clock. Nothing from Kenny, though.'

'Must get to see them, before Christmas.'

'That'd be nice. But won't it be awkward with the fight coming up?'

'I'll write next week. And I'll fix up visits for after the fight. Take the Lonsdale Belt. That should cheer 'em up. Least it'll show I've not be wasting my time while they're banged up.'

'They know you're not wasting time, Johnny. It's not your fault they went down.'

'No. But I should've gone with them.'

Mary shook her head. 'What good would that've done? They love you, Johnny. They're proud of what you've done, what you're doing. They didn't want you locked up. That,' she emphasised, 'would've been a waste.'

'I know, I know. But I can't help feeling bad. It's wrong. Me out here and them... well, it doesn't seem right.'

Mary put her arms around him. 'Oh, Johnny, Johnny.' She rested her head on his chest. 'Just get out there and do your best. Win the British title if you can, but stop feeling angry at yourself. Don't tear yourself apart.'

Willis kissed the top of her head and they held each other in silence. Mary was first to move away.

'I've gotta get Ma's tea. She'll be hungry when she gets in. Oh, didn't tell you, did I? She's got a little job. In Boot's, the chemists in town.'

'I don't believe it! Ma working!'

'She's had a few jobs, Johnny, be fair.'

'Yeah, as a barmaid until the landlord chucks her out. She drinks the profits.'

'That's nasty. She's changing, Johnny, believe me. She's not drinking as much and she's really smartened herself up. You ought to give her a chance.'

'Chance! Look – no, I'm not gonna argue. It's not worth it. We see things differently, that's all. Leave it at that.'

Mary looked at her brother with sad brown eyes. She sighed. 'As you wish.'

She took a potato peeler out of a drawer. 'I've gotta get on. What're you doing now?'

Willis looked at the kitchen clock. It was nearly five.

'I'm gonna see Ron. Tell him the news. I'll be back in about an hour. Can you book a taxi for seven thirty? We'll go to Mario's. They'll squeeze us in.'

'Okay. But I'll ring Mario's as well. May as well book a table to make sure. It is Saturday night.'

Willis kissed her forehead. 'I'll be about an hour.'

Upstairs, Pete heard the BMW drive off. He got out of bed and started to dress as Mary came in.

'What's he doing home?'

'Come to take us out.'

'What?'

She sat on the end of the bed and watched him pull on his jeans.

'He's celebrating. The British title.'

'What?'

'Is that all you can say?'

'What? I mean, when? The British title?'

'Next month. At the ice rink.'

'Great! Champion by Christmas. Who's he fighting?'

Mary thought. 'He didn't say. It's not that friend of his, Brian.'

'I know. He's banned. Poor bugger failed another scan.'

'Anyway, I told him you were working tonight.'

'Yeah. Can't really get away. Might finish a bit early though, about eleven?'

'Don't worry. We're going to Mario's and then coming to see you. But you don't know that. I'm phoning you at six but I'm not to tell you that Johnny's here.'

'Why are you phoning me?'

'I'm not, stupid. Johnny was gonna phone you when he got here, so I told him I'd already arranged to call you. Be great, your phone going off in this room, wouldn't it?'

Payne looked at his mobile phone on the bedside table. 'Jeez. Never thought about that.' He stepped into his black slip-on shoes. 'Isn't it time we told him? About us, I mean?'

'Not yet. Let him get the title fight out of the way. We'll tell him at Christmas, like we said. When we get engaged.'

'You're the boss.' He picked up his phone to dial for a taxi and smiled. 'Wouldn't have mattered. It's switched off, look. Didn't want to be disturbed.'

We nearly was, she thought. Now *that* would've been a surprise for Johnny.


Connie sat on the upright chair next to her bed. She slipped off her shoes and rubbed her tired feet. Nine hours. Long time to be standing. Time was when I'd dance the night away and not feel a thing, she thought. Never tired.

She sat upright and rolled her shoulders, rubbed the back of her neck. Closed her eyes. She ached. When Mary's finished in the bathroom I'll have a nice, long soak, she thought. Bingo at the club tonight. At least I'll be sitting.

She looked at the clock. Nearly seven. Mary said Johnny'd be here about six. Men! Always late. Just then, she heard a car door slam and footsteps on the path.

'I'm back.'

Willis walked to the back room. It was empty except for Connie's dirty crockery on the table. He returned to the passage and paused at his mother's door. It was ajar. He could see her reflection in the wide mirror above the fireplace. She looked weary.

Connie looked up. She saw his reflection, too. They gazed at each other, two shimmering ghosts. She went to speak but Willis abruptly turned away and mounted the stairs.

'You in the bathroom, Mary?'

Dinner was superb. Pasta and veal for them both and a shared bottle of red. Not house wine, the good stuff.

Mary wore a royal blue dress with a tight, high-necked bodice and a mid-calf-length skirt, split up her left thigh. She listened to Willis as he spoke.

'You should see Michael's house. God knows how much it cost. But he's a millionaire. Says I can be a millionaire in a coupla years. Can you believe that?'

And... 'These characters at the dogs. Shoulda seen them. Straight out of a gangster movie. Real laugh. But they gave me a good tip. Made four hundred quid.'

And... 'Natalie, that's Brian's sister, she's fun. Knows everybody in Soho. There's a club, just a disco place really, run by a poof. Funny bloke, if that's the word. Name's Ginny. Got ginger hair, see. Well, he's a laugh. All "darling" this and "darling" that. Even calls me darling. "All the best looking guys are straight," he says. Never pay a penny in there. Always sends over a bottle of wine. Plonk, not like this stuff, but Natalie says it's the thought that counts.'

And... 'Freddie's a good bloke. I mean, he's a great trainer, really knows his business. But he's really hard on his lad, Wayne. Not a bad boxer, only seventeen, but Freddie's always at him. "Do this, do that, you're not doing it right." I had a word with Freddie the other day. "Take it easy," I said, "you're too hard on him." Know what Freddie said? "Nah," he said. "If he can't take his old man pushing him, he's in the wrong fucking game." Got a point, I suppose.'

And... 'This girl, Mandy's her name. All shy like. But then she asks me for an autograph. "Sure," I says, and she gives me an old Albert Hall programme with my picture in it. Turns out she'd been at the fight with her boyfriend. "Do I sign it for him, then?" I says. "No," she says. "I blew him out that night." Do you know why? You'll never believe it. Bold as you like, she says, "He was jealous 'cause I fancied you." And I thought she was shy.'

And... 'Little Smithy in the flat above me, Gary Smith, bantamweight, all skin and bones. And he's as ugly as shit. Nice guy, but ugly; can't pull a bird. Anyway, he pays for a prozzie. Not even a looker. Hard sort. Pays her hundred and fifty to stay the night. He's really gonna make a pig of himself. An all-nighter. Guess what happens? He does the job a coupla times and then falls asleep. It's not even midnight. So she takes the money and creeps out. Probably the most she's ever had for a coupla bangs. So embarrassing for Smithy. Daft thing is, he tells us about it. Can you believe it? Not only ugly, but thick as well.'

It was nearly eleven when the taxi dropped them outside The Casino.

'Good to see you, Johnny,' said Bomber on the door. 'It's busy in there tonight. Reckon I'll be putting the block on soon. Can't have it too crowded, can we?'

Payne spotted them as they walked down the stairs towards the gaming area. Rather, he saw the flash of Mary's thigh. He kissed her and shook Willis's hand.

'What you doing here?' he said.

'Come to make sure you're not slacking. Keep you on your toes.'

'What?'

'Just kidding. Got some good news. Let's get a drink.'

Willis ordered lager for himself, white wine for Mary and tonic water for the worker. Then he told Payne about the title fight.

'Dillon's a useful scrapper,' said Payne. 'Saw him when he won the welterweight title. Remember, you were on that show? In Nottingham. Beat Ricky Walsh, you did. Two rounds.'

'Yeah, he's gotta be half-decent. But he's only just come up to light-middle and I'm a big light-middle. Truth is, Pete, it's a bit of a struggle to make eleven stone these days. Have to watch my diet.'

'Better not have too many of those, then,' said Payne.

Willis picked up his lager. 'Last blow-out. Six weeks on the wagon after this. Weak tea and water only. Nothing else'll pass my lips.'

'I'll get in touch with Greene's office next week. Fix up the tickets. Should be a good earner for the lads.'

'Sure. No idea about the prices. Won't be cheap, though.

Don't even know what the ice rink holds. D'you?' asked Willis.

'For a fight? Hard to say. Been to wrestling there but they don't put many seats out. I'd guess around three thousand.'

'Three thousand! That's more than enough. Won't fill that.'

'Dunno. British title. Haven't had many of those around here. You might be surprised. Anyway, I'd better keep circulating. Going on the tables?'

'Reckon we'll have a little dabble. I feel lucky. Get some chips, pal.' He handed over four hundred pounds – the profit from the one dog.

Willis persuaded Mary to take five ten-pound chips and she cautiously placed bets on the roulette table. A run on red, four consecutive numbers, trebled her money.

Her face was flushed. 'Think I'll stop now.'

'No, keep going,' said Payne, appearing at her shoulder. 'Could be your lucky night.' He gently squeezed her left buttock.

Mary switched to black. Gambled fifty and won. She hopped up and down, clapping her hands.

'That's lucky. Just one more.'

Black again, another winner. She couldn't hold all her chips. Willis had only a few left. He wasn't so lucky, after all. But he smiled at Mary's unconfined joy and put fifty next to her chips. Still on black. They won.

'That's really it now,' said Mary.

She piled up the chips. Must be three hundred pounds. Such a lot of money, she thought.

Willis placed a hundred on zero. Odds 36–1.

'Why've you done that?'

'Impulse, Mary. Just a feeling.'

'No more bets, ladies and gentlemen, no more bets, thank you,' said the croupier.

Mary was transfixed by the spinning wheel. Willis casually looked around the room. Ping, ping. The ball bounced around the numbers. Ping. It settled. Now Willis looked as the wheel slowed to a halt.

'Zero, ladies and gentlemen, zero.'

The croupier paddled in the losing bets, before pushing stacks of chips towards Willis's hundred.

'Tray please,' he said calmly. The croupier stacked the winnings in a tray and handed them over. He took out a twenty chip and tossed it to the croupier. 'Be lucky,' he said.

Mary watched, speechless as Willis added her chips to his tray.

'C'mon. Let's cash in.'

'How much've you won? Lots, ain't it?'

'Between us, there's about four grand here.'

'No! Oh no! Not that much.'

Willis smiled. 'Told you I felt lucky. Things are starting to go my way.' He collected his winnings in fifties and twenties. He peeled off ten fifties. 'Put those in your bag,' he said to his sister.

'No, I couldn't,' said Mary. 'It's your money.'

'Don't be silly, sis. You won as well. Take it. It'll be useful at Christmas. Buy something nice for Pete. In fact, take this as well.'

He added another five fifties. Mary looked at the money in her hand and kissed her brother's cheek.

'Thanks, Johnny. I'll get you something nice for Christmas, too.'

'Don't waste your money on me. Get me a shirt or something. Seeing you happy is my best present.'

Payne joined them at the bar just before one o'clock.

'Hear you had a tickle, Johnny.'

'Yeah. Have some champagne.' He filled the empty glass that had been awaiting his pal's arrival. He and Mary had already finished one bottle. Mary was giggly and leaning into her brother. Now she grabbed Payne's arm.

'Ah, there y'are, lover boy. It'sh been great. Johnny's won thoush-ands. Thoush-ands! Int' that great?'

Willis raised an eyebrow at Payne. 'Lover boy?' he said.

'That'sh right. Pete's my lover boy. Int' that sho, lover boy?' She slapped an arm around his waist.

Payne put an arm on Mary's shoulders and held her tight against him. 'You certainly seemed to have enjoyed yourself,' he said.

'Why not?' Mary sat upright, indignant. 'We're *shellebrating*. Johnny's won thoush-ands. Thoush-ands an' thoush-ands. An' he's gonna be British champion. Int' that right, Johnny?'

'Right on, sis. Everything's just great.'

'Oops.' Mary put a hand to her mouth. 'Pardon.' Another belch. 'Oh dear.' She slid off her stool. 'Toilet. Going toilet.'

Payne walked with her, holding her by the waist. Willis smiled, sipping champagne. He'd never seen her enjoy herself so much.

Five minutes later, she sat back on the stool. Fresh pink lipstick, hair brushed around her neck.

'No more for me. Woo,' she exhaled, wafting a hand in front of her mouth. 'Never had sho much to drink. S'gone to my head.'

Willis grinned. Payne looked concerned.

'We'll get off, then,' said Willis as he downed the last of the champagne.

'No, s'all right. Avanother drink.'

'It's gone one, Mary. We'll get a cab,' said Payne.

'Shure?'

'Sure. I'll order it now. Won't be a tick.'

They waited five minutes, Willis grinning at Mary's earnest attempts to speak soberly.

'C'mon, Pete's probably talking to Bomber and the lads on the door,' said Willis. 'Cab should be here now.'

Mary stood and steadied herself. She clutched her bag under one arm and held Willis's left hand as she walked carefully up the stairs. No stumbles. Fresh air blew through the open double doors. Bomber and a colleague stood massively on top of the steps, looking down at the street, hefty hands by their sides. Payne was on the middle of the five steps, talking to three men. Drunks.

'Sorry, chaps. Place's full. Another night, eh?'

'Give over. We've seen fuckers coming out. There's gotta be room. Let us in.'

'Sorry. Not tonight.'

'Look,' said another, rocking back on his heels. 'There's two more coming out.' He pointed at Willis and Mary.

'Problem, Bomber?' said Willis.

'Pissheads,' he hissed from the corner of his mouth, eyes still watching the men on the street. 'Won't take no for an answer.'

'Last time,' said Payne. 'Nobody else's coming in tonight. Just go home, or find somewhere else, there's good lads.'

'Fucking hell! Only want one more drink.'

'Not in here. Not tonight.'

'Hey, look who it is,' said the biggest of the trio, tie askew, hair blowing in the breeze. 'If it ain't that turd, Johnny Willis.'

Uh oh, thought Bomber.

'That's enough,' said Payne. 'We don't want any trouble.'

'Trouble? With that shit?' The drunk elbowed past his mates. Payne put a restraining hand on his chest.

'That's far enough,' he said.

The drunk looked down at Payne's hand. He raised his right arm and pointed at Willis.

'He's a fucking rat. Lets his bruvvers do time for him.'

Willis's eyes narrowed. 'What'd you say?'

'Leave it, Johnny,' said Payne. 'We'll handle it.'

Mary tugged at Johnny's sleeve. 'C'mon. Back inshide, Johnny. Leave it. Do as Pete says.'

The drunk carried on. 'You fucking heard, shithead. I was in the Falklands, mate. Fucking glad you weren't by my side. Bleeding coward.'

Willis pounced. Three savage punches and it was all over. Flat out on the pavement, blood smeared the drunk's face. His pals tottered back.

'Christ!' said Bomber.

'Shit!' said Willis. Pain in his right hand. Not again. Fuck it.

# Chapter Fourteen

Thomson shook his head and sniffed. 'Too much swelling to tell.' He ran a thumb gingerly over the back of Willis's right hand. 'Could have busted a metacarpal. Little bones from your fingers to wrist. Is that what happened before?'

'Yeah. Before I was supposed to fight Brian Adams.'

'What happened?'

'Had an operation.'

'No, my son. How did it happen this time?'

'Fucking loudmouth called me a coward, so I whacked him.'

'Could be an expensive whack.' Sniff.

'What do we do?'

'Get it X-rayed. Tell Michael we've got a problem.'

'Can't that wait? We don't have to tell him yet. It might be okay in a few days.'

'Michael should know. The whole show revolves around you.'

'A few days won't hurt.'

Thomson thought for a moment. 'If it's broken, there's no way you'll be able to fight in six weeks.'

'What if it's not broken?'

'Training will be affected. You can't punch with it. Probably not for three weeks, two at best. And that's supposing it's only bruised or sprained or sumfink.'

'Don't tell Michael. Let's see how it goes, okay?'

Thomson rubbed his bristly chin. 'What's today?'

'Now who needs a calendar? It's Monday.'

'You did it Saturday night.' Sniff. 'We'll leave it until Thursday. No later. If the fight's off, you'll have to tell Michael. He'll go fucking ballistic.'

'Don't worry, Freddie. I'll tell Michael I did it training, not whacking some idiot. Okay?'

'Right. Meantime, you'd better get plenty of ice on it. Be careful what you're doing. Go for a run but, otherwise, stay indoors. I'll see you Thursday morning. Eleven sharp.'

Willis walked along the road to his flat, filled an ice bucket from the refrigerator and sat on the sofa, hand plunged in the bucket between his knees.

Three days indoors. I'll go crazy, he thought. He picked up the phone. She answered after four rings.

'Natalie, baby, it's Johnny. You doing anything the next coupla days?'

Thomson was worried. He knew Greene should be warned, and it was his job to let him know. By Wednesday morning he'd decided. He phoned Greene's office.

'Sorry,' said Vanessa, 'Michael's in Westhampton, seeing the council to sort out the site for the Willis fight. Then he's having lunch with a reporter up there. If it's important, you can get him on his mobile.'

'No, it's not that urgent,' Thomson lied. 'He doesn't like being disturbed in meetings. When's he back?'

'Tomorrow. Press conference at noon.'

'Course there is. Forgetting. Well, I'll see him there, then. Cheers, Vanessa darling.' Freddie put the receiver down. A press conference to announce the fight. If it's still on.

Mercer was surprised to receive a telephone call from Greene. Usually, Greene's office sent out press statements. Provincial guys like him rarely got to deal with the promoter direct, except at press conferences and shows.

The even bigger surprise was Greene's invitation to lunch.

'I'm in Westhampton on Wednesday and I'd like you to have lunch with me, Bob. Few things to talk over. Say twelve thirty at the Regent Hotel?'

Over pre-lunch drinks – lager for Mercer, tonic water for Greene – the reporter was given his exclusive. By the time coffee was served, Greene had offered six pairs of special ringside tickets for a reader competition.

When Greene shook hands before leaving, he had one request.

'Sit on it until tomorrow, Bob. I wouldn't want it leaked before the press conference. What time's your first edition?'

'Hits the streets about midday.'

'That's fine, then. Gives you plenty of time to get a good story together.'

'Yes, thanks Michael. I'll give Johnny a ring at his flat.'

'Sure. But don't speak to Dillon's people. Wouldn't want it out in Nottingham, would we? You can see them at the press conference tomorrow.'

Greene's Bentley transported him back to London and Mercer called a taxi. He had a big story. It was worth a free ride back to the office.

'Good lunch, Bob?' The sports editor didn't look up from the page proof he was scribbling on.

'Very good, thanks Mac.'

'Story in it? Or was it just social?'

'Don't think Michael Greene would ever come all the way up here just to socialise. Certainly not with me.'

McKenzie looked up, pulling the pipe out of his mouth. 'So, what've you got, laddie?' he asked, interested.

'Johnny Willis fighting for the vacant British title at the ice rink. Second Saturday in December.'

'The ice rink? Saturday, you say.'

'Yeah. Saturday night, live on satellite.'

'That's a pity. Been better midweek.'

'It'll be too late for the Sundays. Even if they were bothered that much. Anyway, the nationals will be full of soccer. It's a big 'un for us.'

'Um. Who do City play that day?' Mac swivelled in his chair and ran his pipe stem down the football fixture list pasted on the wall above his desk. 'There's lucky,' he said. 'No game until Monday.'

Mercer's eyes rolled. 'Well, that is lucky.'

McKenzie ignored the irony. 'Editor's overnight meeting in an hour. Give me a note of the facts.'

'Sure, Mac. By the way, it's exclusive.'

'Thought it might be. This Greene guy, what's he like?'

'Knows what he wants and works to get it. Come on strong the last two or three years. By the way, he's offered six pairs of tickets for a competition.'

'That's good. The ed likes reader involvement.'

'And there's a press conference in London tomorrow.'

'Right. Give me that note for my meeting.' He turned back to the page proof.

Mercer's exclusive was the lead story on Thursday's back page. The editor also decided that Willis's thumbnail photograph should appear on the front page. Two paragraphs revealed the facts and referred the reader to 'Bob Mercer's full, exclusive story on the back page'. Last time Willis's picture appeared on the front page, he'd been arrested. What a difference a year makes.

Mercer caught a mid-morning Intercity train to London. Willis and Thomson went by taxi to Dominion Road and the restaurant where the press had been summoned. Apart from a yellow bruising, Willis's right hand looked normal, but it felt far from it.

'It'll be okay,' he told Thomson. 'Say nothing to Michael.'

'Watch the handshakes,' Thomson sniffed. 'I'm gonna tell Michael you've bumped it on the bag. Nothing to alarm him. But he needs to know something.'

'I'll tell him.'

They met Greene in the restaurant foyer. He was alarmed.

'How bad is it? Here, let me see. Show me,' he said.

'It's not serious, Michael. Just a bit of bruising.'

Greene looked. 'What do you think, Freddie? Will it be all right?'

'Should be. We're resting it. Not punching. Give it a week or so and we'll know for certain.'

'Week or so? Shit! He's gotta be fit for this. Dillon's no mug. I don't want him going in there one-handed.'

'Michael, you worry too much,' said Willis, smiling. 'I'll be fine.'

'You'd better be right,' said Greene. 'There's a lot riding on this. I'd rather call it off than take a risk.'

'There's no risk. Trust me.'

Greene looked at Thomson. 'Well?'

The trainer sniffed. Why ask a pair of gamblers? he thought. But he said nothing.

'Hell, the world's going potty. Saddam Hussein's taken over

Kuwait, Maggie Thatcher's being eased out and I've got a one-handed fighter boxing for a title.' Greene's neck twitched. 'Right. C'mon, let's meet the media mob. It's the room in the back. Dillon's already in there.'

The final sparring session was on Wednesday, three days before the fight. Willis had managed only eight days of sparring and no heavy bag work.

The big training gloves provided extra protection. Even so, he felt some discomfort and used his right hand sparingly.

'Truth time,' said Thomson. He unwrapped Willis's hands. 'Tell me how it feels.'

'Sore. But not too bad.'

Thomson fingered the back of his fighter's hand. Willis flinched. 'Not good,' he sniffed.

'It'll be okay, Freddie. I'm not pulling out. I'll beat the bastard with one fucking hand.'

'It's not the way to tackle a big fight, my son. Twelve rounds is a long time when you're fit, let alone firing on one cylinder.'

'I'm fit. And I won't need twelve rounds.'

'It's your choice. You'll pass the doc, okay. But I think we need some insurance.'

'What's that, then?'

'Insurance, my son, bit of protection. In short, painkillers. Injections. It'll keep the pain off. Deaden it, at least.'

'Sounds good.'

'One problem, my son – the drug test. You know, the piss sample you give after title fights? It could show up.'

'That's out, then. I'm not gonna be stripped of the title. Stick your painkillers.'

'Not so hasty, my son. There's a way around it. It's been done before. Just takes a bit of practice and a lot of nerve.'

'Tell me about it.'

'Okay, but no blabbing. Not even to your pals. Just between me and you, my son. If word gets out, we're both fucked.'

Thomson checked Willis's weight at nine o'clock, two hours before the official weigh-in. Eleven stone one pound.

'Shit! That's what I feared.' Sniff. 'I'll ring Ron, get him to open the gym. C'mon.'

Brown met them at the Friar gym at nine thirty.

'Johnny's never been overweight before. What's happened?'

'Knocked his hand up weeks ago. Bound to affect his training.' Thomson sniffed. 'It's only a pound. He'll skip it off.'

An hour later, they left the gym for the ice rink and the weigh-in. It was a minute past eleven when they arrived. Greene was already there, pacing.

'You're late, Freddie. Where've you been?'

'Traffic.'

'Should've left in good time. I've been here since ten. You weren't in your rooms.'

'Went for a walk,' lied Willis.

Dillon was first on the scales. Wearing his tracksuit trousers and socks. Ten stone twelve pounds.

'Still not much more than a welter,' Mercer said to Brown. The trainer nodded.

Willis stripped to his briefs, inhaled deeply and stood on the scales. Ten stone thirteen and a half. Made it with half a pound to spare. There were cheers from a band of supporters.

'Go get him, Johnny.'

'Perfect,' said Mercer.

Brown nodded. I wish, he thought.

Boxing started at seven thirty. Willis, Thomson and Brown drove up in Greene's Bentley at eight. Greene had gone to the arena at six. Hundreds were milling around the ice rink entrance. Cars jammed the streets. The car park attendant raised the barrier, admitting the Bentley and Graham, the burly chauffeur, eased the car into their reserved space at the rear of the arena.

Brown banged on the tradesman's entrance. Inside, they turned right. Graham led the way, shouldering through the incoming spectators. Brown and Thomson flanked Willis, shielding him from back-slapping supporters.

The locker room was a ladies toilet. A familiar tattooed character stood guard – one-time pub thug, now a member of the Willis security firm.

'Good luck, Johnny,' he said.

'Cheers, Tom.'

The trio settled into their improvised changing quarters and Graham headed for ringside. 'I'll let Mr Greene know you're here,' he said.

Five minutes later, Greene bustled in. 'Everything all right?'

'Sure, Michael,' said Willis. 'Saddam's released the hostages, ain't he?'

'What?'

'The world's not going so mad.'

'Ah, right!' His neck twitched. 'But Maggie's gone. Ousted for that John Major.'

'New champion, eh?' Willis grinned.

Greene allowed himself a weak smile. 'You could be right.' He sat down on a wooden chair next to his boxer. 'Seriously, how's the hand?'

'Feels good.' Willis made a fist. 'Good enough to take care of Dillon.'

Greene slapped Willis's thigh and stood up. 'Glad to hear it. I'll be back in an hour. Remember, Freddie, in the ring for nine thirty. First bell at nine forty.'

'Sure, boss,' Freddie sniffed.

Greene left. Brown cut and stuck lengths of one-inch adhesive tape on a mirror. Rolls of gauze, supplied by the Boxing Board, stood on a chair. Thomson told tattooed Tom not to let anyone in.

'Knock on the door if it's anyone important and wait for us to open it. Okay?'

Brown had everything ready to wrap Willis's hands. Thomson opened his holdall. He lifted out a red plastic box, opened it and withdrew a syringe.

'Let's get it done, my son.'

The roar that greeted Willis even drowned Queen's 'Another One Bites the Dust'. Spotlights danced around the darkened arena, sweeping over the excited crowd, who were on their feet, waving and chanting.

'Will-is, Will-is, Will-is.'

Two leggy girls in Bunny-style uniforms, carrying flags of St George, headed the parade to ringside. Then Greene, followed by Thomson. Willis's gloved hands on his trainer's shoulders, head bowed, wrapped in his crimson robe. Brown brought up the rear. Six security guards flanked the group.

Ahead, Dillon waited. Wearing a blue gown, head hooded in a white towel, shuffling his feet. His back was turned on Willis's entrance.

The lights flared as Willis ducked through the ropes and skipped into the middle of the ring, both hands pumping in short hooks. The crowd went mad. Dillon glanced over his shoulder, then turned back and smiled at his corner men. He'd seen it all before.

Willis went to his corner. Thomson offered him water but Willis shook his head. He looked down at ringside, saw Mercer, winked at Payne. Then he noticed a long black case in front of a dinner-jacketed official. The Lonsdale Belt's in there, he thought. Be round my waist soon. Fucking great!

Dillon was introduced. Cheers from the left, the Nottingham crowd. Willis still looked out into the arena. Not many empty seats. At the sound of his name, he spun round, right arm raised, to a cacophony of applause.

Thomson stripped Willis of his robe and passed it to Brown on the outside of the ropes. Greene leaned to whisper in his ear. 'Be lucky. It's your night,' then clambered out of the ring to sit in the front row.

The wiry, grey-haired referee called the boxers to him. Last minute instructions. Willis didn't take in a word. Dillon's head was bowed, avoiding eye contact. He was at least three inches shorter. They touched gloves.

'Seconds out…'

Brown fed him his watered mouthpiece as Thomson ducked through the ropes. He turned, leaned on the top rope.

'This is it, my son. Fucking enjoy it.'

Willis struggled to find his range. Dillon bobbed, weaved, backed off and scored with some quick but light jabs.

'Lack of sparring,' Thomson said to Brown. Neither took their eyes off the action. 'He'll get into it. Fucking hell—'

Willis was on all fours. The crowd was quiet, stunned. Then the Nottingham quarter found their voices.

'Yer've got 'im Gary! Gaa-ree, Gaa-ree.'

A short right uppercut-cum-hook had whistled under Willis's left lead, catching him flush on the chin, coming forward. He'd stumbled, clutching at Dillon's legs as he pitched forward.

What the fuck! What am I doing down here? How fucking embarrassing. In front of all these people, he thought.

Dillon went quickly to a neutral corner. The referee picked up the count from the timekeeper at 'three'. A second later, Willis was on his feet. Gloves rubbed clean on Grey Hair's white shirt.

Dillon moved in. Narrowed eyes of a gunslinger, shoulders rolling.

'On yer bike, Johnny,' Brown yelled from the corner.

Willis reacted. Swayed as if to move left but switched direction. Dillon was flat-footed. Willis walked along the ropes, out of distance. The bell!

The crowd buzzed as Thomson ducked into the ring. He doused Willis in water. Brown, outside the ropes, held the ice pack to his neck and removed the mouthpiece with his other hand.

'It's okay,' said Willis. 'I'm okay.'

Thomson looked deep into his eyes. Spoke quietly, matter-of-factly.

'Keep away from him. Find your legs. Jab. Get a rhythm.' He towelled Willis's face, pushing his damp black hair off his forehead.

Greene's neck twitch was working overtime as he looked up at the calm activity in the corner.

'Seconds out…'

'Gaa-ree, Gaa-ree.'

'Will-is, Will-is.'

Dillon stalked. Experience told him Willis had probably recovered from the flash knockdown. He'd been up quickly. Had a minute's rest. Still, apply pressure, keep him on the back foot.

First two rounds to Dillon.

Willis was still moving, circling, in the third. Found the range with his jab as Dillon rolled forward. Anchored his feet in the fourth to unleash a volley. Jab, right cross, left hook, all to the head. All landed. Got some respect.

His big right hand shook Dillon early in the fifth. Dillon's left eye closing. Solid jabs. Little coming back. Feeling good. Boom! Another right. Spot on.

After six, Willis was in front. Dillon now on the back foot. Breathing heavy.

Start of the seventh, left hook to the short ribs. Heard him gasp. Holding on. Feint to repeat body shot. Switch with hook to his ear. Rocked him. Jab. Jab. Knocked his head back. Jab. Now the big bang. Right shoulder turning, hip coming through. Total weight shift. Shit! That hurt, he thought. First real pain in the hand. Still, Dillon's down.

Thomson halfway up the ring steps. Count at six. Dillon crouching. Eight. Up he gets.

Got his hands high. Peering through. Left eye almost closed. Left hook thumps his ear. Right straight through the middle of his guard. He's staggering back into the ropes. Slumping. Left, right, left, left... white-sleeved arms grabbing hold, pulling. Finally lets go. Referee switches attention to Dillon, lolling on the ropes. Corner men in the ring.

It's over.

'Fucking champion!' Payne yelling at him, in the ring, grabbing and hugging. 'You're fucking champion, Johnny!'

Brown removed the mouthpiece. In the corner, Thomson grinned. Greene rushed up the steps. The crowd was on its feet, shouting, chanting.

The opened black case was pushed under the bottom rope into the ring. The Board inspector stooped to remove the Lonsdale Belt.

My belt.

Yes, Pete. Fucking champion!


Willis stood at the far end of the bar, Thomson at his side. He surveyed the room. People were enjoying themselves, celebrating his victory. His right hand was sore. From hitting Dillon, from innumerable handshakes.

'Awright, my son?'

'Never better, Freddie.'

'Hand okay?'

'Bit sore. Injection worked. Didn't feel it until the seventh.'

'Didn't give you too much.' Sniff. 'No problem with the test?'

'No, went a treat.'

'Good. Don't think it'll be the last time we work that trick. That's the trouble with you bangers, my son. Knock your hands up.'

Willis raised his tender right hand and waved. 'There's Mary, my sister,' he said.

Mary and Pete edged through the throng at the bar. Mary, in jeans and roll-neck sweater, slung her arms around Willis's waist and kissed his cheek.

'Well done, Johnny. I'm ever so proud of you.' Her eyes were dazzlingly warm.

'Cheers, sis. Did you watch it on TV?'

'Tried to, but I couldn't. Couldn't stay in the room. Kept going in the kitchen. But Ma watched. She's thrilled.'

'I'm Freddie.' Thomson held his hand out to Mary.

'Pleased to meet you. Johnny's told me a lot about you.'

'Nothing good,' said Willis.

'Why doesn't that surprise me?' he sniffed.

'You do tell fibs, Johnny. I've never heard you say—'

'Don't, sis. His head's big enough.'

'See, nothing good,' said Thomson.

Mary laughed. 'You're a matched pair, I can see that. Wow, Johnny. The belt, it's lovely. I couldn't believe it when Pete showed it me. Looks real classy. Expensive, isn't it?'

'Finest belts in boxing,' said Thomson.

'World title's worth more,' said Willis.

'Know what you mean, my son. Title's worth more but Lonsdale's the best belt. By far.'

'Where did you put it?' asked Willis.

'Ma's got it in her room. She's really proud.'

Before Willis could speak again, Payne joined the group, handing Mary a glass of white wine. 'Cheers, Johnny.' He raised his pint of lager. 'Didn't know you were buying all the drinks.'

'Just this once.'

'What?' said Freddie. 'And all I get is a tonic water? After all I've done for you.' He raised his voice. 'Landlord. Mine host. Double gin over here, my son.'

The group laughed. Willis, turning to nod at landlord Doug Jones, noticed a raven-haired girl at the opposite end of the bar. She smiled at him.

'Hang on. Be back in a minute,' he said. He walked towards her. People stood aside, offering congratulations as he passed. 'Thanks,' he said. 'Thanks a lot.' Eventually he reached the girl.

'How are you, Shirl?'

'Fine, Johnny, fine.' Shirley Collins's distinctive, husky voice. 'Didn't know you were having a party here. Thought you'd be at The Casino. That's your hangout, isn't it?'

'Go there a bit. But this little pub's just fine. Guv'nor's on our books. You know, the security business. And he sells a lot of my fight tickets, He's a good man.'

'Well, he won't need security tonight, will he?'

Willis glanced around the room. 'Right, most of 'em are here,' he agreed. 'What brings you in?'

She chuckled. Throaty. Sexy. 'Believe it or not, I went to the fight. Gang of us from work. They're over there in the corner. You didn't work with us for long, but they remember you. You're a star, after all. Anyway, one of the lads said they usually serve a late one in here. So, here we are. I'm just getting a round in.'

'Put your money away. Drinks are on me,' he said.

'No, it's all right.'

'I insist. For old times.'

'Old times. Makes it sound a lifetime ago.'

'Five years or so, Shirl. Must say, you've not changed much.'

'Come off it, Johnny. Look at me.' She stepped back a pace, drawing open her long leather coat. Black tailored trousers. Dark sweater, V-neck exposing the swell of her breasts. 'I've put weight on. Least a stone.'

'You look well on it.' His eyes lifted from her chest to the pools of her violet eyes.

Shirley let the coat close around her. 'I do believe you're turning into a bit of a gentleman, Johnny Willis. There's hope for you yet.'

'There's always hope, Shirl. Can't give up on hope, can we?'

'Suppose not. But – no.'

'What?'

'I was pretty low on hope once. Remember?'

Willis nodded. 'Guess so.' He paused. 'Tell me, what happened? I mean, I got your card. At Wembley.'

'Hah!' She smiled. 'Thought you might have asked before now. You know, after you'd won that ABA title.'

Willis shrugged. 'Didn't seem to matter then. You know, everything was all right. No baby, like. And I didn't think you'd want to know me any more.'

'Johnny, Johnny,' she said, almost under her breath and shook her head slowly. 'I loved you.' She paused. 'Ah well, that was then.'

Silence.

'Well?' he said.

'Well what?'

'What happened?'

'The baby, you mean? I miscarried.'

'Shit! I'm sorry.'

'Probably for the best, wasn't it?'

'Couldn't have been nice.'

'No, it wasn't.' Shirley's eyes misted over. She sighed. 'At least I was on the toilet. Happens a lot, apparently.'

Willis took her left hand. 'I am sorry. Really.'

'I guess you just might be.' She stared into his face. 'You know something?'

'What?'

'Your nose is broader.'

They laughed. Willis pulled her to his chest, putting his left arm around her shoulders.

'Reckon it'll get flattened some more before I'm finished,' he said.

'Willis!' A smoky voice barked across the room. 'Put her down. She's supposed to be getting the drinks.'

'You always was an impatient bugger, Sid.' He released Shirley and joined the supermarket crowd. 'Good to see you all.'

'Good fight, Johnny,' said Sid, his flat cap pushed back on his head. Stock controller for twenty years, he was nearing retirement. 'You had us worried in the first.'

'Don't remind me. I just wanted to get up before anyone saw me.'

The supermarket crowd laughed.

'Still,' said Shirley, putting a tray of drinks on the table. 'All's well that ends well. That right, Johnny?'

He looked at her, smiling coquettishly up at him.

'Guess you could say that,' he replied.

# Chapter Fifteen

Christmas morning. Crisp with a pale sun. Willis jogged into Johnson Close wearing a black tracksuit, trainers and a woollen bobble hat pulled over his ears.

He sprinted the last hundred yards and at the gate to number 36, he inhaled deeply and looked around. Unkempt gardens, drab brick houses with faded curtains. Battered cars, one standing on house bricks. What a shit'ole, he thought. Happy Christmas!

Inside the house, a cassette of carols played in the back room.

'That you, Johnny?' came the voice from within.

'It's not Santa Claus, Mary.'

Mary sat at the table, eating toast and drinking tea. 'Had a good run?' she asked.

'Yeah. Nice morning. Cold but dry. Didn't see a soul.'

'Well, it is Christmas morning. Want a tea?'

Willis pulled off his bobble hat and ran a hand through his damp locks.

'Yeah, then I'll have a bath. That's if Ma's not in there. Or is she still in bed?'

'No,' said Mary, pouring tea into a mug. 'She's in the kitchen. Preparing dinner.'

'What? You've gotta be kidding me.'

Mary smiled and placed the mug before him as he sat down. 'She's been in there about half an hour. She says I've got to do nothing. It's her treat.'

'Amazing, bloody amazing. Not before time, mind.' He took a gulp of tea. 'Surprised she knows where the pots and pans are. Can she cook?'

'You really are blinkered, Johnny. Ma's always cooked. You've forgotten, or perhaps you don't want to remember. Selective memory.'

'I remember a few times. Not many. Anyway, I'm glad you're having a rest for once.' He got up. 'I'll have a bath, then.'

'Do me a favour, Johnny. Be a bit nicer to Ma. She's trying, you know.'

'So you say.' He paused at the door. 'I'll do my best.'

'Thanks.'

Dinner was a quiet affair. Just the three of them. The absent Kenny and Colin were in their thoughts.

'The screws all wanted a look at my belt. Even asked for my autograph. Cheeky bastards!' said Willis.

'I thought Col looked a bit thin,' said Connie.

Willis was surprised. 'When did you see him?'

'Last week. And Kenny. He seems okay.'

'Didn't know you'd bothered to visit.'

'Ma's been lots of times. We both have,' Mary said.

'Lots?'

'Twice a month.' Connie placed her knife and fork on her empty plate. 'That wasn't half bad,' she said.

'It's lovely, Ma. Turkey's done to a treat,' said Mary.

'All right for you, Johnny?'

Willis nodded, chewing his last Brussels sprout. 'You've done well, Ma. Thanks.'

Mary smiled.

Christmas night. It was raining. Willis offered another can of lager to Payne as Mary, in the kitchen, piled cold turkey sandwiches and sausage rolls on plates and Connie slept in a chair in front of the television.

'Just time for this one,' Payne said, taking the can, 'Got a taxi booked for twelve thirty.'

'Why don't you stop over? There's a spare bedroom.'

'Mary suggested that. But I told Mam and Dad I'd be spending Boxing Day with them. If I stay over, it'll probably be lunchtime before I get home.'

Mary brought in the plates of food.

'Look at that lot. You trying to make me into a heavyweight? I'll have to go for another run in the morning,' said Willis.

'You've got nothing else to do.' Mary handed a plate to Payne. 'Anyway, it gives you something to train on.'

'Trouble is, sis, I'm struggling to keep my weight at eleven stone. I haven't been in the gym since winning the title. It's gonna be hard work.'

'You'll get it off.' Payne bit into a sandwich. 'Got anything fixed?'

'No. Spoke to Michael on the phone two days ago. He's looking for something in February; a ten-rounder at the Albert Hall.'

'Got more than a month then.'

'I'll need it. Must be over twelve stone now. Can hardly do up my jeans.'

'Lie on the bed and do them up.' Connie stirred in her chair. 'That's what we women do. S'easier that way. Anyone want a tea?'

'I'll get it, Ma.'

'No, Mary, you sit still. You've got supper already. I was gonna do that.'

'You've been on your feet all day. No wonder you fell asleep.'

'That's the warm fire and boring telly. They never put anything good on.' She walked towards the door. 'Have you told Johnny your news?' she added.

Mary and Pete looked at Connie and then each other.

'Guess not,' said Connie. 'Better tell him now, then.' She headed for the kitchen.

'What news?'

'Mary and me. We're getting engaged,' Pete said.

Willis looked from one to the other. 'Engaged?'

'That's right. Engaged.' Mary brushed a crumb off her chest. 'Aren't you gonna congratulate us?'

'Engaged,' muttered Willis. 'Well, I never. Of course,' he said, putting down his plate and standing. He bent to kiss his sister and offered his hand to Payne. 'Congratulations. Well done, Pete, old pal. When you doing the deed? Giving her the ring an' that?'

'Soon as your mam comes back in.'

'I'm here.' Connie walked over to Mary. 'Give us a kiss, Mary.'

Payne pulled a small box from his jeans pocket. He opened it to reveal a cluster of diamonds surrounding a sapphire.

'You've gotta ask her properly,' said Willis. 'Down on one knee.'

'He's done that already,' said Connie. 'Weeks ago. Before your title fight.'

'That right? Why didn't you tell me?'

'Mary didn't want to bother you.' Payne slipped the ring on his fiancée's finger. 'Said you should concentrate on the fight.'

Mary held her hand out in front of her. The jewels sparkled under the Christmas tree lights. 'Like it, Ma?' she asked.

'It's a lovely ring. I hope you'll both be very happy.'

'Yeah,' said Willis. 'Hope you'll be happy. Jeez. That means you'll be getting married.'

Mary laughed. 'That's the general idea.'

'When?'

'Not for some time,' said Payne. 'Summer after next, maybe.'

A car horn sounded outside. Payne looked at his watch. Twelve twenty.

'Probably my taxi. Bit early,' he said.

'I'll have a look.' Willis walked to the front door and opened it. 'Yeah, Pete. Taxi's here.'

Payne kissed Mary goodnight on the lips, and kissed Connie on her cheek. Willis walked with him down the path towards the taxi.

'Well, that was a fucking surprise. I knew there was something between you two. But engaged!'

'She's a lovely kid. I'm a lucky fella.'

Willis put an arm around his pal's shoulders.

'She's in good hands.' He paused. 'Have you, you know, have you two – no, don't tell me. I shouldn't ask. Look, you're a good bloke. Take care of her. She means the world to me, you know that.'

'And to me.'

'Yeah, sure. Just don't do anything to hurt her. Okay? Know what I mean?'

In the wet, under the shadowy gloom of the streetlight, Payne looked at his friend's stern face.

'I know,' he said.

'Good,' said Willis, grinning a big white-toothed smile. 'That's okay then. See you later, Pete.'

Payne looked through the taxi window. Willis stood at the

gate. Mary on the doorstep. They all waved as the car drew away.

'Thanks, Johnny,' said Mary as Willis closed the door.

'Why thank me? I mean, it was a shock. I didn't know what to say. But I do hope you'll be happy. Really, I'm happy for you, for you both. I just told Pete that.'

'That's good. But I didn't mean that. I meant for being nice with Ma.'

Willis shrugged. 'It's Christmas.'

Julie O'Sullivan had a captivating smile. Generous mouth with very white, slightly protruding teeth. Big, blonde hair fell below her shoulders and her breasts, bouncy but firm, were high and proud.

And she was tall, about five foot nine in fishnet tights. Julie's legs, in fact, were mainly responsible for her height. They were long with strong, spectacular thighs. Willis noticed her legs first of all, between the fourth and fifth rounds.

He twisted on his stool to spit water into the bucket and a flash of fishnet thighs beneath a lemon pelmet skirt distracted him. He looked beyond Thomson and watched Julie strut away, hips swaying, tiny skirt flapping, barely covering her buttocks. His gaze didn't get above her waist.

Between rounds five and six, he noticed the shoes. Pink high heels. And, of course, the legs.

Come the interval between six and seven, he saw the blonde hair and white crop top. Bronzed midriff. Bet the legs are, too, he thought.

The smile got him in the next interval. As she passed by, arms aloft holding the round-eight card, she looked down at him, and smiled. Great white teeth. He watched the legs stride away. Knee crossing knee, foot crossing foot, exaggerating the hip swing.

In that round, he noticed her sitting ringside. She looked up at him as he bullied Miguel Martinez into the ropes. The Spaniard was ranked fourth in Europe, two places above Willis, but he was no bullfighter. Rather meek, in fact, ultra defensive. Willis had long been bored with the fight. Now he leaned on the Spaniard and looked at Julie's crossed legs. What heavenly thighs, he thought. Get between them, my son, as Freddie would say.

He missed her next circuit as Thomson crowded over him.

'C'mon, Johnny. Step on the gas. You can stop this guy. He's a patsy.'

Then, as Julie approached, Brown's hand came across and smeared Vaseline into his eyebrows. Blast!

Martinez took a count in the ninth – a breather really – then back-pedalled to see out the remaining fifteen seconds.

It was busy in Willis's corner before the last round. Waistband pulled off his stomach, more grease on the eyebrows. Towel rubbed on the chest, mouthpiece in. He looked across at the Spaniard, saw his tired legs stretched out between his cornerman's stance. And Julie, right leg lifting over the middle rope then the left leg. She walked down the steps, draped a jacket over her shoulders and sashayed up an aisle. Job done for the night.

A little over three minutes later, the Albert Hall crowd warmly applauded Willis. Not an explosive night, but a clear winner. Nine rounds with one drawn. Good enough for a move up the European rankings.

Fifty minutes after that, Willis joined Greene in the sponsors lounge. Media interviews over, he was showered and dressed in black slacks, a red sports shirt and black leather jacket.

Greene worked the room, introducing Willis briefly to the money people. Overweight, most of them, with perfumed women in tow of various shapes and ages. Some wives. Some, well, who knows?

Eventually, Greene finished touting him around the small room.

'Have a drink with Freddie and Ron at the bar,' he said. 'You've earned it. Good win. The Spaniard's no mug.'

'Cheers, Michael.' The Spaniard was a mug, he thought. 'I'll have an orange and be off. I'm whacked.'

'Sure, I'll speak to you later.'

He made slow progress across the crowded room. People congratulating, requesting signatures on programmes. Willis was polite, obliging but, inwardly, wanting out of there.

'Excuse me.' His path was blocked. Cerise shirt, blonde hair below her shoulders.

'Sor-ree.' Light London accent. She turned and smiled a

generous smile. Willis was rooted to the spot. But his brain and mouth operated.

'You're the ring girl, aren't you?'

'That's right.' She faced him squarely. 'And you're Johnny Willis. Couldn't help seeing you but I'm surprised you noticed me. Thought you'd be occupied out there.'

'Not all the time,' he smiled. Good smile, but it couldn't compete with hers. 'Anyway, you know my name. What's yours?'

'Julie.'

'Pleased to meet you, Julie.'

He offered his hand. She switched an empty wine glass to her left hand and they shook, her delicate soft palm lost in Willis's broad grip.

'Would you like another?' He took the glass.

'I was just saying goodnight to Katie here.'

Willis looked at Julie's companion. Dark hair, cut around her jawbone, green eyes. And much shorter.

'Hi,' said Willis.

'Hi. I'll be getting off then, Julie. See you around. Bye.'

'What about that drink?' he asked.

'Why not?'

Willis led the way to the bar, avoiding his two trainers and ordered white wine and an orange juice.

'You must be one of Gillian's girls.'

'That's right. I'm on her books. How'd you know?'

'Michael wouldn't use outsiders. Keeps business in the family.'

'Michael? Oh, Gillian's husband. The whatsit, promoter.'

'That's him. My promoter, in fact.'

'Right.' She sipped the white wine. 'I've only been with her for three months. First time I've done ring work. Bit scary, all those blokes.'

'You didn't look scared.'

'You know how it is. All show. Big smile and wiggle your bum.'

'I noticed.'

'You did? When you've got a bloke trying to beat your brains in? I find that incredible.'

'Sometimes it's hard to keep concentrating. You sort of switch off. Go on automatic pilot. Honestly, some fights I don't know what round it is.'

'Really? Amazing.'

'But I knew tonight.'

'You did? Why?'

Willis grinned. 'You helped.'

'Oh.' She covered her mouth with a hand. Coy, innocent but her eyes were flirting. 'You must think I'm thick. I mean—'

'No, not at all. Far from it. Most people wouldn't understand what goes through a boxer's mind in a fight.'

'Suppose not.' She took another sip and placed her glass back on the bar. 'And what went through your mind tonight?'

'Truthfully?' He was stalling. Is she for real, or what? he thought.

'Truthfully.'

'I thought I'd ask Michael who you were.'

'I see.' Another sip left a pink lipstick smear on the glass. 'Well, now you don't have to ask him.'

'True. So I'll ask you.'

'Ask away.'

'For a start, Julie what?'

'O'Sullivan.'

'What's that, Irish?'

'Was originally. My great-grandfather came to England years ago. Since then most of us have been born around London. I'm from Paddington.'

'Don't know the area. Railway station. That's about it.'

'Right. Paddington Bear, eh? Well, there's the waxworks. And the Planetarium. But it's a dump, really. I want to get out of the place. Live somewhere better.'

'Like where?'

'Oh, I don't know. You name it – Chelsea, Knightsbridge, Crouch End. But that takes loads of money. It's just a dream. Anywhere would do for now. Just not Paddington.'

'How about Islington?'

'Islington? Hmm. Some nice places around there. Never thought about it.' She paused. 'Where d'you live?'

'Westhampton. The Midlands. But, when I'm down here, Islington.'

That generous smile again. 'Ah! I see. You're not inviting me to see your etchings, are you?'

Willis saw Thomson wave and point at his watch. Time to go.

'I don't have any etchings but you're certainly welcome any time,' he said.

He lifted his left hand, palm facing Thomson. Julie turned her head and saw Thomson and Brown looking across at them.

'They were with you in the ring.'

'In the corner. My trainers. Freddie, the tall one, he's driving. Wants to go.'

Julie looked at her watch. It was nearly one and the room was emptying.

'Time for us all to go, I think.'

'Do you want a lift?'

'No, that's all right. Wouldn't want to trouble you or your friend. Besides, I can take a cab. All expenses paid, this job.' Big smile.

'If you're sure.'

'Positive, thanks. I'll get my gear and be off. Been nice talking with you. You're not like I imagined a boxer would be.'

'That right?'

'Yeah. Thought boxers were all hard. Brutal. Know what I mean? But you're a sweetie.' She lifted a hand to his cheek and kissed his lips, briefly but firmly. She turned to leave, wiggling her fingers goodbye at him.

'Perhaps we'll meet again some time.'

She half turned. 'I'd like that.'

On impulse he asked, 'How about tomorrow?'

Julie returned to the bar and requested pen and paper from the barman. 'Here, my number. Call in the morning. Not before ten, though. Must get some beauty sleep.'

Willis took the paper, kissed her lips again and watched her hips wiggle towards the exit. Peachy!

Julie wasn't on duty in late March when Willis dispatched New Yorker Vince Sheldon in five lopsided rounds. But she was at the

Manchester ringside, in the guest section. And Willis had a double bed at the hotel.

At Willis's special request, she was working when he returned to the Albert Hall on the fourteenth of May. It was, after all, his twenty-fourth birthday and Julie was a significant part of his celebration plans.

It was a low-key fight. Not even top of the bill. Ugly Gary Smith had that honour for his European bantamweight challenge. Won it, too. Another champion for the Greene stable.

Willis faced Ray Petersen in a ten-rounder. Sellers had not renewed his contract with the Southern Area champion. Although rated at number seven for the British title, Petersen was considered on the slide. He had accepted the fight because the money was good. And Greene promised a title shot if he put up a decent show. The promoter told Willis a different story.

'It's just a warm-up for the European title. You've been nominated as number one challenger. Two months and you'll have another championship.'

So Willis trained hard and weighed in exactly on the match stipulation of eleven stone three pounds.

Mercer wrote that Willis should halt Petersen and go on to his European challenge. The publicity of the impending title fight prompted an invasion of Westhampton fight fans to the capital. They'd cheer on their local hero, not just against Petersen but to conquer Europe.

Petersen was spirited from the start. It was his big chance. He crowded Willis, refusing to concede an inch. Willis rammed his jab into Petersen's face but the veteran shrugged them off. He was teak-tough, for the first two rounds.

In the third, Willis landed heavily and consistently with right hands. Petersen didn't step back but he fell increasingly into clinches. Towards the end of the round, Petersen ducked inside a jab and his head crashed clumsily into Willis's face. Blood!

Willis blinked, his vision blurred. Wiped his left eye with a gloved thumb. Petersen jabbed at the cut. Willis pulled him in close and turned his head, keeping the injury away from Petersen's head. The bell rang.

Thomson applied a swab, soaked in adrenaline chloride 1:1000 solution. Pressure staunched the blood flow. Outside the ropes, Brown leaned in to towel down Willis's blood-spotted chest and offered the water bottle.

Willis sensed Thomson's concern. 'Is it bad?'

Thomson was calm as he pressed a fresh swab to the eyebrow. 'Watch his head. Keep your distance,' he sniffed.

Confirmed. It was bad. Shit!

Thomson wiped grease along the undamaged right eyebrow and removed the swab. No trickle of blood.

Willis didn't hear the ten-second warning to the cornermen. He certainly didn't notice Julie as she strode by. She wore her professional big smile, but inside, was concerned.

But she couldn't see Willis. Thomson and Brown blocked her view.

Petersen had a target. He fired a jab. Willis, head moving, felt it slide through his hair and responded with a left hook to Petersen's ribs.

'On yer bike, Johnny,' shouted Brown from the corner.

'Jab, Ray, jab,' came from Petersen's corner.

Another minute safely negotiated. No blood. Freddie's done a good job. Bollocks! He's done it again, Willis thought.

The referee stepped in. 'Watch your head, Petersen.'

Willis blinked as blood again seeped into the corner of his eye. Bastard nutted me on purpose, he thought. Stiff jab stopped Petersen's advance and a right hook straightened him up. Left hook missed. Clinch. Break!

Referee looked at the blood flowing. 'Time out,' he shouted to the timekeeper and led Willis to his corner. 'Clean it,' he told Thomson.

Thomson, already on the ring apron with a towel, pressed it on Willis's eyebrow, just for a few seconds. The referee peered up close.

'S'okay ref,' said Willis. Don't fucking stop it, he thought. There's a European title fight at stake here.

'Okay.' Referee turned and pointed to timekeeper. 'Box on.'

The crowd roared as Willis shook Petersen with a combination. Left hook off a jab and following right. Jeez. Fucking hand! That's all I need, he thought. He bit hard on his mouthpiece. Jab.

Jab. Sloppy left hook. Willis paid for it with a smack on the eye. Brown shouted, 'On yer bike, Johnny. Get away, fer Chrissakes.'

Thomson joined in. 'Jab and move, jab and move.'

From Petersen's corner, 'Beautiful, Ray, beautiful.'

Greene's neck twitched as Petersen landed another jab. It's all going wrong. Yet another jab. Willis was blinded by his own blood. Referee stepped in to send him back to the corner again. The crowd was buzzing.

'Stop it, ref,' yelled Petersen supporters.

The referee called up the doctor. Shit! This is bad, thought Willis. The crowd was now almost silent as the doctor dabbed the eye with a gauze pad. He shook his head.

'Sorry son.' The referee turned, waving his arms and raised Petersen's hand as his supporters cheered. The rest of the crowd howled and groaned.

Willis slumped on his stool as Thomson applied another swab. Greene came up the steps. Julie put the round-five board back in the pack. Mercer closed his notebook. Payne left ringside, heading for the changing rooms. Spectator Sellers sat, a wry grin on his face. Who'd have thought it? There's your luck! he thought.

Petersen came across. 'Bad luck,' he said. Willis didn't look up. Petersen turned to Greene. 'Don't forget your promise.'

The promoter steered him away. 'You'll get your shot.'

Willis accepted warm applause as he trudged back towards the dressing room. What a fucking birthday!

## Chapter Sixteen

Greene faxed the European Boxing Union in Rome with a plea. Willis's first defeat, after twenty-seven wins, had been on a cut, caused by a clash of heads. An accident. Willis should not be denied his European championship bid.

Early in June, the EBU nominated another challenger. Willis was to meet the winner, if he won his next contest.

It was all the promoter could expect. Willis, having had four-teen sutures in his wound, was satisfied. One more fight. One more win. Not too much of a delay. It could have been worse.

Three days after the Petersen defeat, he went home. By then his face didn't look too damaged and Mary was relieved.

'Ma watched it on TV. She said it was bad. Lots of blood. But it doesn't look so bad.'

'It'll be all right. Doc's done a good job. Few weeks of rest and it'll be healed, good as new.' Hopefully, he thought.

Connie, home from work, was surprised to see her son. Willis was even more surprised when she hugged him and kissed his cheek, surprised that he even let her. He couldn't remember her ever doing it before. Mary was pleased, for both of them.

After three days, Willis returned to London. He'd make the most of his enforced break. Enjoy himself, rest, relax.

Julie had an all-over tan. A sunbed tan. A bronzed goddess in a tiny turquoise bikini, stretched out on the beach at Newquay, she was even more delicious spread out on white hotel sheets, naked.

Willis's swarthy skin turned a deep brown watching the surfers on Fistral Beach. Five lazy days. The hottest, sunniest days of the summer, as it happened.

Benny, Terry and Arty gave him a warm welcome at the dogs. And two winners.

'Missed you, John,' said Benny. 'Not seen you since your

fight. Bad luck, that.'

'Yeah. Bit of a blow.'

'So, what've been up to?'

'Not a lot. Had a bit of a holiday.'

'Anywhere nice?' It was Terry.

'Newquay.'

'Never been there. Southend, Brighton in the old days. Spain's the place now – Marbella. Well, Fuengirola, really.'

'You ought to try it,' joined in Arty. 'We can fix you up. Know people out there who'd be happy to put you up.'

'Thanks. I'll remember that.'

Mandy was delighted to see him. She was wearing a light, flowery summer frock, cut low at front and back. Bare legs in low-heeled white slingbacks.

In the car, heading for Islington, she said, 'I'm not wearing any knickers.'

Willis kept his eye on the traffic but his left hand slid along her inner thigh. 'Naughty girl.'

In the flat, she kicked off her shoes and stepped out of the dress. Ten frenzied minutes later, she rested her head on Willis's tanned chest.

'You're nicely brown,' she observed.

'Had a few days at the sea. Newquay.'

'I could do with a holiday, somewhere really warm.'

'Why don't you go, then?'

'No one to go with.'

'Aah, poor baby.'

'It's true. My pals are either married, poor sods, or knocking about with fellas.'

'Where would you fancy?'

'Spain. There's places I can stay.'

'That's funny. Some guys I know said they could fix me up in Spain. Let me think. Where did they say…'

'Fuengirola?'

'Yeah, that's it. How'd you guess?'

'Benny. He's my brother.'

'What?'

'Yeah. He's ten years older than me. I musta been a surprise.'

She kissed his chest. 'Shall we go? Could be fun. You and me in the sun.'

The villa sprawled in the hillside. In enclosed grounds, the red roof and white walls were barely visible behind wrought iron gates. A figure-eight azure pool dominated the rest of the property.

Alec was in his fifties with a sun-bleached thatch of fair hair, white moustache and leather skin. Crows feet around his eyes from squinting in the sun. He had a small paunch in his shorts but, otherwise, he was fit. He greeted Mandy like an uncle.

'You're looking as gorgeous as ever, Mand,' he said as they hugged and kissed. 'How's Benny? Well, I trust.'

'Just fine, Alec. He's sent something for you. It's in my case.'

'That's Benny. Always sending gifts. And you're Johnny, the boxer.' He shook Willis's hand. 'Seen you fight. Wonderful this satellite TV. Keeps me up to date with things back home. Come and meet the missus.'

In a lounger by the pool, Yvonne looked twenty years younger than Alec. Tanned, midnight hair, she wore shorts and bikini top, dark glasses with Spanish gold at throat and wrist. But no wedding ring.

They were perfect hosts. Breakfast on the patio, drinks at the poolside, salad lunches and barbecues in the evening. Always people popping round. Other Londoners. Talking about the old days. People they knew. What they got up to. Cops and robbers stuff. Old Bill and blags. But this was the life now. Who needs dirty old, rainy London? Even the English papers are printed here. Same-day news.

Sometimes they went to restaurants and met friends. Always in a group. Four, five hours at the table, with plenty of food, wine and gossip. Mandy beamed at Willis's side. When the bill came, the men generously peeled off pesetas and tossed them on the table. Except Willis. He wasn't allowed.

'You're guests,' said Alec. 'Mandy's almost family. We're happy to have you here. Ain't that right, Von?'

'Course, Alec. You young 'uns enjoy yourselves.'

So the week disappeared in a social whirl. Relaxing by the

pool, Alec relating old fights he'd seen, quizzing Willis about the modern game and about Michael Greene.

'Come up quick, ain't he?' he asked. 'Knocking old Jacobs off his perch. Had to happen some day.' He told Willis he'd been in Spain nearly ten years. Been in cars and clubs but sold the lot and come out here. Best move ever.

The last night, Mandy packed their cases and put a bulging jiffy bag in hers, from Alec to Benny.

'What's that?' asked Willis.

Mandy straddled him. 'Betting money,' she said hurriedly, pelvis grinding. 'Alec likes a flutter on the dogs.'

'Your brother's lucky at the dogs.'

'Usually. Depends what I hear.'

'You?'

'Yeah. When Albert's talking to the trainers, sorting out the card. Amazing what you can pick up.'

So that's how it works. 'Gotcha. Inside info.'

Mandy nodded. Eyes closed, rhythm increasing. 'You've got it,' she panted. Then, leaning forward, whispered in his ear. 'Kiss my tits.'

How could he refuse? One good turn deserved another.


Mary was excited. She'd never been to London. Now she was pulling up outside her brother's flat, in his new silver Mercedes. Pete couldn't get away from The Casino. But celebrating her twenty-first birthday in London with Johnny would still be a special weekend.

Willis gave Mary a quick tour of the flat. Just a look. They wouldn't stay long. He'd booked two rooms in a central hotel, off Trafalgar Square.

'More convenient,' he said.

Friday night they ate expensively in a French restaurant, then on to Ginny's club. Natalie and three friends joined them – two dancers he'd met before and Samantha, a statuesque platinum blonde, who was a new face. A pretty face at that and sexy in a crop top and lycra cycling pants.

Mary eased into the company. 'Sorry about your brother,' she said.

'Yeah, thanks,' said Natalie. 'Bit of a bummer. But he's okay.'

The girls danced, all except Samantha. She sat with Willis.

'Natalie tells me you're a boxer. British champion. That's great,' she said.

Willis accepted the compliment with a smile. 'What about you? What d'you do?'

'Actress. Like Natalie.'

'Is that how you met?'

'Sort of. We've been in the same films but never worked together.'

'Sorry, I don't understand.'

'I only do girl-girl. Natalie's not into lesbian. So, I've never done a scene with her.'

'Gotcha. Never fancied men, then?' Willis wondered aloud.

Samantha tossed her blonde tresses and rested a hand on Willis's arm. Focused on his eyes.

'Oh yes, I've fancied men all right.' A finger lightly doodled on the back of Willis's hand. She suddenly withdrew it, leaning back. 'But men only want one thing. Brains in their groin. Because I'm in porn they think I'm easy. Well, I'm not.'

Pretty, but hard, thought Willis. She drained her wine glass and placed a hand back on Willis's arm.

'No offence meant.'

'None taken. It's your life. Do as you want.'

In silence, both watched the gyrating bodies as Samantha's finger again traced over Willis's hand.

'Want to dance?' she asked.

Three numbers later, they all returned to the table. The girls noisy, warm and breathless. Willis ordered champagne and toasted Mary at midnight. The girls sang happy birthday and kissed Mary's cheeks. She glowed. Not too much champers, though. Remember The Casino!

Ginny appeared, carrying another bottle.

'Here's to the most beautiful table in the room, And,' he said, turning to Willis, 'that includes you, too, darling.'

'You never give up, do you Ginny?' laughed Natalie.

'Ever the optimist, Nat.'

'Meet Mary,' said Willis. 'My sister.'

'Enchanted.' Ginny bowed and held her hand to his lips. 'Good looks certainly run in your family. I gather it's your birthday?'

'Yes.'

'Twenty-one,' said Willis.

'Congratulations, darling. That's a special one. I trust you've got something delightful planned, Johnny. Not just this visit to my humble little club.'

'Shopping and theatre.'

'Shopping! A girl's dream.' Ginny clapped his hands together. 'And the theatre! How wonderful.' Noel Coward would have winced at Ginny's performance.

Mary looked at her brother. 'The theatre? Oh Johnny, I can't. I haven't brought anything to wear.'

'That's what we're shopping for. Something special.'

'It's got to be a little black number,' said Ginny. 'Be perfect for you. Match your beautiful hair and those bewitching eyes. What d'you say, girls?'

They all agreed, noisily, enthusiastically. Mary blushed.

'Where will you go?' asked Samantha. 'I know some nice boutiques. I'll give you the addresses, if you like.'

'You could take them,' said Natalie.

'Yes,' said Willis. 'That'd be good.'

'You don't want me tagging along. It's your special day together.'

'I'd like you to come,' said Mary. 'You'll be able to help me pick something suitable. Please?'

It took three hours to find Mary's little black number. And a linen coat. Plus a trouser suit. And evening shoes. Two pairs, of course. All Samantha's suggestions. She also persuaded Mary to add black lingerie, bikini briefs and balcony bra with hold-up stockings.

'Superb. Ravishing.' Samantha admired Mary in the small cubicle. She decided on a similar set for herself, in purple, then protested when Willis paid for the lot.

'Our thanks for your help,' said Willis.

'Thank you.' She kissed his cheek and whispered. 'I'll think of you when I wear them.'

They went to a wine bar in Covent Garden. At five, Samantha kissed them both goodbye and waved down a cab.

'Enjoy yourselves. See you again,' she said.

'Nice girl,' said Mary. 'Are they all dancers?'

'No. She and Natalie are in films. Porno.'

'What? Well, I never! Such nice girls as well.'

'They are,' said Willis. 'Nice girls.'

Mary was breathtaking in her new outfit. Willis, neat in a light grey suit and sea-blue shirt, was proud. They dined in the hotel, fussed over by attentive waiters. Tickets had been left at the theatre box office, arranged by Michael Greene.

Michael and Gillian were waiting when they entered the private box. There were warm greetings and introductions. Gillian, in a dark flowing skirt and sleeveless top, was expensively perfumed.

'Lovely outfit,' said Gillian. Michael nodded his agreement.

'Birthday present from Johnny. He spoils me.'

'Bet it wasn't his choice. Men are useless when it comes to buying women's clothes.'

'But we're good at picking up the tab,' said Greene.

'Yes, darling,' Gillian touched her husband's arm. 'But we're worth it.'

At the interval, the women excused themselves to go to 'the powder room'.

'You're looking well, Johnny,' said Greene. 'Enjoyed your break? Freddie tells me you went to Spain.'

'Yeah. For a week. Very relaxing.'

'Mm.' His neck twitched. 'A word to the wise, Johnny. I gather you stayed with friends of Benny Carpenter?'

'S'right. D'you know him?'

'Of him, know of him. He's a regular ringsider. Point is, he's a bit dodgy. On the edge. Understand?'

'Think so. He acts the gangster, if that's what you mean. Him and his pals. I find them funny, really.'

'Well, believe me, he's not funny. He's serious business.'

'What're you saying?'

'Just be careful.'

Just then, the women returned.

'Careful, Michael?' said Gillian. 'What's Johnny got to be careful of?'

'His eye,' said Greene, his neck twitching. 'When he starts training again next week.' He smiled at Willis. 'Don't want any accidents, do we?'

'No, boss. Although I didn't plan on training next week.'

'You'll need to. You've had the best part of three months out. Seven weeks from tonight, you'll be fighting again.'

'Seven weeks?'

'That's right. And, looking at you, you've got some work to do before then. Lose a lot of weight, chubby chops.'

It was true. Willis was over twelve stone. 'I'll get it off. No problem,' he said.

'Good. Because it's a title defence. Return with Petersen. Okay?'

'Perfect. Then the European, eh?'

'Should be, all being well.'

'C'mon, you two,' said Gillian. 'Enough business for now. Second half's starting.'

Willis found it hard to concentrate on the stage. He thought about Petersen. Put the record straight, then go for the European. Michael sure worked quickly. And then there was Benny. Serious business? Dodgy? On the edge? I'll ask Freddie to tell me about him, he thought.

At the end of the show they went backstage to the crowded artistes' bar. Greene introduced Gordon Mitchell, a tall, middle-aged man, his trim beard flecked with grey. Something to do with the theatre management, Willis didn't quite catch what exactly, but he was friendly with the Greenes. He'd arranged the tickets.

'Enjoy the show?' There was a northern twang in his voice.

'Very good, thanks,' said Willis.

'Brilliant,' said Mary. 'The dancers were superb.'

'That's good. Karen – my daughter – will be pleased. She's one of them,' said Mitchell. 'In fact, here she is.'

Karen glided across the room, healthy blonde hair scraped back into a lengthy swinging ponytail. High breasts jutted under a baggy woollen jumper and black tights clung to athletic legs. She wore small, worn pumps on her feet. She went straight to Gillian with a beaming smile and planted air kisses on both cheeks.

'Wonderful show,' said Gillian. 'Are you enjoying it?'

'Certainly am.' That northern twang again. 'It's hard work with so many routines. You probably noticed, we're hardly ever offstage. But it's exciting. After all this time – it's four months now, you know – I still get a buzz. Hi, Michael.'

Greene kissed a proffered cheek.

'Meet Johnny Willis, one of my boxers. And his sister Mary. It's her birthday. Twenty-first.'

Karen shook hands with Mary. 'Happy twenty-first. Hope you're having a good one. I did. Just last month.'

She turned to Willis next. They held rather than shook hands. Karen had hazel eyes, a dainty nose and wide smile. Under a light tan, she had a clear complexion, scrubbed clean of stage make-up. She wore just a hint of pale pink lipstick.

'Hi,' she said. 'A boxer. Dad's into boxing.'

'Is that right?'

'Yes. He goes to a lot of shows. Perhaps he's seen you. Dad! Have you seen Johnny box?'

'Sure. A few times.'

'See, thought so. Are you any good?'

'Karen!' Her father came closer. 'He's a British champion.'

'Oh! That is good, then.' She looked down. 'But you've got gentle hands. I imagined boxers would have rough hands.'

Willis released his grip. 'It's the way we use them that's rough. It's not rough work, not like digging roads or hacking away down a mine. That's hard work. Hard on the hands. Boxing's quite a soft job, really.'

'Soft? How can you say that? Fighting's soft? I don't think so.'

'You get used to it.'

'But it must hurt. People hitting you, knocking you down.'

Willis shrugged. 'The idea's to hit, not be hit. I don't do too bad.'

Karen studied his face. Nice features, not at all battered. Handsome really; tall, dark and handsome, in fact. Warm brown eyes and a slight red scar-line in his left eyebrow.

'Perhaps I'll see you on TV some time.'

'Maybe. But you work at night as well.'

'I'll get Dad to video it.'

'Video what?' said her father.

'One of Johnny's fights.'

'If you like.' Then he turned to Willis. 'Michael's just been telling me you defend the title next month.'

'That's right.'

'Return with Ray Petersen. That was a bad cut.'

Willis automatically fingered the scar. 'Caught me with his head. One of those things,' he said.

'Didn't it hurt?' Karen was frowning.

'Not really. More of a nuisance. Bet you get worse dancing.'

'Eh?'

'It must be a strain on your ankles and knees. Don't you get twists and sprains?'

'Yes, sometimes, little twinges. But we wrap 'em up and soldier on. Unless it's too bad.'

'Exactly. It's the same with us. Soldier on. All part of the job.'

Karen pondered. 'Suppose so. You could put it that way.'

What an unassuming man, she thought. Not a braggart. Charming really. Quiet, reasoned – and dishy.

'Well, it's been nice talking to you, Johnny,' said Mitchell, offering his hand again. 'We must be getting home. The wife's down with flu.'

'Sorry to hear that. Flu can be nasty. Hope she gets better soon. Nice meeting you. And thanks for the tickets. It's appreciated.'

Mitchell nodded. 'Any time. Just ask Michael.'

'Bye then.' Karen's soft hand caught his again. Mary then received a nice smile. 'I like your dress. Real chic,' she said.

'Birthday present from Johnny. Lucky, aren't I?'

Mm, thought Karen, he's generous as well. She floated through the room alongside her father. Willis watched her go, talking up at her father, a big smile on her face. Willis couldn't hear the conversation.

'Johnny's nice,' she stated. 'Wouldn't think he was a boxer, would you?'

Mitchell smiled, indulgently. 'Seems a nice lad. Polite.'

'Handsome, too, Pops.'

'In a rugged way,' he agreed. I do believe she's smitten, he thought.

Three rigorous weeks later, Willis was down to eleven stone eight pounds. No boxing. Purely physical graft. Hammering the body back into fighting shape. Running and skipping for stamina, pounding the heavy bag, exercises ripping off the pounds, hardening his midriff.

Natalie went to Florida for a holiday and Julie had a calendar shoot in Jersey.

Willis made one Saturday night visit to the dogs.

Benny and his crew were not there. Gone to Spain, said Mandy. No winners. Willis lost a grand and was not happy. But Mandy stayed overnight. Took her doggie style. And stuff the dogs, he thought. Stay away till after the fight. Concentrate.

Occasionally, he found himself thinking of Karen. Nice girl, open, fresh. Like to meet her again, he thought.

Samantha phoned. She'd got his number from Natalie and invited him for dinner. She had an airy apartment in Chelsea with scatter cushions and white rugs on a polished-wood floor. High ceilings. After dinner, he needed the toilet. There was a huge black and white photograph inset into the bathroom door of Samantha, dressed in a basque, wielding a whip with a haughty look on her face. He sat on the pot looking at it. Peculiar.

On a widescreen TV, a video played of Samantha and a red-head performing. Interesting. She left him watching the recording and came back wearing the purple briefs and bra.

'Thought you might like to see your gift.' She paraded in front of him.

They lounged on the floor, kissing. Tongues. Touching, feeling, getting aroused.

'No,' she said abruptly, pushing him off. 'Sorry. Not tonight. Use the bathroom if you like.'

With that picture? Not likely.

'Give me time. Perhaps another night,' she said.

Perhaps, he thought, but not likely. Mixed-up bitch!

Kenny and Colin were released on the Monday before his

Saturday night fight in Manchester. They drove down to watch him train and slept overnight in his flat, on the floor. 'Luxury,' they laughed.

'There's a party on Sunday,' said Colin. Double celebration – our freedom, your victory. Ma and Mary have everything arranged.'

Willis handed them special ringside guest tickets.

At the weigh-in, they gave him the thumbs-up. Both boxers smack on eleven stone.

'He's looking mean,' Freddie told Brown. 'The rest has done him good. It won't last long.'

At the first bell, Petersen took centre ring, as he had in the first fight, but Willis met him there. Jab-jab-hook-jab-hook-cross. All thudded into Petersen's face. Willis was relentless. The veteran buckled and took a count, on one knee, as the round ended.

Repeated solid jabs had Petersen on the back foot. They also puffed and bruised his frowning features. He tried to hold, maul, but Willis shrugged him off. He was strong, contemptuous. A hook off the jab and a right cross split Petersen's nose into a nasty, jagged gash.

One minute into the third round came a jab, right cross, left hook combination which sent Petersen sprawling. Nose and left eyelid were bleeding, dripping on to the canvas. He got gamely to his feet, but tottered. The referee spread his arms.

Petersen lolled into the ropes, hands by his sides, his face pitifully masked in gore.

'Sorry, Ray,' said the referee.

Petersen spat his mouthpiece into a glove and grimaced. Thank Christ that's over, he thought. The kid's fucking good. Something different.

# Chapter Seventeen

Approaching midnight. Willis was ready to go. The media had left. Mercer said it was his best performance as a pro. Devastating, destructive, he'd later write.

Kenny, Colin and Payne had also departed, Colin driving. Only Willis and Brown remained in the stark dressing room. Brown finished packing the kit bags and fastened the clasps on the black case which held the Lonsdale Belt. Thomson was out in the arena with another Greene fighter. The final bout of a long night.

'Ready?'

'Think so.' Brown glanced around. Last check. Nothing left, just discarded hand-wraps, empty plastic water bottles. 'Let's go,' he said.

The door opened and Greene entered. The promoter had been in and out like the weather. Never settled, always on the move.

'Decent at last.' He looked at Willis in jeans, sweatshirt and leather jacket. 'Your new number one fan's been waiting outside for ages to see you.'

'Not now, Michael. I'm done in. Can't you make up some excuse? Me and Ron are going back to the hotel.'

'That's okay. You can give your fan a lift.'

'What're you talking about? You taking the piss? We just wanna get off, have a beer and get to bed.'

Greene had a hand on the doorknob. 'Don't think you'll mind.' He opened the door. 'C'mon. He's dressed now,' he said to someone outside.

Willis looked at Brown, exasperated. He looked back at the door as Greene stood to one side.

'Hi,' a voice said.

She stepped in. Suede jacket and tight tan trousers, long ponytail swinging as she looked around the room.

'Karen! What're you doing here?'

'I've got a week's rest from the show. First break in five months. I was going to watch the fight on TV, but Michael said to come up and I thought, "Why not?" So, I got a train and here I am.' She gave him a big smile.

Willis grinned back. 'Hope it was worth it.'

'Oh yes. Great. Different to the theatre crowd, though.'

'Just a bit. So, what're you doing now?'

'Michael said you might give me a lift back to the hotel. He's booked me a room for the night.'

'Sure. Okay, Ron?'

'Course.' He held out a hand to Karen. 'I'm Ron.'

'Sorry,' said Willis. 'Ron's one of my trainers. Looked after me since I was a kid. So high.' He held his hand out at his hip. 'This is Karen, Karen Mitchell. She's a dancer. From London.'

'A dancer,' said Ron. 'My daughters go to dancing class. They're twins, Angela and Lauren. Thirteen now.'

'What sort of dancing?'

'Tap and stuff. Got dreams of being in showbiz. Not ballet. They're not interested in that. Oh! You're not a ballet dancer, are you?'

'No,' she chuckled. 'Look at me – I'm much too heavy for that. I'm in musicals, mainly. Sometimes variety shows. Summer seasons, chorus work.'

'I've things to sort out,' said Greene from the door. 'I'll take Freddie back to the hotel. See you later, Karen.'

'Okay, Michael. Thanks for everything.'

'C'mon then, Ron,' said Willis. 'Let's be off.'

Brown drove Willis's Mercedes back to the hotel. In an alcove in the resident's bar, they settled in soft chairs. But Brown left after one drink for a lonely drive home.

'Nice guy,' said Karen. 'He must be doing well to have a Merc.'

Willis chortled, his eyes shining.

'What? What did I say that's so funny?'

'It's my car.'

'Oh. Why didn't you drive?'

'Not after a fight. I will tomorrow. Back to Westhampton. Bit of a party at home.'

'Celebrating your win?'

'Sort of.'

Why did I say that? he thought. 'Yes' would have done it. Now I've go to tell her. *My brothers are jailbirds.* What will she think of that? End of relationship before it's started? Stupid bastard. Ah well, here goes.

'It's a double party. My brothers, Kenny and Colin, they're just out of prison.'

Karen sat back and recrossed her legs, right over left. 'Prison? What for?'

'Robbery. A post office.'

'Oh dear.' She picked up her glass of Chablis.

'I'd better explain. If you want to know, that is.'

Karen studied his face. Saw he was earnest, concerned. Frightened, almost. And certainly handsome.

'Tell me,' she said softly.

For twenty minutes, he delivered a potted history of the Willis family. The story according to Johnny. He didn't seek pity. No, never. Just a bit of understanding. He fumbled and fudged at times, left some things out, like Shirley and the miscarriage. But he ploughed on, even admitting his part in the post office raid and how he'd avoided prosecution.

All the time, Karen was absorbed. Her emotions were mixed. Occasionally she asked questions, seeking clarification, reasons. She nodded or shook her head, sometimes sadly, sometimes in disbelief, horror even.

And so, he concluded, boxing was his way out. His chance to make something of his life, to be somebody.

'So, that's it. That's me. My life.'

Karen twiddled with her empty glass. Such a lot to take in, she thought. What a jumbled, crazy life. And what a complex person.

'Want another?' he asked.

'Pardon?'

'Another drink?'

'No, I don't think so. Thanks.'

Willis looked at his glass of lager, untouched. He felt like getting drunk. He'd unloaded his life story on this beautiful girl, warts and all. Why? What possessed him? He'd never done it before, not even with Mrs Riley. What was Karen thinking now? Looking for a way to get out of here, probably.

'I don't know what to say, Johnny.' She looked at him. 'It's not what I expected when I came up here.'

Willis, head bowed, chewed at his lower lip. Slowly he sat upright, hands clasped between his knees.

'I just thought you should know.'

'You did? Why?'

Good question, he thought. Best question in the world. Because, in searching his brain for the answer, Willis realised the truth.

'Because I like you. What I mean is, I'd like to get to know you. Does that make sense? I'm not good with words.'

'I understand.' She paused. 'You felt you had to tell me. Then I either accept you for what you are, where you're from, what makes you tick. The whole thing. Or,' and she paused again, putting down her glass, 'or I just walk away.'

Willis saw Greene and Thomson enter the bar.

'They're back,' he said.

Karen nodded. 'It's time I was getting to bed, anyway.' They looked into each other's eyes. Karen sighed. 'I really don't know what to say, Johnny. There's such a lot to think about. We've hardly met. Yet I came up here, just to see you. That must tell you something. But now... well, I just don't know.'

'You two want a drink?' said Greene from the bar.

'Not for me, Michael, thanks. I'm just off to my room.'

'What about you, Johnny?'

Willis looked at his glass. It was nearly empty now but he couldn't remember drinking any of it. He glanced at Karen as she started to stand up.

'One more,' he said, also getting up.

He offered his hand. She took it. 'Sleep well,' he said.

Her cheeks dimpled above a wry, tight-lipped smile. 'You too.' Then she kissed his cheek. 'Well done tonight. I don't just mean in the ring. Thanks for telling me. I guess it wasn't easy. But it was a decent thing to do.'

Willis said nothing. Didn't know what to say. He'd said enough. Now he watched as she walked away, waving to Greene and Thomson at the bar.

'Goodnight,' they chorused.

His gaze followed her all the way out of the room. You've fucked that up, he thought. Picking up his empty glass, he headed for the bar. But he didn't want to get pissed any more. Didn't even want the drink waiting for him.

He knew what he wanted. She'd just walked out of the room and probably out of his life.

The party was a success. People came and went all night through the ever-open door. Most carried drinks, cans, bottles, and were pleased to see Kenny and Colin. Many neighbours, grateful for past favours, the goods they'd acquired. They were good lads, really. And then there was Johnny. Boxing champion. Lonsdale Belt on display in his mother's room. He was a star.

The brothers had another reason to celebrate. Going legit, as Kenny put it. Johnny outlined his plan that afternoon. He'd supply the money; Kenny and Colin would be the workers. A joint venture. A building business.

Johnny's cash would buy a small lorry, mixer, tools and the rest. Property even. Convert them to flats, bedsits for students.

They knew enough people in the trade – plasterers, electricians, plumbers. And there's Ron, the decorator. Mary would keep the paperwork but they'd get a proper accountant and a separate bank account. Who knows where it might lead? Michael Greene did well with his Islington operation. A sideline for a millionaire. A business for us, thought the boys.

Connie's eyes had a bright light in them for the first time in years. Her boys were gonna make it. Johnny was already on the way, a champion, famous. And not short of money. Now Kenny and Colin could follow. No more prison. They would be businessmen! Now that is a reason to party! A real celebration.

Karen had slept fitfully in Manchester and had room service deliver breakfast. She was avoiding Johnny. She needed to think clearly. Not be distracted by his presence. And, dammit, she had to admit he was attractive.

Case against: a troubled past. Dysfunctional family. Crime.

Case for: it was two years since he'd been near trouble. He was making a success of his career, his life.

Returning to London in Greene's Bentley, she sat in the back with Greene. Thomson was in the front passenger seat.

'What d'you make of Johnny?' she asked.

A minefield question. 'He's ambitious,' said Greene. 'That's really all I need to know.'

'That's business,' said Karen. 'What I mean is, what's he like as a person?'

'Can't really say. I don't know him that well. But he's always polite in company. Presents himself well. Like that night at the theatre. I get the feeling that he somehow knows the right thing to say. It's a sort of streetwise sixth sense. But I couldn't say if that's the real him. Freddie might know better – he works with him every day. Freddie, what d'you think of Johnny?'

Thomson turned in his seat, pretending not to have heard the back-seat conversation. 'Told you before, Michael. Reckon we've got a winner. Could be world champion,' he sniffed.

'Didn't mean his boxing,' said Greene. 'Karen wanted an opinion on his character. What's he like? You work with him.'

'Difficult to say.' He twisted further in his seat, focusing on Karen. Nice looker, he thought. Must have the hots for Johnny. I mean, coming all the way to Manchester. I ask you, obvious or what?

'Why difficult?' asked Karen.

'I mean, we've got a working relationship and I like the kid. He's good to work with. No trouble. We've even had a few nights out, a few laughs. But that doesn't mean I know him.'

'Would you trust him?'

'Trust him?' Now there's a fucking question, he thought. Sniff. 'As much as I'd trust anyone. But, frankly, I'm not big on trust. Cynical, me. That's boxing for you.'

'I see.' She paused. 'Is he honest?'

Gor blimey! Trust? Honest? What questions!

'Don't think he'd tell you a lie. No, he's pretty straightfor-ward, is Johnny. But, as I say, I'm not really that close to him. Not personally. It's work. Daily contact. Know what I mean?'

'Thanks.' She smiled.

'S'okay.

Thomson turned back, staring at the motorway stretching before them. Johnny, you've got a live one here, he thought. Lucky bleeder!

Greene looked sideways at Karen as the Bentley swept into the outside lane.

'Okay?'

'Yes. Fine thanks, Michael.' Couldn't be better, she thought.

They walked hand in hand along Brighton's shingle beach. It was Tuesday, a mild, dry September day. Both in jeans and Karen in her sloppy sweater, Willis in a sports shirt.

'What will you do when you stop boxing?'

'Hard to say. I mean, it depends how well I've done. You know, how much money I've made.'

'Let's say you're comfortable. Rich, maybe. What then?'

'Wouldn't do a lot,' he laughed. 'It's been a lot of hard work so far, so I'd take it easy. Be a lazy sod.'

'But you'd have to do something. After all, you won't be very old, will you?'

'That's true.' He kicked at a pebble. Goal! Like a little kid again, scoring for his school team. 'I've got a few plans, few ideas.'

'Good. Such as?'

'Building. Property. That sort of thing.'

'D'you know anything about it?'

'Some. Well, quite a bit, really. Been looking into it.' He paused. 'In fact, we're gonna start soon.'

'We?'

'Me and my brothers. I'm putting up the cash. They're not really villains, you know. They're builders. Been doing it since they left school. Anyway, we're looking at starting a business. Only small, but it could grow.'

'Everyone has to start somewhere.'

It was getting chilly. They left the beach and found a café. Pot of tea, for two, and toast.

'Your brothers are lucky.'

'How's that?'

'Well, without you, they couldn't start a business, could they?'

Willis stirred his tea, thoughtfully. 'I know you must think we're a strange family,' he said. 'After what I told you the other night, I mean.' Karen said nothing. 'But we look after each other,' he added.

'That much I can see.' She scraped excessive butter off a piece of toast. 'You and Mary, for example. You're obviously close. And I guess what your brothers did – not letting you take any blame for the post office raid…'

'Thought we weren't gonna mention that again? You said so on the phone yesterday.'

'Yes, right, I'm sorry. But it's just another example, isn't it? How you look after each other. Now we won't talk about it again. Book closed.' She smiled.

'Nearly closed,' he said. 'Just one more thing. They've not had my luck. I'm the one getting out.'

'But you've worked for it. Fought for it—'

Willis reached across the small table for her hand and squeezed it.

'Let me finish. Like I told you, boxing's my way to get a better life. I want that for my brothers and sister as well. And, I hope you understand this, I feel I owe Kenny and Col. Starting a business could be the way. Don't forget, they'll be doing the work. It's up to them whether they make it.'

'Yes, I see that. You're giving them an opportunity.'

'That's it that, then.' He leaned back. 'Book closed, as you say.'

'Book closed.'

'Anyway…'

'What's this, a postscript?'

'Whatever… what I was gonna say is, if they make a success of it, so do I. It's a three-way partnership. Another way of making my money work while I don't. I'm not daft.'

They both laughed. That's better, thought Willis. Such a nice happy smile. She's gorgeous.

No, he's not daft, thought Karen. What a smile. Handsome devil.

Willis gritted his teeth. Sweat bubbled on his brow, soaked his vest. Push-ups. Sit-ups. On the reclining board. Thomson pummelling his midriff with a medicine ball. Skipping. In the sauna, wrapped in bin liners, swathed in jumpers and a tracksuit. Shower, dry off, onto the scales.

He didn't dare look.

'What is it, Freddie?' Greene was anxious.

'Hang on.' Thomson peered at the figure. 'Hundred an' fifty-seven.'

'What?' said Greene.

'Eleven stone three. Three pounds over.'

'Shit!' murmured Willis.

'I knew it, I knew it.' Greene paced, huddled in his top coat. 'We should've gone up to middleweight. This is madness.'

'We've got twenty-four hours. He'll dry out.'

Willis stepped off the scales and started to dress.

'What if he doesn't make it? What then?'

'I'll do it,' said Willis. 'Don't worry.'

'Don't worry!' More pacing. 'Don't worry, he says!'

'Calm down, Michael.' Freddie steered the promoter to the other end of the gym. 'Don't panic the fighter. He'll be okay. Just leave it to us. We'll have a test weigh in the morning, early.'

Greene's neck twitched. 'And if he's still over?'

'We'll get it off.'

'How? He's worked his bollocks off. I've watched him. Bastard'll be as weak as a kitten.'

'Freddie,' shouted Willis, sitting on a bench. 'Where's my trainers?'

'Where you left 'em, my son.'

'Can't see 'em.'

Thomson walked back to Willis. He squatted, looking under the bench. Willis bent forward.

'What's the fucking fuss?' he whispered.

'Promoters! All the same. Panic!'

'Tell him to go home. Shag Gillian or something. That'll take his mind of it.'

Freddie grinned. 'Here they are, you blind bleeder.' He stood up, Willis's trainers in his hands.

'Freddie,' Greene called, his arm beckoning. 'Come here a minute.'

'You got everything now, Johnny? I'll be knackered trotting up and down this gym,' Freddie sniffed again.

'Go to your master,' grinned Willis.

'Cheeky sod.'

Greene issued his orders. 'Ring me as soon as you've weighed him. Get me on my mobile.'

'I'll let you know.'

'What time?'

''Bout ten.'

'Weigh-in's at eleven thirty.'

'I know. It's enough time.'

'You know best.'

'Yeah, I do.'

Greene looked at him. 'Right. I'm off.' He walked towards Willis. More orders. 'Don't drink anything. Not anything. Understand?'

'I know what to do, Michael. I've never failed the scales in my life.'

'Maybe not. But this is close. Damn close.' He started for the door but turned back. 'Look, I know it's not your fault. You've worked hard. I'm not blaming you or anything.'

Willis continued towelling his damp hair.

'We'll have a talk afterwards. After the fight,' said Greene.

'Sure, Michael. Anything you say.'

The promoter left.

'He's right, you know,' said Willis.

'I know he is, my son.' Thomson picked up his boxer's sodden training gear. 'You're a middleweight now.'

'Yeah. Shame, innit? I'll win the European title and then give it up. No fucking money in that.'

'True. But there's lots more dough at middleweight. That's a top division; next best to heavyweight. Think of all the champions. Big names – Robinson, Turpin, Monzon, Hagler. Think about it, my son.'

Willis did and liked what he thought. But, first things first. Make the weight and beat the Frenchman.

After his demolition of Petersen, everyone had great expectations. All except those who knew.

Nothing passed Willis's lips for twenty-four hours. Just a dribble of water off his toothbrush. He couldn't summon up a spit. He was ounces over at the test weigh but spot on at the official ceremony. Greene managed to hide his relief, except for one neck twitch at the announcement.

'Johnny Willis – one hundred and fifty-four pounds.'

'Told you,' said Willis. 'You worry too much, Michael.'

'Henri Jacques – one hundred and fifty-three pounds.'

The Frenchman, making his second defence, looked much smaller as they posed for the cameras. Jacques was good at posing.

He did it for most of the twelve rounds, much to Willis's relief, and to the disappointment of the large Wembley Conference Centre crowd. They'd turned up expecting more fireworks from the Midlander. Instead it was a plodding points win, unanimous and wide, but dull.

Mercer wrote as much in his fight report. But the back page exclusive explained the reasons:

Johnny Willis will go down in boxing history as the shortest-reigning European champion.

Within minutes of taking the light-middleweight crown from Frenchman Henri Jacques at Wembley Conference Centre last night, the Westhampton fighter relinquished the crown.

'I can't make the weight any more,' he told me. 'It's been a struggle for some time. Tonight I just didn't have any power out there.

'I'd like to defend the title but it's impossible. I'm moving up to middleweight.'

The 24-year-old Willis, with only one cut-eye defeat in thirty contests, must also surrender the British title. One more successful defence of that title would have earned him the Lonsdale Belt outright.

'That is a blow. I really wanted to make the belt my own,' he admitted. 'But I'll just have to do it at middleweight.'

Willis didn't tell Mercer his real news. He was buying a house. His first house. In Islington. After all, he could afford it. In one year and seven fights with Greene, he'd grossed over two hundred thousand pounds. And there was lots more to come at middleweight.

Besides, Karen was moving in with him.

## Chapter Eighteen

They moved into their three-bedroom home at the end of November. Willis left the choice of furnishing to Karen. He simply wrote the cheques. In fact, he wrote a lot of cheques that month. The Willis Bros Builders account opened with a fifty-thousand-pound deposit.

It all knocked a massive hole in his account. He didn't have much luck at the dogs, either. Benny was suddenly short of good things and information from Mandy seemed to have dried up. At least, it didn't reach Willis. Not since Karen's significant arrival in his life.

Then there was the Inland Revenue. Willis's newly appointed accountant – recommended by Greene – warned him to expect a hefty demand. The house, the firm and the gambling had eaten into the sum earmarked for Her Majesty's Government.

Not that he worried. The next fight would provide the much needed cash injection. Anyway, life with Karen was too sublime to incorporate any worries.

They didn't make love until the first night in their home. The wait was frustrating, but worthwhile. When they came together it was tender, prolonged and sensual. Tantalising, too. Willis was rampantly eager, but Karen led them gently, passionately along the path of total mutual exploration. Only then, with both perfectly aroused, did she spread to welcome penetration.

At climax, for the first time in his life, Willis savoured not only physical release but a fusion of minds. He kissed her brow, nose and lips and looked gratefully into her hazel eyes. They shone contentedly back at him.

'I love you,' he said.

Karen cupped his face in her soft palms, drew him towards her lips and gave him a soft, brief kiss.

'Good,' she said. 'It's nice to know.' Then she smiled, playfully chiding him. 'It's only taken two months for you to say that.'

Twenty-four years actually, he thought.

Karen's parents visited for Sunday lunch; the one day in a week when Karen and her father were not at the theatre.

Diane Mitchell – 'Call me Dee' – was a former chorus girl. She'd met Gordon in Blackpool when he was a young front-of-house manager. They married and, soon after, produced Karen, their only child. Dee gave up her career and they moved to London when Gordon secured his manager's position with a major company. Karen was twelve.

Dee was now an attractive forty-four. Regular use of a health studio kept her body and legs toned and weekly visits to the hairdresser maintained her layered blonde hair.

At their first meeting, Willis complimented her.

'If daughters really do turn out to be like their mothers, I won't mind one bit,' he said. Dee liked Willis from that moment.

Gordon liked the Islington house. 'You've invested a pretty packet,' he said. Dee admired the furnishings, enthusing over the fully automatic kitchen and the labour-saving gadgets.

Playing host was an unfamiliar role for Willis, but he relaxed in their company. Chatted politely, helped Karen in the kitchen. That also impressed Dee.

'Gordon never does anything around the house,' she said. 'Doubt if he knows where the kitchen is.'

'Don't be unfair,' said Karen, theatrically hugging her father. 'He works very hard, don't you, Pops?'

'Daddy's girl,' said Dee. 'She twists him round her little finger, Johnny. Watch it. She'll do the same to you.'

Willis grinned at Karen. 'I can think of worst things in life,' he said.

Mary and Pete came down by train and taxi the next weekend. Karen had a matinée, so Willis showed them round. Upstairs, he started with the bathroom. Then the master bedroom, with its walk-in wardrobes and en-suite shower room.

'That's the smallest room,' he said, pointing along the landing. 'It's empty,' he added, opening the door to the second bedroom. 'This is for guests. Your room.'

Mary and Payne exchanged glances, startled.

'C'mon, I'm not stupid,' said Willis. 'D'you think I hadn't guessed? You've been engaged long enough, for Chrissakes.'

That evening, they watched Karen on stage from seats in the circle. Mary had come prepared this time, with the blue dress, split up the left thigh.

'Another lovely dress,' said Karen in the artistes' bar. 'Johnny buy that, too?'

'Yes, some time ago.'

'For your birthday last year,' said Payne.

'Look at me. All I've got is rags,' said Karen. She wore familiar post-show sloppy jumper and black ski pants.

'But you've got me,' said Willis, wrapping an arm around her shoulders. 'What more could you want?'

'How much time have we got?'

'Listen to you,' said Mary brightly. 'You're like an old married couple.'

'Married!' said Karen, mockingly. 'Me? To your brother? Heaven forbid!'

'You should be so lucky,' said Willis, pulling Karen close. And me, he thought.


Greene pressed the British Boxing Board to nominate Willis for an immediate middleweight title challenge. Willis's previous stature as national and European light-middleweight champion warranted preferential treatment. That was the claim.

The Board didn't agree. Instead, they sanctioned an eliminator against the official number one contender, Nottingham's Carl Rhodes. Promoters had until 31 December to lodge contracts. Failing that, purse offers to be received by 16 January 1992.

Greene swiftly concluded a deal. George Barnett managed Rhodes and Greene proposed a joint promotion. Greene would be senior partner, arranging the venue (Sheffield), TV date (early February), tickets, programme and publicity. Plus, three other major bouts featuring his boxers. Barnett would organise the six-fight undercard and liaise with the local Area Council of the Boxing Board. He'd receive a quarter of the net profits. Rhodes was to earn fifteen thousand pounds for the ten-rounder. Barnett agreed.

Contracts were signed and lodged with the Board. Willis was to get thirty thousand; three thousands pounds a round. He turned that into five thousand when Rhodes was retired on his stool at the end of the sixth. Knocked down in the third, twice in the fifth and again in the sixth, he'd suffered enough.

A month later, in Cardiff, Willis outpointed Conrad Woodbury, a durable black American from Philadelphia. In the main event, Gary Smith lost his European bantamweight title to local hero Dai Jones. It was sad for Ugly Gary but not so sad for Greene. He also promoted Jones. A no-lose situation.

That wasn't the case for Willis at the dogs. More of a no-win situation. The occasional greyhound obliged; overall, though, the bookies collected large lumps of Willis's bankroll.

'Go easy, my son,' said Thomson. 'Your dosh's going quicker than the fucking dogs.'

'My luck'll change,' said Willis. 'What d'you fancy in this? The five dog?'

Thomson screwed up his nose and sniffed. 'Nah. The three.'

Willis placed five hundred on his choice, at three to one. Thomson bet fifty on his selection at evens. Three minutes later, Willis tore up his ticket and Thomson stood in line to collect.

'No luck tonight, John?'

'Not a sniff, Benny. D'you know anything?'

'As it 'appens, I hear the one dog in the last is up for it. Might be a tickle. Take twos. Any higher, forget it.'

'Cheers, Benny. How's Mandy?'

'Mand? She's okay. Got a new bloke in tow.'

'That's good.'

'Not really. He's a tosser. Fucking yuppie. Pad in the Docklands somewhere. Got a stupid two-seater, all tyres and exhaust. I mean, where's the fucking comfort?'

'He must be doing all right.'

'All show. La-dee-fucking-dah. Thinks five quid's a big bet. Mand'll blow him out soon. Not her sort, really. Not like you, John. How's your love life?'

'Fine.'

'Thommo tells me you've bought a drum.' It was Arty.

'That's right. Still in Islington, not far from the gym. It's handy.'

The crowd in the bar started to disperse for the last race.

'Right,' said Willis. 'I'm away. The one dog.'

'Be lucky,' said Benny. 'Remember, no more than twos.'

Willis nodded. 'Twos it is. See you later.'

As the handlers paraded the runners, the fancy was a point higher. Three to one. All along the line. As they led the animals behind the traps, the grey one dog was marked down to twos. Five to two at places. Willis fingered the four hundred pounds remaining in his pocket.

'Done anything?' Thomson appeared at his side.

'Been looking for you. Benny says one dog.'

'Bollocks,' he sniffed. 'I've done the four.'

The first two dogs were in their traps. Willis thrust his four hundred at a bookie. Five to two. Willis watched the familiar flurry of betting activity just before the off. He noticed Benny's little man in the hat. He shrugged his shoulders at Willis and mounted the steps, back to the bar. No bets. The one dog was back to threes. Even seven to two.

The grey was fast away. Led at the first two bends. Streaked along the straight, then skidded slightly at the next bend. The pack closed and the crowd groaned as the one and two dog bumped coming into the home straight, nose to nose. Four dog fast on the outside.

'Photo... photo.'

'What d'you reckon, Freddie?'

'Fucking close. Two dog, maybe.'

He was wrong.

'Result of the photo-finish for the last race. The winner, number four, Joanna's Pet, second, number two...' came over the tannoy.

'Yes, go on, my son!' shouted Thomson. 'You little beauty!'

Willis crumpled his ticket and tossed it on to the terracing. Thomson stood in line. Fifty at twos.

What did Brian Adams say? Betting's a mug's game. I believe him, he thought. But try telling that to Freddie. Lucky bastard!

The income tax demand stunned Willis. It would virtually wipe out his bank account. He asked his accountant, 'Is this right? Seems a lot. See what you can do.'

Good news. The investment in Willis Bros Builders would reduce the figure. Not a lot. But it was something.

More good news. The Boxing Board had ordered Matt Gibson to defend against Willis.

Gibson was managed by Lew Sellers. And Harry Jacobs offered Willis seventy thousand pounds. Incredible, Greene told Willis. Eighty and it's a deal, he told Jacobs. Fuck off, Jacobs had rasped, but three days later, he came back. Seventy-five thousand. Last offer. Done, said Greene. And you have been!

'I'm leaving the show,' said Karen, standing at the kitchen sink after breakfast. She washed as Willis watched.

'Why? Have you got a new show?'

'No. It's doctor's orders.'

'What? What's wrong?'

'Calm down. Nothing's wrong.'

'What is it then?'

'People don't pay good money to see fat women dancing.'

'Fat? You're not fat.'

'Not yet. But I will be. Pregnant women do get fat. Haven't you noticed?' That big grin again.

'Jeez! Pregnant! When? I mean, when's it due?'

'August. About the fourteenth. Happy?'

'Are you?'

'Course I am. If you are.'

Willis took her in his arms. She peeled off the Marigolds and dropped them on the drainer. They kissed.

'It's great news, Karen. We've gotta celebrate.'

'No drink for me.' She patted her flat stomach. 'Got to take care of baby.'

'I'm not drinking either. Strict training. But we can go to bed, can't we?'

'We've only just got up.'

'So? We've had breakfast. I fancy something else now.'

'You always do. That's why I'm in this condition.'

'Complaining, are we?'
'I will be if you don't get a move on. Up those stairs – daddy.'

# Chapter Nineteen

Mercer's experience told him that, in nearly every champion's career, two things would surely happen.

There would be one rival who would always push him to the limit. However many times they met, it would always be hard. Like Ali and Frazier. Mercer knew that Willis had yet to meet such a man.

And there would be a peak performance. The career high spot. Not necessarily the biggest triumph, like winning a world championship, but the fight when everything came together. Power, skill, class. Mercer suspected Willis's battering of Ray Petersen was that fight.

Until, that is, the April night in 1992 when Willis confronted Gibson in Manchester.

Gibson was a Marvin Hagler clone. Shaven-headed, black, a southpaw. And tough. He was the British and Commonwealth champion from Salford; the local boy. He had massive support in the vast auditorium. Even Willis's large following, around two thousand, was outnumbered.

A world lightweight championship was the billed main event. But, in the arena, the atmosphere was fuelled by the dominant Gibson–Willis factions. Taunting, chanting. High in the cheaper seating, spasmodic fights broke out, brief flurries of punches, pushing and shoving. Security guards were alert, busy, defusing emotional time bombs.

In the bowels of the arena, Willis and Gibson sat quietly in their dressing rooms, contemplating. Mentally preparing.

Gibson shared his room with a stablemate. A novice heavyweight. A TV monitor flickered in the corner, showing preliminary bouts. He didn't watch, not even when the heavyweight won.

Willis's room was small. No TV monitor, just two rickety wooden chairs and a worn massage table. Willis sat on one chair,

Greene on the other. He would take his ringside seat only for the Willis fight.

'Making us feel welcome, aren't they?' said Greene.

'Luxury,' said Thomson.

A Board inspector watched over the wrapping of Willis's hands. Done to his satisfaction, he ink-stamped them and signed with a felt-tip pen.

New eight-ounce gloves lay on the table. Brown picked them up and loosened the laces, but Willis shook his head.

'Not yet, Ron.'

Willis shadow-boxed, throwing a few jabs into the palm of Thomson's hands. Smack, smack.

'What's the time?'

Greene looked at his watch. 'Nearly nine.' Twenty minutes to go.

'Okay, Ron.' Willis sat down. 'Let's put 'em on.'

Karen sat with her father, ringside. Greene's empty seat was next to Gordon. The arena lights dimmed and the crowd hummed with anticipation as two spotlights concentrated on one corner of the hall. Suddenly, loudly, the sound system blared. Queen. Willis was on his way.

*Are you ready…? Are you hanging on the edge of your seat…?*

Karen was. Hands clasped over her stomach, turned in the direction of the spotlights, she strained her neck, looking for Johnny.

'Will-is, Will-is, Will-is.'

A mighty roar greeted Willis as he stepped into the pool of light. Greene, neck twitching under the collar of his dark suit, led the way. Then Thomson, Willis's gloved hands on his shoulders. Brown at the rear. All flanked by a posse of security men.

Willis bounded up the steps as the ring lamps illuminated his workplace. He was wearing a new scarlet robe. White towel hooded over his head. Arms pumping in short hooks. His customary entrance. The fans responded, bellowing support.

The ring plunged into darkness again. The spotlights swung to another corner of the arena. But Karen had eyes only for the silhouette in the ring. Willis leaning his back into the ropes, testing, jigging on the canvas, testing. Back to his corner, nodding as Greene spoke into his left ear.

The sudden flare of the ring lights startled Karen. She hadn't even noticed the massive volume of shouts which marked Gibson's entrance. Now she looked. No gown, black shorts, glistening, muscled body. Mean and moody as he raised one arm in mid-ring. Willis walked towards him and Gibson glared at him. Cold brown eyes met cold brown eyes. They didn't speak.

'To your corners.' The referee stepped into the six feet of space between the boxers and pointed with both arms raised.

'You're mine,' said Willis, unblinking.

Brown gripped Willis's right arm and tugged.

The referee looked from one fighter to the other. Before he could say 'Corners' again, both started to walk backwards, eyes still fixed on one another.

The bell. Clang, clang, clang. The MC began his introductions.

Thomson smiled to himself as he removed Willis's robe. Kid's got some fucking balls, he thought.

Don Murray fed Gibson his watered mouthpiece. Sellers leaned over the top rope.

'Be positive, Matt. Go for him. Don't let him settle.'

At the bottom of the steps, Brian Adams looked up. Easier said than done, he thought.

What followed would be described by Mercer as '...savage mayhem. The collision of two supreme athletes bent on destruction'.

Willis struck first, with two solid jabs. Gibson ripped a left hook to the ribs. A powerful blow but Willis didn't even notice. He snapped a long right to Gibson's temple and the champion's backside bounced off the canvas.

There was pandemonium in the crowd.

Still sitting, he glared across at Willis in a neutral corner and sprang to his feet at the count of six. Not hurt. See how I jumped up? he seemed to say.

Willis pounced. Jab-jab-hook. Gibson backed off, grinning. Another Willis jab, flush in the mouth, and another. Blood dribbled from Gibson's nostrils. Gibson landed his right lead, high on Willis's brow. Willis jabbed again. Gibson curved a hook over Willis extended arm and sliced Willis's eyebrow. He felt blood, warm, trickling.

Thomson reached into his medicine bag for a swab.

'Bloody hell,' Brown shouted above the crowd's roar.

Thomson looked up. Gibson was face down. He rolled on to one side and reached for a rope to haul himself up. On his feet again, he was swaying.

The referee wiped Gibson's gloves on his shirt front.

'You okay?'

Gibson nodded. 'What round is it? asked the referee.

'First.' The referee stepped back. 'Box.'

Willis stalked, jabbed, looking to land one more right hand. The killer blow. Gibson grabbed and held on. His head was clearing.

Murray banged a brawny fist on the canvas and shouted, 'Last ten, Matt! Last ten!' In fact, twenty seconds remained to the end of the round.

Willis stepped back from a clinch. Hands fatally low. Gibson seized the opportunity and slammed a right onto Willis's gashed eyebrow. A left uppercut ripped under Willis's chin.

Willis looked at the canvas. Blood dripped, only inches away. Fuck! On all fours, he raised his head and looked to his corner. Thomson, swab stick between his teeth, urged him to get up.

'Six...'

Karen raised both hands to her mouth. Gordon stared at Willis. Greene sat, straight-backed, on the edge of his seat.

'Seven...'

Willis was up.

'You okay?' The referee looked at the laceration and debated a time out. It's nearly the end of the round, he thought. Let it go.

Gibson charged behind a wild right but missed. His head bumped Willis's cheek. The bell clanged.

Bedlam.

Thomson applied the adrenaline chloride swab. Brown leaned in, squeezed water on Willis's neck and sponged his chest, washed the mouthpiece.

'Okay, my son?' Thomson was calm, one hand pressing the swab, the other pulling at Willis's waistband. 'Deep breaths.'

Murray stuck cotton in Gibson's nostrils and doused his face with water. 'Right hand over the top, Matt. He's a sucker for it,' he said.

Gibson landed two jabs. But he gasped as Willis slammed a right hook under his ribs. Heads bumped and they exchanged searing hooks to the body. A furious toe-to-toe brawl. The crowd hollered. Karen gasped. Could this be the same man who gently held her? Made love so tenderly? The father of the child growing in her tummy?

Bump! Body met padded flooring.

'Eight... nine...'

It was all over. There was chaos at ringside. Greene was out of his seat, racing up the ring steps. Security guards on the ring apron, looking out into the frenzied crowd. Reporters gabbling into telephones. Camera shutters clicking, clacking. The bell. Clang, clang, clang.

The clamour abated for the MC's announcement. 'By count-out after one minute, twelve seconds of the second round, the winner and new British and Commonwealth champion – John-neee Will-is!'

Another Lonsdale Belt strapped around his middle, Willis bathed in the glow of adulation and enjoyed the fruits of his brutal labour.

And, he thought, now the taxman can have his pound of flesh.

Willis was famous. The sensational fight, his dramatic victory, catapulted him into the public eye. Television embraced him. Guest appearances on a sports quiz, inter-round expert at big fights and a commercial endorsing a new sugar-free drink.

Gillian secured an advertising contract. A photo-shoot for a range of men's boxer shorts. A lissom blonde model lounged at Willis's feet. Head turned, looking up at him, she wore only boxing boots and briefs. Boxing gloves, draped around her neck, covered a small bosom. Willis stood, legs akimbo, arms folded beneath his glistening, oiled chest. He gazed straight at the camera, naked except for the boxer shorts. An eye-catching advertisement, on the underground, street hoardings and in newspapers and magazines.

Feature writers interviewed Karen, swelling with pride and pregnancy, on life with a champion. Photographed at home, she was glossy and glamorous. The showgirl and the sports star.

In May, they flew to Gran Canaria, taking Mary and Payne. It was Mary's first holiday abroad and she tanned a golden brown. Karen relaxed, mainly in the shade. The bump was expanding. Willis and Payne ran daily through the dunes of Maspalomas, exercised in the hotel's mini-gym and swam.

Three weeks later, Willis was back in the Islington gym.

Greene negotiated with Westhampton Council for use of their athletics stadium. An open-air show for the first Saturday in August. Willis would make a voluntary defence of his championships against the number four contender, Paul Nelson.

A twenty-eight-year-old Geordie, Nelson had been out-pointed in a title bid three years earlier. He'd had only eight fights since, winning six but losing in Paris and Madrid.

Greene was confident Willis would prevail. His gamble was on the expensive promotion, and the weather. Tiers of seats were erected on a mass of scaffolding and crowd capacity was set at four thousand.

A sprinkling of early morning rain gave way to a fine afternoon and evening. Greene was relieved when the local weather bureau predicted a clear night. Only ten per cent chance of a shower.

Greene estimated that only four hundred seats remained unsold when boxing began at eight. Shortly before Willis was due in the ring at ten, half of those were also occupied. Willis's battalion of fans was growing into an army.

But Karen, two weeks from the scheduled delivery, wasn't at ringside. She'd kissed Willis on Wednesday morning before he and Thomson drove to Westhampton and The Post House Hotel, then went to stay with her parents.

Willis telephoned on Friday evening. They wouldn't speak again until Sunday morning. It would be too late after the fight and Karen needed her rest.

Nelson was first in the ring. As Willis emerged into the cool night air, a sudden wind rippled the ring canopy. When he climbed the steps for his familiar, bounding entrance, raindrops speckled the vociferous crowd.

Willis dominated the opening round. Jab, jab, constantly, solidly into Nelson's face. A roll of thunder accompanied the bell at the start of round two and lightning speared the skies. Rain swept into the ring on a rising wind and spectators covered their heads with newspapers or programmes. Jab, jab. Nelson slipped to the canvas. The referee called for a towel. He wiped the boxer's gloves, wet from touching the canvas.

Thunder clapped overhead in round three. Puddles formed on the canvas and both boxers slipped. Nelson went down again at the bell, this time shaken by a short right.

In the one-minute interval, four security guards mopped the sodden canvas with towels. Thunder rolled in the distance. The rain eased.

'Take my boots off, Ron.'

Brown scissored through the laces, pulling off the boots and white socks.

The television producer loved the barefoot Willis. It presented him with unusual, dramatic pictures. The drenched crowd roared as Willis planted his feet securely enough to end the farcical proceedings with a left hook.

The rain stopped. The Willis reign continued.

Gordon Mitchell rewound the tape. It was the second time he'd watched the fight. Dee was in bed. It was now nearly one o'clock on Sunday morning.

The telephone buzzed.

'Gordon? It's Johnny.' His voice was anxious. 'I've just got the message to ring. What's wrong?'

'Nothing's wrong.'

'Thank God for that. I panicked when reception gave me the message. Thought something might be wrong with Karen.'

'No, she's fine. Couldn't be happier. Congratulations, Johnny. You've got a daughter.'

'What? Karen's had the baby?'

'That's right. At ten twenty tonight. Well, last night now.'

'Is she all right?'

'Yes. They're both fine. Baby's healthy.'

'What happened? It's supposed to be another coupla weeks.'

'She started about teatime. I was at work, but Dee drove her to the hospital and I met them there. We didn't get home until midnight. That's when I left the message at your hotel.'

'Jeez! I can't believe it. A daughter, you said?'

'Yes. Six pounds, five ounces.'

'What a night! Have you got the number? I'll phone Karen now.'

'I wouldn't do that, Johnny. Best leave it until tomorrow. I think maybe she'll be sleeping now.'

'Course she will. What an idiot! Not thinking straight.'

'It's understandable, Johnny. I remember when Karen was born…'

Willis heard the voice but not the reminiscence. He was thinking of now. What to do? His small celebration party was warming up in the bar. He'd order champagne, get pissed. No, can't do that. Gotta get back to London.

'I'm coming home,' he said as Gordon finished. 'I'll go straight to the hospital.'

'Get some rest first, Johnny. You've had a busy night. Congratulations, by the way. Clever move that, going barefoot.'

'Yeah, thanks. Weird bloody night, wasn't it? Okay, Gordon. Thanks for letting me know. I'll let you get to bed now.'

'Right. Careful how you go.'

'Sure. By the way, sorry for making you so old.'

'Old?'

'Yeah. You're sleeping with a grandmother now. See you later.'

Gordon replaced the receiver and chuckled. He picked up his glass of whisky. 'Cheeky bugger.'

Willis ordered champagne and announced the news. They all toasted the health of Karen and the latest member of the family and congratulated the proud father.

Kenny handed him his mobile phone. He'd phoned Mary.

'What's going on, Johnny? Kenny says you've got something to tell me.'

Mary listened as Willis told her the news.

'Oh, wonderful! What you calling her?… I'll get Ma for you… Okay, I'll tell her in the morning… Give my love to Karen.'

Karen sat in a bedside chair, the warm bundle in her arms and wondered when Johnny would telephone. It was seven. Perhaps he wasn't awake yet.

'Hi.'

Willis bore flowers and sheepish grin.

'Hi, champ.'

Willis kissed Karen's lips and looked down at the small face in the crook of her arm. Wispy blonde hair and Karen's tiny nose, but his brown eyes.

'Hope you're not too disappointed it's not a boy.'

'God, no. Don't be silly. She's perfect. Just like you.' He smiled. 'Anyway, there's plenty time for that – or them.'

Greene was concerned. The European Boxing Union had ordered Alberto Canzoneri to defend against Willis. Promoters had until 30 August to agree contracts. Otherwise, purse offers by 12 September, fight by 31 October. But the Italians were being difficult.

He'd faxed a good offer, but they didn't respond. On the phone they were dismissive. Later, they countered with a trivial sum. It was heading for purse offers.

Damn! Don't want to go to Italy, he thought. Hard to get a result over there.

Round one to the Italians. Their bid won. Bologna, San Remo or Rimini were the proposed sites. For 16 or 23 October. Greene hoped it wouldn't be Bologna. Canzoneri, born in Sardinia, had lived in Bologna since he was three.

Now twenty-nine, Canzoneri had twice defended the European championship. He was undefeated in forty-eight contests, blemished only by two early-career draws. Thirty-three stoppages. But a shortage of recognised, class opposition. And he'd never boxed outside of Italy. He'd had a carefully manipulated career. It had paid off, too. He was ranked in the world top five and rumoured to get his big chance if he retained his title against Willis.

In all, Greene considered the odds stacked heavily against Willis. But Willis wasn't concerned.

'Don't worry, Michael. It doesn't matter where we fight. It's just me and him.'

Anyway, thought Willis, the pay was fantastic. The bid, in Swiss francs, converted to a staggering hundred and four thousand pounds for Willis.

But Greene was wary. He demanded that two-thirds of Willis's money be deposited with the British Boxing Board before they left England, one week before the fight.

Promoter Roberto Musso disliked the inference.

'I'm within my rights,' countered Greene.

Musso was already stumping up for three return-flight tickets, plus three hotel rooms for six nights, plus meals. Reluctantly, he agreed to Greene's demand.

But Greene wasn't finished. 'The rest of the purse must be lodged with the Board forty-eight hours before the contest.'

He faxed details to the Board, requesting their support. 'Protect our interests,' he asked.


Vita Nenci introduced himself to Greene, on the phone, late at night.

'I am manager of Alberto Canzoneri. Associate of Roberto Musso. I understand you have concerns with financial arrangements. I do not understand this. Do you no trust?'

'Frankly, no.'

'But, Mr Greene, I and Roberto Musso have been in this business for nearly forty-five years. That, I believe, is many years longer than you have lived. Certainly, it is many years more than you have been involved in boxing. Is that not so?'

'Yes. But it doesn't mean I don't know my business.'

'Mr Greene, listen. I would not suggest such a thing. You, I understand, are a successful young man. I, too, was young once. Back then, I did business with Mr Harry Jacobs. A good man. A good businessman. We've been happy to do business many times over the years. Talk with him. He will tell you, you have nothing to fear. Will you do that?'

'I don't discuss my business with Harry Jacobs.'

There was silence at the other end of the line. Then Nenci spoke again.

'Mr Greene, I make this call in the hope we can have a better understanding. I wish only that we can work comfortably with each other, as I have done for many years with Mr Jacobs. However, it seems I have wasted time and money. For that, I am sorry.'

'Mr Nenci, I don't intend to cause offence. I appreciate your call. But I must do business as I see fit.'

'Of course you must. So must we. I will tell you, Mr Greene, that in forty-five years we have given no cause for complaints. Our word is our bond. What we say will happen, happens. *Capisce*? You have nothing to worry about. Believe me, Mr Greene, everything is in order. All is taken care of.'

The connection was broken. Six days later, Greene received a fax from Italy.

Canzoneri (champion) v Willis (challenger)
European middleweight championship.
Friday, 16 October 1992, San Remo.
Three return-flight tickets for three persons in Mr Willis's party. From London Heathrow to Genoa via Milan. Road transport provided from Genoa.
Three hotel reservations. Five nights (12–16 October inclusive). Meals included. Any additional rooms at personal expense. If notified in ten days, Mr Musso will oblige by booking rooms.
Gymnasium available for Mr Willis. Sparring partners can be arranged on request.
Mr Willis must attend brief press conference on arrival (12 October) and press conference on 14 October.
Boxers in ring at nine thirty local time. First bell at nine forty, in accordance with Eurovision Sport television contract.
Four ringside complimentary tickets for Mr Willis. Others by payment, if available.
Mr Willis's monies being lodged with British Boxing Board of Control in accordance with agreement with Mr Michael Greene, adviser to Mr Willis.

It was signed by Roberto Musso. Everything was, indeed, taken care of.

*PART FIVE*

H E SAT HEAVILY on the stool. Odd this, he thought. Usually, the minute between rounds provides a welcome haven. A time of rest, respite from battle. One minute in which to regroup and recover for the next three minutes of battle.

Not tonight.

Each time I come back to the corner, it gets worse. Still no solution and the clock's ticking away. Ten rounds gone already. It's flying by. Going too quickly.

'Six minutes more.' Those familiar eyes bored into him, intensely. 'Your whole future hangs on these six minutes. It's up to you. It's in your hands.'

My hands. If only that was the case, he thought.

He glanced again at the ringside crowd. A sea of faces, staring up at him. Bit of anxiety here and there, but mostly blank. Just looking.

'How're the hands?'

Painful. Bloody painful. You know that. But that's a minor problem. That you don't know.

'C'mon. Grit your teeth. It's all or nothing, my son. All or nothing. You're a warrior. Do or die.'

Bloody hell! Do or die! Where'd those words spring from?

He got to his feet. Final glance at the crowd. Can't give up hope. There's still time. Not much. But some.

'Seconds out... for round eleven...'

# Chapter Twenty

'Half! Be lucky to bank half!'

Willis paced the lounge carpet, then stopped himself. Jeez! I'm getting like Michael, he thought.

Karen, blouse open, nursed Suzie on the leather sofa.

'You're still getting a lot of money, Johnny.'

'Yeah, but fifty grand? That's a lot to lose.'

'You're not losing it. It's business. It's costs, expenses. There is a difference. Anyway, it might not be that much. Accountants always paint a black picture.'

Willis slumped on to the sofa and looked again at the figures on the notepaper. Greene's commission, Thomson and Brown's wages, Brown's travel and hotel expenses, sparring partners. Other training costs. Income tax.

'D'you know what Michael said? He said I could save some if Ron didn't go.'

'Well?'

'Jeez. That's only about two grand. Anyway, I want him there. He's been with me all along.'

Karen worked her palm on Suzie's back.

'That's it, then. Accept it. Get your mind on training. The fight. If you win the title, you'll get lots more money.'

'*When... when* I win the title.'

'Yes, of course.'

Suzie burped, dribbling at the mouth.

Willis smiled at his daughter. 'You don't care, do you? If your dad has anything to do with it, you'll never worry about money.'

'You shouldn't be worrying, either. There's millions of people who'd love to earn fifty thousands pounds in one night.'

'One night? I've worked—'

'Yes,' she interrupted. 'I know. You've worked a long time for this. I appreciate that. But you know what I mean. And, God willing, Johnny, there'll be a lot more to come. But look at you.

You've come a long way. You're only twenty-five, got a house, posh car, a successful career. That's not bad, is it?'

'You're forgetting the best bit. I've got you two,' he said. But, he thought, I'd like to keep more of my money.

It was a damp October morning. Willis, in heavy boots, pounded the streets of Islington. Dark tracksuit, woollen bobble hat. Nearly home. Five more miles in the stamina bank.

The rear doors of a blue Renault saloon opened and two characters emerged. One tall, lean. The other squat. Both in scruffy jeans and zip-up jackets. They walked to the pavement and watched Willis approach.

'Johnny?' The tall one spoke first.

Willis eased down to a walk. Watchful.

'Who wants to know?'

'Benny sent us.'

'Benny who?'

'Benny. You know Benny. Says you'll help us out.'

'Like he's helped you,' said Squat.

Willis eyed them both. 'What sort of help?'

'Look after some stuff. Just for a few days. Week or so.'

'What sort of stuff?'

'Some bags. In the boot.' Tall One nodded at the car.

The driver stared straight ahead along the road.

'Stop pissing about. What's in the bags?'

'Money,' said Squat. 'There's twenty grand for you.'

Willis blinked. Twenty grand! He said nothing.

'Just for a few days. Benny says you'll keep it safe.'

'Let's have a look.'

Willis walked towards the car. Tall One tapped on the car roof and the driver pulled a lever. The boot clicked open. Squat looked up and down the street. It was deserted, except for a stray dog sniffing in the gutter.

Tall One raised the boot lid, halfway. Willis looked in and saw three large bags.

'Must be a lot of money.'

'Yeah. And two shooters.'

'What?' Willis stood back.

'S'okay. Ain't been used.'

'Don't know about that. Money's one thing, shooters another,' said Willis.

'C'mon, Johnny. Twenty grand's yours.' Tall One looked along the road. 'We don't wanna hang around out here. Okay? Let's get 'em in the house.'

Willis looked at his house. Still in darkness. Karen must still be asleep. What the hell! Twenty grand's not to be sniffed at.

'Bring 'em to the door. Quiet, like. Don't want the missus to know, do we? Then piss off. I'll see Benny later.'

'Cheers, Johnny.'

Willis opened the front door and slid the bags quickly into the hall. Karen switched on her bedside lamp. Tall One and Squat returned to the car. Willis went inside and he heard Karen moving about upstairs. Shit! Gotta hide this stuff, he thought.

Karen opened the curtains and watched the strangers get into the dark, dirty Renault and drive off. She belted her housecoat and went to the bathroom.

Willis parked the bags behind the sofa. In the kitchen, he filled the electric kettle with water.

'Morning, love. Just making a cuppa.'

'Lovely,' said Karen. They kissed.

'Who're they?' she asked.

'Who?'

'Those blokes I saw leaving.'

'Oh, them? Just some people I see at the dogs. Fight fans.'

'What did they want?'

'Wondered if I was going to the track tonight?'

Karen glanced at the kitchen clock. 'Bit early for that, isn't it?'

'They're working round here somewhere. Saw me finishing my run.' He lifted two mugs from a cupboard.

'What are they? What do they do?'

'I dunno. Brickies or something. Why? What's it matter?'

'I didn't like the look of them,' she said.

Willis laughed.

'I'm serious, Johnny. Sometimes I think you know some funny people. You mix with strange characters.'

Willis kissed her tousled hair. 'Strange people hang around

boxing. It attracts 'em. It's full of characters. I can't help that.'

Karen looked at him but said nothing.

'Come here, silly. They're just blokes, that's all. Hardly know 'em, really.' Willis kissed her firmly but quickly on the lips and patted a firm dancer's buttock.

'I'll have a shower before breakfast. Scrambled eggs and toast will do. Suzie still sleeping?'

'Yes. Try not to wake her. We might get a peaceful breakfast together.'

'Sure.'

Willis closed the kitchen door behind him, then gathered the bags from behind the sofa, climbed the stairs, eased open the loft cover and pulled down the metal steps. Listened. Good, he thought, Karen's switched on the television in the kitchen.

He took a quick peek. Jeez! Must be hundreds of thousands. Used notes. He sniffed the sawn-off barrels. Not fired. He shoved the booty into the loft and replaced the steps and cover. He showered quickly and dressed in jeans, T-shirt and trainers.

Karen cooked his eggs as he drank tea. They ate and watched TV news. Thousands still dying of famine in Somalia.

An armed raid on a security van made the second item. Forced off the road in Bayswater. No shots fired, but two guards beaten, clubbed. They were in hospital with head, arm and leg injuries. Police were seeking six men and appealing for witnesses. A transit van was found abandoned two miles from the scene. They believed the raiders switched to two other vehicles. One, a dark blue saloon, possibly a Renault.

Karen stiffened and looked over her tea mug at Willis.

'What? What's up?'

'You heard what they said. Possibly a blue Renault.'

'So?'

'Those men. They were in a Renault. A dark one.'

'Christ, Karen! There's thousands on the roads. What d'you think I am? A bloody hold-up man?'

'You've been close before. You and your brothers.'

Willis rose angrily. His chair tumbled and clattered on the tiled floor. 'I don't need to do that any more,' he shouted. 'None of us do. And I don't need this shit from you.'

He flung open the kitchen door and marched out. The front door violently slammed behind him. Suzie cried out. Karen trembled, startled, frightened by Willis's rage.

She sat there for a minute, maybe two, confused. She wiped tears from her eyes. Must comfort her baby. Shouldn't have said that about Johnny's past, his brothers. Anyway, he'd been running this morning, not robbing. Probably all a coincidence, the men and the car.

'Mummy's coming. It's all right, darling.'

Willis walked for thirty minutes. Head down, thinking. He didn't notice the cold. His temper eventually cooled and was replaced by remorse. What've I done? he thought. Shouldn't get involved. Who needs twenty poxy grand? Why didn't I just tell 'em to fuck off? Jeez, Johnny, you're a bloody idiot. And Karen. She doesn't deserve this crap from me.

'I'm sorry.' Willis stood in the lounge doorway. 'I shouldn't have stormed off like that.'

Karen nurtured Suzie. She looked across the room at him, eyes dulled by anguish, her normally full-lipped mouth now pinched.

'I'm a bit uptight. It's a big fight, this Italy thing.' He paused. 'With Suzie crying at nights, I haven't been sleeping too well. I'm just on edge. When you started on I just snapped.'

'I'll take Suzie to Mum's,' she said coldly. 'We'll stay there. You'll be able to sleep then.'

'No, that's not what I want. I want you here with me. And Suzie. I'll be okay. There's no need for you to go anywhere.'

'Fine, if you're sure.'

'Certain.'

'I shouldn't have said that about you and your brothers. I know that. It's in the past,' she relented.

'S'okay.'

'But, and I mean this Johnny, I'm telling you straight. If you get up to any funny stuff, I'm out of here. Me and Suzie. Like a shot. Understand?'

'There's no funny stuff. Never will be. Not any more.'

'Good. Why don't you go upstairs. Get some sleep. I'll wake

you in time for the gym.'

Willis walked to the sofa and squatted in front of Karen. She softened her lips for a brief kiss. Suzie burped.

At the top of the stairs, Willis glanced at the loft cover. Must see Benny, he thought. Get that gear shifted.

Benny wasn't in his usual place at the bar. Nor Terry. Nor Arty.

He found Mandy in the office, alone, behind her desk.

'He's in Spain,' she said. 'Went this afternoon.'

'When's he back?'

'Dunno, didn't say. Usually goes for a week. Sometimes longer. Looking for a tip?'

'Have you got one?'

She walked towards him. Breasts jutting beneath her sweater. Provocative. Available. 'What's it worth?' she asked.

'Thought you'd got a fella.'

'I have. Look.' She flashed a ring. 'Thinks the world of me, he does.'

'That's good. I'll give you a tip, then.' He bent and kissed willing lips, then patted her trousered buttocks. 'Be a good girl. See ya.' And he was gone.

Mandy shrugged her shoulders. Only gonna tell him to watch his step, she thought. Best tip I could give him.

October twelfth was a long day. Three airports, two flights and a weaving ride around mountain passes from Genoa to San Remo. Willis had risen from his bed at five thirty for a five-mile run. It was five in the afternoon when they reached the Italian Riviera.

Greene had complained that the travel arrangements were disruptive, too time-consuming. Musso was politely dismissive.

'The best we can arrange for that date, Mr Greene,' he said.

A flight to Nice, followed by a drive north across the border to San Remo would have halved their travel time. That was the special charter route organised for Willis's two hundred travelling supporters.

'They're messing us about,' agreed Thomson at Heathrow. 'We lose a day's training.'

Willis didn't object. He relieved the boredom by listening to

Brown and Mercer as they discussed fights, fighters and, in particular, how British hopes had fared on European travels. Waiting in Milan for the flight to Genoa, the conversation focused on San Remo.

'Bit of a graveyard,' said historian Brown. 'Bunny Sterling and Kevin Finnegan both lost European middleweight title fights there.'

'It's not been all bad,' said Mercer. 'Maurice Hope won a world light-middleweight championship fight. Stopped Rocky Matiolli.'

'When was that?' asked Willis.

'Think it was in '79. Long time ago.'

'Nobody won since?'

'Not that I recall. Not in San Remo. Fact is, we've not had many wins in Italy.'

'Which doesn't mean you can't do it,' said Greene.

The promoter's injection of optimism prompted positive reactions and a roll call of winners. Winstone, Charnley, Honeyghan, Cooper and Bugner. They'd all triumphed in Italy. Thomson sniffed. All a long time ago, he thought.

Willis closed his eyes, leaned back into the airport's uncomfortable plastic seat and hunched his shoulders. So the odds are stacked against me, he thought. Nothing changes.

At the hotel, Musso had assembled the Italian media. The promoter was a heavy man, built like a heavyweight with massive, rounded shoulders. His thinning black hair was slicked back over a huge domed head.

He greeted Greene warmly and shook hands with all five travellers. Then he flicked podgy fingers at a minion and in rapid Italian dispatched him to complete the hotel registrations for 'my guests'.

Greene cast a glance at the media scrum gathered in the lounge. Musso insisted on a brief session.

'It's been a long day. The boxer needs to rest,' said Greene.

'But of course, Mr Greene. Just a few moments. That is all that is required. I am sure you appreciate the value of publicity. We promoters must have it. Is that not so?'

The 'few moments' amounted to twenty minutes. Greene

fielded most of the questions while Willis's eyes roved the room, indifferent to the questions and whirr of camera shutters. When required to answer questions, Willis was polite, respectful of all things Italian and of Canzoneri in particular. Mercer smiled when Willis referred to past British defeats.

'I'm expecting a hard fight,' he said. 'We always expect that in Italy and Canzoneri is a good champion. His undefeated record speaks for itself. But I have come to beat him. Whether I can or not, we'll find out on Friday night.'

'Should be a diplomat, my son,' said Thomson as they stepped into the lift for the third floor.

'Only told them what they wanted to hear,' Willis said.

'Exactly.'

'Didn't mean a fucking word of it.'

He gave a similar performance at the main press conference two days later. But he was more concerned this time with sizing up Canzoneri.

The Italian was two inches shorter and barrel-chested beneath a tight-fitting sweat top. He had black cropped hair and thick eyebrows fused a broad, flattened nose. But no visible scar tissue.

Canzoneri was relaxed and smiled freely as he answered his adoring media in his native tongue, although he spoke in halting English when speaking to the foreign press. Six British national newspaper writers and the Press Association agency reporter had arrived at lunchtime.

The meeting broke up after the two boxers posed together for the photographers. Canzoneri smiling, Willis stern. Hands linked but not gripping. All done, they nodded at each other and turned away.

'Let's get outta here,' Willis told Brown.

Greene stayed on for discussions with Musso, Nenci and two other members of team Canzoneri.

'All monies have been lodged,' said Musso.

'Thank you,' said Greene. He knew that. He'd telephoned the Boxing Board to check.

Musso related details of the weigh-in, rules meeting, transport arrangements to the arena and the names of officials. The judges were from France and Switzerland. Referee from Austria.

'I trust you have found our arrangements satisfactory,' said Nenci. He was stocky. Walked slowly, importantly and his piggy eyes missed nothing. 'The gymnasium, the automobile, the hotel. No complaints?'

'No complaints, so far,' said Greene.

'That is good.' He nodded. 'Perhaps you would care to join us for lunch?'

'Thank you but I must decline. I'm going to the gym with my boxer.' Greene looked at his watch. 'In an hour.'

'So be it. Perhaps after the contest. We have arranged a late supper at a fine *ristorante*. It is close by the Piazza Colombo. You and your party are most welcome.'

'Your offer is appreciated. But, perhaps you might wish to reconsider if the night does not turn out to your satisfaction.'

'That is not a consideration.' Nenci's eyes never flickered. 'Our hospitality does not depend on the outcome of the contest. We simply make the gesture. It is you who must decide.' The Italian stood and offered his hand. 'We must detain you no longer. You have the business with your boxer to attend to.'

'Indeed.' Greene accepted his hand.

'Should you have any needs, any problems, do not hesitate to contact us. Myself or Mr Musso.'

'I won't. *Ciao*.' Don't trust them one inch, he thought.


Willis and Canzoneri each scaled eleven stone, five pounds at the weigh-in held in the plush San Remo Casino.

Willis handed two complimentary tickets to Kenny and Colin who had arrived on the charter trip. After the fight, a fleet of coaches would return the British fans to Nice for an early-morning departure. No overnight hotel. Tiring, but cheaper that way.

'How's business?' asked Willis.

'Good,' said Colin. 'One place almost done. Got the accommodation agency sorted. They reckon we'll have no bother renting 'em out.'

Back at the hotel, Willis had chicken and pasta and he viewed a Canzoneri video in his room. He'd watched it several times before. Now he repeatedly hit the fast-forward button. He'd seen enough, really. Knew what he had to do.

# Chapter Twenty-One

The Italian crowd greeted Willis's walk to the ring with near silence. They tolerated the cheers from his small band of supporters, but they whistled derisively when Willis launched into his arm-pumping routine mid-ring.

'Haven't got many friends here, my son,' said Thomson.

Canzoneri received a hero's welcome. In the ring he raised both arms on a circuit of the roped square. Willis sat on a wooden corner stool, unconcerned, waiting for the real show to begin.

The pattern of the early rounds was quickly established. Willis jabbed and Canzoneri blocked most of them with his high guard. The champion tucked his chin into his chest and his brawny left shoulder provided further protection as he plodded forward, weaved, bobbed, aimed for the body. Every punch was greeted with a roar of approval. Willis's busier work went unheralded.

Canzoneri opened up in the sixth. He rushed at Willis, barged him into the ropes and clubbed at his body and head and the tactical switch surprised Willis. He was better prepared in the seventh, employing jab, jab, right cross to effect. But Canzoneri was robust. Punches bounced off the top of his head.

The eighth round sparked furiously as Canzoneri grazed Willis's left eyebrow. The smear of blood inspired the champion and he increased his volume of punches to the frenzied joy of the partisan crowd. But that weakened his defences. Willis took advantage, connecting solidly for the first time. The final seconds of the round were fought with toe-to-toe ferocity. The din drowned the sound of the bell.

Willis returned to his corner. Thomson was already in the ring. But there was no stool. Thomson shouted down at Brown.

'Where's the fucking stool, Ron?'

Brown looked around him. The stool was his responsibility. Where was it?

Thomson pointed over the top rope. 'That bastard's sitting on it.'

Brown looked at a grinning spectator, yards away in the aisle. He was squatting on Willis's stool.

'Get off,' shouted Brown.

The Italian shrugged his shoulders and garbled something, arms opened wide.

'The stool.' Brown pointed. 'Get up.'

The trainer moved in, ready to knock the offender off his illegal perch. The spectator stood, picked up the stool and handed it to Brown, grinning. Twenty valuable seconds of rest had been lost.

Thomson pressed a swab on the injury. It was nothing serious, yet. He ignored the ten-second warning to leave the ring. The Austrian referee was still urging him to leave when the bell sounded.

'Fuck 'em,' said Thomson.

Brown fed Willis his mouthpiece and the round started. Ten seconds of rest had been stolen back.

'Watch the stool,' ordered Thomson.

'I'm sitting on it,' said Brown. He looked over his shoulder. No sign of the offending spectator. He'd disappeared. Cheating bastards, he thought. But clever, he grudgingly conceded.

Willis had different thoughts. Make 'em pay, with jolting jabs and hooks. Canzoneri covered and retreated for the first time. It was the same procedure in the tenth.

'That's the way, my son. You've got him now. Keep working behind the jab.'

Across the ring, it was all Latin passion – urgent, demonstrative. At the bell, a final reminder to the Italian. His world title challenge was at stake. Canzoneri raised his effort. Willis dug in, refused to concede ground. It was a physical and mental battle.

The intimidating crowd urged their champion to even greater effort as the boxers touched gloves before the final round. Their cheers propelled Canzoneri on. But his left eye was swollen and his vision impaired. He couldn't see the punches. Willis jabbed, jabbed, jabbed.

Keep moving. Win the round. Win the fight, that's what Freddie said. Coasting it. Jab, jab. Not long to go. Jab, right cross, clinch. Mauling, heads banging.

Thomson thumped his right palm on the ring floor. 'Stick and move, Johnny, stick and move,' he yelled.

Canzoneri whacked a right to the ribs. Willis gasped. Another clinch, wrestling. Butted! Blood dripping. Jab, jab. Keep him off.

'Last ten.'

Locked, like two stags, their heads rubbed together. Too weary to land a decisive blow. Too proud, too determined to back off. They collapsed together at the bell. All over, except for the verdict.

Brown doused Willis with water, poured from the bottle, as Thomson applied the adrenaline swab.

'I'm fucked,' said Willis. 'Where's the stool? Not gone again, is it?'

'Keep on your feet, my son. Just a bit longer. Don't let 'em see you're knackered.'

Greene, in the ring, leaned over the ropes and looked down at the officials totting up the scorecards. Musso, by his side, turned away and gestured to Nenci at ringside. Thumbs up.

'What's the score, Michael?'

'Couldn't tell, Freddie. It's close.'

'Great! We know that.'

Clang, clang, clang. Crowd hushed.

Piercing whistles followed the MC's announcement that the Austrian referee had voted 118–117 for Willis. Cheers greeted the French judge's 116–112 for Canzoneri.

'What?' said Greene. 'No way we lost eight rounds.'

Just the Swiss judge left – 117–117.

'A draw. It's a bloody draw,' said Greene. His neck twitched. 'What a turnover.'

The crowd erupted as Canzoneri allowed the referee to raise his weary right arm. Still champion, he bowed to all four sides of the arena and received a bouquet from promoter Musso.

Thomson held the ropes open for Willis's exit before the promoter could present their bouquet. Polite applause followed him to the dressing room. His own supporters chanted. They knew injustice when they saw it.

Nenci approached Greene with his hand outstretched. Greene

swallowed his anger and took it.

'You have a fine fighter, Mr Greene. A worthy adversary.'

'Tell that to your French judge. I'll be lodging a protest. He should never work again.'

Nenci shrugged, palms open, but said nothing.

Greene shook his head and walked away. I was right. Can't trust them an inch, he thought.

It was Saturday evening, a week after Willis had returned from Italy. He sprawled on the sofa, watching TV. Karen was upstairs, preparing Suzie for bed.

Door chimes roused Willis. He reluctantly tramped to the door and opened it. Tall One stood in the shadows.

'I've come for the gear, Johnny.'

'Not now,' he hissed. 'It's a bad time.'

'We've gotta have it. We're getting out.'

'Can't be done tonight. The wife's here.'

'Tomorrow, then.' He was insistent. 'Must have it by then.'

'Come to the gym. About ten.'

Willis closed the door and rested his back on it, thinking.

Karen peered through the bedroom window. She recognised Tall One as he eased into the rear seat of a red Escort. Not the blue Renault. She sat on the edge of the bed, wondering, until Suzie slept.

Willis, downstairs, lounged on the sofa. He looked relaxed, but he wasn't. Karen entered. Wearing a knee-length leather skirt and white shirt tucked in at the waist; she was quickly getting her figure back. She sat in an armchair.

'Who was that at the door?' she asked.

Shit! Willis had hoped she hadn't heard.

'One of them double-glazing pests. Said we weren't interested.'

'Don't lie, Johnny. He's been here before. The day we had that row. What's going on?'

Willis swung his legs off the sofa and leaned forward, elbows on his knees. He laced his fingers.

'It's nothing for you to worry about. Just a bit of business.'

'What sort of business makes you lie to me?'

Willis looked at his hands and sighed in resignation.

'I didn't want another row.'

Karen hitched forward to the edge of her chair.

'Tell me the truth.'

He did, but he didn't the mention the shotguns. Or how much money was in the bags. Or his twenty thousand pound payoff.

'It'll all be over tomorrow. I'm meeting them at the gym. Giving the stuff back.'

Karen was ashen-faced. 'I can't believe you've been so daft,' she said. 'You must realise you're an accessory.'

'We don't know that,' he said quickly. 'You're just assuming it's from that hold-up.'

'That one or something else. It doesn't matter, does it? It can't be legal.'

Willis shook his head. 'I don't know,' he said slowly. 'Suppose not.'

'Suppose not? Course it's not! You know that much.' Karen stood up and walked to the door.

'Where're you going?'

'Bed,' she said sharply. 'You'd better sleep in the spare room.'

Thomson was surprised to see Willis. Ugly Gary was one of three boxers preparing for a session. The trio commiserated with Willis over the San Remo affair. 'Robbed,' they said.

Willis pulled his trainer to a corner of the room. In hushed tones, he told him about the favour for Benny and his arranged meeting that morning to hand back the stuff.

'Bloody hell, Johnny. You shouldn't bring this on our doorstep,' Thomson sniffed. 'Where's the stuff now?'

'In my car. The boot.'

'Well, get out of here. Wait for them outside. We don't want them in here.'

The red Escort pulled up as Willis walked out. Tall One and Squat joined him at his Mercedes as he unlocked the boot.

'Have you taken yours, Johnny?'

'No. I don't want any. I've never even seen the stuff. Take it and piss off.'

He got behind the wheel, waited for the boot to be closed and drove off. He hadn't noticed Greene park Gillian's Cavalier outside the gym.

'What's Willis up to?' Greene asked Thomson.

'What d'you mean?'

'I saw him outside with that lowlife Sam Fisher. You know him, one of Benny Carpenter's crowd. He was with another bloke. Tall. Didn't recognise him. They took some bags out of his car and then he just drove off.'

'Don't know nothing about it. Johnny popped in for a minute. Said he's taking another week off. Back in training after that.'

'I can't work him out. He mixes with some rum people. Jekyll and Hyde, that's what he is,' said Greene.

'Enigmatic.' Thomson had been studying his *dickshunary* again.

The house was empty when Willis returned and Karen's Metro wasn't in the garage. At one o'clock he telephoned her parents.

'Is Karen there, Gordon?'

'Yes. But what's going on, Johnny? Karen won't talk about it but she's upset. Distressed, in fact. What've you done?'

'I've done nothing to her. I know she's upset but we can sort it out. Can I speak to her?'

'Afraid not. Karen says it's all over between you two. She says you know why. And she doesn't want you anywhere near her or Suzie.'

'That's ridiculous.'

'Not according to Karen and, unless you give me a good reason not to follow her wishes, I'm also telling you to stay away from my daughter.'

'This is crazy. Let me talk to Karen.'

'Hold on.' Mitchell held a hand over the mouthpiece. Willis heard muffled voices. 'No, Johnny. She refuses to speak to you. We don't want any trouble. I'm going to put the phone down now. Goodbye.'

The line went dead.

Willis slammed down his receiver.

Mitchell dialled Greene's number.

'Sorry to disturb you on a Sunday, Michael, but I've got a

problem. You might be able to help.'

'What's the matter?'

'Johnny Willis. I know he's a boxer, but is he a violent man?'

Five minutes later, Greene put the phone down. His neck twitched. What the hell's going on? He dialled Willis's number. No reply.

Willis was in his car, heading for the motorway and Westhampton.

Kenny drained the last of his beer and placed the bottle on the table. Mary sagged in her chair.

'Reckon yer best out of there,' Kenny said, looking at his youngest brother. 'Steer clear. Stay away. They might get away with it but yer know how hot coppers are on big jobs like that. Telly says they got around a million, could be even more. It's big stuff.'

Willis scratched at his throat. 'It's a bleeding mess. But I couldn't tell 'em to piss off, could I? Wish I'd taken the twenty grand now. Least that way I'd have something for my trouble.'

'No, Johnny.' Mary sat upright. 'You don't want anything to do with that money.'

'Mary's right. The money puts you in the frame.'

'Guess you're right.'

'We are,' said Kenny. 'You've gotta make a clean break. Come back here, if you like.'

'What about Karen?' asked Mary. 'She knows. Will she say anything?'

'Don't think so. She's not even told her dad. I don't think she will.' He paused. 'She just wants away from me; her and Suzie. I can't even talk to her.'

Kenny looked at the clock. It was nearly seven.

'I'm gonna pick Col up. He's at the house. Plasterers are finishing off. Come and have a look round, see what we've been doing. Then we'll have a beer.'

Gordon Mitchell answered the phone. Shortly, Karen came on the line.

'Hello, Mary. If Johnny's with you, I'll put the phone down. I won't talk to him.'

'It's all right, Karen, He's not here. It's just me.'

'Right. I'm not being rude to you. You've done nothing wrong. I suppose Johnny's told you we're finished.'

'Aren't you being a bit hasty? I know you're upset, but so's Johnny.'

'Upset? I don't want anything more to do with him. I warned him, but he took no notice. He lied to me. Sorry, Mary, but I'm not getting involved in his... in that life. I'm not a gangster's moll.'

'Johnny's not a gangster. Look, Karen, I know he isn't perfect, but he's not a bad man. He's just easily led sometimes. Doesn't think things through properly. But he's trying to make something of himself. It's not been easy for him, you know.'

'I know what you're saying, Mary. You're his sister, his flesh and blood. You're bound to love him—'

'I thought you loved him.'

'I did... in a way, I still do.' She paused, then spoke again, in a quieter, softer voice. 'But I won't be dragged into that sort of life. I told him – warned him – but he still did it. He lied, Mary. He tried to cover up. No, I can't live like that. I've got Suzie to think about. Thank God we didn't get married.'

'What are you going to do?'

'I'll probably move back here. Live with my parents again. I'll go back to work. I'd always planned that but now I'll do it a bit earlier. Mum will help with Suzie.'

'What about Suzie? Johnny's got a right to see her.'

'No way.' Karen's voice was terse. 'It's a clean break. I don't want him anywhere near her. Never.'

'But you can't do that.'

'Oh yes, I can. And if he challenges me, I'll tell the courts why I don't want him around. Then he'd be in trouble. Real trouble. You can tell Johnny that.'

'I will. But I'm sorry you feel that way.'

'You tell him, Mary. Tell him to stay away and I'll never say anything. Not a word to anybody. Okay?'

'Okay... But it's all so sad.'

'Yes, it is.' Her voice broke. 'I didn't want it this way. It's not my fault.'

Mary listened to the sobs, the heartache down the wires.

'I've got to go, Mary. Sorry. I really like you. We could've been good friends. I hope you have better luck with Pete, I really do. Bye.'

'Bye,' said Mary. Oh Johnny, Johnny, she thought, what a mess you've made.


Willis woke. A vice squeezed his skull and hammers knocked at his temples. He'd never been so hungover. He reached the bathroom just in time. As he wiped his mouth, he looked in a mirror. Red-rimmed eyes. Grey complexion.

'Never again,' he muttered.

Can't drown your sorrows in booze, he thought. Pathetic. Doesn't change anything. You've got to face facts. Turn the page, start a new chapter. As Karen says, that book's closed.


The new chapter started with a phone call to Greene's office on Monday morning. He arranged with Vanessa to meet Michael at eleven on Thursday. Then he phoned Mercer. Would he have another word with Lew Sellers?

'What's happened, Johnny?' asked Mercer.

'Don't wanna say too much. Let's just say things have gone a bit sour down there. I'm coming back home. I need a change.'

'Sellers wasn't too happy when you joined Greene. I reckon it's best if you approach him direct. Not through me.'

'Is he pissed off with me?'

'He didn't like it when you turned him down. Of course not. And he was annoyed about the Greene business. They're not exactly buddies, you know.'

'Not good, then?'

'They might see this as an opportunity to get one over Greene. You're still a champion and the San Remo robbery really didn't do you any harm. Give him a bell. Talk to Lew. That's all you can do.'

His next move was to drive back to Islington on Wednesday. From there he phoned the Mitchell house. He told Gordon he would sign over the house to Karen. She could sell it or continue to pay the mortgage as she chose.

'It's up to Karen. She'll make a big profit either way. But that's all she's getting. If I can't see Suzie, that's it. Tell her the book's closed.'

Thursday morning he met Greene and in thirty minutes their partnership was dissolved. In two years and twelve fights, Willis had grossed nearly half a million.

'Thanks a lot, Michael.' They shook hands. 'It's been a good two years. But it's all gone sour for me down here. I'm going back to Westhampton,' he said.

Greene knew he couldn't alter Willis's decision. In a way, he was relieved and he said as much to Gillian.

'He's a good ticket seller. Good fighter with some big ones still left in him. But he needs to sort himself out or he'll be in big trouble.'

An hour later, Willis shook hands with Sellers. The veteran manager asked what had gone wrong with Greene.

'Nothing. The deal with Michael was that I lived in London. But that's not possible now – I've had a few problems. Personal problems, nothing to do with boxing. Fact is, my girl's left me and taken our kid with her. But that's all sorted now and I'm going back to Westhampton.'

Sellers insisted on a three-year contract. No payment up front and no guarantees on purses.

'You're a top-line championship fighter now. You don't need that.'

Willis assured him he wouldn't sign for any other manager. He sealed it with a wet palm and thanked him.

'You won't regret it,' he said. 'I still want that world title.'

'One other thing,' Sellers said as he walked him to the door. 'Training and trainers. You've gotta sort that out. We've got good sparring in our gym. You can come down anytime. But, if you stay in Westhampton, you pay for sparring. It's gotta be quality stuff. And you pay the trainer, the corner men.'

Willis organised that on Friday morning.

'Ron'll look after you,' said Thomson. 'I work mostly for Michael, as you know. But it's not exclusive. No contract. I'll be happy to work the corner with you. Two per cent or flat fees –

whatever. We'll work it out.'

That left only one other detail – leaving the Islington house. He spent the afternoon emptying drawers and wardrobes, stopping only for a few minutes to use the telephone.

'Hi, Natalie. Doing anything tonight?' he said.

'No. Hallowe'en party tomorrow at Ginny's, but tonight's free.'

'Great. We'll have a meal and then come back to my place. How's that sound?'

'Stuff the meal, honey. I'll bring a pizza. We'll eat it in bed.'

Saturday evening, Natalie helped Willis load his bags into the Mercedes. Then he strolled with her to the high street and put her in a cab.

'Sure you won't come to the party? Be great fun.'

'No, thanks. I've gotta get home. Enjoy yourself and give my love to Ginny. On second thoughts, better make that "my regards".'

Back at the house, Willis collected the black case containing the Lonsdale Belt from its hiding place in the loft. He also picked up a supermarket carrier bag. The doorbell rang.

'Trick or treat, mister.'

Three urchins at his doorstep; couldn't be more than nine years old. Willis laughed and he dug his hand into the carrier bag.

'Here, how's that for a treat?'

He handed them each a ten-pound note, then closed the front door for the last time.

The happy trick-or-treaters waltzed down the path and shouted back over their shoulders, 'Thanks, mister.'

Willis put the Lonsdale Belt and supermarket bag under the front passenger seat. Watched the kids wander down the road.

What's thirty quid when you've treated yourself to five grand? he thought. Them bastards won't miss that out of a million or so.

## Chapter Twenty-Two

In late November, Willis signed two contracts. The first was with Lew Sellers. The second secured a three-bedroom detached house. Westhampton Golf Course was at the end of the long, rear garden and to the front was a horseshoe drive and a double part-integral garage.

The Islington house transfer had gone through and it had been sold again. Karen's solicitors wrote that she didn't want any furnishings, so Willis had until mid-December to remove anything he wanted. He had most of the furniture transported to his new home.

One bedroom was set aside for Mary.

'I'll stay some weekends,' she agreed. 'You'd be amazed how Ma's looking after herself these days. Even cooks Sunday lunch for us all. She's a changed woman.'

'Not before time. She knows you won't be around for ever. Have you sorted a wedding date yet?'

'No. We haven't talked about it lately.'

'I'll have a word with Pete. Buck him up a bit.'

'No you won't, Johnny,' she said, alarmed. 'If you do, I'll never speak to you again.'

'Only kidding, sis.'


Willis also found a new workplace. He couldn't train at his old amateur gym, although Brown still occasionally helped Vic Grant with the Friar youngsters. The solution was an old fight factory above the Hare and Hounds pub in the centre of Westhampton. It had been there for ever.

Clive Yeoman, a featherweight from the late sixties, now paid the rent. He was both manager and trainer to five professionals. A one-man band, at forty-five he still dreamed of finding a star. He'd had no luck in twelve years, however, just a succession of willing but limited hopefuls from the Westhampton area.

'Be glad to have Johnny here,' he told Brown. 'My kids might learn something from him.'

Brown offered to help with their training.

'Great, Ronnie. Some nights when I'm away at shows the other fighters have to look after themselves. That's not good. If you're here, Ronnie, that'll be great. Cheers, Ronnie.'

The room was shabby. Fading fight posters peeled off brown walls. The ring was small and the kit dilapidated. There was one leaky shower cubicle, rarely used. Willis fell in love with the place. It was basic, no frills, an ideal place for a hard profession.

But he made changes. He bought a heavy punchbag, a floor-to-ceiling ball and a reclining exercise board. A workman needed proper tools. One weekend, Brown painted the walls white and put up new posters, but he managed to preserve a couple of the older bills. They had Yeoman listed at the bottom.

'It's great.' Yeoman looked around at the transformation. 'Thanks Ronnie, Johnny. What a difference a lick of paint makes. Fresher, innit? And the kit, Johnny. Quality stuff. Can't thank you enough, Johnny.'

'That's okay, Clive,' said Willis. 'Take it as our thanks for letting us use the place, Clive.' Jeez, it's catching, he thought. Clive this, Clive that.

Willis knew two of the boxers. They'd joined Friar in his last year as an amateur. The other three had never boxed amateur. Rough-and-ready lads; one from the other side of the Burnmoor Estate. He remembered Kenny delivering a new TV.

'Years ago. I was just a kid. Great big colour set. Still got it.'

The quintet ranged from lightweight to light-heavyweight. Willis sparred with them all. Nothing heavy, but it kept him ticking over. And the lads appreciated working out with a champion.

Christmas Day was celebrated in the new house. Mary and Connie spent much of it in the kitchen. Kenny, Colin and Pete drank plenty of beer, but Willis restricted himself to orange juice and a glass of wine with the turkey.

The two elder brothers introduced extra company in the evening. Sharon and Donna, two fun-loving girls they'd met weeks earlier at a club. Just good friends – good between the sheets, too, as it happened. Willis thought briefly of Karen. He'd posted a card to her and sent a giant cuddly toy to Suzie. Karen sent him a card to Johnson Close, signed 'Best wishes'. He didn't put it on display.

Willis's first fight under Sellers's management, in January 1993, was staged three thousand miles from home. Bill Clinton was moving into the White House when Willis arrived in Atlantic City, America's east-coast version of Las Vegas.

Don Murray brokered the deal. Apart from Willis, he took two other boxers to appear in six-round bouts at Resorts Casino Hotel. It set up a mini USA–British match. The preliminary boxers gained valuable experience. Willis grossed one hundred and fifty thousand dollars, all expenses paid, staying in Resorts for three nights.

Opponent Mike Donovan was the main attraction. With only one defeat in twenty-six contests, the Irish New Yorker was being groomed for stardom. He was eleventh in the world ratings. Willis was seventh following the draw in Italy.

'You're the name opponent,' said Murray. 'They want you on Donovan's record. That's why we're being paid. A win for him and he'll shoot into the top ten. But he's not up to it. You'll do him, okay. American TV exposure is our bonus.'

Willis listened and nodded. But he was more concerned that Canzoneri, promoted to second in the ratings, was lined up to challenge for the title in Bologna next month. I was that close, he thought.

Thomson hadn't made the trip. It wasn't a financial proposition. Brown, Murray and Sellers would be in the corner. Murray in the ring as senior cornerman, the other two working outside the ropes.

The ten-round fight would be broadcast live on TV at four o'clock on Saturday, before the punters headed for dinner and the tables.

On Friday night, in Murray's room, Willis viewed two video clips of Donovan. The matchmaker had watched Donovan fight in Boston.

'Look at his left hand,' said Murray. 'His pet punch is the left hook. So, he holds it low. Brings it back even lower after jabbing. Your quick right over the top will do him.'

Maybe, thought Willis, maybe.

Willis dominated the first two rounds with solid jabs and occasional rights to the jaw. Donovan was slower in thought and action. But the hurtful rights forced him to hold his left hand higher. He was defensive, not aggressive.

In the third, Willis double-jabbed and feinted to throw a following right. Instead, he stepped in with a cracking left hook which felled the ginger-topped Donovan like a giant redwood.

'I can't believe how easy he made it look,' said Sellers when Mercer phoned him at seven. It was midnight back home. Mercer was pleased with the result, but annoyed that the *News* declined to pay for his journey to New Jersey.

'He's some fighter,' Murray said to Brown over dinner. 'I knew he was special when he roughed up Matt Gibson. That was some battle. But, tonight, he made it look easy. Believe me, that Donovan's no slouch.'

To round off the American adventure, Willis won three thousand dollars on the blackjack tables and then entertained a grateful cocktail waitress in his room when she took her supper break at midnight.

The land of opportunity, mused Willis. They got that bit right.

American Joey Robinson and his outraged handlers left Bologna in fury. The world championship had been taken from them on disqualification in round six, for persistent low blows. Robinson was a renowned body puncher. 'Sonofabitch jumped on 'em. Made 'em low,' he said.

A defence of his British and Commonwealth titles was next for Willis. He battered Shaun Metcalfe to a second-round defeat. The Leeds fighter was outgunned and outclassed. Victory earned Willis the Lonsdale Belt outright. Thomson had worked the corner again. 'Something to treasure, my son,' he said.

'Sure,' said Willis. 'But I need something bigger than this. There's nobody in Britain to touch me. I want the world title.

That's where the real treasure lies.'

World champion Canzoneri officially relinquished the European championship on the day Willis beat Metcalfe. Two weeks later, the EBU announced that Willis and Spaniard Jose Carreno should meet for the vacant championship.

Murray drove Sellers to the Hare and Hounds gym. Yeoman was effusive in his greetings. Lew this, Don that, Lew the other. Willis smiled as he wrapped his hands. Yeoman even made a sales pitch. Two of his fighters, both welterweights, were ready for a London airing. Murray listened, non-committal.

'I'll bear 'em in mind, Clive.' Could be useful fodder, he thought.

Later, Sellers and Murray sat with Willis and Brown in a corner of the pub. The manager proposed the deal. Seventy thousand pounds for the European title fight.

'It's a good purse and Harry can work around that. He'll make a deal with the Spaniards. Failing that, at least he'll have a chance of winning a purse bid. We don't wanna go to Spain if we can avoid it. Let's fight at home.'

'Dunno,' said Willis. 'Seventy grand sounds reasonable. But I'll go to Spain if there's more. I'll fight anywhere. We did okay in America.'

'That was different.' Murray lit a king-sized cigarette. 'The Yanks paid well and I knew you'd take Donovan. It was good business for us. The thing with the European fight is to make certain we win. Get the odds on our side. Let them do the travelling, live in a hotel, eat strange food. Have no real support. You know what it's like.'

'Yeah. But, in the end, it's only me and him, wherever we fight.'

'True.' Murray inhaled. 'Didn't work out in San Remo, though, did it? Everyone knows you won that. Close, but you won. Except you didn't get the decision. Didn't get the title. At home it would have been different. That's why the Italians paid you. Kept the odds in their favour. Now look at Canzoneri. He's the world champion. Could've been you.'

'I know what you're saying. But this Spaniard ain't Canzoneri.

I won't need any judges.'

'Joey Robinson didn't. Canzoneri got him disqualified.'

'Okay, I understand. But I still think I'll take care of this Spaniard anywhere. Don't you?'

'As a matter of fact, I do. We all do.'

'Well then? What's the fuss?' Willis leaned back, satisfied.

Murray stubbed out his cigarette, only half-smoked. 'Let me put it this way. Generally, there are obvious dangers about boxing abroad. Record books prove it and, believe me, we've experienced all manner of shenanigans over the years.'

'More than enough,' said Sellers the sage. Brown thought of San Remo. The missing stool.

'In your case,' Murray continued, 'we know you're capable of winning away. Like you did in America. What we also know is that you're damn certain to win at home. I'd bet my house on it. That's why you should fight the Spaniard here. In London, at Wembley. We're not asking you to fight for peanuts. That's not our way.'

'I'm not complaining about seventy grand. But I'd take more if I can get it. That's what I mean.'

'Fine. We understand that.' Murray lit another cigarette. 'But consider this. What if the Spaniards win a purse bid but it's only a bit more? A grand, say? It might only be a few hundred. Is that worth the hassle?' Murray didn't wait for an answer. 'The main point,' he went on, 'is that, once we've got the title, we'll make money. Believe me, we know what we're talking about. We've been there, many times.'

'Yeah, I know that. But what sort of money are we talking?'

'We have a strategy,' said Sellers. 'A plan to land the world title.' He looked from Murray to Willis. 'I'll explain. When you're European champion, the EBU dictate mandatory defences. They take it out of our hands. Once every six months you must defend against their nominated challenger. But we can make voluntary defences. That's when you cash in. Challengers come cheaper then. The guys in the bottom half of the rankings grab the chance. They might never get a mandatory nomination, see?'

Murray stubbed out his smoke and took over the plot.

'Two defences inside four months, say. Hundred grand each

time. That's two hundred and seventy thousand in total, guaranteed. Not only that, by then you'll be solid in the world ratings. We'll be pushing for a world title shot. Now isn't that better than taking a risk, however small, of fighting in Spain?'

Murray was convincing. Willis agreed to the seventy thousand.

Two days later, he sat in the same seat. Mercer had watched him train and a *News* photographer had recorded his workout.

'How's it going with Lew?'

'Fine, Bob. But, to tell the truth, Don seems to do most of the business.'

'The power behind the throne.'

'Something like that.'

'Don's the worker, the pusher. You've got to remember that Lew and Harry Jacobs are not young men. They're both in their seventies. Jacobs hasn't been in the best of health for some time – heart problem. Though a lot of people say the old bastard hasn't got one.'

Willis smiled. He'd only met the promoter a few times. Hard-boiled, he thought. Mercer continued.

'Don's worked with them for years. Now they're letting him get on with things. They have the final word but they're giving him his head. He's got a few fighters of his own, as you know, and I reckon he's also into Lew's fighters. A small percentage, maybe.'

'Not with me. My contract's just with Lew.'

'But that doesn't stop Murray from having a piece of Lew's action. That's their deal. Understand?'

Wembley was nearly sold out when Duncan Anderson, a London-based Scot managed by Sellers, outpointed American Mike McCormack in a world light-heavyweight final eliminator. In the chief supporting bout, Willis forced Carreno into submission. The Spanish champion, from Barcelona, retired on his stool after seven rounds. Willis was European champion again, three days before his twenty-sixth birthday.

Five weeks later, French champion Andre Martin was knocked out in the fifth at Wembley Conference Centre. Martin was ranked eighth in Europe.

On 7 September, German champion Karl Jansen got his chance. He lasted five rounds at Wembley until the referee called it off, blood pouring from Jansen's numerous wounds. Willis moved up to the fifth spot in the world ratings.

His career record showed thirty-eight wins in forty fights. One cut-eye defeat and the controversial draw in San Remo were the only blemishes. In only eight months and five fights with Sellers, he'd grossed three hundred and seventy thousand pounds.

Willis put the money to work. Kenny and Colin started conversion work on two more houses. They also contracted for extensions, repairs and other minor building works, employing sub-contractors but they turned the pub security business over to Payne. He'd earned it. Willis also paid off his mortgage, parked a new blue Mercedes in his garage and bought Mary a Metro. She didn't want anything larger or more powerful.

In October, Willis was summoned to a meeting in Sellers's office. The EBU had nominated the new Italian champion, Cosimo Belotti, as mandatory challenger, but Sellers had other ideas.

'We're stalling,' said Sellers. 'Don's working on something bigger. It could get us some grace, especially as we've defended twice already.'

'Something bigger?'

'Duncan Anderson's fighting for the world title next month. The date's still to be firmed up. But it's in New York. Madison Square Garden. Don's trying to get you on the bill in an eliminator against Howard Miller, the number three. But these things take time.'

'An eliminator at Madison Square! That's special, Lew.'

'If Don can fix it. Point is, we're asking the EBU for time. World eliminator takes precedence and all that jargon. They might buy it or they might insist you defend.'

'What if they insist?'

'If we get the eliminator, stuff 'em. If we don't, we'll defend. But we're trying to get the eliminator and go there as European champion. It's best that way.'

'Something to fall back on, you mean?'

'Sort of. Titles are hard-earned, Johnny. Let's keep 'em as long as we can.'

'Sure.' Willis nodded. 'Where's Don now?'

'At the gym, seeing one of his fighters. Pop along if you like. He'll be there most of the afternoon.'

Brian Adams was walking to the gym as Willis paid his cab fare. They shook hands and entered together. Adams had just finished a stint in the bookies. Now he wore his assistant trainer's hat, just for an hour. Willis rapidly explained the reason for his visit.

'Pleased for you,' said Adams. 'We'll have a cuppa in the caff later. If you're in no rush, that is. Nat's coming in for a lift home.'

Déjà vu, thought Willis.

'Mind you, if you're there, I'll be going home alone,' Adams laughed.

Murray immediately cut short a conversation with another boxer and strode across to greet Willis. Different from their first meeting. Murray 'had to fly' then. I must be a star! thought Willis.

'Lew phoned to say you were coming. Good to see you, Johnny. I haven't got any more news at the moment. Another two or three days. That should do it.'

'What're the chances?'

'Good, I'd say. Promoter wants it and our end's pretty well tied up. Depends on the other lot. Come into the office. We'll talk in private.'

The office was no more than a partitioned wood and frosted-glass erection in one corner of the gym. An hour later, after several phone interruptions, Willis emerged, in time for a cuppa with Adams. And Natalie, of course.

She shrieked when she saw Willis.

'Johnny – how y'doing, honey? You're looking great.'

'So are you, Natalie. Like the coat.'

She was wearing fake leopard skin with a matching beret and black knee-length boots.

'It's cold out there, honey. A gal's gotta keep her bits warm. Still, it's okay in here.'

She dropped her duffle bag and discarded the coat, revealing black hipster pants and red crew-necked sweater. Her bust, incredibly, seemed even bigger. Four hours later, she was naked in Willis's arms. In Ginny's flat.

*Déjà vu.*

## Chapter Twenty-Three

Sellers phoned with the news on Saturday afternoon. Willis was watching TV. Racing from Catterick. He'd got an interest, one hundred pounds on the favourite in the third race.

He quickly forgot about that.

'We've got the eliminator,' said Sellers, '26 November.'

The purse was two hundred and fifty thousand dollars and Murray had nailed the promoter for three return flights and two hotel rooms for six nights. Thomson and Brown could share. Sellers and Murray were contracted to go a week earlier with Anderson.

Willis replaced the receiver. Must let Ron and Freddie know, he thought. Make sure they can get away. Just then, the phone rang.

'Hello?'

'Hi – is that you Johnny?'

'Yeah. Who's this?'

'Julie, Julie O'Sullivan.'

A vision of long legs flashed through his mind.

'You do remember me, don't you?'

'Course I do, Julie. Long time no see. How are you?'

'Fine. Hope you don't mind me calling but I bumped into a friend of yours yesterday. She gave me this number.'

'Yeah? Who was that?'

'Natalie. I had a swimwear shoot and she came to the studio to meet a friend of hers; another one of the models. Anyway, to cut a story short, we all had a drink together and Natalie got talking about you to her friend. You saw her the other day, didn't you?'

'That's right. I was in London on business. Didn't expect to see her.'

'So I gather. She said it was a surprise. She hadn't seen you in a long while. Anyway, I said I worked for Gillian and that I knew you, but that I hadn't seen you in ages. So she gave me your number. Nice of her.'

'Natalie's a nice girl.'

'Yes. I can see why you like her. Bubbly personality and big knockers.'

Willis envisaged Julie's generous smile. 'She hasn't got your legs,' he said.

'Anyway, I rang to ask you something.'

'What's that?'

'Another time you're down this way, will you let me know? I'd like to see you again. Have you still got my number?'

'Should have.' Willis flicked through the pages of his address book. 'Yeah, got it.'

'Good. Well, bear me in mind, won't you?'

'Sure will. Tell you what, if you get the time, come up here. Stay over. I'd love to see ya. It's been a long time.'

'I'll do that. Make a change to get away from bloody Paddington. I'll check my diary. Next month maybe?'

'After that, Julie. I've got a big fight in New York next month. Just been fixed today.'

'New York? How exciting! Always dreamed of going there. They don't want any round girls, do they? Only kidding.'

'Wouldn't have you, anyway. You put me off. Ruin my concentration.'

Julie's laugh tinkled down the wires. 'Okay, Johnny. It's been nice talking to you again. All the best in New York.'

'Thanks. I'll see you later.'

'Look forward to it. Give me a call when you're back.'

'Sure thing. Bye.'

Willis put the receiver down. Well, well. Nice girl, he thought.

Racing had finished on the TV. Willis flicked to the text pages and called up the Catterick results. No good – third. Still, it's only a ton. Nothing compared to a quarter of a million dollars.

He dialled Brown's number.

'Hello, it's Johnny. Is that Lauren?'

'No, it's Angela.'

Willis always picked the wrong one. The twins sounded so alike on the phone.

'Right, sorry Angela. Is your dad there?'

'No, he's at the hospital.'

'The hospital? What's he done?'

'Nothing. He's all right. He's gone to visit old Mrs Riley. Dad called at her home this afternoon – he often pops round – and the neighbours said she'd be taken to hospital. On Wednesday, I think it was.'

Mary Riley had pneumonia and pleurisy. She was pale and frail in the small hospital bed, but her light blue eyes twinkled when Willis walked in, carrying flowers and grapes. Brown sat on a bedside chair.

'What a surprise. Lovely to see you, Johnny.' Her breathing was shallow, laboured. It was clearly an effort to talk. 'I'm so proud of you. Harry would've been, too. You're doing really well. And you've kept out of trouble.'

If only, he thought. 'It's down to you, Mary.' He gently held a bony hand and stroked it with his thumb. 'You put me right. That chat we had.'

'You're a good boy,' she said softly.

'When I fight for the world title, I'll dedicate it to you and Harry. Just you see.'

Her cracked lips formed a small smile.

'But how're you? I didn't find out until an hour ago.'

'Getting better. I couldn't get out of bed for days. One of my daughters, Betty, popped round. She called the ambulance,' she coughed. 'It's just my chest now. Sore, you know. I'll be back on my feet soon.'

After twenty minutes, Willis and Brown left. The old lady needed rest. On the way out, Willis told Brown about New York.

'I'll take as much time off as you want,' said Brown. 'There's not a lot of work about at the moment, Christmas is coming. They're thinking decorations, not decorating.'

They headed for the car park.

'You'll need some good sparring for this one. Top class stuff.'

An ambulance sped past towards the emergency entrance. Blue light flashing.

'Some poor sod,' said Willis.

The phone rang as Willis entered the lounge.

'Johnny, it's Mary,' an agitated voice said. 'I've been trying to get you for an hour.'

'I've been out. What's the panic?'

'I'm at the hospital.'

'What? I've just come from there. What's happened?'

'It's Ma. Think she's had a heart attack. She collapsed in the kitchen. You've gotta get here. She's in intensive care. Kenny and Col are here.'

'I'm on my way,' he said. Got to be there for Mary, he thought. She needs me.


There were wires and drips everywhere. Monitors bipped, beeped. Connie's eyes were closed. Brothers and sister turned as Willis walked in.

'How bad is it?'

'They've done tests,' said Kenny.

A nurse appeared. 'It's a bit crowded in here,' she said. 'Sorry, but if you don't mind, perhaps you'd take it in turns? Two at a time, maybe. Okay?'

Willis retreated to the door. 'C'mon, Mary. Let's get a cuppa tea.'

Willis fed coins into a vending machine for two polystyrene cups of a weak, tasteless brew. They sat side by side on plastic waiting-room chairs.

'What happened?'

'I heard Ma cry out, so I rushed into the kitchen and she was on the floor. Hand to her chest, all scrunched up. I phoned for an ambulance and then went back to her. It was horrible. I didn't know what to do. She was breathing but couldn't talk. Her eyes kept closing and I was frightened, thought she was gonna die. When the ambulance came, they put a mask on her. Oxygen, I suppose. Think they gave her an injection. Anyway, I came in the ambulance with her. They took her away and told me to wait. So then I started ringing you. I got Kenny on his mobile. They were working but they got here just before I managed to get you. I'm sure it's her heart.'

'I'm not surprised.' Willis sipped his tea. 'It had to happen, the way she's carried on.'

Mary looked at him. He seemed cold, detached. She shook her head.

'It's serious, Johnny. Don't be so hard. She's not had it easy, you know.'

'Easy? You must be joking. She—'

'No, Johnny, no.' Her voice was severe, angry. 'Not again. Don't bad-mouth her. Not now, not here. She's fighting for her life and you don't know the half of it. You really don't.'

Willis watched as Mary stood and venomously tossed the cup into a waste basket. Tea dregs splattered the wall.

'Now look what you've made me do,' she said. She turned back and stood over him, her brown eyes glaring. 'One day... one day, Johnny, you'll understand. I hope it's not too late.' She spun away and walked towards the door.

'Sis – wait. Look, I'm sorry. I know you're upset. You've cared for her all these years—'

'Don't say any more. Not a word.' Mary studied his face. 'I'm the only one who knows the truth. I wish you knew, wish you could understand. But I can't tell you.' She resumed her slow walk but glanced back over her shoulder. 'Are you coming?'

Willis followed her back to Connie's room. Kenny and Colin vacated their seats and, grim-faced, they silently shuffled out.

Mary sat and bowed her head. She closed her eyes, muttering. Willis stood at the end of the bed. She's praying, he thought.

He looked at Connie's face. Ashen and lined. Blonde matted hair pushed back and spread on the pillow. Looks old, he thought, older than fifty-three. Then, he could swear, her eyelids flickered. They opened a fraction and her dull eyes looked at him. The lids opened wider, in surprise. A small twitch at the edge of her mouth. Lips moved. She was trying to speak but the effort was too much. The eyelids closed. But a smile creased the corners of her mouth.

Connie went home after ten days. She'd been lucky; given a warning. Rest was ordered. She had tablets and hospital appointments. More tests to monitor her progress.

Mary took time off work but two weeks later she returned.

Connie was brighter and could fend for herself.

'Don't fuss, Mary. I'll be all right,' she said.

Willis sometimes visited. He wouldn't normally have bothered, but he'd been shaken by Mary's verbal attack. It was the first time she'd spoken sharply to him.

Mostly he trained, hard. Three times a day. He imported two sparring partners from London. Thirty pounds a round and six rounds a day. They boarded in a small hotel for three weeks. In total, it cost him over three thousand pounds, but he flew to New York in superb condition. Sharp, honed and eager.

Only one worry nagged in the back of his mind. He kept hearing Mary's voice.

*I'm the only one who knows the truth… I wish you knew… but I can't tell you.*

Manhattan amazed Willis. The towering skyline, Broadway and Times Square. All bustle in the day, a neon spectacle at night. The clattering subway, yellow cabs, gridlocked traffic, so many people! And Madison Square Garden. There it was, a massive ten-storey building on Seventh Avenue and Thirty-Third Street, above Pennsylvania Station, the busiest railway station in America.

Okay, so it wasn't the original Garden. The fourth, in fact, opened in 1968. But Ali and Frazier had battled there. The greats of showbiz – Elvis, Sinatra, The Stones, John Lennon – had appeared in concerts. Now, Willis thought, I'm here. A kid from the Burnmoor Estate fighting in front of twenty thousand people in the world's most famous arena.

Willis and Anderson shared a locker room; large, clean with wooden benches and lockers. Willis was in the third fight on the programme, Anderson in the fifth. Both were on satellite TV beamed back to Britain. For once, all the Willis family had to be content with an armchair view.

'Stay with Ma,' he'd told his brothers. But the gesture was aimed at Mary.

The vast arena was barely two-thirds occupied when Willis made the long walk to the ring. He'd warmed up in the changing room and sweat glistened on his brow as he short-hooked under the fierce ring lamps. The New Yorkers had seen it all before. Limey lamb to the slaughter.

Howard Miller was tall; six feet two inches. All ebony muscle with long arms. No wonder they called him 'The Spear'. He'd earned his number three ranking on the back of thirty wins, no defeats. Twenty-two inside the distance.

The MC started his announcement.

'Twelve rounds of boxing... an eliminator for...'

Willis gazed into the arena. Must be fifteen thousand out there. He saw Mercer at ringside, sitting alongside the other British press, and winked at him. Mercer smiled back.

'...from New York City, undefeated in...'

Thomson removed the towel from Willis's head. The crowd cheered and whistled as Miller raised his right arm at the end of his introduction.

'...with a record of thirty-eight wins, one draw and...'

Murray pulled Willis's head towards him and whispered in his ear.

'Remember, you're champion of Europe. He's not even a champion. Get into his ribs. Shake him up,' he said.

'...champion of Europe, Great Britain and the Common-wealth... John-kneee Will-issss!'

The spattering of British fans cheered and waved their flags. America sat and waited.

Miller poked out a lazy left lead. A range finder. Moved to his left, then switched. Drifted to his right. Always on the move. Dropped on to his heels. Whiff-whiff-whiff. Three quick, light punches and away. All three had landed on Willis's gloves.

Willis edged forward. Rolled from the waist and jabbed at the midriff. Miller knocked it away with his right hand. Moved back. Whiff-whiff. Flicked jabs at Willis's head and scooted to his right. Willis stepped across. Whipped a left hook under the ribs. Miller gasped. Bumped a retaliatory right on to Willis's head and drifted away to his left.

'Good work, my son.' Thomson smeared grease into Willis's eyebrows and over his bristled cheeks. 'Keep tight. Hunt the body.'

'Don't follow him.' Murray leaned across the ropes. 'Cut him off in the corners. Make him fight.'

Whiff-whiff. Over Willis's head. Miller side-stepped one way, then the other. Whiff-whiff, as he moved clear. Willis jabbed at the body and stepped in with a solid upward jab. It landed under the chin, jolting Miller's head back. Thumping right to the stomach. Crunching left hook. Miller retreated, felt the ropes on his calves and back and started to slide away. Willis hammered at the body. Miller dropped his elbows to block the blows. Bingo! A whipped left hook to the right ear sent Miller down on to his left knee.

Miller up at count of seven. Backed off, still on the move. Willis jabbed the throat. Right hook to the ribs. Left to the back of the ear. Miller grabbed and locked Willis's head in the crook of his right arm. Miller on the move at the bell.

Connie sat on the edge of her seat. Colin passed another can of beer to Kenny. Pete shook his head. Mary stood in the kitchen and looked at the clock. Just after two. Could be another forty minutes. Be lucky, Johnny!

Connie sipped her brandy. Medicinal.

'You okay, Ma?'

'Fine, Kenny. Why shouldn't I be? Johnny's got that bloke in his pocket.'

'Long way to go yet. Twelve rounds.'

'Pfff. No way. He can't live with our Johnny.'

Gordon Mitchell drew on his cigar and lifted his glass of gin and tonic. I don't know what you did to upset my daughter, he thought, but you're one hell of a fighter.

Karen, legs curled beneath her on the sofa, looked at the familiar face on the TV. He was in close-up, in the corner. Eyes staring. Intent, listening to Freddie. Still a handsome bastard, she thought.

Brian Adams rolled his shoulders, then his neck.

'You all right?'

'Yeah. Just a bit stiff, Nat. It's all this sitting, watching TV all night. Not used to it.'

'Know what you mean,' Natalie yawned. Stretched out her arms. Mammoth bust expanded under her bathrobe.

'Won't be much longer, will it?'

'Shouldn't think so. Reckon Johnny's got his measure. But Dunc's not on for another hour.'

'I'm not stopping up for that. Johnny's all I'm interested in.'

'I know that, Nat.'

Willis blazed into action. Miller tried to grab the bullying Brit but Willis pushed him off and clubbed at the wilting, black body. Miller bit hard on his mouthpiece and slung a right at Willis's head. Missed. Right hook under the ribs buckled Miller's legs. Right uppercut jolted his head. The American didn't see the left hook.

'By count-out after twenty-six seconds of the third round…'

Connie shouted to her daughter. 'Mary, Mary, c'mon! Quick! It's all over.'

Mary glanced at the clock. Nearly twenty past two. That didn't take long. She raced to the back room.

'What happened?'

'Johnny won in the third,' said Payne.

'Shush,' said Connie. 'Look, they're gonna talk to him.'

Willis stood at ringside. There was sweat on his brow but he was breathing evenly. His eyes were bright in triumph.

'A great win, Johnny. Were you surprised to win so quickly?'

A microphone was pushed towards him.

'Thanks… well, honestly, I didn't think it'd be that quick. I'd trained for twelve rounds and felt real strong in there, you know… I dunno, I just felt, well, sort of inspired. I mean, look at this place.' He turned his head, glancing around the arena. 'It's fantastic. If you can't turn it on here, where can you do it?'

'You certainly turned it on tonight. You've done Britain proud.'

'Yeah, well, thanks. I've got great supporters. I know many of them couldn't be here tonight. It's a long way to come. But, to everyone back home watching, I just wanna say thanks. And a big

"Hi" to my family. I'll be home soon. Love you all.'

'We hear that your mother's not been too well lately.'

'That's right. But she's okay now.'

'Your win tonight should be a tonic for her.'

Willis brushed his mouth with a robed arm. 'Yeah, well… I hope all the people back home, 'specially those in Westhampton, feel like I do now.' He grinned.

'Look at that monitor over there, Johnny. We'll show you the finish. Talk us through it, will you?'

'Right. Wow, good uppercut, eh? Bang! I knew he'd never get up off that hook. What a beauty.'

'Let's bring in your manager, Lew Sellers. Lew, come in here…'

Mercer followed Willis back to his locker room. The pair chatted as Willis showered and changed.

'Your best performance yet,' said the reporter. Might even be the peak fight of his career, he thought. But Willis was still young and improving all the time. Who knows what's to come?

When Anderson made his way to the ring, Willis tagged along and settled into a spare seat in the guest section. He couldn't soak up enough of the atmosphere.

Anderson soaked up too many punches. He was stopped in the eleventh. Sellers hadn't got another world champion.

Not yet, anyway, thought Willis.

# Chapter Twenty-Four

Willis decided it was time for the family to leave the Burnmoor Estate. He confirmed it when he saw a four-bedroom house for sale, less than three hundred yards from his own home. It was vacant; a previous buyer had pulled out. The vendors now wanted a quick sale.

'It's ideal.' Willis looked over the house with Kenny. 'Plenty of room for you all and I'm just down the road.'

'Yeah, it's ideal all right. Ideal for you.'

'What d'you mean?'

'You should live here.'

'I'm okay where I am.'

'You're not thinking straight. Listen to your big brother. By the time you buy this place, you'll have lived in the other house for more than a year. As I understand it, that means you won't pay any of those extra taxes – capital gains or whatever – if you sell it. So, move in here and do the same thing. Make it your address for at least a year. See what I mean?'

'That's okay. But this has four bedrooms. Mine's only got three. You don't wanna carry on sharing a room with Col, do you?'

'You've taken too many punches, Johnny. Addled your brain, it has.' He paused. 'We're builders, ain't we? We'll stick another bedroom above the garage. That'll put more value on the house. You win both ways.'

'You could be right.'

'Course I'm right. Besides, one day you'll sell it. Let's face it, Mary's gonna marry Pete, Ma's not gonna last for ever and, well, me and Col might find ourselves nice birds to settle down with.'

'See what you mean.'

'Good. Glad you're not completely out of it.' Kenny slapped an arm around his brother's shoulders. 'It's great you're looking after us, Johnny. But you've also gotta look at these things as an investment.'

'You know, you're wiser than I thought. I always thought Col was the clever one. You know, the planner.'

Kenny laughed. 'Jeez! He's got us in enuff trouble in his time, ain't he? Nowadays I just let 'im think he's the brains.'

Julie visited for the weekend. She admired the house, the view over the golf course.

'So roomy and airy. It's like being in the country. Not grimy and penned in like bloody Paddington.'

Willis showed her the new house and she was even more impressed.

'You're doing well, Johnny. Must be a lot of money in boxing. Big house for one man, though.'

'Plenty of room for visitors,' he said.

'Nobody permanent, then?'

'No. Been there. Didn't work out.'

'Yeah, I know. Natalie told me about – oh, what's her name?'

'Karen.'

'Yeah, Karen. And the baby. Suzie, is it? Don't you see them?'

He shook his head. 'Clean break. It's a closed book, you might say.' He paused thoughtfully. 'Anyway, enough of that. What about you? Thought you'd have a special fella by now.'

'Not me, no way. I'm only twenty-two. Plenty of time for Mr Right to discover me. Until then, I'll enjoy myself. So, what've you got planned for us? Or is that a silly question?'

'Thought we'd go to the opera tonight. The ballet tomorrow.'

'What?'

Willis grinned. 'Gotcha!'

Friday night they dined out. Saturday it rained, so they stayed in bed. Willis used the bedside phone to order Chinese food. Julie trailed fingers down his back, tickling his spine.

'I'm glad it rained,' she said.

At night they went to The Casino. Julie won thirty pounds but Willis lost. Just a few hundred. What the heck! There's a lot of money in boxing, he thought.

Sunday he drove her to the railway station. Bought her a first class ticket. She's worth it, he thought.

Canzoneri was ordered to meet Robinson in a rematch. Early in December, the Italian faced his first fight on foreign soil, at Caesar's Palace, Las Vegas, on a triple world title programme. He triumphed on points in a bruising battle. All three judges gave it a close call, but there were no disputes. It was unanimous.

Mary kept in touch with Karen. After all, Suzie was her niece. Mary posted birthday and Christmas cards to them both and Karen responded. She sent Willis a Christmas card. Mary had given her the correct address.

The card disturbed Willis. Still signed 'Best wishes', but inside was a photograph of Suzie. Chubby face with blonde hair and brown eyes, snuggling up to a giant cuddly toy.

In January, Willis made the delayed defence of his European title against the Italian Belotti. At Wembley Conference Centre, a sledgehammer right accounted for the mandatory challenger in two minutes four seconds. It also caused Willis great pain. The old hand injury flared again.

A month later, Connie had tears in her eyes as the last of her furniture was loaded into the removal van.

'It's been my one true home,' she said as she and Mary embraced in the hollow emptiness of the front room. 'When I was shuttled around as a kid, I always dreamed of settling in one place. This was it.'

'I know, Ma. But you love the new house. You always said so, from the day Johnny bought it. It's better than living on the estate.'

'Nothing wrong with the estate.' Connie wiped her eyes with a tissue. 'Some good people here, Mary. They look after each other and they've been good to me. Don't ever forget it.'

'I won't, Ma. But it's time to move on. Somewhere better to live in your old age.'

'Old age! I'm not for the knacker's yard yet, my girl. There's plenty of partying left in me.'

'Oh Ma, you're impossible.' Mary smiled. 'C'mon, let's get out of here. There's work to do up at the house.'

'Right. You got the kettle?'

'It's in the car. Like you said, I didn't pack it.'

'Good. I could murder a cuppa. But watch them removal men. They'll drink tea all day and we'll never get straight. Just one cup for them, when they're finished. Not before.'

Connie closed the door of 36 Johnson Close for the last time. The neighbours waved.

'Good luck, Connie. Come back and see us some time,' they shouted.

'You can bank on it. See you later,' she said. If it wasn't for Mary, she thought, I wouldn't be going.

Canzoneri's hero status in Italy was magnified when he retained his title with a sixth-round knock-out in Modena, just north of Bologna. The victim was the ninth-ranked Mexican, Kid Morales.

Two months later, in April, he bludgeoned Ramon Gomez to a fifth-round defeat back in San Remo. The Argentinian was ranked seventh.

A boxing magazine profiled Canzoneri. He'd opened a *ristorante* in Bologna, a popular eating-place where the champion greeted his customers. The magazine photographed him there. Gorgeous women surrounded him. *La dolce vita*. It wasn't all punchbags and bloodied noses.

Willis read the article. Canzoneri was clearly a millionaire and enjoying his lifestyle. And I beat the bastard, he thought. Would do again, given the chance.

That opportunity moved a step closer when Willis and Robinson were matched. An official final eliminator, one fight from a world championship challenge.

Time for another deal. Just in time to pay the Inland Revenue!

Robinson flew in to Heathrow from Detroit on 1 April 1994. But he was no fool. The American had eleven days to settle in, acclimatise and round off his preparations. A comfortable timespan. Not too long to get bored or homesick.

The British press, Mercer included, were allowed only one day to watch him training. He was impressive, in and out of the ring. Two sparring partners travelled with him and the ex-champion handled them with ease.

He was also articulate with the media. Said he respected Willis. Knew he'd given Canzoneri a hard time. The victory over Miller in Madison Square was excellent. He's a good European champion, he said.

'But I want my title back. I know I can beat Canzoneri,' he grinned. 'I guess your man thinks the same. It'll be interesting.'

Willis trained for the last three weeks in Sellers's gym. He and Brown had a suite of rooms in a Piccadilly hotel. They had to get away from Westhampton. The small Hare and Hounds gym had been packed daily with his fans and it was hard for Willis to concentrate.

Payne couldn't get enough tickets. Sold five thousand. Nice earner for him and the doormen. Wembley was sold out even before Robinson arrived. Harry Jacobs was on a winner.

Willis had only one worry; his right hand. It pained him after sessions on the heavy bag and sometimes in sparring. He abandoned the heavy bag and used the floor-to-ceiling ball. It was good for timing. Hand and eye coordination. And not so painful, either.

'I'll need some insurance, Freddie.'

'No problem, my son.' Sniff. 'You're quite an expert now.'

It wasn't a secret between them any more. Brown knew. Sellers and Murray, too. Mercer guessed something was being done to alleviate Willis's recurring problem.


Robinson was past his best. Experienced ringsiders, particularly those in the press seats, quickly formed the opinion that he'd come to London for one last big pay day.

The American wanted to win. He called on his experience and fighting heart in a bid to master Willis. But he wasn't prepared to risk all. In the heat of battle, he sought sanctuary in clinches and wouldn't trade with his younger, more powerful foe. He'd been to the well once too often.

Willis concentrated on his jab. It was authoritative and point-scoring. Left hooks and occasional rights earned respect. Round after round, he did enough to stay on top. He edged his way to victory and that's all that mattered.

At the final bell, with Robinson having initiated another

clinch, the American sportingly raised Willis's hand. He knew. So did everyone else in the packed arena. The three judges awarded it to Willis by a wide margin; two by eight rounds and the third by nine. Conclusive.

The crowd hadn't seen the dramatic, exciting Willis. But he'd won and they celebrated. They went home happy, already discussing his prospects of beating Canzoneri.

Willis was drained, mentally fatigued. He'd fought virtually one-handed and still beaten the ex-world champion. I'd have slaughtered him with two, he thought. Sellers knew Willis was a tired fighter and told him so next morning, before the post-fight press conference.

'Have a rest, Johnny,' he said. 'You've earned it. The last fifteen months have been hard work. You've had some big fights. Forget boxing for a while. Go away and recharge your batteries. Have a holiday.'

'But what about the world title? I've gotta stay in some condition.'

'Don't worry about that. It'll be near the end of the year before that happens. Canzoneri's been a busy champion. He'll be given at least another six months before he's ordered to meet you and the Italians will take all the time they can get. They're in no rush to meet you again.'

'That's a long wait. I can't go six months without fighting. I'll be stale.'

'Leave that to us, Johnny. We'll fit in another fight, nothing strenuous. But right now you need a rest.' He put his hand on Johnny's shoulder. 'Take the advice of your old manager, son. I know what's best.'

'Okay, Lew. I can just about afford it after tonight. A week in Southend. Somewhere like that.'

'My heart bleeds for you.'


At the airport, the customs officer checked his passport. He studied the photograph and then looked at Willis.

'Thank you, Mr Willis. Good luck when you fight for the title.'

'Thanks a lot,' said Willis. Julie beamed at her celebrity

companion.

In the departure lounge, a trickle of people requested autographs. They wished him well and smiled at the blonde beauty sitting at his side.

In Florida's theme parks, Julie was stunning in shorts and flimsy tops. She loved the parade at Disney. Loved the dolphins and manatees even more at Seaworld.

Willis drove them along the Gulf Coast and they lazed on the beaches at Clearwater and Sarasota. Julie tanned golden brown in a variety of mini bikinis, Willis turned a deep chestnut colour.

'Shame about the white bits,' she said as they showered together.

'Dunno about that,' he said, soaping her curves. 'They're my favourite bits.'

They celebrated his twenty-seventh birthday in Key West. Eating room-service breakfast on their fifth-floor balcony, Julie presented him with a card and a gold boxing glove key ring.

'You shouldn't spend money on me,' he said.

'I wanted to.' Large smile. 'Anyway, you've spent an absolute fortune on me. It's the least I could do.'

'Well, thanks a lot. It's nice.'

'No, thank you. For my best holiday ever.'

'Glad you're enjoying it.'

Julie leaned to kissed his cheek. 'What about you? Are you enjoying it?'

'Sure. It's fun.'

'C'mon, then,' she said, taking his hand. 'Let's have some birthday fun. Let's play with our white bits.'


Refreshed and relaxed, Willis returned to Westhampton in early June. He was also overweight but it didn't matter. Sellers told him there was no news about a Canzoneri fight.

'Harry's been in touch with his manager but nothing doing. They're planning to defend again in August. We can only wait for the board to set a date.'

'I'll need another fight, Lew. It's a long time since April.'


Canzoneri's fourth title defence was set for the sixth of August in

Bologna against Jerry Mendoza from Fresno, California. But, the Board said, the winner must defend against Willis within ninety days.

Willis shed weight and prepared to defend his European title in September against Frenchman Jacques Lamora. Sellers was anxious. Defeat would ruin the world championship bid. But Willis and Murray were unconcerned.

Lamora lasted four rounds at Wembley. Mendoza had bowed out in the fifth in Bologna.

Jacobs resumed negotiations with his old friend Nenci. Time to recall past favours.

# Chapter Twenty-Five

Don Murray doffed an imaginary hat to Harry Jacobs. The veteran promoter had bid one million, four hundred and fifty thousand dollars. The Italian tender was fifty thousand less.

'How did he do that?' Murray said as he sat in the office with Sellers. 'I was sure the Italians would outbid us.'

Sellers leaned back in his chair. 'Harry called in a few favours. It's a long story. Goes way back to the late fifties. Vita Nenci was quite new to the game when Harry came across him in Rome. Nenci had a heavyweight. Big, ambling sort, not a puncher, though. Harry offered to help develop the fighter. He brought him to London, had him schooled in the gym and got him a couple of knock-out wins. He sent him back to Italy and gave Nenci a list of suitable opponents. Nenci's partner was Roberto Musso – a new promoter – and, with Harry's advice, they built the heavyweight's record. Two years on, he was a star over there.'

Murray lit a cigarette. 'Hard to believe Harry was so magnanimous. Doesn't sound like the old bastard.'

'He didn't do it out of kindness. Remember, Harry managed Doug Chandler at the time – the European champion. Well, he took Chandler to defend the title in Italy. Nenci knew his fighter wasn't up to it. Although Chandler had seen better days, it was easy for him. Point is, thanks to Harry, Nenci and Musso established themselves and, as you know, they've picked up good fighters over the years. Harry never took a penny from Nenci or Musso. Course, he got good money for Chandler's easy win. It was good business all round. They've worked together, on and off, ever since. Anyway, Harry's looking to retire, you know. He told Nenci he wanted to go out with a big show. Boost his retirement fund. Willis against Canzoneri fits the bill.'

'Crafty old bastard.'

'Experience and contacts, Don.' Sellers smiled. 'Nenci told him they'd come for a million dollars. So, Harry pitched his bid accordingly.'

'And we've done a deal with Willis for two hundred and fifty grand.'

'Harry cuts about forty grand off the purse. Helps make it a viable promotion.'

'Boosts his retirement fund.'

Sellers shrugged. 'Whatever. But Willis has a great chance of winning. Much better than in Italy. He could make millions after this.'

'Then you'll retire.'

'You've got it, Don.' The old manager spread his arms. 'Then all this will be yours.'

The evening before a press conference to announce the fight, Sellers briefed Mercer. Not all the details, but just enough for the *News* to run a front-page exclusive in their early editions.

Johnny Willis's challenge for the world middleweight boxing championship against Italian Alberto Canzoneri is heading for Westhampton.

I understand London promoter Harry Jacobs has secured the fight with a bid of nearly £1 million and he is now seeking a suitable venue in the city.

One possible site is the new £15m Civic Centre which will be officially opened on Monday, 31 October. The city council is finalising a week-long programme of events at the 12,000-seat arena including a pop concert, all-star basketball match and professional five-a-side soccer tournament.

The world title fight – the first to be staged in Westhampton – could be the climax to those celebrations on Saturday, 5 November.

Willis, the 27-year-old European, British and Commonwealth champion, boxed a draw with Canzoneri in San Remo two years ago. Canzoneri was then European champion and, in his next contest, took the world crown from American Joey Robinson. He has made four defences.

A city council spokesman said this morning: 'I can confirm that a boxing promoter has made enquiries about using the Civic Centre on 5 November. I cannot confirm any more details but, if it is for a world title fight involving Johnny Willis, then the council would be delighted to host such an event.'

> Promoter Jacobs is holding a press conference later today when it is expected he will announce the Willis–Canzoneri fight.
>
> Willis, who is believed to be in London for the announcement, will receive the challenger's mandatory 30 per cent share of the purse, around £290,000.

Willis, in fact, travelled to London that day on a train with Mercer and Brown as companions. Boxer and reporter worked on a story which would appear under Willis's byline in the next day's *News*.

> Great to be getting my big chance in Westhampton... Fans are terrific... Thought I'd done enough to get the decision last time... But Canzoneri is tough, the hardest opponent of my career... Worthy world champion... I'm looking forward to becoming Westhampton's first world champion boxer...

Willis trained for a month in London. Michael Greene insisted that Thomson carried on working with his boxers in the Islington gym.

'Nothing to it. I'll reorganise,' Freddie sniffed.

Willis started at one thirty and, two hours later, Thomson dashed to Islington where he'd arranged a four thirty start for Greene's boxers. Thomson's schedule eased when Brown packed away his paintbrushes and joined Willis for the final two weeks of preparation.

A daily procession of reporters, photographers, TV and radio crews turned up at the gym. There was always someone wanting an interview, a picture or soundbite. Willis found it relaxing, at the start. In the second week he complained. He didn't want to keep answering questions.

'Let me do my work and get out of here,' he told Sellers. 'They've got enough quotes now. Let 'em wait for the press conferences.'

The message was relayed, politely, to the media. Willis had to concentrate on his training.

Sellers was pleased. Willis was getting edgy. He was spoiling for a fight. Look out, Canzoneri.

Canzoneri and his entourage arrived ten days before the fight.

Jacobs made the effort to meet Nenci and Musso at Heathrow.

'Good to see you again,' said Nenci. 'How are you, my old friend?' They shook hands and embraced. Musso did likewise.

'I've had better health.' Jacobs had a grey pallor. 'But you are looking well.'

'It is thanks to the climate. In Italy we do not suffer as you do. Come, let me introduce Alberto.'

Canzoneri, in a three-quarter-length coat and a scarf at his throat, shook hands with Jacobs. The promoter quickly turned back to Nenci.

'I am not troubling you with the press until tomorrow morning. You received my fax?'

Nenci nodded. 'The arrangements seem most suitable.'

'Good. I will ride with you to the hotel. Tomorrow morning we have the press conference and then you will be driven to Westhampton.'

'That I understand. But, tell me Harry, how long is the journey from London?'

'Not long. Maybe two hours.'

Nenci and Musso settled into the rear of Jacobs's chauffeur-driven Bentley. Canzoneri, his trainer and two wide-shouldered friends climbed into a second limousine. The baggage and two sparring partners were loaded into a white van.

'Your boy has done well. I hear he has a restaurant.'

'This is true. A fine *ristorante*. He has indeed done well. We all have. But, my friend, I must confess that we do not always feel comfortable. We have our worries.'

'Ah, Vita, we always worry about the boxers, particularly when championships are at stake.'

'True, very true, Harry. But, you must understand, with Alberto, it is not his ability as a boxer that causes concern. Alberto is a good fighter. A much improved fighter since he and your Willis fought in San Remo. No, his boxing is of no concern. It is other matters. How you say – outside influences?'

'Saw his picture, with all those girls. The king playboy of Bologna, eh?'

'The girls.' Nenci nodded. 'But that is normal, is it not? Fighters are... *maschile*. Macho! They desire beautiful women. And certain of the women, they find the boxer irresistible. But, alas, not the old manager or the old promoter.' Nenci laughed and slapped Jacobs's knee. Harry grinned.

'So what's your problem, Vita? If it's not wine, women and song?'

'His friends, if that is the word. We are not sure of them. They are our concern.'

'Like those two in the car?'

'I see that you are still, as you say, on the ball. You observe. Truth to tell, Alberto has become – what shall we say – difficult? Yes, difficult. Roberto and I, we suspect his friends may have influence.'

'Influence?'

'That is right.' Musso entered the conversation.

'Once we have no difficulties. Alberto was… compliant. But now, this past twelve months, well, it is not the same.'

'And you put this down to his friends?'

'I am afraid it is so,' said Nenci firmly. 'His family friends, shall we say?'

Jacobs then guessed why Nenci had agreed to leave Italy for this defence. It wasn't just old favours being repaid.

'Is your contract in danger?'

'We have six more months.'

'I see.'


The Italians were booked into The Post House at Westhampton. Murray sent Brian Adams to stay with them as a liaison officer. His rôle was to report any problems or requests to Murray.

The matchmaker arranged with Clive Yeoman for use of the Hare and Hounds gym.

'Sure, Don. We'll be glad to have them, Don.'

The sweetener was a place on the bill for Yeoman's two welterweights. It wouldn't harm local ticket sales.

Canzoneri obliged with one training session for the media. Otherwise, he trained behind closed doors.

The final press conference was scheduled for Thursday afternoon, the day Willis returned to Westhampton. The first floor of The Post House was virtually taken over by the fight promotion.

But Willis and his trainers were booked into The Rateby Country Hotel, on the outskirts of the city.

Mary pasted more cuttings into her latest scrapbook. It was the sixth. She flicked through the pages and paused at a picture. It was of Johnny, with blood flowing from his eye. Mary shuddered.

'What's wrong, Mary?' Connie had noticed.

'This picture of Johnny. Blood all down his face. I hope there's nothing like it on Saturday, I couldn't bear to see it.'

'But we must be there. It's the biggest night of his life. It'd be wrong not to go.'

'I know, but I'm dreading it. You know I can't even watch him on the telly. It's all right for you. It doesn't bother you.'

'Oh yes, it does. I don't want to see Johnny hurt but I'd rather watch than just sit wondering. I used to get all knotted up when he first started. That's one reason why I had people round or went to a party. It stopped me thinking too much.'

The telephone trilled and Connie lifted the receiver.

'Hullo. Is it possible please to speak to Mrs Willis?' A foreign accent.

'Speaking.'

'Ah, Mrs Willis, pleased to speak with you. I am Federico Serti, a journalist from Italy.'

'Yes, Mr Serti, what can I do for you?'

'Ah. I am in England to write about the boxing match. I am a feature writer and my newspaper wish me to interview you.'

'Me? What for?'

'It is thought we could talk about your son, Johnny, yes?'

'What d'you wanna know?'

'Sorry, Mrs Willis. I did not quite hear that. But what we wish is for an interview with you. Understand?'

'Yeah, er, yes. When?'

'When? We wish to entertain you. Lunch tomorrow? We talk over lunch. It is more pleasant, yes, with food and a little wine?'

Connie put a hand over the receiver. 'Some eye-tie reporter wants to take me to lunch.' She smiled at Mary. 'Could be my lucky day.'

'Is that acceptable to you, Mrs Willis? We would be most

grateful.'

'What d'you wanna know?' Connie asked again.

There was a momentary silence.

'Ah! What we want to know! We wish to discuss Johnny. What sort of boy he was. How you think of him and boxing. You must be proud. Your *bambino*, he become a successful boxer. We wish you to tell about him, yes?'

'Okay. Where do we meet?'

'Not meet. We send a car. Bring you to the hotel. We are all staying here. Many Italians. British reporters too. We have lunch, talk and a car will deliver you home.'

'Sounds fine.'

'Excellent. The car will be with you at twelve thirty. Is that suitable?'

'Twelve thirty it is. I'll be waiting, Mr…'

'Serti. But, please, call me Freddie.'

'Okay, Freddie. Twelve thirty tomorrow.'

'One other matter, Mrs Willis. We wish to take photographs. That is permissible, yes?'

Connie agreed and ended the conversation.

'They want to take my picture. What shall I wear, Mary?'

'Your best black dress, I'd say. And your pearls.'

'Yeah, good thinking. Wonder if I can get my hair done?'

'Stop panicking, Ma. You had your hair done this morning, remember?'

Connie laughed, lifting a hand to her newly tinted blonde locks. 'Course I did. Ready for Saturday. Silly me.'

'Where's this lunch to be, then?'

'Some hotel. He said they've all come for Johnny's fight.'

'That'll be The Post House. Johnny says everybody but him's staying there.'

'He sounded dishy. Call me Freddie, he said. Smooth bugger. Now, what's his real name? Ah, yeah… Federico Serti,' she said. 'Federico, Federico. Sounds better than Freddie, don't you think? Yeah, I'll call him Federico. Not Freddie.'

Connie grinned to herself. Knowing my luck, he'll be fat and greasy, she thought.

*PART SIX*

H E WATCHED THE champion turn away and trudge to his corner. I could take him. He's done for. I'm tired but he's knackered. Out on his feet.

A hand gripped his forearm and tugged. He responded, turning to walk back to his own corner.

'Good round.'

A wet sponge was wiped over his face and the adrenaline swab pressed to his eyebrow. Not bleeding now.

'C'mon, breathe in. Deep breaths.' Hands pulled at his waistband. 'That's the way.'

So this is it. The last three minutes. And still I don't know. Jeez! I can beat the bastard. Know I can, even with these hands. What shall I do?

'Keep your left hand in his face. It's close but a big last round will do it. It's all down to these three minutes. It's up to you.'

Don't I know it, he thought.

He looked into the crowd. Still just blank faces. And the two empty seats. Hopeless. It's too late now. Time's ticking away. Like a bomb.

Do I take the risk? The biggest gamble of my life – but not just mine. What would she want me to do? Take a chance or play safe?

His mouthpiece was thrust into place. He stood and took another last, desperate look across the ringside faces.

'Seconds out... for the twelfth and final round...'

## Chapter Twenty-Six

The car was a taxi. It arrived just before twelve thirty. Connie was disappointed; she'd had visions of a long, black limousine with tinted windows. She'd dressed for the occasion in the sleeveless black dress with a scalloped hem. Two strings of pearls rested on her cantilevered cleavage.

She drained the remains of a second brandy as Mary helped her into a woollen jacket.

'You look great, Ma. Enjoy yourself, but don't drink too much.'

'Make your mind up.' Connie's eyes glistened. She fluffed up her hair. 'What's it to be?'

'Okay. Have a drink and enjoy yourself.'

'Good afternoon, Mrs Willis,' the driver said as he opened the rear door. 'How's Johnny?'

'Fine, I think. He's been in London for a month. Only came back yesterday.'

The driver was a fight fan. Remembered Johnny as a kid. Had watched him box many times at the Friar and even went to London for the Robinson fight. He'd got a ticket for tomorrow's fight. Expensive, ain't they? Still, it's a world title fight. Looking forward to it. Johnny will win. Should've got the verdict in Italy. Draw? It was a travesty.

Ten minutes into his monologue, Connie interrupted.

'This isn't the way to The Post House.'

'Post House? I'm not taking you there. My instructions were to pick you up and take you to The Craven.'

'Oh, I thought it was The Post House. Must've got it wrong.'

'Must have. As I understand it, a character came in the office this morning and paid cash in advance. Said it was important we picked you up by twelve thirty and got you to The Craven by one.'

'Right.'

302

'Craven's a nice place. Posh.'

'Mm.'

Connie opened her handbag, pulled out a compact and checked her make-up in the mirror. When the taxi pulled up on the hotel's gravel forecourt, she freshened her red lips, ready to meet Federico. Whether he turned out to be a greaseball or not, it was a nice hotel.

She strode into the foyer, heels clicking on the terrazzo surface and headed for the reception desk.

'Mrs Willis?'

She stopped and turned to her left. Thank you, God!

'Yes. Federico?' There, she'd said it. In her poshest voice, too.

'Mrs Willis, so pleased to meet you. Thank you for agreeing to the interview. May I say, you look enchanting.'

Connie smiled as the tall, dark-haired Italian put a hand under her left elbow. He wore a dark suit and a striped blue and white shirt, with the top two buttons undone, showing a hint of curled chest hair. Mid-forties, she guessed.

'This way, if you please.'

He walked her to the lift. Inside he pressed the floor-three button.

'We have a suite of rooms. I thought it more private if we dine there. It is better for the interview, don't you think?'

'Whatever you say, Federico.'

He used a key card to release the door catch, opened the door and stood aside, allowing Connie to enter. The room was spacious. Two armchairs and a four-seater sofa surrounded a glass-topped coffee table. In one corner, a television. Beneath the picture window to the left, four chairs at a round, polished dining table. On the far wall, an open drinks cabinet.

One of the several doors on the right wall opened. A stocky, bespectacled gent entered, casually dressed, in slacks and a blue sports shirt.

'Ah, my colleague. Mrs Willis, this is Hugo. He is the photographer.'

'Enchanting,' he said, lightly shaking her hand.

Popular word, thought Connie, smiling.

'Please. Allow me to take your coat.'

Federico removed the woollen jacket, releasing a waft of Connie's musky perfume. He opened another door, to the bedroom, and laid the jacket on the bed.

Hugo was at the drinks cabinet. He turned and held out a glass.

'A fine red wine,' he said. 'Italian, of course. I hope you like.'

Connie sipped. She'd prefer a gin and tonic, but wine would do for starters.

'Yeah. Very pleasant, thank you.'

'Please.' Federico gestured towards the sofa. 'Be seated. Be comfortable.'

Connie placed her drink and handbag on the coffee table and lowered herself into the centre of the sofa. She kept her knees together, legs at an angle. The scalloped hem settled revealingly at mid-thigh. As she reached for her drink, Federico gazed at the exposed swell of her white bosom.

'If it pleases you,' he said, 'we will start the interview now. We will order our lunch later. Unless, of course, you wish to eat now?'

'Later will be fine.' Connie took another sip. 'The drink's okay for now. Cheers.'

Federico placed a small tape recorder on the table and switched it on as Hugo poured more wine into Connie's glass.

'I find the recorder more relaxing, Mrs Willis. Much simpler than writing. If you would please say something, I will arrange the sound level. Then we can forget all about it. As if it was not there. Yes?'

'Sure, as you wish. You're the expert. What d'you want me to say?'

Federico adjusted a knob as she spoke. 'That's fine, Mrs Willis. It is now arranged.'

Connie chuckled and drank more wine. 'Very smart, that. Please, call me Connie. Mrs Willis sounds so starchy.'

'Starchy?'

'Yeah. All stiff and formal, like. Let's relax.'

'But of course. Relax.' Federico settled into one of the armchairs. 'It is best to relax. Makes for a charming interview, I find.'

Hugo poured more wine.

'Aren't you having a drink, Fed… Federico?'

'Presently. With our lunch. At the moment, I must keep the clear head. Work before pleasure, yes?'

'Of course, dearie. Just seems odd drinking on me own. What about you, Hugo? Course, you're working as well. Silly me. Where's your camera?'

'He will take the photographs later,' said Federico. 'First, we talk. Hugo will take a few Polaroids. It helps for the lighting. He is very professional. If I may say, Connie, he wishes to do justice to your beauty.'

'Get away with yer! Me, a beauty? Once upon a time I was. Long time ago now, Feddie.' Federico was too much of a mouthful.

The Italian raised both hands, palms towards Connie and waved them side to side.

'No, no, Connie. You have beauty. We Italians, you know, we recognise the magnificence – if you will pardon my saying so – the magnificence of maturity.'

'Mamma's boys, eh?'

Federico shrugged. 'It is maybe so.' He paused. 'You have other *bambini*, I believe. Johnny is not, how you say?'

'The only child? No, he's not. He's my third son and my youngest child is a daughter. Mary. Now, she is a looker…'

Hugo topped up Connie's wine glass from a fresh bottle. Her tongue was loosened.

Blimey! This wine's good stuff, she thought. Quite gone to me head.

Hundreds of supporters turned up for the weigh-in at the new Civic Centre. At exactly ten o'clock, twelve hours before the first bell, Willis stepped on to the scales. Eleven stone, five pounds. Canzoneri was spot-on the championship limit at eleven stone six.

Photographers jostled for pictures as the two shook hands. Both looked into the lenses but did not smile. They parted without speaking.

Radio stations pressed Willis for his final comments.

'It was a hard fight last time. I'm prepared for another battle. I believe I'm a better fighter now than I was two years ago. And I reckon I was robbed then. Tonight I've got the chance to put the record straight.'

'You're the champ, Johnny!' A shout from the eavesdropping crowd.

'Cheers,' said Willis raising his right fist and smiling. He spoke again into the microphones. 'I'll be doing my best to give Westhampton their first world champion.'

The crowd cheered again and chanted, 'Will-is, Will-is, Will-is.'

Sellers nodded at Brown. He and Thomson guided Willis through the well-wishers towards one end of the hall. There, at the base of the first section of tiered seating, his brothers stood guard over his clothes and holdall. Willis took off his robe, donned sweatshirt and jeans and reached in the bag for his footwear.

'Anyone seen my trainers?'

'Blimey, my son. You're always misplacing those sodding trainers,' Thomson sniffed. 'Where'd you leave 'em?'

'Thought I put 'em in my bag.'

'Have you looked properly?'

As Willis rifled through his bag, his hand struck an unfamiliar, square object. He lifted it out. A brown-paper parcel. He turned it over in his hands and saw the scrawled message. *Open in private.*

'Here they are.' Thomson stood up, trainers in his hand. 'In your bag? You'd left 'em under your coat.'

Willis dropped the mystery package into his bag, turned and took the trainers from Thomson.

'Cheers, Freddie.'

'S'all right, my son. People have been known to nick things. Souvenir hunters. Even just plain old tea leaves. Whatever. Gotta be careful in a crowd.'

Yeah, thought Willis, that's why Kenny and Col watched my gear. So how did the parcel get in my bag?

'Anyone come near my kit?'

Kenny and Colin exchanged glances and shook their heads.

'Sure? I mean, you were here all the time?'

'Yeah,' said Colin. 'Well, we stood on those chairs to have a look when you weighed in.' He pointed twenty yards away to the last row of seats on the main floor.

'Why, something wrong?'

Willis shook his head. 'No,' he said. Not now, he thought. Not now I know somebody had the chance to leave me a parcel. Wonder who it's from?

Connie lay on the bed, legs spread, skirt riding high. Her chest undulated with the steady rhythm of her breathing. Hugo stood over her with an empty syringe in his hand. It was four o'clock on Saturday afternoon.

'How is she?' Federico entered the room.

They conversed in their native Italian.

'She is fine. Should sleep for another six hours.'

'What did you give her?'

'Same as before. Same as she had in the wine. Like I told you, it's a psychoactive drug. Benzodiazepines they are. This one's Diazepam. Suppresses the central nervous system. The dosage dictates. You can induce anything from mild impairment to deep sedation.'

'She's had a lot. Sure it's safe?'

'Alcohol helps the effects. Apart from her drinks, the drug dosage she's had is like another bottle of spirits. What I've injected will make sure she stays quiet.' He looked at his watch. 'She's been unconscious since midnight. Sixteen hours. She won't feel good when she wakes. A colossal hangover. But the way she drank, I don't think that will be something new to this lady.'

'We'll stay with her until seven. Then we must leave for the boxing. Everything is packed and the bill is paid. I told reception we are leaving early in the morning, before breakfast.'

The two Italians donned surgical gloves. Then they washed the drinks glasses, wiped down all wooden surfaces, door handles and panels, the window ledge and light switches, Finally, they cleaned the drinks bottles, including the discarded red wine and gin bottles.

Willis was curious. He was also hungry. And food was the priority. He ate chicken and vegetables followed by fresh fruit. He drank water, orange juice and tea. It was nearly one o'clock when they all finished eating. At five, he would eat grilled fish and more fruit. But now, he left his trainers, manager and matchmaker discussing fights and fighters.

'I'm gonna get some shut-eye,' he declared. 'Give me a call at four thirty, Ron, okay? See you later.'

'Cool customer,' said Murray, watching Willis leave the dining room.

'Always been the same,' said Ron. 'Even back when he was a kid. He used to tell me and Harry Riley – remember old Harry? – he used to tell us "You worry too much." Can't think of anything that'd faze Johnny Willis. No, sir, not a thing.'

In his room, Willis fished into his bag. He turned the package over in his fingers, balancing it in the palm of his right hand. Not very heavy. He started to tear at the brown paper, then stopped. Idiot, he thought. I know how it got there. Course I do. Kenny or Col put it in my bag. Jeez! Kenny's right. I've taken too many punches. He smiled and continued unwrapping.

A Polaroid picture fell out, spiralled and landed on the carpet, face down. He unveiled a small plastic object. A tape machine. Small, like the ones reporters use. They've recorded a message, he thought. He bent to pick up the photograph. What the fuck? he thought.

Connie, in her black dress, stared out of the picture, all legs and bosom. She was beaming and a red wine glass was held aloft in salutation.

What's this all about? I don't need this rubbish, he thought. He tossed the photograph on to a chair and lay back on the bed, placing the small recorder on his stomach. He closed his eyes.

Why should she send me a picture and message? As if I care.

'I'm worried, Kenny. Something's happened to Ma.' Mary looked at the kitchen clock. 'It's four o'clock and we've heard nothing. Surely she'd let us know where she is?'

'You know Ma, sis. Goes off on a bender at the drop of a hat.' Kenny poured a mug of tea. 'Want another?'

'No, no thanks. I'm drowning in tea.' She brushed her dark fringe out of her troubled eyes. 'I can't believe she'd do this now.

Not today. Not when she's going to the fight.'

'That's Ma.'

'What if she's had another attack?'

'We'd have heard, sis.'

'Tell me again,' said Colin. 'What did The Post House say?'

Mary sighed. 'They said they had nobody named Serti staying there. And no dinner reservation. But Ma might have got his name wrong.'

'Or the hotel.'

'No, she wouldn't – wait a minute. Come to think of it, she didn't say it was The Post House. I only assumed that because this Serti fella – or whatever his name is – he said there was lots of Italians staying there. And British newspaper blokes. It could be another hotel, couldn't it?'

'Could be,' said Kenny. 'But most of 'em are at The Post House. Canzoneri's staying there.'

'What about the taxi?' said Colin. 'They'd know where they took her.'

'I didn't look. Don't know which firm it was. I could start ringing round.'

'Nah, sis. Leave it a while. She's got plenty of time to turn up. She'll breeze in here, you see. Five minutes later, she'll be ready to get off to the fight.'

'You could be right,' said Mary. But she wasn't convinced.


Willis woke at four. He swung his legs off the bed and sat up, sending the recorder tumbling to the floor. It landed heavily, depressing the play button. The tape started to play.

*Johnny always said he'd be world champion. That's been his aim in life...*

Willis stooped to pick up the machine. He listened to his mother's voice, bit tipsy, but proud. That he could hear.

*...it's driven him on. He's not had an easy life. Full of ups and downs. But he's stuck to his guns. He's a real fighter, is Johnny. Any mother would be proud to have him as a son...*

She stopped. The tape was still coiling. He looked for a rewind button and gaped at the machine when a new voice began.

*You will recognise the voice of your mother...*

A strange voice. Muffled. Disguised even.

*...You will, of course, recognise her picture. It is not our wish to harm her...*

Harm her? What's going on?

*...Do not worry. At the moment she is safe. She will remain safe if you lose tonight. Repeat: you lose tonight. Understand? You must not win. Your mother's life depends on you. Not only that, be assured that you are also in grave danger. A final warning. Do not mention this to anyone. Not to the police, not to family or friends. If you have not understood any part of this message, play it again. Do not attempt to win.*

Willis found the rewind button. He listened again. And a third time. Fucking unbelievable!

The telephone chirped. It was Brown with the four thirty call.

'I'll see you downstairs. In the restaurant at five. Okay, Ron?'

Mary was sitting next to the phone in the lounge. She snatched up the receiver after the first ring.

'Hello, is that you, Ma?'

'Hi, sis. It's me, Johnny.'

'Johnny! Sorry, I was hoping it was Ma.'

'Why? What's happened?'

'Nothing. Nothing for you to worry about. How're you feeling?'

'I'm fine. But you're not. You're lying to me. Tell me, Mary, what's happened to Ma?'

'It's nothing, honest. It's just me, panicking. Kenny's right. She'll probably walk through the door any minute.'

'Where is she?' Silence. 'You still there, Mary?'

'Yeah. Sorry.'

'Well? Where is she?'

'Okay. May as well tell you.' She paused. 'That's the trouble. We don't know where she is.'

Willis gripped the receiver. Sweat moistened his palm. 'Tell me about it,' he said calmly.

Mary recounted the story, starting with the telephone call from Serti on Thursday evening.

'So you haven't seen or heard from her since yesterday lunchtime?'

'No. But Kenny says she's probably gone on a bender.'

'Maybe. Tell me, sis, what was she wearing?'

'Why? What d'you wanna know for?'

'Just tell me.' Willis looked at the photograph as Mary described Connie's outfit. Jeez! This is serious, he thought.

'Right. Now, listen. There's some things I want you to do.'

'I'm listening.'

'I want you to stay there until Ma turns up. Kenny and Col can come to the fight. I'll be here until eight. Phone me any time until then. I'll be in the restaurant between five and six but I won't phone in case she's trying to get through. Okay? Got that?'

'Yes.'

'If it's after eight when she shows, phone Kenny on his mobile. Make sure he's got his mobile. Then he can let me know she's okay. Right?'

Mary had listened. Not only to the words but to the urgency in her brother's voice. 'You're worried, aren't you?' she said. 'I've never heard you like this. Not about Ma. You think something's wrong, don't you?'

'I don't know. But there's one more thing I want from you.' He paused. 'Tell me her secret. The story no one else knows.' Silence. 'I'm waiting, sis.'

It was almost five o'clock when Willis hung up the phone. He sat, staring at the photograph. His mother's smiling face. All that pain. Shuttled from one family to another, not wanted. The abuse, the fucking abuse! Losing the man she loved. Because of one mistake, one slip. Fuck! We all make mistakes. And still she smiles.

The phone chirped. He snatched it up.

'Hello? Mary?'

'No, it's Ron. Thought you'd fallen asleep again. It's ten past five. We're waiting in the dining room.'

'I was expecting Mary to ring. She'll probably do it later. Okay, Ron. I'll be right down.'

Suddenly he didn't have an appetite. All he wanted to do was punch a hole in the wall. Release his anger.

I'll save it for that bastard Canzoneri, he thought. Or can I? What happens if I beat him up? Is this for real or is it a joke? Shit!

At seven, the two Italians closed the door to the suite. They checked the 'Do not disturb' sign on the handle and made for the back stairs. They wore dark suits and carried overnight bags. Hugo also had a small black medical case. Connie was still unconscious.

## Chapter Twenty-Seven

Willis showered, dressed and packed his holdall, but resisted the temptation to telephone Mary. At eight o'clock he got into the passenger seat of his Mercedes. Brown drove, Thomson and Sellers sat in the back. Matchmaker Murray had left in his Jaguar two hours earlier. The show started at seven thirty.

Two bouts had already finished when Brown parked in their reserved spot. Fireworks and bonfires lit up the night sky.

A steward led the small party to the dressing room. Their footsteps echoed as they tramped flights of concrete stairs to the rooms on the second floor. Bomber, on a night off from The Casino, stood guard at Willis's room. Willis patted the doorman's brawny shoulder.

'Be lucky,' growled Bomber. 'Your brothers are waiting inside.'

Thomson and Brown dumped kit bags on a table in the middle of the room and Sellers started an inspection.

The room was large. No windows but fluorescent ceiling tubes provided bright light. There were wooden benches and three plastic chairs. Clothes pegs and hangers on the white walls. The manager pushed open a door to an adjoining room.

An open shower bay faced him, with three toilet cubicles next to that and a latrine on the left wall. Behind the door, three handbasins and a long wall mirror. To the right, another door leading to the corridor. Sellers tried the handle. Locked. He returned to the changing area and opened that door. Bomber's massive frame turned.

'I say, son, that door along there – the one to the toilets – it will stay locked, won't it?'

'Unless you want it open, Mr Sellers. I've got the key.'

'No. Locked is fine. We don't want anyone getting in. Understand?'

'No fear of that. There'll be another two guys joining me

later.'

'Good. Unless it's an official, someone to do with the show, don't let them in. Knock first and wait for us to answer. Got that?'

'Couldn't be plainer, Mr Sellers.'

Willis had walked straight over to his brothers who sat side by side on a bench. Two laminated tags dangled on thread around their necks. Green, for the guest seating area. Gold, to admit them anywhere in the arena.

'Any news, Kenny?'

'Not yet.' He held up his mobile. 'Switched on, ready and waiting. But don't worry. You know Ma. She'll be here. You concentrate on winning the title.'

'Let me know as soon as you hear from Mary. Even if it's during the fight. Got that?'

'During the fight? That might be difficult.'

'Why? Where're you sitting?'

'Near your corner,' said Colin. 'I've checked it out.'

'How near?'

'About four or five seats away. To your left as you sit on the stool. Second row. There's me and Kenny, Pete, Mary and Ma. We're all together.'

'No problem then, Kenny. You can let me know.'

A loud rap on the door. Sellers opened it and admitted Mercer and Payne. Payne hugged Willis and Mercer shook his hand, lightly. Never squeeze a fighter's hand before a contest.

'Bob, I've gotta question for you.' Willis walked Mercer to a corner of the room. 'You've been hanging around the Italian journalists. Have you come across a guy named Serti?'

'Serti?' Mercer shook his head. 'Can't say that I have. Why?'

'It's not important. Just something I'd like to check.'

'I'll have a word at ringside, if you like. See if any of the lads know him. Serti, you say?'

'Yeah. I'd like to know but don't go to any trouble. I know you've got a lot on tonight.'

'Not as much as you. Anyway, I just popped in to wish you well. Feeling okay? No problems?'

'I'm fine.'

'Hands okay?'

'They'll do,' Willis smiled. 'Thanks a lot, Bob. It's been a long road but we've finally got here.'

'Just one more hurdle, Johnny. Just one more. There's thousands rooting for you out there. Not like in San Remo, eh?'

'Big crowd, is it?'

'Just about full now. Getting on for twelve thousand.'

Murray bustled into the room. Jacobs made slower progress behind him. Both were in dinner jackets.

'You'd better get ready, Johnny,' said Murray. 'The steward will want to supervise hand-wrapping soon. Who's going to watch the Italians?'

'I'll be doing that,' said Sellers. 'How're you, Harry?'

'So-so.' The promoter looked at Willis. 'How're you, son? Ready to get us the title? It's cost me enough.'

'I'm ready, Mr Jacobs. They tell me it's a big crowd out there.'

Jacobs nodded, acknowledging Willis's observation. The show was profitable. He turned to Sellers. 'See you later, Lew. Must call on Nenci. He's sure to have a moan about something, even if it's only the weather.'

The small group of visitors left together.

'Better get the business done.' Thomson picked up his medical pouch. 'In there, I think.'

Willis accompanied him into the shower room. Good timing. He needed a pee, anyway.

Mary was dressed for the fight, in leather trousers, boots and black high-neck ribbed sweater. She sat on the sofa. A trench-style coat lay at her side.

The preliminary bouts were on the television. She could watch boxing if it didn't involve Johnny, but tonight she couldn't concentrate. Her gaze flicked between the TV set, the clock and telephone. The action on screen was lively. The clock hands moved relentlessly towards nine o'clock. But the phone was static. Silent.

The last of the cleaning staff signed off at The Craven. Alice reported to the manager that she hadn't 'done' the top-floor suite.

'The "Do not disturb" sign's been hanging on the door all

day,' she said.

'That's all right, Alice. We know about that. They're moving out early in the morning.'

'Good night, then. See you tomorrow,' said Alice. That was one less job, she thought.

In the dark of the third-floor suite, Connie stirred on the bed. Her first movement in hours. She turned on to her right side and drew her knees up into the foetal position. She groaned but she didn't open her eyes.

It was nine thirty.

In rooms fifty yards apart, Willis and Canzoneri stood at latrines, both naked except for socks, boxing boots and bandaged hands. Both wanted to urinate but they managed only dribbles. Tension. Butterflies.

Next they pulled on jockey shorts, leather groin protectors and boxing trunks. Crimson-coloured for Willis, blue for the Italian.

Thomson rubbed oils into Willis's torso as Brown read through the pile of greeting cards and notes. It seemed as though everyone Willis had ever met had sent their good wishes, from Natalie and Ginny to Karen and Mary Riley.

Canzoneri asked for a drink. Nenci picked up one of three water bottles. They'd bought them at The Post House and, immediately, Nenci had sealed the tops with adhesive tape to prevent tampering. Then he'd wound more adhesive around the middles. Easier for wet hands to grip.

The world champion gargled and spat into a wash basin. He looked in the mirror and shadow-boxed. Didn't see his reflection. It was Willis, the enemy. Pow, pow. You're finished.

Willis warmed up as a television crew relayed his final moments of preparation. It was fifteen minutes to ten.

Mary watched her brother on the screen. He looked so determined, so focused. Amazing. He can't really be so cool, she thought.

She looked again at the telephone. C'mon, ring, damn you. Where are you, Ma?

Connie moaned. Her eyelids flickered, opened. The room was in darkness. God, I don't feel well, she thought. Bloody awful, in fact. What happened? Must've drunk hell of a lot. Haven't felt this bad in years. I'll sleep it off.

The vast arena was plunged into near-darkness. Lights in the domed ceiling twinkled like stars as a laser light show began. Bursting, cascading fireworks and soaring rockets.

Behind the scenes, Willis and his handlers were led along the corridor by security and two uniformed policemen. Past Canzoneri's closed door, they descended the stairs. Noise in the dim distance. Murray waited for them at the entrance to the arena. In the auditorium, a spotlight shone on the massive black-out drapes. Murray checked his watch and nodded to a man wearing headphones. The man relayed the message. 'Willis ready. Cue music…'

The curtains parted and the entourage moved forward. A television cameraman walked backwards before them. His pictures of Willis's entrance appeared on all four sides of the giant canopy surrounding the ring lights. The welcome was deafening.

Willis removed his gloved hands from their customary position on Thomson's shoulders and raised his head to look around at the cheering throng. His chest swelled with pride. Jeez! If Ma could see me now.

Tears welled in Mary's eyes. That's our Johnny. Look how they love him.

Connie struggled to get off the bed. Must get to the bathroom, she thought. Her stockinged feet touched the carpet. Strange! That feels thick. She moved her toes among the pile. That's not my carpet. Where the hell am I?

She wriggled gingerly forward. Hands by her hips, pushing into the mattress. Dress rucked up to her groin. She stood, wobbled, tried to balance herself, arms outstretched like a tightrope walker. She toppled backwards, sliding down the side of the bed. The jar spasmed through her body. She bent and retched, then rested her back against the bed, her eyes adjusting to the dark.

This is no good. Gotta get up.

She steadied herself, left hand on the bed, and stood. The room still oscillated. She reached cautiously for the wall and shuffled along, feeling for a light switch. Wood! Must be a door. Where's the knob? She twisted it one way, then the other. That's it. Her left hand pulled the door open, her right hand rested on the wall.

Pale light seeped into the room. From a window on the far side of another room. This isn't home. C'mon, Connie, think. What've you been doing?

Flash! Bang! Woosh!

Fireworks? Connie leaned into the doorjamb, right hand held at her thumping forehead. Can't be? Not 5 November. Not Saturday night. Where's the bloody light switch?

Mary's quandary: to watch or not? The referee was giving final instructions. A minute after ten, the first bell rang. She muted the sound.

Willis looked ringside towards Kenny. Nothing. Thomson bent between the ropes, the last to leave the ring. Willis glared across at the opposite corner. Only me and him now.

The first three rounds passed in a mental fog. Willis would never remember them. On automatic pilot, his thoughts were elsewhere. But Canzoneri knew he'd got a battle on to retain his championship.

The Italian made his planned aggressive start. But Willis countered him with solid jabs and hurtful hooks to the body. One right cross in the third round thumped heavily against Canzoneri's left cheek and it started to swell. Between rounds, a cornerman worked a cold iron on the injury.

'You're doing fine, my son.' Thomson smeared grease into Willis's eyebrows, cheeks and nose. 'Jab him to death.'

Canzoneri's aggression sneaked rounds four and five. But it was hard work. He needed a breather, but he didn't get it in the sixth. Willis increased his work rate.

If I must lose this fight, he thought, I'm not gonna make it easy for him. Bollocks to that.

Connie found the switch. The flood of light made her blink. She looked around the room. Sofa, armchairs, coffee table, drinks cabinet.

It's coming back to me, she thought. Bloody journalists. Got me pissed. Red wine and gin. What else happened? Connie felt between her legs. Panties still there. I need the toilet, she realised. Which door was it? No, not this one, it's a kitchen. Next one? No, ironing board and mop, a cupboard. Must be this one. She pushed the door and almost fell into the bathroom. Steady, old girl! Bloody blokes. Always leave the seat up. Uh, uh! Good job this time. Connie lurched forward, fell on to her knees and vomited into the bowl.

At the interval between rounds six and seven, Mary turned up the sound. The commentator thought it was even but the expert by his side had Willis one round ahead. She muted the sound again.

The sudden intrusion of the telephone tone startled her. She picked up the receiver and glanced at the clock. Twenty-five past ten.

'Hello, hello?'

'Sorry. Think I've got a wrong number.' The connection was broken.

Connie replaced the receiver. Engaged. Still, somebody's home. Probably Mary.

She staggered back to the bathroom and dipped towards the bowl once more. This isn't good, she thought. She wiped her mouth with the back of a hand and looked at the bath. The shower. That's it. A cold shower.

Slowly, Connie undressed, stepped into the shower cubicle and started the water. She flinched as the icy jets struck her chest, but gingerly revolved, reviving under the flow of cold water.

Willis was in trouble. The effects of the Novocaine were wearing off and both hands pained him; the right most of all. The vulnerable scar tissue on his left eyebrow had split again. Five rounds still to go.

Canzoneri, too, felt the effects of the punishing contest. His left cheek was swollen, his vision on that side impaired. He had to turn square-on to see and that gave Willis a bigger target. Still, the British bastard was cut.

Willis rammed jabs into Canzoneri's face during the ninth. An easy target to find. A big round.

Mary waited until the tenth round, then she went to the bathroom. Couldn't wait any longer. As she flushed the toilet, she heard the phone. Damn! She raced to her bedroom and snatched up the extension phone.

'Hello? Hello?'

'Mary?'

'Ma! Thank God. Are you all right?'

'Yeah. Been better, but I'm okay.'

'Where are you? What's happened?'

'Slow down, girl.' Connie took a deep breath. The nauseous wave passed. 'I'm in a hotel. The Craven.'

'What y'doing there?'

'It's where I met that eye-tie reporter and his photographer pal. Fuck knows where they've gone. I woke up on me own in the bloody dark.'

'I'll come to fetch you.'

'Right. What time is it?'

Mary looked at the illuminated bedside dial. 'Twenty to eleven.'

'What? Christ! What's happened to Johnny?'

'They're still fighting. Tenth round. Look, I'm on my way, okay?'

Mary replaced the receiver, careered down the stairs and snatched up her coat as her brother answered the bell for round eleven. She slammed the front door behind her and fumbled to insert a key in the car door. Less haste, more speed, Mary. The door opened and she flopped behind the wheel.

Stupid idiot! She banged the steering wheel with both hands. You've gotta phone Kenny.

Connie switched on the television. She stood in front of the set, operating the remote control with her right hand. In her left hand, she held the bath towel and rubbed her damp hair.

'C'mon, c'mon. Which bloody channel is it?'

Her son's face filled the screen. Thomson held a swab to his left eyebrow. Johnny's eyes were fixed on the trainer's face.

'On my card,' came the commentator's voice, 'Willis is a round in front. He can't afford to lose this last round.'

Connie dropped the remote and used both hands to vigorously rub her hair. Whoa, steady, girl. The room stabilised again. Must've been one hell of a session, she thought.

Mary raced back into the lounge and punched the numbers for Kenny's mobile.

'Hello, Mary. What's happening?' Kenny's voice was almost obliterated by the din from twelve thousand voices.

'Ma's okay,' she shouted. 'Can you hear?'

'What?'

'Ma's okay. She's all right.'

'Ma's okay, did you say?'

'Yeah. That's right. I'm gonna fetch her now.'

'Fetch her?'

'Yeah. Look don't bother about that. Tell Johnny she's okay. Got that?'

'Got it. Fuck! They're gonna start the last round.'

Connie let the towel drop to her feet. Naked, she looked at Johnny, leaning over the ropes. Kenny was in the crowd, shouting at him.

'This is amazing,' said the commentator. 'The bell's gone for the start of the last round but Willis is talking to someone in the crowd. Quite unbelievable! Now the referee's pulling at his arm. Canzoneri's in the middle of the ring, waiting. He can't believe it either. At last, Willis seems ready to carry on. I've never seen anything like it...'

## Chapter Twenty-Eight

It took Willis nearly five minutes to reach the sanctuary of his dressing room, A posse of security stewards, uniformed police, his cornermen and brothers herded him through the boisterous crowd.

Now he slumped in a plastic seat, legs wearily stretched out as Thomson held another swab to the leaking wound above his left eye.

Kenny and Colin leaned against a wall. They beamed with pride at their kid brother.

'What's Mary and Ma doing? Are they coming here?'

'Dunno,' said Kenny. 'Sis said something about fetching Ma. It was hard to hear out there. Bloody noisy.'

Payne kneeled between Willis's legs, rocked forward and kissed the championship belt strapped around his best friend's waist.

'You always said it, Johnny, now you've done it. Champion of the world. I'm thrilled for you.'

'Cheers, mate.'

Thomson removed the swab and peered at the wound 'It's been worse. Not a lot.' Sniff. 'We'll see what the doc says but I reckon you're best going to the hospital.'

Hospital? That's better than the morgue, Willis thought. Bloody death threats. Still, that's all they were, threats. Now just one more bit of business – the urine sample – and it's all over. I could sleep for a day. No, a week!

Mercer, notebook jutting out of his jacket pocket, rested a hand on Willis's left shoulder.

'Congratulations,' he said. 'I'd shake your hand but I guess it's a bit painful right now.'

Willis hauled himself to his feet. 'Come here. Give me a hug.' He embraced the reporter and whispered into his ear. 'Thanks for everything, Bob. You're a nugget. Been a real help.'

Mercer smiled and poked his spectacles back on to the bridge of his nose. 'It was some punch you came up with.'

Willis looked at his tender right fist, still encased in gauze and tape. 'Best right I've ever thrown. Soon as it landed I knew it was all over. He couldn't get up from that.'

'Only twelve seconds left, you know.'

'Is that right? Was I winning?'

Mercer flicked through pages of notes and totted up his scoring.

'Before the last round, I made it five–four with two even. But I don't know how the judges scored it. What did you think?'

'He needed the last to be certain,' Sellers interjected. 'But what's it matter? He bombed the guy out. First time Canzoneri's been stopped. It was some punch.'

Willis sat again. Brown untied the new champion's boots and removed them, while Thomson carefully cut off the hand bandages.

'Get in the shower,' said Thomson. 'I'll fix your robe.'

A babble of voices came from the corridor as Murray entered the room. He closed the door behind him.

'You've gotta let the press in for a few minutes. They're all outside.'

'They can fucking wait,' said Thomson. 'Let's get sorted first.'

Clean towel draped around his shoulders, Willis went for his shower. The hot, sharp rays speared his skin, stinging back and shoulders. Rope burns. He closed his eyes and let the water soothe him. He had never felt so spent after a fight.

'Everything okay?' asked Thomson from the doorway.

'Fine.'

'There'll be no problem with the test. You've done it before. If he gets too nosy, you know what to do.'

'Don't worry, Freddie. It'll be a piece of piss.' He smiled. Again felt the pain in his bruised face. Bloodied lips. Cut mouth.

'Fucking wise guy. Anyway, the press'll be in soon. Get dried and put your robe on. Make sure it stays tied, okay?'

'Yeah, yeah.'

But it wasn't okay. More questions. Fucking hell, he thought, I'm shattered. Knackered. Can't they just leave me alone? I told it all at ringside. It's gone out on satellite TV. Still, the reporters have a job to do. They've been fair to me.

He switched off the water and towelled his aching limbs. Jeez! No way am I going to any celebration party.

Mary's Metro crunched to a halt outside The Craven. She leaped out, pushed through the hotel doors and raced to reception.

'Can you tell me which room Mrs Willis is in?'

'Who?'

'Mrs Willis.'

'I don't think we have anyone of that name staying here.'

'No, sorry, she isn't staying. She came for an interview with—'

Just then, the lift doors opened.

'Mary! Haven't been waiting long, have you?'

Connie carefully walked towards her daughter. She'd brushed her hair into some semblance of tidiness, applied lipstick and eye-liner, but her dress was crumpled.

'Only a few minutes, Ma. Where's your coat?'

'I don't know.' Connie fluttered a dismissive hand. 'What's it matter? Where's the car?'

'Just outside.'

'Good. C'mon then. Let's go see your brother. The new champion of the world. Great, innit?'

'Champion? Johnny's won?'

'Yeah. Don't you know? Knocked the eye-tie out in the last. Bam! Great walloping right hand.'

'I didn't know. I was driving over here. Right, let's go. And you can tell me what you've been up to. We've been really worried.'

'Wish I could, Mary, wish I could. I know one thing. My head's banging like a million drums. Give me your arm.' They linked arms and walked towards the door.

'Excuse me… sorry, excuse me.'

Connie turned back to face the receptionist. She fluttered another theatrical hand. 'Not now, dearie. Got places to go,' she said.

Sellers, Murray and Jacobs answered most of the press enquiries, but Willis found the energy and spirit to provide some quotable responses.

'It looked for a time as though Canzoneri might steal it. How did you see it, Johnny?'

'Through blood, at times.' He fingered his eyebrow as the press ranks laughed. 'Yeah, he was a hard nut. But I expected that from last time. Let's face it, no mug wins a world title and he's no mug.'

'Did you think you were winning?'

'I reckoned I was just in front. Perhaps a round or two. But it was hard work. I've never felt so knackered. I'm just glad I found the strength to throw that right hand.' He smiled. 'That stopped any arguments.'

'It was a cracking punch, Johnny. Made up for the draw in San Remo, didn't it?'

'Yeah, could say that. But that's all in the past. I'm looking to the future.'

'What about that? Would you give Canzoneri a return?'

'Not thought about it, not yet. All I'm thinking about is having a bloody good rest.'

Sellers took that as a cue to wind up the session. Jacobs had the last word.

'See you all at the press conference tomorrow,' he rasped at the retreating backs. 'Twelve thirty at The Casino.'

Finally, the door was closed on the journalists, but one stranger remained. Stocky, smart in dark suit and pale blue shirt. Mid-forties with grey hair at the temples. A swarthy, continental look that wouldn't be out of place in the movies.

Willis studied him. The stranger stepped forward.

'*Scusi.* Are you ready now, Mr Willis? I need two samples of the urine.'

Willis noticed his lapel badge. The World Boxing Board's emblem. The man held a small black case in his right hand. Willis wrapped his robe tightly round him.

'Two? Don't know about that. I'll give it a go but you might have to settle for one.'

'I understand. Dehydration. It is not unusual after such a hard fight. Do your best, Mr Willis. If there's enough, I'm sure we can make it into two samples. It's not a problem, really.'

Willis stood up and took a swig from his water bottle. 'That might help.' Barefooted, he walked with Thomson towards the linking door.

'Only you and me, Mr Willis,' said the official. 'No one else is permitted in the room. It's the rules.'

Willis and Thomson exchanged glances.

'Sure, okay by me,' sniffed Thomson. 'I was gonna check that the room's secure. There's a door from the corridor, you know.'

'Yes, but it is locked and there is a security person outside. I have checked. I assure you, we will not be disturbed.'

Thomson stood aside. The official closed the door behind him and placed his case on a washbasin.

'I'll give you one bottle for a start.'

He lifted the case lid and extracted a round, dumpy bottle, unscrewed the top, and handed it to Willis.

Willis ignored the stand-up latrine. A cubicle offered more privacy. Improved the chances of a successful deception.

The doctor followed Willis to the middle cubicle. Willis started to untie the cord around his robe, but faltered. Looked over his shoulder.

'Hang on. Are you some kind of pervert? A peeping-fucking-Tom? Back off.'

'Please, Mr Willis, there is no need for such behaviour. I have to be here. I must be close to pass you the second bottle, yes?'

'Look, mister, I've done loads of these things, and no one has ever been as close as you. Just stand back. I'll tell you when I want the second bottle. Understand? Stand back.' Willis glared. The man took a handkerchief from his breast pocket, dabbed his brow and stepped away. 'That's better. Now I'll see what I can do.'

Willis turned and smiled to himself. Not bad acting. Perhaps I should be in the movies. He finished loosening his robe. Now for the tricky bit, he thought. Piercing the condom.

The condom had rested against his left thigh for the last half-hour. It contained the urine he'd deposited moments before Thomson injected Novocaine into his hands. Thomson had then knotted it and stored it in his holdall. While Willis showered after the fight, Thomson had safety-pinned the contraceptive inside the boxer's robe.

Now Willis held the bottle in his right hand. With his left, he withdrew a pin from the inside of his robe. He poised the condom over the bottle, pierced it and urine dribbled into the receptacle. Piece of piss, indeed.

Traffic was chaotic outside the Centre, but Mary managed to edge the Metro into the car park. She spotted Johnny's Mercedes and parked in the nearest vacant space.

They got out and a fresh-faced police constable approached as Mary locked her door. The constable looked at the blonde woman, unsteady on her feet and hardly dressed for a cold November night.

'Are you all right, ladies?'

'Which is the way in? I'm Johnny Willis's mother. You know, the world champion.'

'I know who you mean. What are you doing out here?'

'We've just got here. It's a long story.' Another wave of a fluttering hand. 'We've gotta see him.'

'Can you tell us where to go?' asked Mary.

'Follow me.' The policeman walked towards the arena, passing Willis's car. Mary and Connie hurried in his wake. Connie stumbled but Mary grabbed her arm. An exit door was ajar. A shaft of light. The policeman pointed. 'You can get in that way.'

'Thank you, officer.'

Inside, the arena was almost deserted. The ring was already being dismantled. Mary spotted a yellow-bibbed security steward.

'Excuse me,' she shouted.

The steward turned. One of Payne's doormen.

'Mary! What're you doing down here?'

'We're looking for Johnny's dressing room. D'you know where it is, Jimmy?'

'This way.'

Willis glanced over his shoulder. His vigilant new friend was still at a safe distance. Back at the washbasin, he was attending to something in his case.

Willis dropped the pin into the toilet bowl. Most of the liquid had found its new home. He stopped the flow, squeezing the teat of the condom with the thumb and forefinger of his left hand. He'd enough left for the second bottle.

'Okay, give me the other one quick.' He half-turned, right arm extended, offering the first bottle.

'Yes, good.'

The doctor stepped across the room. They clumsily exchanged bottles and he retreated to his case.

Willis released the last few dribbles. Home and dry! He shook his shoulders and sighed.

'That's it, pal. There's no more.'

Bomber heard the urgent clack of heels reverberating along the corridor. He recognised the two women and tapped on the door as the trio approached, Jimmy leading the way.

The women were breathless. 'Hi, Bomber,' gasped Mary.

The door opened a few inches and Payne peered through the gap. His eyes widened. 'Mary! You've made it at last,' he exclaimed.

They embraced and kissed in the doorway. Connie brushed past into the room. She looked round and saw Kenny and Colin.

'Where's Johnny?'

'He won't be a minute, Ma. Where've you been?'

'Never mind that.' Connie's face was flushed and her bosom heaved as she battled for oxygen. 'Where is he? I wanna see him. Where's my boy?'

'You must be Mrs Willis,' said Sellers, walking towards her. 'Johnny's mother?'

'That's right. I know you. You're his manager. But where's Johnny?'

'He's next door, giving a sample. You know, for drug testing.'

Connie looked to her right, at the closed door. 'In there?'

'Yes. He won't be a minute.'

Connie stepped towards the door.

'I'm sorry, you can't go in,' said Sellers.

'Can't go in!' Connie almost screeched, affronted. 'He's my son. Don't you think I haven't seen his willy?'

She reached for the door handle.

Willis released his hold on the empty condom. A dribble of urine seeped down his leg as the deflated vessel flopped against his thigh. He folded the robe around him and prepared to turn, bottle in hand.

'Johnny!'

The scream almost caused him to drop the bottle.

But it did stop the startled, stocky man from thrusting a knife into Willis's ribs.

Connie lurched from the doorway. She vaguely recognised Hugo. He looked different without spectacles. Heels skidding on the tiled flooring, she lunged at him. Instinctively, Hugo thrust his arm up. The blade entered just below Connie's left breast. He staggered under the weight of her desperate attack.

Willis launched at the assassin. His left hand gripped Hugo's throat and his right palm thumped into the muscular chest. Willis violently shoved him back towards the washbasins.

Connie slipped to the floor, a dark, sinister wet patch forming on her black dress.

With a sickening thud Willis drove the man's head into the mirror above the basins. The knife bounced on the tiled floor. Willis banged the head twice more and the mirror shattered.

Kenny loomed into the room and he saw his brother wrestling with the doctor. Connie was crumpled on the floor, her white thighs exposed, one arm extended and the other limp across her breast. Blood seeped along the tiles.

'You bastard!' shouted Johnny. He slammed Hugo to the floor, only feet from Connie's contorted body, using both hands to pound his head on the floor. His right fist then pummelled the man's face. Hugo's thin nose squashed beneath the blows. Willis didn't feel any pain. He punched furiously before Kenny and Brown intervened.

The back of Hugo's pulverised head was a gaping mess. The skull was shattered. Blood matted his hair. His nose was smashed, teeth broken. He was unconscious, barely alive.

Kenny grabbed his brother's shoulders and struggled to hoist him off. Chest heaving, arms trembling, Willis sobbed as he shouted.

'Bastard... the bastard's killed Ma.'

He kicked the man in the groin and the inert body lifted on impact.

Payne held Mary at the doorway. Brown and Thomson knelt next to Connie. Thomson felt for a pulse in her pale neck. Murray shouted at Bomber.

'Use those fucking radios! Get the medics up here, and the police. Be quick. And keep the corridor clear.'

Colin took in the scene. He walked purposefully towards the knife. Brown sprang to his feet and grabbed at him and they fell into a heap by the latrines.

'Don't be bloody stupid, Colin.' Brown pinned him to the floor. 'You'll do no good stabbing him.'

'For fuck's sake,' hissed Thomson. 'Don't bother about him. Your mother needs help.'

Sellers stooped to pick up the knife, using a handkerchief. Connie moaned, a dribble of blood appearing in the corner of her mouth.

'It's all right, Mrs Willis,' Thomson said gently, pressing a towel on her wound. 'Help's on its way.'

Willis removed his robe and draped it over his mother's body. Naked, he squatted and gently took Connie's limp left hand, stroking the back of it with his thumb.

'You'll be okay, Ma.' His voice was hoarse. 'Hang in there. You're a fighter, I know you are. It's where I get it from.'

Connie's eyelids opened. Her head turned to look at her son's blood-smeared, swollen face.

'You're a champ, son... my champ...' A weak, spluttering cough.

'Don't say anything, Ma. Save your strength. We'll talk later.'

The two lines of smudged red lipstick parted in her ashen face. A smile, of sorts. 'You're a good boy, Johnny. Always have been, I love you... love you all.'

Mary, followed by Payne, went to Willis's side and draped a towel over his shoulders. Her eyes were dry. She leaned forward and whispered to her mother.

'You'll be okay. Love you.' She kissed a damp cheek.

Paramedics hustled into the crowded room.

'Can we have room? Please, move back.'

Willis remained kneeling by his mother's head. The medics went to work. Connie was lifted onto a stretcher, still draped in Willis's robe.

'I'm coming with her,' he said.

'Okay, son, but you'll need some clothes.'

Another ambulance squad arrived. They leaned over Hugo. 'He's in a bad way,' said one.

A police constable conferred with two detectives in the doorway. The uniformed officer's radio squawked. He walked down the corridor, talking into the instrument.

In the dressing room, Willis hastily pulled on jeans, sweatshirt and trainers. Mary joined him and they merged into a silent hug. Both started to sob.

Mercer turned away. Grief is private, thought the reporter. But what a bloody story. How do I write this?

The constable, his head shaking in bewilderment, returned to the detectives. 'We've found a man bound and gagged in a storeroom. He's not hurt. Shaken and frightened. Seems he's some sort of boxing official.'

The detectives nodded and surveyed the room. Two bodies. Man and a woman. Blood everywhere. A knife wrapped in a handkerchief. Some crime scene. Forensics would go potty. It's a mess that will take some sorting. They looked over at Kenny and Colin. Colin guessed what they were thinking.

'We haven't a fucking clue what's gone on,' he said.

'We'll need statements from you all,' said one detective.

The paramedics lifted Connie's stretcher. Warming blankets replaced Willis's robe. Thomson picked up the gown. The police stepped into the room, allowing the stretcher-bearers to pass.

Willis, followed by Mary, came back into the room and saw Connie being removed.

'C'mon, Mary. Let's go.'

'We need to know what happened, Johnny,' said one of the detectives.

Willis looked into the officer's eyes. 'Sure you fucking do. But not now.' He paused. 'In my bag, you'll find a tape. Listen to it. That'll do for starters. You can take it from there. You know where I'll be.'

Willis turned but the detective held his arm.

'I don't know what's gone on here,' he said, 'but, well, I'm sorry. You know what I mean.' He looked into the fighter's eyes and debated. Was this the right time? The right thing to say? He pressed on. 'You win a world title and then – well, it's wrecked what should've been a great night for you.'

Willis settled his right hand on the detective's left shoulder. 'Thanks. But I'll tell you this, when someone you love's in danger, world titles don't mean shit.' He grasped Mary's hand and they hurried off down the corridor.

'We're coming, Ma,' he shouted.